MW01135905

Fragile

Battling Demons, Volume 3

Kris Morris

Published by Kris Morris, 2016.

FRAGILE

First edition. September 28, 2016.

Written by Kris Morris.

Thank you to my dear husband for believing in me, my sons for inspiration, and my friends Carole, Abby, Janet, and Anneke for ceaseless encouragement and tolerating my insecurities.

Special thanks to my dear friend, Abby Bukofzer and my son, Karl for countless hours spent assisting me with editing. And to my talented husband, Tim, for designing my book covers.

I love you all!

Chapter 1

Sunlight lit up Jan s Henry's tow head as he gambolled across the grassy field atop R carrock Hill. He stopped occasionally to pluck a yellow buttercu from the thin skin of soil covering the granite rock underneath efore running towards his mother to present her with the gift.

Martin str e closely behind him, his hand poised to grab the child should venture towards the cliff's edge. His wife, relaxing on a bench i r the Coastal Path, gave him a smile and a nod of her head i acit approval of his paternal attentiveness. Then, wrapping t ir son in her arms, she made a display of her pleasure at receivi the hand-picked bouquet.

"Goo God, Martin," his father's voice sneered from behind. "Are yo aising the boy to be a big girl's blouse?"

M. n whirled around and Christopher Ellingham's eyes looke im up and down, his lip curling as he shook his head. "Lik ther, like son. Do something about it now, before it's too late

e lderly man took a step forward and snatched the d nutir posy away from Louisa, slapping it into his wife's l h M rgaret let the flowers drop to the rocky path before us n her hands in disgust.

She gave er son a disdainful glare and walked towards him. His heart b n to pound as her shoes ground the delicate buttercups int he gravel under her feet. "I'm not surprised your wife walked ou n you. What would any woman possibly want with someone lik ou?"

Louisa's po t. flicked side to side. "Martin, are you going to allow them to ea o you that way? Don't just stand there!"

*His father pulled James from Louisa's arms and strode down
the path with him. "I won't have any grandson of mine prancing
about the meadow this way. I'll make a man out of him if you
won't."*

*"Martin! Do something!" His wife's eyes pleaded silently for
him to act.*

*"Stop!" he cried out as he tried to force his unwilling legs to
move. "Bring—James—back! Now, Dad!"*

*Christopher spun around, casting his grandson into the grass
before taking several steps towards his son.*

*Martin squeezed his eyes shut, waiting for the inevitable
impact. Nothing. He held his breath as he opened them. His
father was gone. James sat in the grass, sobbing and red-faced,
reaching his arms out for him.*

*A descending whine caught Martin's attention and he turned
his head to see a large lorry rising up over the hill, racing towards
him. He tried to run for his son. But again, he was frozen in place.*

*A tremendous jolt of energy coursed through his body, sending
searing pain racing up his legs. He was trapped. Pinned in the
wreckage again. He pulled at his arm as he felt a warm current of
blood pulsing across his hand.*

He bolted upright in his hospital bed. "No!"

"Dr. Ellingham ... Dr. Ellingham."

A soft voice and a hand on his shoulder nudged him from
his morphine-enhanced slumber.

"It's all right, Doctor. It was just a bad dream is all."

Martin blinked as his eyes darted around the room. He fell
back on to his pillow, and then, covering his face with a broad
palm, he turned away from the nurse and pulled in a ragged
breath.

The woman filled a glass with water and pulled his hand
away before pressing the glass into it. "Dr. Ellingham,
nightmares after a car accident as horrific as what you
experienced are to be expected."

"Mm."

The cool water soothed his parched throat as he tried to forget the dream. "Thank you," he said, unable to look the woman in the eye.

"I just came in to change out your IV. Can I get you anything else?"

"No. No, I'm fine."

The nurse straightened his blankets and laid a hand on his arm before leaving the room.

An occupational therapist came by a short time later, introducing herself as Katie Gardner. She took a seat in the chair by the bed. "I understand Mr. Christianson's hoping to have you on your feet by the end of the week."

"Yes, that's the plan," Martin grumbled.

"Even so, I'm sure you realise you'll be using a wheelchair to get around most of the time ... at least for a while."

He screwed up his face. "Of course, I do. I'm not an idiot."

The therapist let her patient's irritability slide. "It'll be helpful if you can get up using a walker though, just to help you get from the bed to the wheelchair. How far will your bed be from the lavatory?" she asked as she manipulated Martin's wrist.

"There's an en suite bathroom. I would guess ten feet or less. I'm not sure. We'll be using my aunt's cottage until I'm more ambulatory."

"Oh?"

"Mm. The previous owner was confined to a wheelchair, so the necessary adaptations have already been made," Martin said, wincing as the therapist rotated his hand.

"Great," Katie said nodding her head. "That'll make it easier for you to be independent. I would imagine you'd prefer to get to and from the loo on your own?"

Martin gave the young woman a scowl. "That's an asinine question."

The therapist had been briefed beforehand about Martin's forthright nature, but his size and commanding presence unnerved her. She swallowed. "All right then, let's see what we can do to get a bit more strength and flexibility back in your arm and hand. Can you get this brace on and off yourself?"

"I don't know. I haven't tried."

"Let's give it a go then, shall we? Before you start, make sure you have your elbow resting on the table. Your loose shoulder might not support your arm once the brace is removed," she said stepping back to watch as her patient worked to remove the orthotic.

The movement necessary to reach the clips and Velcro closures pulled on the muscles and ribs that had been severed during the thoracotomy. Martin set his jaw, as he doggedly worked at the fasteners until he was able to free himself of the brace.

"Excellent, Dr. Ellingham. Now, lay your arm on the table, but let your hand hang down at the wrist. Then I want you to pull your knuckles up towards your forearm and make a fist."

Sweat began to form on Martin's brow as he willed his muscles to fire, and his fingers twitched slightly.

"Good. Repeat that ten times." The young woman gave him an encouraging pat on his good shoulder, causing him to flinch. He hissed a breath through his nose as the furrow between his brows deepened.

Katie pulled her hand away and laced her fingers together in front of her while she waited for him to complete the exercise. "Good. Now I want you to rotate your hand, palm up."

Martin's thumb rotated towards the ceiling. "Bloody hell!" he sputtered as intense pain shot through his arm.

"I know it hurts, Doctor, but try to repeat that movement ten times."

Martin blinked the tears from his eyes, as he completed the repetitions.

"Would you like a glass of water, Dr. Ellingham?"

He rested his elbow on the table and dropped his head into his hand, waiting for the light-headedness and waves of nausea to ease. "Yes, please," he said, closing his eyes and swallowing back a flood of saliva.

"I spoke with Tim Spalding," she said as she filled a glass and handed it to him. "He worked your legs pretty hard yesterday evidently, so we'll give you a break from that today. He can torture you some more tomorrow, hmm?" she said trying unsuccessfully to coax a smile from him.

The therapist went through several less painful exercises, having Martin touch each of his fingers to his thumb before laying his palm on the table and moving each digit up and down.

She then took out a box filled with items, varied in size and shape, and dumped them out on to the table. Martin's task was to pick them up, one by one, and put them back into the box.

Nerves had been damaged in the accident, leaving his arm and hand numb, and he found it maddeningly difficult to control his fine motor movements, often dropping the objects before they made it close to their final destination.

The therapist had him close his eyes and feel around for the pieces before picking them up.

"I can't do this," he said, embarrassment and anxiety quickly building in him.

"Just keep trying, Dr. Ellingham. This will take time and practice."

Martin could hear the pieces rattling around on the table as he bumped them with his fingers, but it felt as if he was grasping at air, and he inadvertently knocked the items off on to the bed.

His frustration with his inability to perform this simple task left him feeling weak and vulnerable. And the pain and stresses of the last weeks, which he had managed to keep fairly well hidden up to this point, were bubbling to the surface. The exercise forced him to face the severity of the injury to his arm as well as the possible long-term consequences, and it terrified him.

It was all released in an explosion of emotion. He swept the objects off the table with his good arm, flinging them forcefully across the room. He then gave the tray table a shove, sending it toppling to the floor.

"Get out! Sod off and leave me alone! And take your infantile game with you!" he screamed as he pressed his hand against his head.

The intimidating man Katie had been cowed by moments before suddenly appeared helpless and vulnerable. "I'll have someone come in after a bit to tidy up and help you with your brace," she said before slipping quietly from the room.

Martin collapsed back on the bed, feeling an immediate sense of shame for his behaviour. He waited until the door closed before fully releasing his emotions in ragged sobs.

Louisa was experiencing her own trials back in Portwenn. She had been anxious to get home and get James bathed and off to bed the previous night, so she had forgone her plans to pick up nappies at the market when they passed through Wadebridge. This, however, meant she would have to buy them at the chemist, and she knew Mrs. Tishell would be full of questions.

As she wheeled James's pushchair through the shop door, the cowbell announced her arrival to the proprietor. The woman's singsong voice could be heard coming from upstairs. "I'll be with you in a minute!"

Louisa gathered together several other items that she was in need of while she waited. She glanced over at a display of mouthwash, and her thoughts turned to an exchange of words with Martin shortly after their ill-fated taxi ride. She was still standing in the middle of the shop with an amused smile on her face when the clomping of the chemist's heavy-soled shoes could be heard on the steps. She shook her reverie from her head.

Mrs. Tishell emerged from behind the wainscot wall to see the GP's wife standing on the other side.

"Why, Louisa Ellingham, what a pleasant surprise!" the woman gushed. "And little James, too!"

"Hello, Mrs. Tishell. I'd like some nappies, please ... size four. And I have a few other items." Louisa laid her purchases on the counter before placing a protective hand on her son's head.

"Of course, I'll just go and get those for you," she said, taking a step towards the stairs. She turned. "And how *is* ... Dr. Ellingham?"

"Better, thank you."

The woman wandered back, and leaning over, she rested her arm on the counter. "I was *just* thinking about him, as a matter of fact," she said, staring out the large bay window as her fingers migrated towards the top buttons of her cardigan. She sighed. "What an unfortunate turn of events that accident was. Our good doctor has been sorely missed, I can *assure* you."

The chemist clicked her tongue and shook her head. "There *have* been ... rumours traveling around the village. Of course, I didn't spread them any further, mind you! All lies, I'm sure."

Louisa's ponytail flicked. "What ... sort of rumours?"

"Well, *some* have suggested Dr. Ellingham had been ..." Mrs. Tishell leaned across the counter and whispered conspiratorially in the younger woman's ear. "... on—the—lash ... so to speak," she said.

The ponytail whipped around again as Louisa quickly turned her head away, pursing her lips. "If you could just get my nappies, Mrs Tishell."

"Oh, yes," she said, throwing up her hands before thumping back up the stairs. The cowbell jangled again, and another customer entered the building.

The chemist returned with the requested nappies, and Louisa paid her bill.

"Of course, I told the individual spreading the rumours about Dr. Ellingham that they had it *all* wrong," Mrs. Tishell said. "Not our good doctor ... not in a *million* years, I told them."

"Yer sprog sure do look like 'is daddy, Miss!" said the fisherman waiting behind Louisa.

"Yes, he *is* a handsome child, isn't he," fawned the chemist.

Louisa felt heat rising in her cheeks, and she hurried out, slamming the door behind her.

By the time she headed up Roscarrock Hill she could feel the sting of tears building in her eyes. As she approached Large Restaurant, she heard Bert's jovial voice call out.

"Hello, Louiser!" he said, gesturing to her with a wave of his hand.

She groaned internally, but she had put the man off once already, so she picked up her son, folded up the push chair and headed down the long flight of stone steps.

"Have you had your high tea yet?" Bert asked. "We do a lovely high tea, you know."

Louisa smiled him. "No, Bert. I'm afraid it's a bit late in the day for me. James and I were just heading home for an early dinner. We had to make a stop at the chemist first ... nappies," she said, holding up her shopping bag.

"I tell you what, you can have dinner here—on the house. That way you won't have to worry about cookin'."

"That sounds lovely, Bert. And it's so kind of you, but—"

"Oh, it's my pleasure. You just take a seat right here, and I'll bring you a menu," he said, pulling out a chair. "May I offer you a starter, perhaps?" he asked, spraying a bit of saliva in her direction.

"Erm, no Bert. I think I'll eat light tonight."

"Right then. I'll be right back with a menu." Bert waddled off, and Louisa breathed a resigned sigh. She settled James into a high chair and pulled out a piece of Melba toast for the boy to gnaw on.

The restaurateur returned and handed her the menu before plopping himself down in the chair across the table.

"So, how's the doc doin'? Any better?"

"Yes, every day is a bit better now. The first few weeks were very difficult ... for both of us. Martin had a lot of setbacks, but hopefully it's full speed ahead now," she said, forcing a smile.

Bert leaned forward and placed a plump hand on her arm. "And how about you? Are you doin' all right? You look a bit peaky ... and a bit stressy, if I may say."

"Oh, Bert. It's just ... *this village!* And the stories going around about Martin. I just found out from Mrs. Tishell that people are saying Martin had been drinking when he had his accident. Martin doesn't touch alcohol."

Bert tipped his head to the side and raised his eyebrows. "Well, I'm not sayin' I believe all that goss goin' round, but I do recall a little incident a few years back. Caused quite a stir, if I recall," he chuckled.

Louisa could feel the blood rushing to her face again. "That was my fault, Bert! Martin wasn't used to alcohol, and I kept filling his glass with wine. I *wanted* to get him drunk so maybe he'd be less inhibited ... finally make a bloody move on—"

She cleared her throat, realising she had shared more information than she had intended. "That was awful—what Pauline did. Taking that picture of Martin—passed out on his kitchen floor with that stray dog that used to follow him around." She flopped back in her chair and pulled her arms across her chest. "Letting it make the rounds through every mobile in the village." Her ponytail slapped her cheek. "That was *awful*. Just plain mean-spirited."

She gathered her composure before adding, "Martin had not consumed *any* alcohol what—so—*ever* when that lorry hit him. And I'd appreciate it if you would get *that* bit of information circulating through the village grapevine," she huffed.

"Oh, sure—sure. I'd be happy to. I didn't mean to upset you, girl." Bert heaved himself up from his chair and pulled his notepad and biro from his apron pocket. "Well, you just pay no attention to all that tittle-tattle. And give a whistle if I can be of any assistance ... anything a'tall."

"That's very sweet, Bert. Thank you." She placed her order and handed the menu back to him.

By the time she had hurried through her meal, James was smashing his peas with his fist and finger painting with his applesauce. Both sure signs he'd had his fill as well.

She gathered their belongings together, thanked Bert, and hurried on up the hill to the surgery.

It was nice to not have a meal to prepare, but she had paperwork to do and laundry that was piling up.

She was coming down the stairs after putting James to bed that evening when her mobile rang. A smile came to her lips when she saw her husband's name on the screen.

"Hello, Martin," she said breathlessly.

"Hello. Did I catch you at a bad time?"

"No, not at all. I just put James down for the night. How are you?" she asked as she sat down on the bottom step.

"Mm, tired."

"So ... tell me about your day."

There was a long sigh at the other end of the line. "An occupational therapist came in and discussed some considerations in regard to the move back home ... er, to Ruth's—mostly ambulation issues."

Louisa waited anxiously for his next words. She could hear a despondency in his voice. "Martin, what is it? Something's wrong. Did something happen? Have you had another setback?"

"*No*. It's just that ..." He let out a soft groan. "I'm sorry, Louisa. I lost my temper with the occupational therapist."

"What do you mean, you lost your temper?"

"I embarrassed myself. I threw some things ... yelled."

"Did he do something to upset you?"

"She ... it's a she. No, she was quite professional. I—I—well, she dumped all these bits out on my tray table—blocks, paper clips, pencils, that sort of thing. I was supposed to pick them up with my right hand and put them back into the box. It was so hard to get my fingers to function normally, Louisa.

"Then she told me to close my eyes and do it and— God, I *tried*, I really tried. But I couldn't do it. I couldn't feel a thing. I could feel the table a bit—against my arm, but nothing with my fingers. I couldn't feel all those little pieces.

"It was so—so humiliating! I kept knocking things off on to the bed, but I wasn't able to pick a bloody thing up! Not a single bloody thing!"

Louisa leaned forward, her chin resting in her hand. "I'm sure that was unsettling."

"*Unsettling!* I'd been hoping to have the option of performing surgery again someday. Now I'm finding myself wondering if I'll be able to practice medicine at all! I can't even be a GP if I only have one usable hand. How would I suture cuts, reduce a dislocated shoulder, start an IV?" he sputtered. What am I going to do if I can't even be a bloody GP?"

"Martin, you're just getting started with the therapy. You need to give it time ... give your body time to heal. I can certainly understand why you're upset. This must be frightening for you. It is for me, too, you know. This not knowing the final outcome. But please understand this, Martin

... I am only frightened for *you*, for how this will affect *you* ... mentally and physically. All I care about is whether or not you can be happy, and I'm afraid this accident will be the straw that breaks the camel's back."

"I'm sorry, Louisa. I didn't intend to add to your worries. I didn't mean to do that." Martin was silent for several seconds before adding, "I'll be fine. I'm fine. Please don't worry."

He shifted his weight from his right side. "I miss you when you're not here," he said softly. "I miss your warmth. I miss your softness, your smell, the way you look at me."

"Are you sure you're all right, Martin?"

"I'll be fine, Louisa. If we're together, I'll be fine, no matter what happens. When you're here I don't worry about this, but when you go back home, I start thinking that ..."

She could hear another heavy sigh. "Martin, I promise you, I will *not* leave you. If it would help, I could stay on the phone with you all day."

"Mm, that would be impractical. You wouldn't get any work done. And if you're not getting any work done, you could just as well be here."

A small smile came to her face. "I know, Martin; I was joking. Seriously, though, would you like me to come and stay with you until you can come home?"

What Martin wanted and what he knew to be sensible were two entirely different things. Louisa needed time to get things organised for his return, both at home and at the school.

"No, I think you should stay there. I'm feeling better now. It helps to hear your voice."

"Okay, but call me anytime you want to talk. I mean that, Martin. *Anytime.*"

"Mm, you may regret those words; I haven't been sleeping well. And I miss you at night."

"I miss you, too. I love you, Martin."

"Mm. I love you."

Chapter 2

Martin pulled the earbuds from his ears and snapped the lid shut on Chris's loaned laptop when Dr. Newell came through his door Wednesday morning.

"Sorry to disturb you," the psychiatrist said as he gave his patient a clinical once over.

"Mm, it's okay. I was just watching a surgical video." He wagged a finger at the computer. "Subintimal angioplasty."

"Ah, interesting. Do you feel up to a short visit?" he said, setting a stack of journal articles, which he hoped Martin would find useful, on the dresser by the bed. He suspected scientifically controlled studies would do more to sway his cerebral patient's thinking about the circumstances of grandfather's death than the well-intentioned sentiments of friends and family or the counsel of a psychiatrist would. "I've bookmarked a number of pages I thought would be of particular interest to you."

He picked up the periodical on top of the pile and handed it to Martin. "I want to draw your attention to an article in here on a study done by Lawrence Kohlberg, a Harvard psychologist. He found that moral reasoning falls into six identifiable stages of sophistication."

Martin flipped the magazine open to the pink sticky tab between pages fifty-five and fifty-six.

"In the first, or least sophisticated stage, people will conclude that what's right and good is that which enables them to be rewarded or avoid punishment. That, of course, is the stage you would have been in at the time of your grandfather's death. As a seven-year-old, you would have based decisions on whether the most influential people in your life would reward you or punish you for a particular behaviour."

Dr. Newell pulled a chair over and took a seat. "It turns out there was a flaw in Kohlberg's study ... a pretty major flaw which has made his work somewhat controversial. Even though he maintained a good cross cultural representation, one hundred percent of his subjects were male. There's still a lot to be gleaned from the man's work, though."

Martin shook his head. "I'm not sure this ... this Goldberg fellow had it right. Even having just turned seven, I knew my grandfather was dying ... that if I didn't get help he wouldn't survive," he said, flicking his thumb across the edge of the magazine.

"Yes. You knew that, and you had to make a moral choice. Remember how a seven-year-old makes moral choices.

"Your parents had told you not to interrupt their rows or you'd be punished." The therapist leaned forward, resting his elbows on his knees. "I'm curious, Martin ... how were you punished the times you *did* interrupt your parents' arguments?"

Martin rubbed a hand over his forehead before turning his head away.

"Can you remember, Martin? What would your punishment have been?"

"It only happened once. They were in their bedroom. A man came to the door wanting to speak with my father. When I went upstairs to get him, they were in the middle of a disagreement. I tried to tell him about the man waiting for him downstairs, but he didn't notice me. I tugged on his sleeve to get his attention, and he backhanded me ... caught me in the mouth with his knuckles."

"Did it injure you?"

Martin squirmed uncomfortably. "It knocked out a couple of teeth and split my lip." He shrugged his shoulders. "I'm not sure he intended to hit me as hard as he did though."

The psychiatrist's thumbs tapped together as his brow furrowed. "Martin, children equate the severity of their punishments with the egregiousness of their alleged misdeeds. I don't have to tell you that, as a child, you probably felt interrupting your parents was a very serious offense, considering your father's reaction.

"Your parent's expectations would have outweighed your grandfather's pleas for help. Also, opening the door of that study and interrupting your parents would have had an immediate and *certain* consequence. Whereas, sitting by your grandfather's side would result in a delayed and *less* certain consequence. You knew how your parents would react if you interrupted their row, but how they would react if you stayed put was unknown. Perhaps the punishment wouldn't be as severe if you waited where you were supposed to ... stayed out of their way. Now, think of your choices in moral terms. Which would have seemed more morally just to a seven-year-old?"

Martin's eyes flitted, unseeing, as he processed the information.

"I think you've been remembering the incident through your seven-year-old eyes," Dr. Newell continued. "But you've been judging that seven-year-old boy through your adult eyes ... and your adult definition of morality."

Martin grunted and then began to thumb through the journal as the doctor leaned back in his chair. "So ... how are you doing overall? Is Ed Christianson happy with your progress?"

"Yes, I think so. The first several weeks were a bit bumpy, but there's been steady improvement over the last few days," Martin said as he tossed the magazine on to the stack of books and periodicals. "Ed hopes to get me up on my feet by late this week. The sooner I can get ambulatory, the sooner I can go home."

"And mentally, how are you doing ... with the depression and sleep issues?"

"It's a little hard to tell about the depression," Martin said as his brow pulled down. "I do have times when I feel discouraged ... depressed, but I would think that's normal after a trauma like this. As far as sleep ... I was doing fine until they cut back on the opioids."

The therapist cocked his head. "Withdrawal issues?"

"No, no, no, no, no. It's just hard to sleep. The last week's been difficult. I see my grandfather's face when I close my eyes. Nights get long. I'm so tired I can't keep my eyes open, but as soon as I start to fall asleep, it's the same image."

"The same image?"

"Mm. My grandfather's face."

"Let me talk with Ed and see if we can get you something to help with that. You're on a pretty complicated cocktail already, so we'll need to make sure we don't have any problems with drug interactions. How's the confusion and anxiety been since they cut back on the morphine?"

"Better. But my cognitive skills are still dulled. It takes me longer to process a question."

"A little slow on the uptake?" Dr. Newell asked, giving his patient a sympathetic smile.

Martin scowled. "That's the general idea. I get confused when I wake up in the night. It takes me a while to figure out where I am ... why I'm here and not at home."

"You're going to be on the morphine for quite some time, so you might want to talk with the occupational therapist about some ways of dealing with the sluggish thinking."

Dr. Newell got to his feet and stretched his arms in the air. "You've had a tremendous amount to deal with recently, both physically and emotionally ... a lot coming at you at once. Don't be ashamed to ask for help when you need it."

The therapist glanced at his watch. "I'd better get back to my office. I'll stop back in a few days to pick up the books and journals. Call me if you'd like to talk before then, all right?"

"Yes. Thank you."

Dr. Newell walked to the door and put his hand on the knob before turning. "Well done, Martin," he said as he left the room.

"Mm, yes."

Martin spent much of the rest of the morning either scanning the literature his therapist had left with him, or napping. Sleep came in the form of brief interludes, dovetailed between the morality plays that were his nightmares.

Tim Spalding stopped by late in the morning.

"We need to work some more today on getting you ready for weight bearing later this week, probably on Saturday," he said as he repeated the previous session's exercises with Martin's right leg.

"Mr. Christianson mentioned your surgeons from Imperial may be down this weekend as well. I would imagine they want to check out their handiwork."

"Oh, goody ... an audience."

The therapist smiled at the dour look on the face of the big man. "Aw, it won't be that bad. Think of them as your cheer squad."

"Yeah, right."

"Okay, Doctor. Let's work this left leg," Tim said as he moved to the other side of the bed.

The laceration to Martin's thigh had been causing him discomfort in the last days, and the physiotherapist's manipulations seemed to be exacerbating the problem. He was growing more and more agitated by both his rapidly worsening pain and the young man's chatter.

Tim began to regale him with tales of his recent trip to Africa, traveling with Doctors Without Borders. Martin tried to tune out the verbal travelogue, but his head was now pounding, and a sudden sharp stabbing sensation shot through his leg.

"*Shut—up!* I can't get a word in edgewise with you prattling on like that!" he exploded.

The therapist was knocked back on his heels. "Sorry, Dr. Ellingham. What did you want to say?"

Martin gritted his teeth as another jolt of pain shot through his leg. "That my bloody— God! My bloody thigh hurts," he said groaning and grabbing at his throbbing appendage.

"All right, let's take a break and we'll ice it," Tim said as he hurried out the door to get the needed cold packs.

He returned quickly with his supplies and hurriedly wrapped his patient's thigh in the chilled, gel-filled pouches. "I'm going to let you rest a bit, and then I'll be back to see how you're doing."

Ed arrived a few minutes later. "How's it going, Martin?"

Martin brought a trembling hand to his face and shook his head.

The surgeon pulled the blankets from his patient's legs and removed the ice packs that had been placed there by the therapist. "Spalding called me—said you're having some pain in that thigh.

"Tell me about it. Sharp ... burning ... has it been persistent?" Ed palpated the area around the repaired laceration.

"Geesh!" Martin yelled as he slapped the surgeon's hand away, taking in a gasp of air. "That hurts!"

Ed knitted his brow. "Describe the pain for me."

"Consistent burning. And like periodic elec—trical impulses."

"When did *this* start?"

Martin glanced over at him. "A few days ago."

"Martin, do you listen to me at all? I've told you you need to tell me when you're having pain."

"It's likely postoperative peri—pheral nerve pain. It'll pass," he said, his jaw clenching. "I *don't* want any more—drugs. I can't think straight the way it is."

"All right, genius. What exactly is it you need that famous medical acumen for at the moment? You're sleeping most of the day away."

Martin cast a fiery glance at his surgeon. "None of your business."

Mr. Christianson's fingers drummed on the bed rail as his patient squirmed in agony.

"I need to think some things through," Martin finally sputtered. "I have trouble with my memory when I'm getting a higher dose of morphine."

Ed stood pensively for a moment. "All right, I hear you. Well, I don't see any sign of infection."

"I could have told you that," Martin grumbled.

"How 'bout we put in a nerve block? I suspect the severed nerves are healing, which is a good sign, but until those nerves have healed completely, it's going to be painful."

"Fine. Let's do the nerve block."

Martin was lightly sedated before an area in his groin was prepped for the procedure. Ed threaded a tiny catheter through the skin, positioned to feed anaesthetic to the nerve bundle leading to his leg.

It was a quick and relatively simple procedure, and when Martin woke a short while later he was much more comfortable. The fog left by the sedative had just begun to clear when he heard a familiar nasal voice in the hallway. "Oh, gawd," he groaned.

"You can't go in there, sir. Visitors have been restricted to immediate family, unless approved by the patient," a nurse said.

"This is official police business ma'am." Joe Penhale flashed her his badge, hurrying into the GP's room before she could say any more.

"Hello, Doc!" Joe said, giving his "friend" an oafish grin.

Martin was at a distinct disadvantage with the residual sedative still in his system.

"Penhale, what are you doing here?"

With a jangling rattle, Joe hoisted up his tool belt. "Here on a police matter. Thought I'd drop by ... keep you company for a while."

Martin had a sinking feeling in the pit of his stomach.

The PC scrutinised the doctor's visible wounds, eyeing the brace on his arm with curiosity. He squatted down slightly, peering up at the underside before taking a step towards the head of the bed, standing on his toes to see the top of the brace.

"That's quite a fancy contraption you've got there, Do-*c*."

"It's a brace, Penhale. It keeps my shoulder from luxat— slipping out of the socket."

Joe wrinkled up his nose. "Doesn't sound like much fun."

"No, it's *not* much fun. Is there a purpose for your visit, Penhale?"

"Like I said, just here to keep you company. And I guess in my official capacity as the person responsible for the safety of the citizens of our community, it's my duty to check up on you." Joe hooked his thumbs over his belt. "That's not the only reason I'm here, of course. You and me have a special relationship, don't we, Doc? You bein' in charge of keeping the people of Portwenn healthy and me bein' in charge of keeping 'em safe. Just here to cheer on the team ... so to spea-*k*." The officer gave the doctor a hesitant pump of his fist.

"Oh, gawd." Martin watched in dismay as the constable pulled up a chair and sat down.

"So ... how are you feelin'? A bit sore, I bet?"

"I was hit by a lorry for God's sake!"

"Saw the accident report. You're lucky to be alive, you know. I've seen a few auto versus lorry accidents in my line of work. It's not pretty."

The constable winced and held his palms up in front of him. "Not that *you* aren't pretty. I mean you're *not* pretty. You're quite a distinguished looking gentlemen, actually. Always nicely attired. Quite dapper with your tie all ... tied," he drawled.

"Penhale," Martin moaned.

"Sorry, Doc." Joe fidgeted in his chair. "So, Louiser says you took a bit of a bashing; broke both your legs."

Martin heaved out a heavy breath. "Yes."

"Hmph. Shame, that. Well, you just say the word ... if there's anything I can do to be of assistance ... anything at all."

Martin blinked as a thought popped into his head. "There is something you could do."

The policeman's tool belt jangled as he jumped to his feet. "Anything, Doc. Happy ta help out."

"Could you stop by and check up on the Hanleys for me? Make sure Mr. Hanley's abiding by the rules the SPCC laid out? Check on his children?"

"Sure, Doc. I'll do all three of 'em."

"Good. Thank you." Martin gave the constable a sideways glance. "But Penhale ... be cautious. Hanley's a mean drunk."

"Will do, Doc. Gotta new Taser last week. I'll make sure she's charged up."

Martin looked at him askance and then scratched at an eyebrow. "Erm, Penhale ... my wife told me you were a big help to her the night of my accident. I want to ... to thank you for that ... for driving her over here."

"No problemo. It's the least I could do for the other half of the dynamic duo." He gave Martin a slightly too firm pat on his bad shoulder.

"Ow! Penhale!"

"Sorry there, Doc. You're pretty tender, aren't you." He looked him up and down. "Kind of a mess, actually."

He put his palms up in front of him again. "No offense. I just mean ... well, even you gotta admit you're just a bit ..." He grimaced and then gave Martin a crooked grin. "Well, I'm sure they'll get you set to rights, Doc. Eventually. Eh?"

"Penhale!"

"I'll just be goin' then. Don't you worry about a thing. I'm holding down the fort while you're gone."

"What ... you're treating patients in my absence, are you?"

"I *could* do, if it'd be helpful. You just say the word."

"Yeah, *rright.*"

Chapter 3

The sweet chortles and giggles from her son as he played in his cot across the hall prodded Louisa from her sleep Wednesday morning. She rolled to the side, reaching an arm out for her husband, and a feeling of emptiness came over her, as it had every morning since that horrible night.

She pulled his pillow to her and nuzzled it in his stead, hoping to draw in a scent which had evaporated many days before. Then she forced herself from the warmth of the bed to begin what was to be a very busy day.

Carole Parsons had called the night before. Their discussion about Martin's childhood experiences brought about a flood of emotions for Louisa, and it was well after midnight before she had completely unloaded to her friend about her concerns for Martin, as well as her worries about how the accident would impact their marriage.

She had tossed and turned for the better part of an hour before pure exhaustion took over, and she finally drifted off.

Her anxieties had now been replaced by excitement, however. Martin would be home soon, and they would be returning to some semblance of normal life. She had a laundry list of things that needed to be done before he was discharged from hospital, and she hoped to have the two most pressing requirements completed by day's end.

She and Ruth needed to get the items each wanted to take with them moved to the other's cottage, and she had several potential home health aides lined up for interviews. Though he would be out of the hospital, Martin would most certainly need continued medical support. The candidates would meet with her at the school over her lunch break.

Louisa was able to finish up with the paperwork she had failed to get done the previous night as well as to wash and dry a load of clothes before Poppy arrived. She was folding the last of James Henry's jumpers when the childminder came in the door.

"Good morning, Poppy," she said.

"Morning, Mrs. Ellingham. Looks like you've been busy already."

"Mm, there's a lot to get done. In fact, I won't be home for lunch today. I have several health aide candidates coming in for interviews." She transferred the stack of folded miniature garments to a laundry basket and set it aside. "Would you like to have a cuppa with me before I have to leave?"

"Yeah, that'd be nice. It's kind'a chilly this morning," the girl said, rubbing her arms, vigorously.

"I know. It's hard to believe fall's almost here ... sad actually. It was such a nice warm summer."

Poppy slipped her coat over a peg behind the door before going to greet her small charge. "G'morning, James."

The boy blew out a string of bubbles and kicked his feet as she took a seat next to him.

Louisa set two cups of tea on the table, adding milk to hers before passing the small plastic jug to the childminder.

"Poppy, I need to discuss our plans for Martin's homecoming with you. Since he'll be using a wheelchair to get around most of the time, we've decided to switch cottages with Ruth. Just until he's able to bear full weight on his legs again."

Poppy stopped buttering her toast and looked at her. "Why do you want to switch cottages?"

"It seems Ruth's house is already wheelchair accessible. We'd have to make some costly and difficult changes to this house to make it work for Martin, so Ruth suggested this as a possible solution. Martin and I thought it was a brilliant idea."

"Yeah, that makes sense." She hesitated before peering up at her employer. "Erm, I've been wondering ... will you need me to look after James during that time or ..."

"Definitely, Poppy. If you're comfortable with that." Louisa picked up her plate and cup and carried it to the sink. She turned, giving the young woman an understanding smile. "There'll be a health care worker here to help with Martin's needs ... at least for a while. So, you wouldn't be responsible for any of that, if that's a concern."

Poppy's hunched shoulders relaxed. "I *was* sort of worried. I don't think I'd be very good with ... I mean I'm good with babies, but I don't think Dr. Ellingham would like me to ... you know."

"Poppy, I hope you realise Dr. Ellingham likes you. I think he was impressed when you told him you wanted to learn about first aid ... to be properly prepared for any emergency that could arise with James. Martin has an affinity for anyone who has an interest in medicine ... or just wants to learn for that matter."

Louisa glanced at her watch and grabbed her satchel before placing a kiss on the top of James's head. "I better get going. I'll see you this afternoon, Poppy," she said before racing out the door.

She hurried off towards the school, passing Ruth at the bottom of the hill.

"What's the latest word from my nephew?" the elderly woman asked as she brushed a wisp of wind blown hair from her eyes.

"Martin called last night. Would you be available to go over to Truro with me on Friday? Dr. Newell thought it'd be helpful if you and I could be there for Martin's four o'clock therapy session."

"I think I could make that work," Ruth said as she began to move away. "I'll see you tonight at five then?"

"Yes, we'll meet at your cottage ... move your things first. Poppy's going to stay late tonight and watch James."

"Good enough!" Ruth called over her shoulder.

When the first of the home health aides arrived, Louisa knew immediately the woman would not be compatible with Martin. She had too many mannerisms that would raise her husband's ire. She was far too chatty, her flow of conversation incessant. And she had a rather dishevelled look about her with an oversized handbag to match. The handbag was immediately plopped on top of a neatly organised stack of papers on Louisa's desk, sending them sliding across to land on the floor on the opposite side. Louisa quickly dispensed with the ill-suited candidate, thanking her for her time and showing her to the door.

She gave the young man sitting on the sofa outside her office a smile, and he stood and introduced himself.

"Hello ... er, Mrs. Ellingham? I'm Jeremy Portman; I'm here to interview for the health aide position."

Louisa gave the fellow a quick once over. So far, so good. "Hello, Jeremy. Come on in. Have a seat, please," she said, gesturing to the chair in front of her desk. She sat down and quickly scanned his curriculum vitae to refamiliarise herself with the information she had gone over the day before.

"I see you received your nursing degree six and a half years ago, and you've been working at the Royal Cornwall as a nurse up to now. Why is it that you're making the change to home health care work?"

"I've learned a great deal working in hospitals, but I'd like to get a better understanding of what patients face when returning home.

"I want to be upfront with you, Mrs. Ellingham. As you can see by my CV, I've never worked as a home health aide, and I don't really intend to continue with this sort of work. But I've found during my time in hospital that our health care system doesn't do an adequate job of preparing patients for their return home. I'm hoping to learn more about patient needs and where our medical system's failing to provide for those needs."

Louisa was impressed by this candidate's initiative, and he looked ideal on paper. But would he be able to handle a Martin Ellingham personality?

"Jeremy, have you been made aware of who my husband is ... his reputation?"

The young man smiled at her. "I've actually read some of his papers. I have an uncle who's a cardiologist. He passes his *BMJs* on to me."

This is the person I want caring for my Martin, Louisa thought.

"Yes, he *is* well known for his surgical skills, but there's another side to his reputation. He can be quite ... challenging to work with. He's very forthcoming, too much so at times. It's hard for people to see past his rather crusty exterior to the very kind man he is underneath. That crusty exterior is something many people can't deal with."

"I understand. My grandfather's the same way. I *am* used to the personality type."

Louisa looked at the young man sceptically. "Hmm. Well, I'm impressed with your credentials, Jeremy. I'm just gathering information right now. I'll discuss everything with my husband. Then I'll let you know of my decision, either way, within the next few days."

She saw Jeremy to the door before inviting the next candidate into her office, but in her mind, the decision had been made.

Katie Gardner stopped to see Martin late Wednesday morning. She said nothing about the abrupt end to their session the day before.

Using the lift, she helped Martin into a wheelchair.

"We're going to work today on how to operate the chair, Dr. Ellingham. It's not as simple when you're the patient sitting in the chair as it is when you're healthy and pushing the chair. And since you only have one arm you can use, things become even more challenging. This is a single lever drive chair, so you'll be able to get yourself around using just your left arm."

The therapist showed Martin how to pump the lever back and forth to propel himself forward. She then had him practice turning the chair by moving the lever left or right.

"If you need to go up an incline, lean your body forward to keep from tipping backwards. Do the opposite when you're going *down* an incline."

She had Martin practice, getting comfortable with managing turns.

After double checking that her patient's legs were securely elevated, Katie waved Martin towards the hall.

"Okay, let's go for a walk," she said, holding the door open.

He hesitated. "Are you sure I'm ready for this?"

"I wouldn't send you out there if I didn't think you were, Dr. Ellingham," she said, giving him a reassuring smile. "Come on, let's go."

They made several laps around the hospital floor, with Martin muttering under his breath at the gawps from the group of registrars they passed by.

"For God's sake, haven't they ever seen a patient in a wheelchair before?" he snarled.

A small smile crept on to the occupational therapist's face. "I don't think it was the wheelchair they were looking at."

"Oh, all the better! Maybe they need to find something more productive to do with their time then." He glanced up at the therapist and softened his tone. "I'm sorry. I feel a bit conspicuous ... in my current condition."

"If it makes you feel any better, I don't think they were in awe of your fixators. They're in awe of you ... *Mr.* Ellingham."

"Nonsense. Are we done here, or are you going to parade me around the other floors as well?" Martin said as they neared his room.

"Nope, we're done." Katie held the door as her patient wheeled himself through, manoeuvring the chair over near the window.

"You did very well, Doctor. I'll let you take a break now. I'd like to have you sit for a while before I help you back into bed. Can I get you anything before I go?"

Martin couldn't allow himself to make eye contact with the young lady after his display of anger earlier in the week. "Yes, my journals over there. And ... if you don't mind, a glass of water."

"Certainly." She gathered the items together and pulled a low table over next to the window before laying them down.

"Thank you," he said, his gaze firmly fixed on the floor.

Katie tipped her head down, trying to see her patient's face. Then she pulled a chair up in front of him. "Dr. Ellingham, I think we should talk about what happened the other day. I know it must have been terribly frustrating for you ... frightening in fact. It must have been upsetting to find you had so little dexterity in your hand. Please try to remember ... we're just getting started with therapy. Things *will* get better."

Martin sat silent but nodded his head.

"When I come back a bit later we'll do some more work with that hand. It's going to take a lot of patience on your part to work through this, though."

Martin squeezed his eyes shut, trying to hold back the emotions the young woman was bringing to the surface again. He wiped his palm down his face. "I was a surgeon. I'd hoped that I would still have the option of going back to it again, but I don't ..."

She nodded. "Like I said, we're just getting started. You'll see big changes over the next week ... a lot of improvement. Don't give up hope so soon."

Martin pulled in a ragged breath. "Okay. Okay."

He sat reading after the therapist left, enjoying the warmth of the sunshine and the occasional gaze out the window. There had been no menu delivered to him, so it didn't come as a surprise when the Parsons walked in with lunch.

"Hey, Mart. It looks like they outfitted you with a new set of wheels." Carole took a seat in the chair vacated by the therapist, and Chris pulled a chair over, settling in next to her.

"Mm, this one I can actually drive. Now if I can just figure out how to get the doors open on my own, I can make a run for it."

"We brought you some lunch," Carole said. She moved Martin's borrowed reading material and set a large bowl of macaroni and cheese down next to him, followed by a tossed salad and heavily buttered, hand baked bread. "Eat up," she ordered. "I had a nice long talk with your wife last night."

Martin peered up. "Oh? What did you talk about?"

"Hmm, let's see. We discussed how we felt about the new lipstick colours for fall, and the practicality of above the knee hemlines when you're a primary school teacher."

He furrowed his brow at her.

"And you might find this interesting ... we discussed an article we'd seen in the latest BMJ about the recent medical advancements in the treatment of excessively curly hair," she said, trying to suppress a smirk.

Martin's head shot up, looking at the woman with a mouthful of bread and an expression of consternation. He quickly washed the bread down with a gulp of water and turned to Chris. "I didn't read that one. Did you read that one?"

"I think she's kidding you, Mart," Chris said, shaking his head at his wife.

Chapter 4

Katie came back to Martin's room shortly after the Parsons had left. Having lunch with his friends had improved Martin's mood considerably. He found a visit from Carole made him feel a bit closer to Louisa. Perhaps it was the bond the two women had formed.

The therapist got her patient back into bed and comfortable before beginning to work his right arm and hand.

"Okay, Dr. Ellingham. Can you get that brace off so we can work through some exercises?" She watched as Martin struggled with the fasteners. "Let me know if you'd like some assistance," she said as she noticed moisture breaking out on his forehead and his face beginning to blanch.

"I'm fine! Just give me a little time here!" he sputtered before adding a softer, "Please."

"Well done," Katie said as her patient pulled the brace from his arm, dropping it on to the bed beside him. "Were you able to get it off to do your exercises yesterday?"

"Yes, twice. But there's no way that I can get the thing back on by myself. I need to have a nurse come in to do it."

"I'm sure you can't. I think you'll probably be rid of the brace before you're fit enough to wrestle that thing back on by yourself. That's all right. Just try to keep your arm against your tummy until someone is available to help you. The important thing is you're getting it off and working those muscles and the wrist joint. I'm going to try to do a little with your elbow and shoulder today as well."

She had Martin work through one of the exercises she had done with him on Monday, but the exercise that had proven so agonising had been eliminated for the time being.

"Okay, Doctor," the therapist said, taking in a deep breath. "Are you ready to try my infantile game again?"

"Mm. I'm sorry about that," Martin said, ducking his head. "That was uncalled for."

"It's all right," she said. "At least you didn't throw them at *me*."

Katie dumped the items on to the table, and Martin tried to pick them up. Not only was it nearly impossible for him to feel the objects, trying to get his fingers to move in the coordinated manner required to pick the items up seemed impossible.

He shook his head. "I can't do this."

"Okay, let's take it in baby steps. See if you can push this block from your side of the table over to me." The therapist placed a one inch square block down in front of him.

"Gawd." Martin turned his head to the side and closed his eyes for a moment before refocusing his attention on the task in front of him.

One by one, he managed to shove three blocks across the table before the little strength he had left failed and his arm dropped to his lap.

"Use your good arm to support the right one if you like. It's not cheating." Katie gave him an encouraging nod. "You can do it."

Martin hissed air from his nose and then reached over with his left hand, lifting the right one up to the level of the table before sliding another block across to the therapist.

"Okay, that's progress!" She set another block down in front of him, and Martin scowled at her, mumbling unintelligibly. "I know it doesn't seem like much of an accomplishment to you, Dr. Ellingham, but it's a first step. And believe me, it's a *big* first step. Let's try again."

The exercise continued a while longer before Katie shifted gears to something less taxing. "This is called Therapy Putty," she said, pulling a golf ball-sized piece of the elastic substance from a plastic container. "I want you working with this as often as you can throughout the day. Squeeze it, roll it out into a snake on the table, pinch it, whatever you want to do with it. You're a doctor, so I don't have to tell you that the more you work the muscles in that hand and arm, the faster the swelling will go down. And the less oedema there is, the less pressure there will be on those nerves."

It was excruciatingly difficult, but Martin forced his hand to close loosely around the ball. The second time, the ball of putty fell out of his hand and on to the table.

"That's okay. Just pick it up with your left hand and push it back into your palm. Then try again," she said.

The therapist let him work for a few minutes before picking up a small pot of cocoa butter. She massaged his fingers and hand, gradually working her way up his arm.

"We'll try to work some of the tightness out of these muscles and move some of the fluid back as well. This should actually feel very nice, so if anything hurts, let me know."

Martin laid back and closed his eyes, the gentle pressure on his aches and pains relaxing him. He woke some time later. The therapist was gone, but the ball of putty had been tucked back into his palm.

When Louisa arrived at Ruth's that evening, there was a red van, emblazoned with the words Large Restaurant, parked on the street, and Al and Morwenna were loading it with boxes of Ruth's belongings.

"Hello Morwenna," Louisa said. "I wasn't expecting to see you here."

"Thought maybe you could use an extra pair of hands. How's the doc?"

"The first few weeks were difficult, but he's beginning to show steady improvement now. How have *you* been doing— finding yourself unexpectedly unemployed and all?"

"I'm doin' okay ... good actually. I've been fillin' in at the fudge shop. One of the clerks went back to school a few weeks ago, so they needed someone to help out ... just 'til the tourist season's over. Best thing's I get free fudge. Nice little perk of the job."

"That's great, Morwenna. I'm sorry all of this has been so disruptive for you," Louisa said, dropping a box on to the floor of the van and shoving it to the front.

Morwenna followed her back up the steps to Ruth's porch. "I *was* kinda worried about makin' ends meet with just the fudge shop job. I couldn't believe it when the doc called and said I'd be gettin' paid as usual."

Louisa whirled around in the doorway. "Martin called you?"

"Yeah, about a week ago."

Louisa didn't say anymore. She decided she better discuss this with her husband. He wasn't thinking clearly a week ago. It would be awkward, but the misunderstanding would need to be sorted out.

It took the moving crew a solid three hours to get everything moved between the houses and reorganise cupboards so the essentials in the bathroom and the kitchen at Ruth's cottage would be accessible to Martin. They also moved the bed out of Ruth's guest bedroom so there would be space to accommodate the adjustable hospital bed that was scheduled to be delivered Friday morning.

Louisa knew they would discover impediments for Martin once he was trying to move around in the house, but they were as ready as she felt they could be.

After treating everyone to dinner at Bert's and getting James off to bed, she picked up her mobile and rang Martin.

"Louisa?"

She smiled, wondering if her husband would ever cease to be surprised to get a call from her. "Hi, Martin. How was your day?"

"It was ... better. I wheeled myself around the floor I'm on ... made several laps in fact."

"How in the world did you do that? You know ... with one arm to use."

"There's a lever on the left side. If I move it back and forth, it propels the chair either forward or backwards."

"That's wonderful, Martin! You're getting your independence back."

"Don't be too impressed; the therapist still needs to help me in and out of the chair."

"You need to be patient, Martin. It *will* happen, but you can't rush it."

"I'm hardly rushing things, Louisa. I'm still stuck in this bed for goodness' sake."

"Yes, but you don't want any more setbacks, right? You need to let people help you."

"I don't *like* people helping me!"

Louisa rubbed a hand across her forehead. "Well, you're just going to have to grin and bear it for a while, I'm afraid. I know you're anxious to have things back to normal, but until then, you're going to be pretty reliant on other people." She huffed out a breath. "How 'bout you try to think of it as being on holiday—you putting your feet up and taking it easy ... letting people wait on you."

He groaned. "Sounds appalling."

"Mar-tin ... *patience.*"

Scowling, he picked up the ball of putty and threw it at the wall on the other side of the room, bumping the pitcher of water on the tray table and spilling it on to the bed in the process. *"Oh, bugger,"* he mumbled.

Louisa heard the clattering in the background. "Martin, what's going on?"

"Mm, nothing ... nothing," he said as he reached out to grab the box of tissues from the dresser.

"Mar-tin?" she asked, her tone admonishing.

"All right! I knocked over the pitcher of water that was on my tray table!" he snapped, blotting at the moisture with the tissues.

"Oh, dear. Maybe you should get a nurse to come and clean things up."

He struggled, trying to hold the mobile on his shoulder while he dabbed at the soaked bedding before throwing the wet wads of tissue on to the floor in frustration.

"No, I've got it." He shook his hand, trying to dislodge the bits of soggy paper that had adhered to his fingers.

"You sure, Martin? It sounds like you're having some tr—"

"I've got it, Louisa!" He wiped his hands on the blankets in an attempt to rid himself of the remnants of tissue.

"Well, I had a good day," Louisa said, the cheerfulness in her voice seeming to add insult to injury as Martin continued to wage war in his bed, the moisture now soaking through to his skin.

Beginning to feel a chill from the wet bedding he pulled at the blankets, trying to throw them away from his body. But his efforts accomplished nothing more than to tangle them around his fixators.

Realising there was nothing more he could do to remove himself from the predicament, he returned his attention to his wife.

"... think he'd be ideal. What do you think?"

He heard his wife's words trail off, and there was a long pause with dead air on his end of the line.

"Martin, are you there?"

"Mm. Mm. Yes. Erm, what were you saying?"

"I was saying, Martin ... I think he'd be ideal, don't you?"

Martin's thoughts were racing, trying to imagine what his wife could be referring to.

"Could you say the whole thing again? I was a bit ... distracted."

Louisa huffed and then repeated her description of the three potential health aides, perturbed by her husband's seeming disinterest.

"So, what do you think?" she asked expectantly.

"Which one do you think we should hire?" he asked, looking around the room, wondering how he was going to explain the mess to the next person to come through the door.

"Martin! You haven't been paying any attention to me *at— all!*"

"I'm sorry. I had my mind on something else. I trust you to make the decision. I didn't meet them, you know."

"Okay, Martin," Louisa said, her ponytail flicking peevishly. "We got everything moved around today, so I'm ready when you are."

"Ready when I am for what?"

"It's an expression, Martin. It means that when you're ready to come home, I'll have Ruth's cottage all set for you."

"I see."

Louisa rolled her eyes. "Well, maybe I should let you go. You sound tired." She sat down and swung her legs up on the sofa.

"Mm, I am. But I like to hear your voice. Will you be coming on Friday?"

"Definitely. I think Ruth will be as well. We'll be there before four o'clock."

"Good. I miss you," Martin said, wishing he could feel the warmth of her—her softness.

"I miss you, too. Goodnight."

"Mm. Goodnight."

Martin set his mobile on the table as the door to his room opened and a nurse entered. She stood, slack-jawed, as she scanned around the room.

"What in the world happened in here?"

"Ah. I had a little spill."

Chapter 5

The nurses woke Martin early on Thursday, drawing blood for tests that Mr. Christianson had ordered. He also had to endure a bed bath as well as the added indignity of a hair wash.

Being fussed over by relative strangers had put him in a foul mood by the time Tim Spalding arrived.

"I spoke with Katie Gardner yesterday. She said you've been doing more with your arm but you're having difficulty with muscle atrophy and some loss of sensitivity. Take the brace off and we'll see what we can do about that today."

Martin wrested himself from the orthosis while his therapist waited patiently.

"Okay, I want you to squeeze as hard as you can," Tim said as he took Martin's hand in his. He cocked his head. "Well, you've got a pretty weak grip—not surprising given the extent of the damage. But the muscles are definitely firing." He scanned around the room. "Katie said she left you with some Therapy Putty. Where do you have that?"

Martin scowled and looked down at his lap. "It's over there somewhere, probably on the floor."

Tim walked across the room, and after sliding a chair away from the wall, he reached down to pick up the small tan ball. "You might want to find a more convenient place to store it," he said, giving his patient an amused smile.

Tossing the used ball in the bin, he washed his hands and then pulled a clean chunk of putty from the can on his cart. "Here you go, Martin. I want you to work with this for the next five minutes. Do what you like with it ... as long as you use your right hand. That way you won't be able to chuck it so far if you decide to give it the heave-ho."

"Very funny." Martin yanked the putty from his therapist's hand as he screwed up his face.

The therapist took a seat in a chair by the bed, scribbling notes in a file. He looked up a few minutes later. "Okay, that's enough." Taking the putty, he rolled it out into a rope. "Now, I want you to work your way along the length of this, pinching it flat," he said, demonstrating with his thumb and forefinger.

Martin's face was taut as he concentrated intensely to get his unwilling digits to respond.

Taking note of the occasional grimace on his patient's face, Tim said, "Is that causing you pain?"

"Mm. It's just muscle pain. I'm fine," Martin said, determined to work to the end of the rope.

"Nope, I think that's enough." The therapist set the putty aside and moved to the bottom of the bed. Grabbing hold of the fixators on his patient's lower right leg, he began the range of motion exercises, pushing his patient's knee towards his chest. "You have a lot less rigidity in these muscles now. Think back to the first day I came in and worked with you. Can you feel the difference?"

"I'm not sure I remember our first sessions. My memory's been a bit sketchy lately."

Tim finished working Martin's legs, then handed him a soft, rubber ball, about three inches in diameter.

"Let's play some catch. This will improve the coordination in that left arm and hand. You're going to be relying on it for everything for a while."

Martin groaned. "I've never been good at sports."

"Well, it's not really a sport; we're just tossing a ball back and forth," Tim said, suppressing a grin. "Just to even things up a bit, I'll throw with my left hand, too. How 'bout that?" the therapist said as he gave the ball a toss.

Latching on to the it, Martin grunted softly before throwing it back.

Tim nodded his head. "You're surprisingly good at this. Must be those surgeon's paws of yours."

Martin's breath caught in his throat as the disheartening start to his morning and the young man's words hit him. He set his jaw and swallowed hard before pulling a hand to his face. "Can you give me a few minutes?" he asked.

"I'll be back in a little while," Tim said before leaving the room.

When he returned fifteen minutes later, Martin was working the Therapy Putty in his palm.

"Should we try again?" he asked, giving the ball a toss.

They continued with the game of catch a while longer before Tim returned the ball to the box on his cart and pulled out the all-too-familiar container of objects the occupational therapist used. He dumped them out on to the table.

"You know how this game works, I think. Don't you?"

"Yes," Martin grunted.

"Katie said this has been frustrating you, so don't worry about trying to pick things up. Just try to grasp on to something. You might start with the wood blocks first. They're generally a little easier to get hold of."

Tim watched as Martin made several unsuccessful attempts.

"All right, it looks to me like we need to work on getting those fingers to open." He shoved the objects to the side and had Martin lay his hand, palm down, flat on the table.

"I want you to lift your arm and hand up, but try to keep your fingers straight when you do that."

Martin's brow furrowed and his jaw clenched with his effort to do what the therapist had asked, but he couldn't keep his fingers from curling into his palm. His arm dropped back to the table, and he squeezed his eyes shut. "I can't do it," he said softly.

Tim pulled the table away." I think I've worn you out. Lay back and I'll see what I can do with the oedematous tissue—get some of the fluid worked out of your arm."

He pulled out a jar of cocoa butter, massaging his patient's hand before working his way up his arm. Martin fought to keep his eyes open but lost the battle when the therapist moved to his feet and legs. The pain relief that resulted from the gentle massaging of his limbs allowed his fatigue to take control.

When he woke late in the morning a nurse was in the room recording his vital signs.

"Hello, Dr. Ellingham. Did you have a good rest?" she asked as she replaced the bottle on his drip.

He rubbed the grogginess from his eyes. "Yes, I did. I was tired."

"I'll go and call Mr. Spalding. He wanted to get you up into the chair once you were awake," she said before hurrying out of the room.

Tim came in shortly and moved Martin to the wheelchair, covering him with a blanket. He then disconnected the IV from his wrist and central line. "Let's go for a walk."

They made their way down the hall to the lift, and the therapist took him down to the ground floor.

"*We* are going to get some fresh air, mate. You've been cooped up in this stuffy hospital for too long."

Tim slapped a hand against the button on the wall and the automatic doors whooshed open. "Let me wheel you through the doorway, Martin, and then I'll let you take over. How's the arm holding out?"

"I'm okay."

They arrived at a bench next to the sidewalk and Tim took a seat. Martin fumbled around, trying to get himself manoeuvered into position alongside his therapist.

"Good job, Martin."

"Hmm, it wasn't very pretty."

"We're not going for pretty yet. The important thing is that you got where you wanted to go ... on your own."

Martin reflexively filled his lungs. The fresh air was wonderful, but it lacked the salt that seasoned the air in Portwenn, as well as the overtones of fish and seaweed that were borne on the nearly continuous winds that pushed their way in over the harbour.

Song birds flitted around a nearby bird feeder, and he found himself longing for the brassy calls of the herring gulls, which he usually cursed. They had an unerring ability to splatter his spotless Lexus with their excrement.

The breeze rippling through the trees overhead didn't share the rhythmic, pulsating quality of the waves that washed in before falling upon the rugged coastline of his little community. And the people scurrying about in their blue jeans and jumpers seemed in stark contrast to the laid-back ways of the fishermen who wandered Portwenn in their brace trousers.

"Gawd, I'm missing the village of the damned!" he said, unthinking.

"What's that?"

"Mm, sorry. I'm just ..." Martin shook his head and waved a hand in the air. "Nothing."

The two men sat a while, soaking in the last warm rays of sun, which would soon be replaced by the clouds, rain and cold of winter.

"Do you think I'll get my dexterity back ... my surgical dexterity?" Martin said suddenly, giving Tim a penetrating stare.

The therapist hesitated as he prepared an honest answer that would not discourage his patient.

"Martin, I won't insult your intelligence by feeding you some stale platitude designed to keep you motivated. You know as well as I do that your chances of getting that kind of dexterity back are not great. But you can better your odds by giving this your all right now.

"Your medical history would suggest your chances of surviving the car accident in the first place were pretty low. From what Mr. Christianson has told me about your condition immediately following your accident, you probably have better odds of getting yourself back into theatre than you had of sitting here with me today. So, don't let anyone tell you that you *won't* get that dexterity back."

Tim leaned over and plucked a dandelion from the ground. He sat back up and looked his patient in the eye.

"Martin, do the best you can and be prepared to accept the outcome. I'm sorry I can't give you a better answer."

Inhaling deeply, Martin breathed out a resigned sigh. "Thank you."

He had been poring over the material left by Dr. Newell when Martin heard the door open. Ed Christianson entered the room and walked to the bed, pulling the blankets back from his patient's legs.

"Let's take a look here, Martin. The big boys are coming down from London on Saturday, so we've got to have you looking your best, eh?"

"Mm."

"Have you seen your wounds lately?" Ed asked.

Martin shifted uncomfortably. "That'd be like carrying coals to Newcastle," he muttered. "I think there are plenty of other people gawping at my wounds."

Ed pulled a chair over and sat down. "You know, I'm not going to let you out of here until you can prove to me you can handle all of this on your own."

"I'm a doctor. Of course I can handle it on my own!"

"Well, then show me. Put some of that famous Ellingham fire into this. How are you going to be able to take care of these wounds once you're home if you can't bear to look at them now? Since you seem to like trite idioms, let me put it this way—you've got to take the bull by the horns."

Martin sat looking at his hands.

"Okay, Martin. I'm going to take all of your bandages off and leave you alone to come to terms with this," he said as he removed the dressings. He got up and walked to the door. "I'll be back in a while, and we can talk about what'll happen on Saturday. But I want you to deal with this now," he said, letting the door swing shut behind him.

Ed met up with Chris in the corridor.

"I put him in time out," the surgeon said, giving a nod down the hall.

"Great, what'd he do?"

"Nothing really. But he needs a bit of an attitude adjustment. I can't let him go home if he can't at least look at his wounds to check for infection."

"Ah, I see. I'm not sure, but I suspect he's feeling kind of insecure. He has this lovely wife, and they've had a rather rocky relationship, do in great part to Martin's behaviour I'm sure. But Ed, the guy's absolutely besotted with her. I don't think he could deal with it if she left him. And I think Martin knows he couldn't deal with it."

"She seems very committed to me."

"Well, let's just say his concerns are justified to some extent. I agree, I think Louisa *is* committed to him. But Martin's insecure, and I *do* understand where he's coming from," Chris said. He sighed. "I was heading down that way, so I'll see if there's anything I can do. We looked at his wounds together a while back. I didn't know it was still bothering him."

Chris paused, trying to decide how much personal information he should divulge to the surgeon. "Martin's had a lot more to deal with than the major physical trauma. There's psychological trauma he's trying to work through as well ...

from his childhood. I don't want to betray a trust, so that's all I'll say about it. I just want you to know, the guy's really trying."

Ed nodded. "I have other patients to check on. I'll finish up with the great Martin Ellingham when I'm done with my rounds."

"Thanks, Ed."

Chris knocked lightly on Martin's door before going in. "Hey, Mart. How's it going?" he asked as he sank into the chair next to the bed.

"Mm, all right. I actually got out of the building today. It was good to get some fresh air."

"Yeah, I'll bet." Chris got back to his feet and leaned over to inspect his friend's wounds. "These are looking a lot better than the last time I saw them. What do you think?"

"Mm, I agree ... better. Still pretty ugly though."

Chris reclaimed his seat. "Are you still worried about how Louisa will look at you?"

Martin sat silent, worrying his bottom lip.

"I can understand if you are, Mart. I know you don't need to be, but I do understand."

Martin's head shot up. "What do you mean, you know I don't need to be? You can't possibly know that! She may see things differently once the pity she's feeling for me wears off."

Chris snorted. "Mart, I've told you before, you're not the pitiful type. Louisa's worried about you. She hates to see you in pain—physical *and* emotional. You're not pitiful ... yet. But if you keep fussing over how she's going to react to you in bed—"

"Oh, for goodness' sake, Chris! I never said anything to that effect!"

"Martin, you know that's what you're worrying about. Just say it!" Chris blew a long stream of air through his nose. "You two have had a lot of ups and downs. You're afraid the effect this accident has had on your body is going to be the last nail in your coffin. Am I right?"

"Maybe," he mumbled.

Chris gave him a stern look before Martin snapped, "All right! Yes!"

"Martin, I know women. Once this is all over, Louisa's going to use those scars as an excuse to plaster you with kisses."

"Since when do *you* know women?" Martin snorted.

"I know a thing or two!"

"Yeah, that's about right."

Chris returned a sideways glance. "It's more than *you* know," he mumbled.

"Look ... I'm sorry, Chris," Martin said, shaking his head slowly. "Maybe I'm not pitiful, but I suppose I *am* pretty pathetic to be worrying about something like this."

They sat for a minute before Chris broke the silence.

"Martin, I do understand where you're coming from. I'd probably be feeling the same way. But you should have seen how absolutely devastated that wife of yours was when she walked into the trauma centre and saw you lying there.

"I'd tried to prepare her for the condition you were in. I told her to focus on your face ... to not look at your arms and legs. But she saw. She *saw*, Martin. She saw your distorted right leg. She saw the exposed bones.

"And I saw the look on her face. There was no pity, no disgust. Just absolute terror to see the agony you were in. All she wants is to have you home with her again. To know you're going to be okay. She's not going to leave you, mate."

Martin gave his friend an acknowledging nod before an expression of dismay fell across his face.

"Chris ... Louisa was in the trauma centre?"

"You don't remember?"

Martin took in a deep breath, shaking his head slowly.

"She was begging me to let her see you, and you were desperate to see her. You were crashing, Mart. The more distraught you got about wanting Louisa, the faster your heart raced. Ed and I didn't think you'd..." Chris gulped back the lump in his throat. "We wanted you to see each other one last time."

Martin sat expressionless.

"Did Louisa know what you were thinking?"

"No. She knew your injuries were serious ... that your condition was precarious, but no, I don't think she knew why we let her come in."

Chris placed his hands on his knees and pushed himself up from the chair. "Well, I better get home, or Carole will have my head for being late for dinner."

As the door swung shut behind his friend, Martin picked up the book that he had been reading. Then, taking in a deep breath, he laid it back down and began to assess his wounds.

Chapter 6

Martin lay in bed Thursday night, trying to suss out the bits and bobs of memories which had been flitting through his head. His inability to distinguish between the genuine recollections of the days and nights after the accident and the scenarios which played out in his dreams was disquieting.

He knew he had been anxious to get home that night. He had been looking forward to a proper kiss from his wife. Why, he didn't know. But the thought now caused stirrings in him as he closed his eyes and felt her warm lips against his.

His friend's words, just hours before, replaced his more carnal musings and a melancholia settled over him. Louisa had been there that night. He knew what she had seen. He'd been witness to the consequences of high speed traffic accidents on numerous occasions. The smells, the sounds, and grisly sights in a trauma centre.

Tears stung his eyes as a deep longing for her set in. He had allowed himself to grow used to having someone who loved him. And it seemed to whet the sting of her absence the way a rare warm and sunny day in January seems to whet the sting of the inevitable cold, dank, and grey days that were sure to lie ahead.

It was the small hours before his need for sleep offset that longing.

Carole stopped in shortly after he woke Friday morning, carrying with her the now familiar white box with the red lid.

"Good morning, Martin. Did you sleep well?" she asked, her cheerfulness chafing at his sour mood.

He sighed and looked with a certain degree of annoyance.

"Sorry. I keep promising I'm going to stop asking you that. Just a habit I guess." She pulled his tray table over and set down a plate of scrambled eggs and sausage with a side of heavily buttered crumpets with jelly. "Chris said you could do with a little cheering up, so I stopped in at the cafe to pick this up for you." Carole handed him a cup and set the box aside before sitting down next to the bed.

Martin mustered a small smile. "Mm, thank you."

"So, what do you hear from Louisa?"

"We didn't talk last night; she had a meeting at the school until late."

"I see. I spoke with her earlier in the week. I guess you know that," she said giving him a sly smile.

He washed down a bit of crumpet with a swig of espresso. "Yes. Lipstick, hemlines, and hair."

Carole couldn't help but giggle at his childish pout, earning her an especially stern look in return.

"Anyway, she mentioned she and Ruth were coming this afternoon. Can they stay the weekend? We'd love to have them."

Martin hemmed and hawed as an anxiety began to build in him. He had been looking forward all week to having Louisa with him at hospital, and he fought his inclination to decline the offer for his wife. He knew better than to make decisions for her.

"Mm, you need to ask Louisa."

Carole leaned back in her chair. "How are you doing Martin? Does it seem like things are improving?"

He poked at a bite of sausage. "Some things are improving. The pain's better than it was at first. The physiotherapy ... it's frustrating ... quite infuriating at times actually."

"I'm so sorry this happened, Martin." She gave him a sympathetic smile. "You and Louisa will get through it, though. I know you will."

"Mm. Has Louisa said anything about how she feels about this?"

Carole cocked her head at him. "Well, I'm not sure what you're asking, but at the moment she feels a great sense of relief that you're going to be all right, and she can't wait to have you home."

He huffed out a breath. "No, I mean about all she's going to have to put up with."

"Martin... put up with? She loves you!"

"What I mean is, it's going to be months of everything revolving around ... this. She might need someone to talk to ... complain to when I get the way I can be—a difficult person. And things aren't going to be the same between us."

"What do you mean by that?"

"Well, I can be ... monosyllabic—gruff—rude."

The corners of Carole's mouth nudged up. "There's some truth to that. But I don't think that will come as a surprise to her. And you have many wonderful qualities, Martin. But that's not what I was asking. I was wondering what you meant when you said things aren't going to be the same between you."

Martin's head dropped to the side. "Well, it's just ... Well, with all this hardware it's not ... you know it won't be easy. The—the physical side of things will ... Oh, come on! It won't be the same! You must know what I mean!"

"Sex? You're talking about sex?"

"Of course, I'm talking about sex!" Martin sputtered as the door opened and a young woman came in to replace the linens in the cabinet on the wall.

"Sorry to interrupt; I'll just be a minute," she said as the colour rose in her cheeks.

Martin turned his gaze to the window until the girl had stepped back into the hall, and the door closed behind her.

Carole got to her feet and stood by the bed. "Okay, I think I know what you're getting at. You *will* work it out Martin. And

I don't think you need to worry about Louisa needing someone to complain to. She might need someone to *talk* to, but I think it's going to be a long time before she complains about you. This accident opened her eyes."

"I'm sorry, I don't follow."

"Sometimes we don't appreciate what we have until we've lost it. Louisa was very fortunate, Martin. She didn't lose you, but she came very, very close. She won't complain."

She gathered the dishes together and leaned over to place a chaste kiss on his cheek. "You *can* be a difficult person Martin, but there's also a sweetness ... a real kindness in you. Let Louisa see that side of you, and she'll be able to look past that difficult side."

Tim Spalding came by later in the morning. Ed Christianson wanted him to step up the resistance exercises and evaluate Martin's readiness for partial weight bearing on his fractured legs.

"Okay, Martin, you know how this one works," Tim said as held on to his patient's heel and began to push his foot forward. Martin gritted his teeth as he worked to resist his therapist.

"Excellent! I'm really impressed with the strength you have in your legs, Martin. You've been doing your exercises."

"I want to go home. If it'll get me home, I'll do it."

"Okay, let's try something different. First, we're going to swing your legs around so you can sit on the edge of the bed."

Martin worked his way down the mattress, pushing off with his left arm, then Tim grabbed the fixators on his legs as he pivoted himself around. The pain that throbbed through his swollen limbs when they were first lowered over the side of the bed was agonising, but the pounding eased after a few minutes' time.

"Martin, we're going to put a small amount of weight on your legs while you're sitting there, just to prepare you for what you'll feel tomorrow," the therapist said as he slid a small adjustable platform under his patient's feet.

Tim raised the device until it was high enough for Martin's feet to rest on top of it.

"How does that feel?"

"It hurts," Martin said as he set his jaw against the pain.

"Is it a deep bone pain or is it pressure in the oedematous tissue?"

"Both. This isn't how it should feel," he said, growing concerned by the strange sensations in his legs.

"That's normal, Martin. Those sensations will be more pronounced when you stand up tomorrow. You'll have some idea of what to expect, though, so hopefully it won't be too overwhelming."

Tim stood back watching his patient's face for any concerning signs of distress. "Mr. Christianson said he talked with you last night about how things will be handled in the morning. Do you have any questions?"

"I'm having some nausea now. Will it be worse when I actually try to stand?"

"Possibly, and that's a very typical reaction. Your body's just overwhelmed by the sensations, and it *will* be painful. We'll have you stand for about fifteen seconds, then we'll have you sit for a while. Catch your breath before we try again."

Martin squeezed his eyes shut against the ache coursing through his lower legs.

"Is the pain getting any better?" the therapist asked.

"A little. But I'm not feeling ... very ..." His face began to blanch and his head fell back. Tim grabbed on to his vest and lowered him back on to the bed as he lost consciousness.

The therapist called a nurse into the room, and between the two of them they were able to get a still unconscious Martin slid back on to the mattress and his legs elevated. The nurse brought a cold wet flannel and laid it on his forehead.

The colour crept back into his face, and his eyelids fluttered open.

"We lost you for a bit there, Martin, but you're okay. We'll let you rest a while before we try again," Tim said as he raised the head of the bed and handed him a glass of water.

"I'm sorry. That was—was— It wasn't what I was expecting." The glass of water sloshed in his trembling hand as he turned his head away.

"Don't worry about that. It's perfectly normal. I was actually watching for it, and we will be tomorrow as well. Your body's weak, you're still recovering from the hypovolaemia, and the pain and those odd sensations are pretty intense."

Tim had Martin sit up several more times, allowing for breaks in between for the nausea and light-headedness to pass. Exhaustion and the pain relief the massage at the end of the session provided combined to lull the patient to sleep.

He woke some time later to the metallic rattle of the trolley that was used by the cafeteria workers to deliver meals to the rooms.

He was finishing his soup and sandwich when Louisa, James, and Ruth arrived.

"You're early!" he said.

Louisa walked over and kissed him. "Hope it's okay. I was anxious to see you."

"No, that's fine. Good!"

Martin didn't smile, but the sparkle in his eyes gave him away. The light seemed to dance in his soft grey-green orbs.

"You look happy," she said, caressing his cheek.

"It's you; you're a pleasant surprise." Martin reached up to press a finger into his son's small palm. "Hello, James."

Ruth walked to the end of the bed and scanned through her nephew's patient notes.

"They had you doing some partial weight bearing I see. Now that's progress!"

"They had you standing today?" Louisa asked.

Martin shook his head. The very thought of his gruelling morning session made him feel tired. "Just the weight of my legs. Tomorrow they'll have me try to stand."

Ruth put the notes down and walked to the head of the bed, leaning over to peer into her nephew's eyes. "How are you doing? I see you had a syncopal episode."

"Yes." Martin pulled his head back and shot her a warning glance. "But just the first time."

Louisa looked back and forth between the two doctors. "A syncopal episode?"

"Neurally-mediated syncope," Martin explained. "I passed out. It's a normal reaction. There were some rather intense sensations with the weight on my legs and that, probably combined with the hypotension caused by the opioids I've been receiving, resulted in a lack of oxygen to my brain."

"Oh, I see," Louisa said. "And what exactly do you mean by intense sensations?"

Martin immediately tried to downplay the effects felt when standing on fractured legs. "Some tingling, similar to electrical impulses. Aching—that sort of thing."

Louisa stared him down with a lowered head and furrowed brow. "Hmm. I think you're being evasive, Martin Ellingham."

He tipped his head towards the ceiling and waggled it side to side. "Louisa, I'm merely trying to answer your question."

Noticing her husband's defensive posturing, Louisa decided to let the issue go. She could get the answers she was looking for from Ruth or Chris later.

"If you'll excuse me, I'm going to get a cup of coffee. Al had me up far too late last night," Ruth said, yawning.

Martin watched the door swing shut behind her before reaching out to his wife.

"I missed you," he said as he pulled her close, giving her a proper kiss.

James Henry took advantage of the opportunity and leaned forward to grab on to his father's ears. Martin tipped his head forward to make contact with his son's.

The tensions about all that was ahead of him eased and Martin's chest swelled. The touch of his wife and son seemed to absorb some of the physical pain and emotional anguish he'd been dealing with. *I have a family—I have a wife, I have a son, and I have Ruth.*

Chapter 7

Louisa could feel her husband's body relax into her shoulder. "Martin. Are you okay?"

He lifted his head slowly, turning away as he brushed at his cheeks and cleared his throat. "Mm. I'm fine. You just—this was nice." He ran his hand over James's head as he blinked away the moisture in his eyes.

"I had an idea," Louisa said, touching her fingers to his cheek.

"Yes?"

"Maybe you could take James and me for a walk. Do you think they'd let you out of here for a while?"

Martin pulled back and peered down at her. "You're serious?"

"Yes, I'm serious. I'd like to see how your wheelchair works for one thing. And it's a lovely day; we should get some fresh air." She stroked her fingertips over the back of his neck.

"Mm. I can't get into the chair on my own you know. I need someone to help me."

"I can help you."

"Noo, you can't. We'll both end up on the floor."

"I'll go and get someone to help then." Louisa picked James up and hurried towards the door.

"Louisa, I really don't—"

She was already out of earshot.

The use of the lift to get him in and out of the wheelchair and on and off the commode was an indignity that had slowly chipped away at Martin's morale. An indignity his wife had not been aware of up to this point. She had never asked any questions about how he got in and out of the bed, and he hadn't offered the information. He was hoping that after tomorrow he would be able to stand and use a walker to transfer himself from the bed to the chair on his own—that she would never see him in such an undignified position.

He began to formulate ways of excusing himself from the outing.

Louisa returned to the room, looking triumphant. "A nurse is going to call Ed Christianson to make sure it's okay. Then they'll send someone in to help get you in the chair."

"Louisa, I don't think I should leave the room. The physiotherapist will be coming in again this afternoon, and we have our session with Dr. Newell at four o'clock."

"We don't have to make it a long walk. I just think it would be nice to do something as a family."

"How 'bout you and James go on your own. I can go with you another time."

"But it's supposed to be a rainy weekend, and it's a nice warm—"

"We'll do it another time, Louisa!"

Her husband's words were angry, but Louisa saw a vulnerability in his eyes.

"Okay. Okay, we'll do it another time," she said softly, brushing her fingers through his hair.

The subject of the walk had been dropped, and Martin sat with James, reading him his naptime story. He laid the book down when the boy's body became heavy against him.

Louisa picked the baby up and shifted him to the sofa cushions she had placed on the floor, covering him with a blanket. "He *is* a good little sleeper," she said when she returned to her husband's side.

Martin shifted himself over, making room for her, putting his arm around her and pulling her close.

"I hope the bed we have for you at Ruth's will be big enough for this kind of activity," she said as she stretched up to press her lips to his.

Martin fidgeted, trying to smooth the bedding covering his legs. "Louisa, that's something we need to talk about."

He kept his gaze averted as she tried to make eye contact with him. "The bed size?"

"No. We—I—er, it will be complicated to have ... as you call it ... activity. All this hardware will make it difficult."

Her husband's reticence to broach a topic with her which he could so freely discuss when in a doctor-patient situation was a trait she found quite charming. She leaned over to place a kiss on his cheek. "Well, *first* of all ... you obviously have a different take than I do on what I meant by *this kind of activity. I* was referring to the activity we're involved in at this very moment. *You*, evidently, are thinking of something requiring a bit more physical contact," she said. "Just what have you been lying in this bed thinking about at night, Martin Ellingham?"

Martin could feel the heat rising in his cheeks. "Well, it is a subject that needs to be addressed!"

"Yes. Yes, it is." Louisa straightened herself and crossed her arms over her chest. "Martin, why is the subject of sex so hard for you to talk about? I remember a certain visit to your surgery when you were full of questions regarding my reproductive cycle. And you seemed completely comfortable asking them then, if I remember correctly."

Martin tipped his head back, shaking his head. "Those were medically necessary questions any doctor would routinely ask a female patient. Especially a patient who happened to be anaemic!"

He huffed out a breath before adding a softer, "If my memory serves me, you accused me of asking questions that were too personal. Then you stormed out of my consulting room, slamming the door behind you."

"And if *my* memory serves *me*, there was some frustration on my part about going 'round and 'round in circles. Hmm?"

"Yes. But that said, you do tend to get a bit tetchy when it comes to discussions about your reproductive system."

"We're not talking about my reproductive system, Martin. We're talking about sex—sexual intercourse between you and me."

"Yes, we *are* talking about sex. But strictly speaking, the primary function of sexual intercourse is a reproduct—"

Louisa kissed him, very effectively and enjoyably putting an end to his discourse on procreation.

"It doesn't matter, Martin. What's important is you've actually been thinking about this. That means you're feeling better ... making progress. And as for how we'll manage the physical logistics of it ... I suspect if we both think long and hard about it, we'll come up with some ideas."

"Mm, yes."

Ruth entered the room, a coffee cup in hand, and Martin quickly moved back an appropriate distance from his wife.

"I think this hospital must be trying to drum up business with the coffee they pour up in that canteen. It's disgusting. Why, it could hardly pass for coffee in China. I could just as well order tea, it makes no difference," the woman said wryly.

James began to stir in his provisional bed and Louisa picked him up, sitting with him while he sucked down the contents of his Sippy cup. When he began to complain about being confined to his mother's lap, Louisa suggested she and Ruth take him for a walk.

"We'll be back after a bit. You just wait here for us," she said.

"It's not like he's going to go anywhere, dear." Ruth gave her nephew a crooked smile before pulling the door open.

Tim Spalding arrived a short time later. With great effort, Martin was able to get himself to the edge of the bed. His left arm, left sore by his efforts with the wheelchair the day before, had begun to give out before he made it to his final destination. "You need to remember, Martin, your left arm is all you have to work with for the next several months. Don't overdo it, or you'll end up with an injury. Only do the things you absolutely have to with that arm. Otherwise, let someone else step in and help out. I let you wheel yourself around yesterday, but you needed the practice before we send you home. If there's someone around who can push you, ask for their help."

Martin groaned internally, imagining being held prisoner in the chair as Joe Penhale pushed him around the village.

Either he was building up a tolerance to the pain or his legs were adjusting to having weight placed on them. Martin found the same exercises to be less gruelling the second time around.

Tim left the room a short time later and returned with the lift. "Let's get you in the chair for a while," he said as he wheeled the device over to the bed.

Martin grimaced. "Is that really necessary? It's—it's—I mean, I'm tired. Couldn't we do that another time?"

The therapist took note of his patient's furtive glances towards the door, and he quickly surmised the reason for his reluctance. "I tell you what, I'll lock the door and get you in the chair. Then I'll come back later to clear the room before we get you back into bed to do the range of motion exercises," Tim said.

Martin swallowed hard and nodded. "Thank you."

When James and Louisa returned to the room, Martin was sitting upright by the window, gazing out at the city. Louisa cocked her head at him as he peered up at her sheepishly.

"Um ... where's Ruth?" he asked.

"She ran into an old colleague from Broadmoor. She'll be back in a bit." She wagged a finger at him. "You're in your chair."

"Yes." He tapped his fingers against the armrest. "We, er ... we could go for a walk here on the floor ... if you like," he suggested. "I need to practice."

"That would be very nice, Martin." Louisa leaned down to kiss his cheek before he moved towards the door.

She watched with happiness and pride as they walked through the hospital corridors together. Her badly broken man was slowly overcoming all that had happened to him—regaining his independence. And she could see a bit of sparkle return to his eyes as he pointed out the helipad to his young son.

James let out an excited squeal when the flashing blue and white lights of the air ambulance appeared in the distance. Louisa knelt down next to the wheelchair, and they watched as the craft approached and hovered in front of them before settling to the ground.

Martin glanced over to see her wiping tears from her cheeks. "Louisa," he said softly. "I wish you hadn't seen it ... in the trauma centre. I'm sorry."

Her ponytail swung back and forth. "I'm not. I think those were the most important seconds I'll ever share with you. I understood just how much I love you that night. How much I need you ... how much you need me."

He stared back at her. "You *do* need me?"

"I do need you ... very much. And if it took seeing you in the trauma centre that night to realise it, then I'm not sorry. It was horrible to see, but I'm not sorry."

"Ah. I see."

She stood up and they moved down the hall. "Martin, Morwenna mentioned you had called her to talk about her salary. Do you remember doing that?"

Martin shot her a puzzled glance. "Well, I should think I would; I made the call."

"You have been a bit fuzzy since the accident."

"Mm. I did call her."

"She said she's going to continue to receive her salary during your absence. I was surprised to hear the CCG approved that."

Martin cleared his throat. "I'm sorry, I should have discussed it with you first. It's just that ... Well, I'd been thinking about her ... worrying."

Louisa stepped in front of him, bringing him to a stop. "*You* were worrying about Morwenna?"

"Yes!" he replied defensively. "Contrary to popular opinion, I do care about people!"

"I know you do. I'm just surprised is all. And I'm surprised the CCG is going to continue to subsidise her salary."

He shifted uncomfortably. "That's what I should have discussed with you. Her salary will come out of my—our pocket."

Martin waited as a group of nurses passed them by before staring pointedly at her. "It wouldn't be right for us not to help her out, Louisa. She doesn't have a family to look out for her. She's on her own and ... and I just want to make sure she's all right," he said, his voice trailing off.

Louisa kissed the top of his head. "You know what that's like ... to not have a family looking out for you, hmm."

"*I* never had to worry about money, Louisa. Morwenna doesn't have a lot. I'm sorry, I should have discussed it with you first."

She gave him a soft smile and then leaned over, her lips touching his.

"I think I can let it go this time. Now, I think we better get you back to your room before they send a search party out after you."

Chapter 8

Tim Spalding was waiting with Ruth when the Ellingham family returned from their walk.

"How did your solo flight go, Dr. Ellingham?" the therapist asked.

"I think I'm getting a feel for it." Martin sought out a position near the window, out of the way of potential collisions.

The therapist glanced at his watch. "Well, we should finish up with your range of motion exercises." He turned to Ruth and Louisa. "We'll be done by about half three. Maybe you could go to the canteen to wait for us."

Louisa settled James back into his push chair and picked up the nappy bag before leaning over to kiss her husband on the cheek. "I'll see you in a bit," she whispered.

Martin grunted and tugged on his ear when his gaze met his aunt's smirk.

Once the room had cleared, Tim pulled a chair over and sat down next to him. "I take it you'd rather not discuss the use of the lift with your wife?"

Martin sighed heavily. "I don't want her to see me that way. I'm hopeful that after tomorrow I'll be able to get in and out of the chair on my own."

"I really don't think your wife would think any less of you if she *did* see you in the lift. But this has more to do with how it makes you feel, and if I can do anything to be of help ... well, that's your call, Dr. Ellingham."

Tim excused himself and returned shortly with the lift. Once his patient was situated in his bed and the device had been returned to it's proper place, the therapist began working the muscles which had again tightened. Then he pulled the tray table back over to the bed and dumped out the box of items in front of his patient.

"Okay, let's see if you can get that hand to grab on to anything today."

Martin closed his eyes and took in a cleansing breath, trying to prepare himself mentally for the seemingly impossible challenge.

He concentrated first on getting his fingers to open, then he tried to pick up one of the wooden blocks. It rattled as it clattered forward, away from his grasp. Lining his hand up again, like the bucket on a steam shovel, he lowered his arm until his palm hovered over the red cube and his fingers touched the table. He then willed his recalcitrant fingers to close around the object without sending it into his lap.

He raised his hand, the block along with it, and swung his arm around so the object was suspended over its target. Concentrating intensely, Martin was able to open his fingers just enough that the block fell with a satisfying rattle into the box.

The left corner of his mouth nudged up as he looked at the therapist.

"Very well done, Martin!" Tim said. That took a considerable amount of effort, but each day will get easier."

Martin felt a sense of accomplishment not unlike what he experienced when witnessing the pinking-up of a body part after he had completed a successful vascular anastomosis.

He kept trying, managing to pick up a golf ball and a small plastic bottle. Fifteen minutes later, Martin was spent, both physically and mentally.

"Martin, you made really good progress today. Your hard work's paying off." Tim cleared the tray table and pushed it aside before retrieving his pot of cocoa butter. Then, lowering the head of the bed, he raised his patient's legs back up on the foam blocks. "You relax and I'll work on the oedema in that arm. Are you having any pain?"

"Mm. A bit."

Tim cocked his head at Martin as he massaged from his patient's fingers towards his shoulder.

"What kind? Ache, sharp, burning?"

"A burning sensation ... and some tingling."

"Let Mr. Christianson know if you need more for the pain. I pushed you pretty hard today; you'll feel it tonight."

The sound of baby conversation was heard in the hall, and Tim got up to allow his patient's family back into the room.

"I was just getting started with the lymphatic drainage technique I usually wrap your husband's sessions up with, Mrs. Ellingham. It'd be good if you were familiar with it. It helps to move the accumulated fluid from his limbs to areas where it can drain away normally."

Tim glanced over at Ruth, who was looking on with interest. "Dr. Ellingham, this is something your nephew might be more comfortable having his wife help him with. But Martin, if you want your aunt to learn as well, we can include her."

Martin grimaced. "No. I think Louisa can handle it, Ruth. Maybe you could ... go away."

Louisa's eyes darted towards her husband before she looked apologetically at the elderly woman. "I'm sure Martin didn't mean it that way."

"Oh, I suspect he meant it in exactly the way it was delivered. I may be getting old, but I do still have my wits about me." She held her hands out. "Here, give me the child. I'll take him down to the lavatory ... change his nappy."

Tim waited until Ruth had disappeared behind the closing door and then turned his attention to Louisa. "This is a technique I would normally teach your husband to do himself, but his injuries won't allow it. The benefits aren't seen immediately, but you should see results within a couple of weeks."

The therapist helped Martin out of his vest and had him lie back, keeping his legs elevated.

"You'll begin by massaging your husband's neck," he said, demonstrating the circular motion required, each movement ending on a downward stroke. "The objective is to open up the pathways in the lymphatic system so that the accumulated serous fluid in his arm and legs can drain away properly. Under no circumstances do I want you doing this with his fractured limbs. Therapists have to be certified to perform the more advanced technique used on injured tissue."

"I've retained a home health nurse. Would he be familiar with this?"

"Possibly. Who have you hired?"

"His name's Jeremy Portman. He actually works here at the moment."

"Yes, I know him quite well. Great guy and very clever ... knows his stuff. I'm sure he's probably certified, but you'll need to check with him." He straightened and gave his patient's wife a nod. "Okay, you give it a go."

Louisa gave the therapist a wary look before tentatively placing her hands on her husband's throat. "Tell me if I'm hurting you," she said, giving him a nervous smile.

Their eyes locked momentarily, and he drew in a breath. "You'll do fine. You always do."

Tim had Louisa continue to work her way down to her husband's upper chest and the lymphatics under his arm.

"You'll need to be very careful, Mrs. Ellingham. The thoracotomy and laparotomy incisions need to be avoided, and try not to put tension on the wounds."

"Wouldn't this be easier and more comfortable for Martin if I had oil or something on my hands?"

Tim shook his head. "No, the objective is to pull the vessels carrying the lymph fluid open. That won't happen if your hands glide over his skin. You want to apply enough pressure to cause his skin to move slightly, and use slow circular movements."

The therapist finished with his training session, and Louisa settled herself on the sofa while Tim massaged the fluid from his patient's legs.

"I think we're done for today, Martin. I'll plan to see you around ten tomorrow morning. We'll try to get you up on your feet."

It was almost four o'clock by the time Tim left, and Louisa could see the growing exhaustion in her husband.

"Do you want to close your eyes for a while … rest a bit?" she asked as she ran her fingers back and forth through his hair.

"If I close my eyes, I'll fall asleep."

Ruth returned with James Henry shortly after Dr. Newell's arrival. The doctor pulled up a couple of extra chairs before taking a seat himself.

"Thank you, Ruth and Louisa, for coming today. Mr. Christianson's been keeping me updated on your progress, Martin. It sounds like things are moving in the right direction now with regard to your physical recovery."

"Mm. I'll put some weight on my legs tomorrow."

"That's a major step." A grin spread across his face. "No pun intended."

He leaned forward with his arms resting on his knees. "In all seriousness, though, I want to make sure we keep moving in the same direction with your psychological recovery as well.

"I wasn't sure if we would get another session in before Martin goes home, and I wanted to give you all an opportunity to express any thoughts or concerns you may have.

"Louisa, how are you doing with your preparations for your husband's return home? There must be a lot to get organised. Changes to be made to the house, equipment to get sorted ..."

"Yes. But I think everything's in place now. We have a home health nurse lined up, and we switched cottages with Ruth. Hers was already wheelchair accessible. It's all working out well."

"Good. It sounds like you have things in hand." Dr. Newell turned towards his colleague, shifting gears suddenly. "Ruth, I was wondering if you could share with us what you remember of your father's death."

She pulled in her chin and shook her head. "I wasn't prepared for this, so I haven't formulated my thoughts, of course." Crossing her legs she laced her fingers over a knee. "I had just returned to London from my previous job in Manchester. I'd barely gotten myself settled in my new flat when I received the phone call from my brother.

"He told me to come to their house right away ... that my father was dead. I was the first to arrive. Margaret, Martin's mother, let me in the door and led me to the study." She glanced over at her nephew and swallowed. "It was a horrible sight—my father dead on the floor.

"The blood pooled up next to him had been smeared across the hardwood. His skin was very dark and his eyes were open, fixed on the ceiling."

Dr. Newell glanced over at his patient. Martin stared out the window as the narrative played out.

Ruth continued. "The police finished gathering the information they needed, and soon after they left, the coroner arrived. Margaret, of course, had the maid in cleaning the room before they had father loaded in the hearse. A young woman, not more than a girl really. Poor thing; she'd obviously never witnessed anything like it before. She probably has never gotten over it. A sight like that at such a young ..." She sighed and glanced over at her nephew, his gaze still fixed on the cathedral spire a mile away.

"I called my sister, Joan, from the phone there at the house. She was, of course, shocked to hear the news and was immediately concerned for Marty ... Martin. I hadn't seen him since my arrival. I assumed he was upstairs in his room—spared from the nightmare."

Ruth turned to her nephew. "I'm so sorry, Martin. If I had known what was going on I would have stepped in to help you."

Ruth pulled a tissue from her pocket before going on. "I wasn't at Margaret and Christopher's again until the day of the funeral. When we arrived at the church, my sister asked about Martin ... where he was, why he wasn't there. Margaret said he was at home with a nanny. She claimed she was afraid all the histrionics brought about by a funeral would be upsetting to him. That should have been our first clue that something was amiss.

"Once we arrived back at the house, Joan went in search of our nephew, but she was headed off by our brother. He said the child had been left with friends for the day."

Martin whipped his head around, pulling himself upright in the bed. "That was a complete fabrication! I was in my room! He didn't want Auntie Joan to see me because he knew she'd ask questions! She would have asked me what had happened to my arm!"

He looked around the room and a flush crept up his neck before he quieted. "She would have wanted to know what had happened to my arm," he said. "I've never liked lies. I'm not any good at it. They knew that."

Martin's expression intensified. "*That's* why they kept her away from me. She would have known I was lying. She would have done something ... gotten me away from them!"

Martin fought tears, and Louisa reached over the bed rail for his hand. Dr. Newell got up to lower the rail out of the way, and the catch made a loud metallic click as it fell into place.

Louisa felt her husband suddenly pull away from her. The anger she had seen in him moments before was gone, now replaced by fear which faded into an expression of utter devastation. He shoved her away and collapsed on to the bed, covering his face with his hand.

"What is it, Martin?" the therapist asked.

Martin turned his head slowly to face him. "I told you I remembered a sound ... when I was locked in the cupboard that day—that it was a familiar sound, but I couldn't think where I'd heard it before."

Dr. Newell nodded. "I remember."

"Uncle Phil had a rifle he used to scare off the foxes that would get at Joan's chickens. It made a clicking sound when he loaded the cartridges into it."

The therapist sat back down. "I'm not sure I follow."

"The day I broke my grandfather's pocket watch ... when we got back home my parents went into the house without me. I didn't want to go inside. I knew they were angry with me, and I didn't want to upset them any further, so I stayed outside.

"There was a stray dog that used to rummage through the bins behind the house. I'd laid down under the trees. I liked to watch the squirrels. That dog came over and laid down next to me. I didn't feel so alone. I put my ear to its chest ... listened to its heart beating.

"The first time I heard a heart beat was when I was staying at Joan and Phil's. I'd had a nightmare and Joan had come into my room. She was holding me on her lap, and I laid my head against her chest. It was comforting ... her warmth and the steady beat of her heart. And that day with the dog ... I just wanted the warmth ... comfort."

"Oh, Martin," Louisa said softly, laying her hand on his arm.

He pulled back and turned away. "My mother would get angry when she'd catch me with the dog. She said it made me stink. She came out that day and found me with it. She yelled at me to get away from it ... to go take a bath and change my clothes. Then she told the groundskeeper, who'd been working in the shed, to get rid of it. He asked her what he should do with it, and she told him, '*Whatever you do with the rest of the vermin that get in the bins. Just get rid of it*'.

"He disappeared into the shed again and came out with a rifle. I pleaded with her to not let him do it, but she pulled me towards the house. I was going up the steps when I heard the click. We went inside and right after my mother pushed the door shut, I heard the gun go off. I never saw the dog again."

The room was quiet for some seconds before the psychiatrist spoke." I'm still not sure I'm understanding how this relates to the noise you remember hearing when you were in the cupboard."

"I thought it was the groundskeeper. I thought my mother had told him to—" He squeezed his eyes shut and swallowed hard.

"You thought your mother was going to have him shoot you for what happened with your grandfather?"

Martin rubbed a hand over his head and huffed out a breath. "*Then,* yes. I know now she never would have done that."

Ruth leaned forward. "Oh, I agree, Martin. Your mother would never stand for it. A groundskeeper in her house ... with a shotgun, no less?" she said, matter-of-factly.

Louisa gave the elderly woman an incredulous glance and then got to her feet, wrapping her arms around her husband.

He pulled away. "I'm fine," he said, his cheeks warming as he glanced at his therapist and his aunt.

His brow furrowed before he groaned softly. "The sound I heard in the cupboard ... I think it was the click of the latch when the coroner raised the gurney." He shook his head. "I don't know. Maybe I'm not remembering things the way they really were."

The therapist leaned back in his chair. "Martin, it really doesn't matter whether or not your memories are completely accurate. What's important is that you can deal with the trauma as you remember it today. Your memories don't need to be neat and orderly to do that."

Dr. Newell began to move towards the door. "Louisa, will you be spending the night here?"

She looked over at her husband. "That's what I was hoping for," she said, giving him a smile.

"Okay, I'll make that happen. And Martin, I'll be back in on Monday. We can talk more then, but call if you need me ... anytime."

After the therapist left the room, Ruth picked up her coat and purse. "Well, I should get back. I have some shopping I need to do yet this evening." Turning to her nephew she said, "Martin, I am ..." She sighed, "I wasn't there for you then, but I'm here for you now." She leaned over and kissed his cheek before hurrying out the door.

Chapter 9

Louisa picked James up from the push chair and carried him to her husband's side. A smile broke out across the boy's face, and he tipped his head, trying to make eye contact with his father. But Martin was lost in thought, trying to piece together the details of his most recent memory.

He had felt a frightening sense of loneliness—of being on his own in the world, knowing he was not just unloved by his parents, but he was loathed by them as well. He longed to be back at the cold, harsh boarding school. The fear he felt there paled in comparison to the ever-present feeling of worthlessness he felt in his parents' home.

He thought about the sensation of the cold, hard earth under him as he lay on the ground that day. About the comforting warmth of the sun's rays as they were absorbed by the navy jumper he was wearing. How he had tried to imagine that warmth as Auntie Joan's arms around him, keeping him safe from the anger and cold stares of his parents.

He thought about the stray that followed him around and the scenarios that his active imagination had created around the animal. The dog racing in to protect him from whichever monster his unfledged mind had conjured up that day. He wasn't meaningless to that mangy dog ... that stupid creature had actually liked him.

Louisa took her husband's hand in hers and pressed it against James's cheek. The sensation returned him to the present, and he shifted his gaze to his son. The child gave him a hesitant smile when he saw he now had his father's attention.

The smile faded and the boy turned away when there was no response.

"Martin, are you all right?" Louisa asked as she lightly stroked the back of his neck.

He closed his eyes and took in a slow, deep breath, shaking his head slowly. "I'm so tired, Louisa. I am just—*so*—tired."

She lowered the head of the bed, and then got up to dim the lights. After picking up several of the baby's books, she settled in on the bed with James between them. "We'll read you a bedtime story. Maybe you'll fall asleep," she said softly before placing a lingering kiss on his forehead.

Daylight was coming in the window before Martin finally woke the next morning. Before he even opened his eyes, he sensed his wife's presence. The softness and warmth of her skin, the silkiness of her hair against his cheek as her head lay heavy on his shoulder, and the intoxicating fragrance that was his Louisa.

Not ready for the moment to end, he pulled her in tight and revelled in their closeness a bit longer before allowing himself to open his eyes.

He turned his head to look at her, hoping to have a few moments to observe her unnoticed before she woke, but his movements caused her to stir.

"Good morning," she said sleepily.

"Good morning. Did you sleep well?"

"I did." She propped herself up on her elbow and studied her husband's face. "You must have been absolutely shattered yesterday. You fell asleep around half five, slept through the hospital staff wheeling a bed in here for me, *and* through a visit from the Parsons."

"Mm, I was tired. I'm sorry I wasn't better company," he said as he looked piercingly at her.

"I believe the last time you looked at me that way, Martin Ellingham, we were on an aeroplane."

"Mm. I was trying to examine your eyes—acute glaucoma."

"Which I might have understood had I met you before ... known you were a doctor. As it was, I just found you creepy."

"*Creepy?*"

"Yes, Martin ... creepy. If I remember correctly, I said you had a problem and found a different place to sit," she said as she gave him a playful poke.

"The *last* time I was merely trying to do what I was trained to do, so that comment was unjustified."

"Hmm, yes. And you were right, I s'pose—acute glaucoma." She tipped her head down and narrowed her eyes at him. "What about this time?"

He hesitated and furrowed his brow slightly. "You might want to find a different place to sit."

Her stern expression softened into a smile. "You're feeling better this morning, aren't you?"

"You have strange curative powers, it seems." He pulled his wife to him and gave her a proper kiss.

"That was very nice, Martin." She sat up and stretched her arms out before slipping off the bed to retrieve her overnight bag. She dug around a bit before pulling out a folded-up piece of paper.

"I had to teach year two for a few hours this week, and we talked about the musculoskeletal system. This was found with the drawings the children made of themselves doing something they use their bones and muscles for. I think it was meant for you."

She handed the item to her husband, climbing back up next to him. Martin raised the head of the bed and then laid the paper on his lap, opening it up with his good hand to reveal a carefully drawn picture of two stick figures walking hand in hand, one tall and one small. The tall figure had what could be construed to be either a suitcase or a bag in one hand, and the small figure had a rectangle drawn over its forearm. The small figure had been drawn with a smile. The tall figure had been drawn with a frown, and over the eyes were short lines, which angled down towards the centre. Below the drawing was scrawled a heartfelt message.

DEAR DOCTUR ELLIGAM
THANK YOU FOR HELPING WITH MY FRAKSHUR. IT FEELS BEDDER.
I HOOP YUR FRAKSHURS HEEL SOON
YUR FRAND EVAN

"I think it's quite a nice likeness of you," Louisa said as she watched her husband's eyes sparkle.

Martin pulled the sheet of paper up closer to his face, furrowing his brow as he peered closely at the drawing. He glanced over at his wife then back at the paper.

"Mm. Best not let Carole see this then, or she'll be force feeding me *two* meals a day." He tried to sound gruff, but the light that Louisa saw dancing in his eyes gave away his true feelings.

She reached out to caress his cheek. "I think you have a new friend, Dr. Ellig-am."

Slipping from the bed, she picked up her overnight bag. "I'm going to take a shower before we lose our privacy."

Mark Mylow, Portwenn's former constable, had asked Martin, shortly after he became the village GP, if he had noticed the way Louisa moved. He watched his wife as she walked across the room. *God, yes. Most definitely, yes.* He breathed out a contented sigh.

As she turned to close the bathroom door, Louisa noticed her husband's fixed stare. "Problem?" she asked.

"Louisa, you look very ... beautiful," he said, lost in a brown study.

She stared back at him for a moment before giving him a coy smile. "Thank you, Martin." Turning, she closed the door behind her.

The Parsons arrived with breakfast while Louisa was still in the bathroom. "Morning, Mart. Did you sleep well?" Chris asked as he carried James over and set him on the spare bed.

"I did ... very well." Martin brushed his thumb across his son's cheek before pressing the backs of two fingers against his forehead. "Good morning, James."

James reached up and grabbed on to the sleeve of his father's vest, pulling himself to a standing position. Martin pulled his hand up reflexively, in part to support the boy, in part to protect himself from any mishaps.

"Well, good morning!" Louisa said cheerfully as she emerged from the bathroom. She quickly spotted James standing up next to his father, and hurried over.

"I don't think this is a good idea, do you ... Martin?" She pulled the boy away and sat him on her lap.

"Louisa, I had control of him. And Chris is standing right there," he said, wagging a finger at his friend.

"I don't care where he's standing, Martin. I'd feel much better if you'd let someone else hold on to him. He's getting heavy, and I don't want you getting hurt." She looked worriedly at her husband. "Please, Martin. Always have someone else holding on to him as well."

Martin scowled and let a hiss of air through his nose. "Yes." He exchanged knowing glances with Chris.

Carole unpacked plates, cutlery, and napkins before setting out a pan of omelettes and a bowl of fruit salad. She had also brought toasted crumpets and marmalade.

She and Louisa watched Martin tuck into his breakfast, happy to see his appetite increasing.

"You better eat up, mate. They're going to work you hard today," Chris said as he jabbed his fork in the air.

"*Yes.* I'm aware of that."

Although he hadn't admitted it, Martin was feeling very anxious about the impending test of his legs. The sensations he had felt the day before were intense and unsettling. Sensations quite unlike anything he had experienced before. He was determined, however, to put the use of the lift behind him.

Chris and Carole gathered together the dishes left over from breakfast and headed out with James. Louisa now had some time alone with her husband.

"Martin ... if it wouldn't make you uncomfortable, I'd like to be here when they work with you today." She sat on the spare bed rubbing a hand across his shoulders.

Martin had been expecting this request and had spent a great deal of time contemplating how to answer. He would be relying heavily on his wife for assistance once he returned home, and she needed to be aware of all the challenges ahead of them. "That's fine. I mean it would be good actually. But ... you should know beforehand that this will be painful. It *will* get less painful as time goes on, though. And the weight placed on the bones increases blood flow to the fractures, speeding the healing process."

"What do you mean exactly? How painful is this, Martin?" she asked nervously.

"I'm not sure. What was done yesterday was uncomfortable, so I'm just expecting it to be worse today."

She laid her hand on his arm. "Martin, I'm very nervous. I just want to know what I should be prepared for."

"I don't know, Louisa! I've never done it before!" he snapped, his own fears on display.

"Yeah, sorry," she said. She straightened herself, determined to be strong for him. "It's a real milestone, hmm?"

"Yes." He reached over and pulled her to him before burying his face in her neck.

Tim Spalding stopped in around half nine. He focused on the usual range of motion exercises, loosening his patient's joints and muscles in preparation for weight bearing.

Martin was feeling increasingly edgy as the morning wore on. Uncertainty made him uncomfortable, and he had never felt as uncertain as he did today.

"How are you doing with all this? Some trepidation maybe?" Tim asked as he pushed his patient's knee forward.

"I'm a bit anxious. It's hard to know what to expect." The therapist handed him a towel, and he wiped the sweat from his face.

There was a rap on the door, and Will Simpson and Robert Dashwood entered the room.

"Good morning, Martin," Robert said as he walked over and gave his friend's left hand an awkward shake. "This is certainly an improvement over what we saw the last time we were here."

Will stood by the bed, watching as the therapist finished up with the last of the exercises, and then the two surgeons eagerly examined the results of their craft.

Robert removed the brace from Martin's arm and had him squeeze his hand. "Hmm, got some work to do here before you're back up and running normally. Can you straighten those fingers out at all?"

"It's difficult, but it's getting better," Martin replied, glancing over at his therapist.

"He was able to pick up several items from the table yesterday. I've definitely seen improvement," Tim said as he watched his patient being poked and prodded.

Will lifted Martin's left leg, running his hand gently over the most badly damaged areas. "We'll need to touch things up a bit down here once the fixators are off. We'll do a skin graft and muscle flap to cover this wound properly. I'm sure the infection wasn't helpful."

He moved around the bed to join Robert in the examination of his arm. "Wiggle your fingers for me," Will said.

Martin's face tightened as he forced his stiffened digits to move.

"All right. Now open and close them."

The swollen fingers flexed inward before straightening again, and Will exchanged glances with Robert. He gave Martin a smile and raised his thumb in the air. "The arm's going to need more work as well, but overall I'd say things are looking very good."

"Do you think I have a chance of getting full dexterity back?"

Will shrugged his shoulders. "I can't say for sure, but I'm more optimistic now than I was a few weeks ago. Keep working at it ... who knows."

Two male aides arrived to help with safeguarding Martin against falls while he adjusted to being on his feet again.

"Are you ready to give it a go?" Robert asked.

Martin drew in a deep breath and swallowed before giving a sharp nod of his head. "Yeah, let's try it."

The surgeons helped him to the edge of the bed, and Martin squeezed his eyes shut as his legs began to pound.

"Tim, we'll let you direct the show here. This is more your territory than it is ours," Robert said, stepping aside and waving the therapist over.

The young man gave Martin a smile. "I'm going to put a gait belt around your waist so we can hang on to you. But I'll put this pad across your laparotomy wound first. That's gotta be pretty tender yet."

Tim gestured to the taller of the two aides. "Garrett, I want you on his left, and Dave, I want you on his right. I'll stay in front of you, Martin. When you're ready, let yourself slide on to the floor. We'll be there to catch you if your legs buckle."

Tim lowered the bed and slipped the belt around his patient's waist. Then he turned to the aides. "I'm going to be watching his face for any sign of an imminent syncopal episode.

Be ready to help him sit back down if he starts having problems."

Martin looked nervously at Louisa, and she moved closer, giving him an encouraging nod.

He closed his eyes for several moments before looking once more to his wife. "Okay. I'm ready." He let his body drop over the side of the mattress, and his feet touched the floor. The air was sucked from his lungs as the throbbing and pain intensified, but he focused his thoughts on keeping his legs under him.

Louisa watched, her heart breaking as her husband clenched his jaw against the sharp pains shooting through his legs. He let out a long, loud moan and started to tremble as his muscles began to fail him.

Tim jerked his head towards the bed, and the two aides lowered him on to the mattress. "Let's take a break and try it again in a few minutes."

The procedure was repeated several times, the pain and stress showing on Martin's face. Sweat was rolling down his temples and his features were taut. He glanced up at Louisa, tears gathering in his eyes as he tried to blink them back.

"How are you feeling, Dr. Ellingham? Besides the pain ... any light-headedness or nausea?"

Martin nodded sluggishly. His face blanched and his eyes begin to glaze over.

"Hang on to him guys; he's gonna drop," Tim said as their patient's legs buckled.

Martin regained consciousness within seconds of being laid back on the bed. "I need to vomit," he said as he rolled to his side. Tim grabbed the basin he had placed on a nearby table and held it for him.

"Feeling a little better now?" the therapist asked.

He nodded, "Could I have a glass of water?"

"Here you go. You're doing great, Ace," Robert said as he handed the glass to his friend.

Tim gave him a few minutes to recover before they repeated the process again. As Martin's body began to adjust to the new sensations, the pain became more tolerable.

"How are you feeling now?" the therapist asked.

"I'm doing okay." He grimaced as what felt like jolts of electricity coursed through his lower limbs.

"All right. I'm going to bring the wheelchair over, and we'll see what you can do with that." Tim said before placing it parallel to the bed.

"Mrs. Ellingham, when you help your husband, the wheelchair needs to be on his left ... always on his left, because that's his stronger side. I'd suggest you look into getting a couple of assist poles, one for the bedroom and one for the bathroom."

Louisa cocked her head. "I'm sorry. What's an assist pole?"

"It's a tension pole that goes from the floor to the ceiling. It'll give your husband something to grab on to when he lowers himself into the chair and pulls himself up out of the chair."

He turned his attention back to his patient. "Martin, you're going to stand up just like you've been doing, but this time you're going to pivot. Then we'll help you lower yourself down." The aide got a firm hold on the gait belt and gave his patient a nod. "Okay, go ahead and stand up."

The pain was diminishing, and Martin was beginning to feel more confident on his repaired legs. But his muscles had atrophied after three weeks of lying in bed, and he still needed support.

"Now, Martin, you're going to pivot clockwise, but be very careful to keep both feet on the floor. We'll follow you around but you'll do the work."

It was frightening to see her husband standing on his badly broken legs, and Louisa breathed a sigh of relief when he was seated in the chair.

"I should explain, Mrs. Ellingham, what we mean when we say Martin is partial weight bearing," Will said. "He can't put more than fifty percent of his bodyweight on his legs right now. In other words, if he were to take a foot off the floor, the leg supporting him would then be carrying one hundred percent of his weight. His fractured bones can't take that yet. He should have both feet on the floor whenever he's upright. This means no walking, Martin. Understood?"

"Yes, I realise that. I'm not a complete idiot," he grumbled.

Tim moved back to the front of the wheelchair. "Okay, let's sit you back on the bed, then we'll try this again with a walker ... see if you can do it on your own."

By the time the session concluded, Martin was physically and mentally spent. He fell back on the bed and closed his eyes.

"We'll let you get some rest, Dr. Ellingham. Someone will be in to work with you again tomorrow." Tim left the room momentarily and returned with cold packs which he wrapped around his patient's legs.

Robert took Martin's sweaty hand in his. "We'll be in touch about the work that will need to be done after the fixators come off. You know where we are if you need anything, so don't hesitate to call."

"Thank you," he said, mustering a nod of his head as the surgeons headed for the door.

Louisa took her husband's hand in hers. "I brought you some more clothes. Why don't we get you cleaned up and into something dry."

She rifled through a bag on the sofa, returning with several items in hand.

"I spoke with an occupational therapist about getting something more comfortable for you to wear. She suggested the baggy boxers and vest like you've been using, but she also mentioned these." Louisa laid a pair of dark blue warm up pants on the bed. "They have Velcro all the way up the sides, so they'll be easy to get on and off over the fixators."

Martin stared at the item for a few moments. "That's a good idea. Thank you."

He reached up and took hold of her arm, pulling her close. "I'm glad you stayed this morning ... that you wanted to be here with me. It made it much easier."

"I'm glad I stayed, too. And I am so proud of you, Martin." She leaned over, wrapping her arms around him before pulling back. "Let's get you out of those wet clothes."

Chapter 10

By the time Louisa had helped Martin change in to clean clothes, he was exhausted. She picked up her book and nestled in against him as he quickly drifted off to sleep.

When the final chapter drew to a close, she flipped the cover shut. Her gaze lingered on his face, still gaunt. But with his increasing appetite and the daily deliveries of meals from the Parsons, he had begun to put on some weight, filling in the hollows in his cheeks. And his normally close-cropped hair had grown out, revealing its previously hidden wave.

His eyes opened slowly, and he lay for a while, staring at the ceiling. Louisa reached her hand out, running her finger over a small curl behind his ear.

"I've never been good at it, Louisa," he said.

"Good at *it*?"

"Relationships ... getting along with people. I just don't seem to be very good at it."

She looked at him sympathetically as she brushed a hand over his arm. "We'll work on it. Remember, you were going to try to get to know Al better. And you were going to practice with Ruth."

He shook his head. "No, not in that way. I'm ... I'm afraid I'm going to ruin it again."

"Martin ... I'm sorry, I'm not following you. Ruin what?"

"*Us*. I know I'm going to do something to ruin it, Louisa. I don't know how to deal with relationships. I invariably do something to bollocks it up, and it always seems to result in someone getting hurt."

Louisa tipped her head at him. "I'm not sure what you're saying, Martin. Do you mean like your grandfather ... or the dog?"

"Mm." He pulled her closer, and she laid her head on his shoulder.

"I've been thinking about that a lot," Martin continued. "It happens every time. I always muck things up."

Louisa tried to pull back to see his face, but he gripped her tighter and turned away.

"I think ... I think I know I'm going to ruin it in the end, so I guess I save them the trouble ... do things to keep them away in the first place. Or to drive them away if I *do* find myself in what could be called a relationship. I get it over with ... like ripping a plaster off."

The two lay silent for a while before Louisa said softly, "*You* haven't always mucked things up, you know. The way your parents were is all on them. Remember that. And what about Joan and Ruth ... Chris and Carole?"

"I did muck it up with Joan ... in a way. She was hurt badly because of me."

Louisa sat up. "What do you mean?"

He sighed and laid his hand on her thigh. "The affair Joan had was with a man named John Slater. She loved him. In fact, she was still in love with him when he showed up in Portwenn a few years ago. She gave him up thinking my father would allow my visits to continue.

"But he used it as a way to punish her ... get even with her. They never got on well, and it was the perfect opportunity to hurt her. It was pure spitefulness. He didn't care about my moral development!" he spat through clenched teeth.

"But how is that your fault, Martin? That was all on your father."

"It was a result of her relationship with me. He wouldn't have had any control over her if it hadn't been for me."

"And Chris and Carole? You haven't mucked it up with them, have you?"

"Carole tolerates me because of Chris. And Chris ... Well, he's like that *stupid* dog that used to follow me around when I was a child. Eventually, he's going to end up getting himself hurt. I've infuriated him on more than one occasion, but he just keeps coming back for more. It's his lookout now."

"Louisa stared at him for several moments, her eyes narrowing. "Martin Ellingham, after all he's done for you! How *dare* you talk about your friend like that! He's been here by your side, *every—step—of the way!*" she said, poking him in the arm with each accented word. "He's been there for *me* and for *James* ... and for *Ruth*, too! Who do you think is responsible for pulling in the top orthopaedic and vascular surgeons in the country to give you every chance to have fully functioning limbs? Hmm, *Mar-tin?*"

She stopped suddenly when she noticed her husband pulling back and wincing with each jab of her finger ... the tears in his eyes. She softened her tone. "Martin, I'm terribly disappointed in you." Her lips were pursed as she stared down at him. She huffed. "I *am* disappointed in you, but don't you think for one minute that I don't love you anymore."

Sliding from the bed, she worked her feet into her shoes. "I'm going to cool off. When I come back we're going to talk about this."

Martin watched as she disappeared through the door before sinking back into his pillow. He pressed a hand to his face, feeling a sense of shame and guilt. Not just for his words but for his festering anger, which had been directed at his best friend. A discomfort grew in the pit of his stomach.

He waited, for what seemed an eternity, for Louisa to return. He became anxious about what she was thinking of him, and with each passing minute, the anxiety intensified. He turned away when she finally walked through the door.

She stopped part way into the room and watched him for a few moments. "Martin, are you ready to talk?" she asked softly.

He wanted to say something ... to apologise, but words failed him.

She came around and crawled up on the spare bed. "I know you didn't mean what you said about Chris, so why did you say it?"

Closing his eyes, he shook his head. "I don't know. He's ... he's a good friend."

"Maybe this is something you should talk about with Dr. Newell. Could be you're trying to speed the process up a bit. Hmm?"

Martin stared absently, considering her words. "I don't know."

She slid over closer to him and stroked his chest with her fingertips, hesitating before asking, "Martin, does it scare you when I'm angry?"

He pushed her hand away as a wave of humiliation washed over him.

Louisa sighed and then tucked her body against his before leaning into his shoulder.

"Maybe this is something else that should be addressed with Dr. Newell?"

"Mm." He pulled her in closer and kissed the top of her head. "I'm sorry," he whispered.

Chapter 11

Louisa waited until her husband had again succumbed to sleep before leaving him to get a cup of coffee from the canteen. When she returned to the room, Chris and Carole had arrived with her son in tow.

"Hello, James!" she said, setting a paper bag down as he reached out to her from his perch in Chris's arms. "Thanks so much for watching him, Carole."

"Chris did most of the watching. I had to get cookies baked for a fundraiser at Dan's school, so Chris and Dan took him to the park."

"How did things go, Mart? Did the legs hold out okay?" Chris asked as he pulled a chair up to the bed.

"It went fine. I won't be running any races for a while, but it'll be good to be more independent."

Louisa handed Martin the paper bag. "I picked up a snack for you," she said as she set it down on the tray table.

"Thank you." He gave her a small smile before removing a plastic-wrapped sandwich from the sack.

"Louisa, I was wondering if you have anything you might need to get at the medical supply store?" Carole asked. "I have a prescription I need to pick up at the chemist. If you'd like to ride along, I'd enjoy your company. I'm sure Chris wouldn't mind watching James while we're gone. Would you, Chris."

He exchanged knowing glances with his friend. "No, that'd be fine."

Louisa picked up her purse. "I really should get over there today, Martin. They might not be open tomorrow."

"Yes, that's fine," he said as he brushed at the crumbs that had fallen on the blankets.

"We'll try not to be gone too long." She passed James to Chris. "You will be careful with him, won't you?"

"Yep, I'll take good care of him," Chris assured her as he aeroplaned James through the air. "We'll have some fun, won't we mate." Giggles bubbled from the child's mouth.

"No, I mean ... that one," Louisa said as she waggled a finger in her husband's direction.

"Louisa, he's a doctor. I'll be fine ... and I have my call button," Martin said.

"Hmm." Her gaze darted between the two men. She hesitated before following Carole towards the hall.

Martin and Chris waited for the door to close before shrugging their shoulders at one another.

"So how did it go this morning?" Carole asked as they dodged the puddles in the car park.

"Robert and Will seemed happy with Martin's progress, but he's going to need more surgery down the road."

"What about the prognosis; do they think he'll have full use of his limbs?"

Louisa slid into her seat and pulled the door shut. "Will says he's more *optimistic* now than he was a few weeks ago. I don't know, Carole. Sometimes it seems like they trot that word out just to pacify the patient. I hope Martin doesn't get his hopes up too high."

"How did it go this morning ... pretty tough to watch?"

"It was horrible. Martin kept at it ... kept sitting down until the light-headedness would pass, then he'd go at it again. He passed out once and vomited once. He says it'll get less painful." She sighed, rubbing her temples.

"Headache?" Carole asked.

"Mm-hmm. Martin's been more temperamental lately … moody, really. I'm afraid he could be getting discouraged. I just hope he doesn't give up."

"Well, that famous stubborn streak he has will work in his favour. He'll keep at it, Louisa," Carole said, patting her friend's knee.

"Yes, I suppose."

"Something else wrong?"

"I'm just worried about him … how he's going to deal with everything. Martin remembered another incident in our session with Dr. Newell yesterday. And remember, this stays between you and me." Louisa said.

"Louisa, Chris and I feel very strongly that what Martin's experienced in his life is his and his alone to share. We've known for twenty years that he had an awful upbringing, and we've never discussed it with anyone. We won't start now."

Louisa worked her purse strap around her hand. "There was a stray dog that Martin had become attached to when he was a boy. His mother didn't want him touching it, but she found him with it one day. She was angry. She told the groundskeeper to get rid of the dog. Martin didn't see it happen, but he saw the man come out of the shed with a gun, and he heard the gun go off. He never saw the dog again."

"Oh, Louisa! How awful for that little boy. That mother of his makes my skin crawl. What a horrid woman!"

"I agree. But that's the past. I'm worried about getting through the next few months without having him implode."

They pulled into the car park next to the chemist, and Louisa walked over to the medical supply store next door.

She ordered the assist poles Tim Spalding had recommended and picked up several other items the occupational therapist said Martin would be needing.

When the two women arrived back at the hospital room they could hear their husbands' voices in serious conversation. Louisa peered in the partially-opened door.

Chris was sitting on the edge of the spare bed holding on to James while the boy stood by his father, one hand gripping the front of his vest, the other firmly attached to his ear.

She put her index finger to her lips to quiet her friend, and they slipped into the room, watching, unnoticed by their husbands.

James was wearing a pair of jeans and the black braces Louisa had purchased on a recent shopping trip with Carole. Martin fidgeted with them, attempting to get the length adjusted properly so that they were even on both sides. Trying to conduct the operation with his left hand, and on a squirming child, was proving frustrating for him.

"These aren't even the same length ... and they're too short! His trousers are being pulled up too high. That's got to be uncomfortable for him." Martin explained to his friend, "You want your braces adjusted properly, or it defeats the purpose of wearing them in the first place."

"Here, Mart. Let me help. You hold the baby, and I'll work with the braces. He turned James around so his back was to his father, and Martin put his arm around the boy's waist. Chris fiddled with the adjusters as James flopped forward, grabbing at his face.

"There, how's that?" Chris asked, a self-satisfied smile spreading across his face.

"Can you hold him up?"

Chris turned the boy around and lifted him into the air.

"Now the other side." Martin made a horizontal circle with his finger, and Chris obliged, spinning James one hundred and eighty degrees.

"Mm. That'll have to do, I guess," Martin mumbled.

Chris lowered the baby and glowered at his friend. "What do you mean, that'll have to do? I think I did a damn good job considering how wiggly your kid is!"

"Watch your language, Chris. Louisa can be a bit Victorian about the use of expletives around the baby."

Louisa looked at Carole, her lips drawing into a thin line as her ponytail flicked. She crossed her arms in front of her. "Everything okay over there?" she asked.

Chris's head shot up and Martin jumped, knocking the open pot of nappy cream off the bed and on to the floor.

He looked at Louisa, wide-eyed. "Yes! We were just ..." Wagging a finger in the baby's direction, he quickly explained, "We were just changing the nappy. We're all done now." He cleared his throat and turned away.

"All sanitary, is he?" Louisa asked, raising her eyebrows at her husband as she took their son from Chris.

Martin fidgeted, straightening the blankets that covered his legs. "Yes. Presentable as well."

"Nicely done, boys. Maybe Louisa and I'll take James down to the canteen while the two of you get the nappy cream cleaned up off the floor." Carole turned and gave Louisa a roll of her eyes before they headed out the door.

Chris grabbed a kitchen roll from the cabinet and returned to wipe up the mess by the bed. He handed Martin the now-cracked pot. "They enjoyed that, didn't they?"

"Yes. I think women take a perverse pleasure in our misfortune." Martin peered over the side of the bed as Chris gathered together the cream-laden paper towels. "I think you missed a spot."

Giving his friend a dark look, Chris gave the floor a final swipe.

The door to the room opened, and two male aides came in. "Hello, Dr. Ellingham. We're here to get you into the wheelchair for a while. Mr. Christianson wants you out of that bed as much as possible this week," said the taller of the two men. "My name's Gavin, and the ugly one here is Bruce," he added as he jabbed a thumb in his co-worker's direction.

Martin started to push himself to the edge of the bed, and the two aides reached out to take his arms.

"I can do it," he said as his batted their hands away.

He worked his way over, painstakingly inching himself across the mattress with his good arm. He prepared himself for the throbbing pain he knew was to come and swung his legs over the side of the bed.

Bruce fastened the gait belt around his patient's waist and he and Gavin prepared to support him during the transfer process.

"Okay, Dr. Ellingham, you're going to pivot clockwise, and we'll lower you into the chair," Bruce said, reaching for the belt.

"No, no, no, no, no. Get the walker; I'll do it myself."

The aides looked questioningly at Chris.

"Go ahead. Let the hot shot give it a try. But Martin, you have to let them hang on to you," Chris said.

"Yes, I'm aware of that!"

He slid on to the floor, clenching his teeth together against the jolts being sent through his limbs.

"How are you feeling?" Gavin asked as he watched his face.

"I need to vomit."

Bruce grabbed the basin they had placed at the ready and held it for Martin.

"Here you go, Mart," Chris said, handing him a wet flannel.

Martin wiped his face before handing it back. "Okay, let's go," he said.

Pivoting, he let himself drop into the wheelchair.

"I *am* impressed, mate," Chris said as the colour returned to Martin's face. "You did that on your own."

"Yes."

The aides cleared the room, and Chris passed Martin a glass of water before pulling up a chair next to him. "So how are you doing? Hanging in there with all of this?"

"I'm ready to go home. Do you think Ed will discharge me this week?"

"You'll have to take that up with him. You've been through a lot, Mart. I don't need to tell you that it's going to take you a very long time to recover completely from this. The immunodeficiency alone is going to cause you problems. We just don't want to send you home too soon."

Chris and Martin looked up when they heard their wives approaching in the hallway.

"Well, it looks like we're all ready to go then." Carole said as she set James Henry down on her husband's lap.

"We're going to get you out of this place for a while, Mart." Chris explained. "I borrowed a van from the care facility next door so that we can take you out for dinner. Seeing you upright again is cause for celebration."

Martin's eyes darted towards his wife. "Did you know about this?"

"That's why I brought the new clothes," she said, slipping a pair of short socks on to his feet.

She gave him a smile and patted his foot. "Let's go."

Chapter 12

"*Wait a minute!*"

Startled eyes turned to look at Martin.

"Do *I* have any say in this at all?"

"Martin, I thought you'd be happy to get out of this place for a while," Louisa said.

"Well *of course* I would—to go home! Not to be paraded around in some restaurant like a godawful exhibit in a sideshow! *No!* Absolutely not!"

He looked up at their stunned faces and took in a deep breath. "Look, I appreciate that you're trying to help, but I don't want to go. I'm not going."

"Mart, we're going to our house ... nowhere else. Just our house and back to the hospital again. Are you good with that?" Chris asked.

Martin shook his head and blinked at him. "Well, for God's sake! Why didn't you say so?" he sputtered.

Louisa turned to Carole. "Could you take James and give us just a minute?"

"Sure. We'll be waiting outside."

As soon as the door closed, Louisa walked around behind her husband, wrapping her arms around him and nuzzling her face into his neck. She held him until she heard his breathing slow and felt his body relax.

"Doing better now?"

"I'm sorry. I embarrassed us both," he mumbled.

"You didn't embarrass me, Martin. I don't blame you in the least for reacting the way you did. And it called my attention to something I'm afraid I haven't given enough consideration to—your feelings. We all got used to making decisions for you when you couldn't make them yourself. Now that you're better we need to let you take the lead."

"Louisa, you know I don't like being the centre of attention in the best of times," he said.

"There was a misunderstanding, or more accurately, a failure to communicate. In retrospect, I would have interpreted things the same way you did. And I can understand why you might prefer to not go out to a restaurant and have people gawping at you. But regardless of our plans, we should have talked to you about this first, not just assumed. Are you okay now?"

"Yes." He hesitated. "But ... I would like to go to the Parsons'."

Louisa kissed his cheek. "Good."

Martin sat in his wheelchair in the Parsons' living room a short while later, next to the sofa where Chris was sitting. Chris was reading the newspaper, and Martin flipped distractedly through a medical journal. His attention was being drawn from his young son, playing on the floor in the middle of the room, to his wife as she moved about the kitchen. She was animated in her conversation with Carole, waving her arms about and gesturing. Tonight, she looked happy. He hadn't seen her look truly happy since before the accident.

Louisa glanced into the living room, and noticing her husband's fixed gaze, she smiled at him, giving him a small wave of her fingers. He gave her a slight upward nod of his head before shifting his gaze back to the periodical in his lap.

Later in the evening, Chris and Carole relaxed on the sofa in the family room, and Louisa took a seat in the recliner next to her husband's wheelchair. Martin listened as the conversation centred on family matters—the trials and tribulations of raising a child to adulthood. James began to fuss at the lack of attention that he was receiving, and Louisa walked over to pick him up.

Martin was mesmerized by her. The soft light in the Parsons' home was in contrast to the harsh fluorescents at the hospital, and it seemed to make her skin glow. The fire flickering in the fireplace was reflected in her eyes. She was stunning.

His thoughts focused on her, he blurted out, "Louisa, you are so beautiful."

She looked up in surprise, and having attracted the attention of his friends, the colour rose in Martin's cheeks.

Carole gave Chris a nudge with her elbow, "Why don't you talk to *me* like that?"

"Oh, now that isn't fair. Martin's on some serious narcotics. Things just slip out," he said in a feeble attempt to defend himself.

Carole crossed her arms in front of her. "Christopher Parsons, that is the most pitiful excuse I've ever heard. You can't murmur sweet nothings to me without the aid of serious narcotics? You're going to end up on the sofa tonight if you're not careful." She picked up a throw pillow and gave her husband a playful slap on the head.

The attention having been diverted away from Martin, Louisa slipped over and placed a quick kiss on his lips before mouthing the words, *I love you.*

His chest filled with air, and he felt a sudden desire to be alone with her.

Her husband's reaction wasn't lost on Louisa. "Martin, maybe we should get you back to hospital?"

She raised her eyebrows at him, and a flush spread up his neck. "Mm. Yes, I am a little tired."

Chris got to his feet and swung James into the air before handing him to his wife. "We need to get you hooked back up to your drip, Mart, and it's about time for this one to go to bed. Eh, mate?" he said, tousling the boy's hair.

James gave him a smile before laying his head against Carole's shoulder.

It was just shy of eight o'clock when they arrived back at the Royal Cornwall. Chris accompanied his friends into the building and assisted an aide in getting Martin back into bed.

The room was quiet now except for the steady ticking of the clock on the wall. Louisa locked the door and dimmed the lights before pushing the spare bed up against her husband's.

"Let's get you more comfortable, Dr. Ellingham," she said as she helped him to rid himself of his warm up pants.

"Okay, now the vest," she said, tugging the garment up towards his head.

Martin lifted his left arm up as he furrowed his brow and cocked his head at her. "Louisa, I sleep with my vest *on*."

"I know you do. I'm just following doctor's orders ... or therapist's orders." She pulled his left arm through the sleeve before tugging the neck over his head. Then she went around to the other side of the bed to unfasten his brace and slip the vest off over his right arm before lowering the head of the bed so that he was lying flat. "There, now we can get down to business," she said as she let her hand glide across his cheek.

He watched as she walked over to lay his clothing on the sofa. Her hair moved gently side-to-side and her hips swayed with each step. She took a moment to remove her cardigan jumper before climbing on to the spare bed. Then she positioned herself where she could comfortably reach her husband's neck and torso.

"You need to lift your chin up so I can get to your throat," she said softly. Putting her hands on the sides of his face, she tilted his head back and then began the slow circular movements the therapist had shown her. Her hands moved continually downward, past his collarbones and across his chest. She raised his left hand over his head and worked the lymphatics under his arm.

"Is it all right if I move this arm out just a bit so I can work on you here?" she asked as she moved to his right side.

His eyes were fixed on hers. "Yes," he answered hoarsely.

"Tell me if I'm hurting you." Her motions were languid as she caressed the skin around the wound on his side. Leaning over, she left a trail of kisses along the developing scar line before her hands wandered back to his torso.

Martin closed his eyes and focused his thoughts on the sensation of her skin against his—so unlike the physical contact he had grown used to over the course of his life, when a touch communicated anger, disgust, or loathing. If not his parents' cruel and painful touches, it was the tormenting touches from his peers at boarding school.

But Louisa's touches communicated something else entirely. They were warm and soft ... gentle. Martin could only feel love in her touches.

Her ministrations continued as she moved her caresses down his torso, her hands circulating around the long wound that ran from his sternum to low on his abdomen. Her lips were warm against his skin as they caressed both sides of the tender incision line.

Martin sucked in a ragged breath. "Oh, Louisa."

Her attention moved to his wounded legs, applying the gentlest of strokes with her fingertips, pausing now and then to allow her lips to flutter ever so lightly against his skin.

She looked up at her husband's face when she heard him moan softly. His eyes were closed, but tears had escaped under his lids. She placed a soft kiss on each of his feet before moving herself back up to where she could wipe the salty drops from his temples.

Martin's eyes opened and his gaze merged with hers. Neither of them moved, suspended in time. They had become one. Louisa leaned forward to kiss him, her breath brushing delicately across his tongue, her lips sweet. He released another soft moan and she reached her hand up to pull his head to hers.

Somewhere beyond the strong reaction he was having to his wife, Martin felt a discomfort building in his broken limbs. He ran his fingers through her hair before they migrated south to toy with the buttons on her blouse.

His hand worked its way under the white lace of her top, and he began to caress the bared skin along her flank, unhurried. A sudden stabbing pain shot through his left leg, and his fingers tightened around her side as he released a low moan.

He moaned again and pulled back from her. "Louisa," he squeaked out.

"Mmm, what is it Martin?" she purred.

"My legs hurt," he moaned. "That imbecile forgot to hook my drip back up."

"Martin! Don't talk that way about Chris."

He groaned and tried to reach an appendage with his left hand. "Not—Chris! That idiot aide! Some of these people couldn't organise a piss-up in a—in a *brewery!*"

The spell had been broken. Louisa hurried around the bed and quickly reattached his IV lines. He had been without morphine since before they left for the Parsons', and the effects of the drug were rapidly wearing off. His face contorted with the increasing pain, and Louisa watched him worriedly. "Martin, should I get a nurse?"

He shook his head vigorously. "No, just wait," he whispered, grimacing as another sharp pain shot through his leg.

A minute or two passed before the medication began to work its magic, and Louisa could see her husband's face relax.

"Getting better?" she asked as her hand caressed his.

"Mm. I think so."

"I'm sorry, Martin. I didn't even think about the morphine."

"It's okay. I forgot it, too." He swallowed hard, trying to loosen the lump in his throat. "I was a bit ... distracted."

As they lay together that night, Martin replayed the events of the evening in his mind, lingering on the special moments he had shared with his wife. *Hmph, Parsons does know a thing or two about women,* he thought to himself.

Chapter 13

Louisa left early on Sunday. Paperwork had been piling up on her desk over the last weeks, and she was hoping to get some interruption-free work time in at the school.

Martin had been reluctant to say goodbye. The days alone at hospital dragged, and he missed his wife when she was gone. But it was more than just loneliness he felt when they were apart. As his physical issues began to resolve, he now had to face the psychological issues from his past. He found Louisa's presence to be like a balm that soothed those still gaping wounds, and her absence left him feeling vulnerable and his emotions raw and exposed.

Ed Christianson came into his room early on Monday morning. "I've had very good reports on your progression with ambulation. I think it's time to start setting some goals for getting you home."

Martin scratched at his head and breathed out a heavy sigh. "I do want to get home, but ... well, I have some apprehensions."

Ed pulled a chair over next to the bed and sat down. "Wanna talk about it?"

"Portwenn is a good distance from the hospital if something were to go wrong. And there are a lot of adjustments that will need to be made."

"We'll keep close tabs on you from our end, Martin. Chris will probably be on his mobile a couple of times a day checking up on you. What adjustments worry you?"

Martin picked up his therapy putty and pressed it into the palm of his right hand. "I'll be home all the time for one thing.

I'm not sure how well I'll deal with that. I'm used to keeping busy with my patients, and I'll have nothing to do. I can be ... well, I suppose I can be a bit difficult at times. It may get to be too much for my wife to have me around all the time ... put a strain on our marriage."

"Try to take things as they come, Martin. Patients who've been through what you have usually struggle a bit when they first leave the hospital. You might feel insecure for a while ... until you're not so dependent on other people. And there'll be frustrations. Allow plenty of extra time for daily tasks. Just putting on your shoes could tire you out. Don't be too proud to ask for help. I can guarantee you, you'll need it."

Ed kicked his feet out in front of him, crossing his ankles. "So, let's set some goals. It sounds like you're able to get yourself into the chair on your own but getting out is a problem. I'm going to have the occupational therapy people bring a couple of assist poles in for you. I want you to try to handle the transfers on your own, but I want someone in here in case you need help. So, no transfers in and out of the chair without someone to supervise. Understood?"

"Yes. Seems simple enough."

Ed stood up and came over to the bed. "Show me how you're coming with that grip," he said, taking Martin's hand. "Squeeze." He gave a nod of his head. "Good, that's coming right along. Keep working on it."

He went to the dry erase board on the wall and picked up the marker. "Here's what I want to see before I'll discharge you, Martin.

"First, I want you to be able to get from the bed to the wheelchair and back again. Unsupervised eventually," he said as he recorded his words on the board.

"Second, I want you to be able to get yourself to and from the lavatory when you need to ... that means on and off the toilet.

"Third, I want Tim Spalding to assess your wheelchair skills ... make sure you can get where you want to go. In Portwenn, that means getting up and down hills." The marker squeaked as Ed continued scrawling out his instructions.

"Finally, and this is probably going to cause you the greatest difficultly, I want you to be able to hold a knife, fork, toothbrush, and if you really want to impress me ... a biro in that right hand.

"I know it's a tall order, but from what I've heard from Spalding and Parsons, you're a pretty determined bloke."

Martin nodded slowly. "So, as soon as I've fulfilled those requirements, I can go home?"

"Yep," Ed said as he walked over to retrieve the tray of instruments he had brought in with him. "But remember, Martin, pace yourself."

"When will you give the okay for weight bearing as tolerated?"

"We'll get some pictures in a couple of weeks. If things look good, I'll give you my blessing. Now, let's take those sutures out of that left leg."

An occupational therapist stopped late that morning and installed an assist pole by the bed, as well as another by the toilet. Having finished the task, he headed for the hall.

"Wait a minute!" Martin yelled.

The OT turned around, startled. "Yes, sir?"

"Is that all your job entails? Installing vertical tension poles? Or do you actually work with patients as well?"

The young man shook his head. "I'm sorry?"

"You're a therapist! Are you going to show me how to use this thing or not?"

The intimidated young man replied haltingly, "I—I was just told to get the poles put in the room. I didn't—I mean, I didn't get instructions otherwise."

"Well, I'm instructing you *now*," Martin said, still chafed. He shifted his focus to getting himself into the wheelchair, pushing himself to the side of the bed, ready to make his transfer.

The OT dropped the tools he had been using on to the dresser. "Sir, you need to wait a minute. I'll get a walker for you."

He dashed from the room, leaving his patient open mouthed, his finger pointing ineffectually at the newly installed assist pole.

"Idiot," Martin grumbled.

Moments later Chris Parsons walked into his room, followed by the therapist.

"Ahh, peace in the kingdom was fleeting," Chris said. "Your reign of terror has begun it seems."

Martin looked at him, bewildered. "What do you mean by that?"

Chris shook his head as he pulled a chair up next to the bed.

"What did I do?" Martin asked, his head cocked to the side and his brow furrowed.

"Let's discuss it in a minute." Chris gave the therapist a nod. "Thank you, Mark. I can take it from here."

The young man gathered up his abandoned equipment and hurried from the room.

Turning to face his surly friend, Chris said, "Martin, you can't just go off on people like that. You'll either put the fear of God in them, or you'll risk getting a fist in your face."

"Well if he'd met even the minimum level of competency he never would ha—"

"Martin, it's the kid's first day! Give him a break!"

Chris moved the wheelchair next to the newly installed assist pole. "Come on, let's see what you can do."

Bracing himself for the agony when his feet touched the floor, Martin slid from the bed. He waited until the pain had abated before pivoting into the chair.

"Nice," Chris said, a smile spreading across his face. "I wouldn't give you high marks for your grace under pressure, but *that* was nice ... very nice. Now, let's get some fresh air and cool that head of yours."

"Mm, no. I want to practice. Ed says that once I've accomplished those four things I can go home," Martin said pointing to the whiteboard.

Chris breathed out a resigned sigh. "Okay, let's get on with it then, Martin. But I *am* going to get you outside for a while when we're done here."

"Yes ... fine!" Martin spat, clenching his jaw against the onslaught of sensations as he stood up next to the pole. He pivoted and sat back on the bed. After resting for a minute or two, he reversed the process and sat himself back down in the chair.

Chris supervised as Martin practiced the transfer procedure again and again. "Okay, let's take a break. I'll buy you lunch," he finally said when he became concerned by the increasing pallor on his friend's face.

"Yes, I'm almost done."

"No, Martin, you're done *now*. You're sweating like a pig in a sausage factory." Chris stepped forward when his friend sat down in the wheelchair and pulled it back from the assist pole. Then he handed him a wet facecloth.

"I need to use the lavatory before we go," Martin grumbled.

Chris threw his head back and rolled his eyes. "Do you *really* or are you just trying to sneak in some more practice time?"

Martin's face flushed. "I need to pee. Are you going to help or should I call a nurse?"

"Fine, fine, fine. What do you need me to do?"

"Put these footrests down for me, then flip them back up when I get in there," he said, nodding his head towards the lavatory door. "I can do the rest."

Having heeded nature's call, Martin headed towards the hallway. Chris hurried to keep up. "Are you coming?" he asked as he slowed and glanced behind him.

"Yes, Mart. It's not a race you know."

Moving through the queue in the canteen was less stressful now that it took more than simple movement to cause him pain, but Martin was ever vigilant, ready to ward off any potential assault with his good arm and a sharp comment. Frequent visitors to the dining room knew to give him a wide berth.

Their lunch trays filled, Martin and Chris found a table in a quiet corner and settled in.

"I know you're anxious to get home Mart, but how are you feeling about leaving the hospital?" Chris asked before taking a swig of milk.

Martin furrowed his brow and squinted his eyes as he puzzled over what it was that had been eating at him. "I'm not sure. I think I'm a bit nervous about not having the medical support that I have here. I'll be rather useless if a problem comes up. The nearest doctor is in Wadebridge, and Dr. Lippolis doesn't have experience treating polytrauma patients."

"You'll need to stay on top of things. Be aware of any changes ... and don't wait to call. If you notice anything at all, call Ed or me straight away. We'll be there for you, Mart. Don't worry."

Martin gulped down a mouthful of fish as his mind focused on his friend's last words. He cleared his throat. "I—I've been wanting to thank you Chris ... for being there for me. For orchestrating everything the night of the accident, for helping Louisa, taking care of James, everything." Martin swallowed back the stranglehold his emotions had on his throat.

"You're welcome mate. I owe you a lot, so consider it payback."

"I don't follow. Payback?"

"Martin, you and I both know I never would have made it through medical school if it hadn't been for your incessant lectures about the importance of keeping my neural pathways free of the effects of alcohol. Not to mention, swotting for exams with me ... drilling me constantly."

"I thought I was being a pain in the arse."

"You were a pain in the arse. And I'm bloody grateful to you."

"Right." Martin cleared his throat again and tapped his fingers on the table. "Are you ready to go then?"

Chris's shoulders dropped, and he breathed out a heavy sigh. "Martin, don't go at this too hard ... please."

Martin blinked back at him. "I just asked if you were ready to go."

"Yes. And I know you. You're going to go back to your room and start in with the exercises again, aren't you?"

"I have to work at it if I want to go home," he said, flicking his thumb across the edge of the table.

Chris raised his hands in front of him. "Fine. Let's go."

Chapter 14

Tim Spalding was just finishing up with Martin when Dr. Newell stuck his head in the door that afternoon.

"Is this a bad time?" he asked.

Tim waved him in. "No, not at all. I'm almost done with him."

"How's it going, Martin? Seeing steady improvement now?" the psychiatrist asked as he waited for his patient to wipe the sweat from his face and drink down a glass of water.

"Yes. Ed's given me some goals," he said as he pointed to the board on the wall. "I can tick off the first one for sure and probably the second one. I just need to get Spalding here to relay the information on to Mr. Christianson."

Dr. Newell glanced over at the physiotherapist.

"He's really got it down pretty well," Tim said, giving his patient a grin. "He must be doing nothing but getting in and out of wheelchairs and beds all day."

"Mm," Martin grunted as his gaze shifted to his lap.

Dr. Newell flipped through one of the psychiatric periodicals he had left with his patient. "I stopped to see if you were done with these things. I'll take them off your hands if you are, but feel free to hang on to them if you'd like to hang on to them."

He pulled up a chair. "Do you have some time to talk?"

"Yes, I think so," Martin said as he looked over at Tim.

The young man moved towards the door. "I'm done with you, Martin, so I'll get out of your way. I'll stop back in tomorrow and we'll give that arm a good workout."

"Yes, thank you."

The psychiatrist turned to his patient. "I'm impressed, Martin. You must be putting a lot of effort into achieving those goals."

"I don't like being away from my family."

The therapist pulled an ankle up over his knee. "We have a lot of work to do unravelling your emotional issues as well. I haven't forgotten about it, Martin. I just thought it was best to wait until the physical trauma had been dealt with before we tried to start in with the more intensive therapy you'll be doing with me."

Martin adjusted the Velcro on his warm up pants, keeping his eyes averted. "Erm, if you have enough time today, there are a couple of things that have come up that I'd like to talk about."

"Certainly, shoot."

"I've, er ... I've been a bit confused by something that happened the other day. I'm not sure why I said what I did."

Dr. Newell leaned forward, his elbows on his knees. "Why don't you set the scene for me first and then proceed."

Martin tried to shift his weight from his right hip. "I was trying to explain to Louisa that I don't trust myself when it comes to relationships ... that I've always mucked it up in the end ... someone gets hurt. She said that I hadn't mucked up my friendship with Chris Parsons."

"And you disagree?"

"No, not really. But I made a derisive comment about him. Basically, that he was too stupid to know any better than to keep hanging around me."

"Is that why you think he's been your friend all these years?"

"No, of course not. He's a reasonably intelligent person. And he's done a lot for me ... been a good friend. He's the reason I had the best surgeons and medical care possible after the accident.

"He told me earlier today that he'd be there for me ... and I know he will. For the last twenty odd years, he's been there whenever I've required his assistance. So, I don't understand where the anger came from."

"You felt angry with Chris?"

Martin grimaced and shook his head. "I don't know."

"What do you mean when you say he's been there for you, Martin?"

"He's been there for me whenever I've need—" He rubbed his hand across the back of his neck. "He's always been a good friend."

"A good friend who you needed in a big way that night several weeks ago. A friend who you still need and will be needing for some time to come."

Martin stared at the man for a moment. "Yes."

"If I were in your position, it might make me feel quite vulnerable to need someone that much."

The therapist continued when he didn't get a response. "Anger can be deceptive. It can mask many emotions we may not want to deal with ... be capable of dealing with at a particular moment in time.

"Three weeks ago, you needed Chris more than you've ever needed anyone. You were about as vulnerable as a person can be. And you still need his help to get back on your feet ... literally and figuratively."

"Yes."

Martin sat silently as Dr. Newell let him contemplate what he had just said.

"But Louisa thinks I'm trying to move the process along.

"Move the process along?"

"With friendships ... relationships. I piss people off to get it over with ... to prevent someone being hurt."

"Hmm." The therapist nodded. "Yes, there are a number of possible explanations for the anger you felt towards Chris.

Perhaps you should think on this, and we can take it up another time."

"What I said about Chris upset Louisa. She was angry ... quite angry with me for what I said. She was lecturing me ... poking me in the arm. It ..." Martin's head dropped to the side. "I could tell that she'd ... Well, she was quite angry. Understandably. I never should have said it."

The psychiatrist laced his fingers over his knee. "You've both been through a very harrowing experience. And the Parsons have gone through it with you. Sharing something like that can create a very strong bond. I would imagine Louisa felt defensive of Chris."

Martin's fingers tapped nervously against the mattress, and Dr. Newell cocked his head at him. "How did you interpret your wife's reaction?"

"She was disappointed in me. She told me as much actually. But she was—she *was* very angry."

"She *told* you she was disappointed in you, but how could you tell she was angry?"

Martin looked at the therapist askance. "I believe I said she was poking me in the arm. And the look on her face made it pretty clear."

"The look on her face?"

Martin hissed out a breath. "For God's sake! The disgust! The jabs at my arm, the anger in her touch! Of course, she was angry!" He whipped his head to the side and fixed his gaze out the window.

"How do you react to your wife's anger?"

"I think it often confuses me. I don't understand why things I say or do upset her. It can make me ... make me anxious."

"Given your background, it would be understandable if Louisa's response to you elicited more than anxiety, perhaps even fear."

"Mm."

"And your reaction to her ... did that have to do with the intensity of her anger or how egregious you felt your behaviour had been?"

Martin sat trying to recall how he felt during the incident, but he was finding himself distracted by his therapist's penetrating gaze. "I can't think about this with you sitting there staring at me," he grumbled.

The psychiatrist stood and headed towards the door. "I'll go get a cup of tea. Mull this over while I'm gone, Martin."

Once the door had swung shut, Martin closed his eyes and tried to replay the conversation he'd had with his wife. He focused on the physical sensations. When she looked at him, he had seen disgust in her . eyes. He felt the mildly painful sensation of her fingernail biting into his arm, the premature beats of his heart and the unpleasant tightness it caused in his chest, the way the air seemed to be sucked from his lungs. He felt vulnerable ... he didn't stand a chance.

Dr. Newell returned a short time later, two cups in hand. "Here you go, Martin. Thought you could use one too," he said as he set a cup down on the table next to his patient.

"Thank you."

The therapist pressed the lid to his cup on a little tighter. "So, did I give you enough time to ruminate?"

Martin shook his head. "I don't like the conclusion I came to."

"Well, let's talk about it."

"The way she looked at me ... like she was disgusted by me, and the way her touch felt, the jabs at my arm. I felt like I was a boy again. The same feeling I had with my parents."

"Try to name the emotions you felt, Martin."

"I felt vulnerable ... defenceless, I suppose."

"When I feel vulnerable and defenceless, I usually feel fear," the psychiatrist said as he tapped his biro against his lips.

"Would you say that Louisa's reaction to your words about Chris frightened you?"

"Mm, yes. That's the conclusion I don't like. I had started to feel ... I guess you could say ... safe with her. But the way she looked at me ... I lost that."

Dr. Newell nodded his head as he reached in his pocket to retrieve his biro. "The way you lost your grandfather, your aunt, even the stray dog—your protectors."

"Mm, possibly."

"Tell me, why did you say you don't like that conclusion?"

Martin shook his head at the man. "Because I should be *her*, as you would say, protector. Not the other way around. And what kind of man is afraid of his own wife?" Martin rubbed a palm over his forehead.

"You should talk with Louisa about what she was feeling at that moment, Martin. Facial expressions aren't always a reliable indicator of how someone's reacting to you.

"You associated your parents' unhappy and angry facial expressions with the degrading words and abusive behaviours directed at you. They made it clear you weren't wanted.

"Your wife has replaced your parents. She's the most significant person in your life now, and it would be quite natural for you to make the same association with her unhappy facial expressions.

"And I can certainly understand how a touch intended to convey that unhappiness could elicit a fearful reaction in you. This is one of those times, Martin, when you need to be generous with yourself."

"I don't like to be touched."

"What about by your wife?"

"Well, of course I like being touched by my wife. I don't like being *poked* by my wife, but I *definitely* like being ..." He cleared his throat and pulled in his chin. "Yes, I like being touched by my wife ... and my son. But ordinarily, I don't like being touched. It's painful."

Dr. Newell leaned forward in his chair. "What do you mean by painful?"

"It startles me, makes me jump and my heart skips a beat. My chest hurts and sometimes..."

Martin closed his eyes. "When my mother was visiting, she put her hand on my wrist. It was like she'd put my hand on a hot hob."

The psychiatrist nodded understandingly. "We have some things to work on, Martin, especially in regard to your relationship with your parents. But you need to heal physically before we get deeper into the emotional issues. In the meantime, we'll deal with things as they come up. "I'll keep stopping by as long as you're in hospital, and I'll send you home with some homework to do. We can touch base by phone as well."

He got up and put his hand on his patient's shoulder. "We'll get this all sorted, Martin."

Wagging at finger at the pile of periodicals, he asked, "How about the reading material? Should I take that with me?"

Martin pulled two books from the top and set them aside. "I'd like a little more time with these, if it's okay."

"Of course. Pay particularly close attention to what they have to say about the effect trauma and stress have on the limbic area of the developing brain." Dr. Newell stopped in the doorway and turned. "Martin, remember ... marriage is all about being there to support *and* protect one another. There's nothing wrong with allowing Louisa to be your protector."

Chapter 15

Louisa and James met Ruth for dinner at Bert Large's restaurant Monday night. "Hello, Ruth!" Louisa said, leaning over to give the woman a hug before lowering James Henry into a high chair.

The elderly woman stiffened as she tolerated the gesture of affection. "I took the liberty of ordering you a salad, and spaghetti for your son. Hope you don't mind." She reached across the table to pour water into Louisa's glass.

"No, that's good! It'll speed up the process at bit," Louisa said as she slipped a bib over the baby's head. "How was your day?"

"A bit dull, actually. Al and I spent the morning crunching numbers, and the afternoon was equally exciting. And yours?"

"It was—"

"Good evening Louiser!" Bert said as he approached the table. "How's the doc doin'?"

"He's coming along, Bert. I can see continued forward momentum with him now. We're actually trying to prepare for him to come home."

"Oh, I been thinkin' about that. You're gonna have your hands full with the doc and with little James here." Bert reached over and tousled the boy's hair with a pudgy hand. "How 'bout I bring dinner over now and again, just to give you a bit of a break."

"Oh, Bert. It's so sweet of you to offer, but Martin's doctors have him on a special diet. Foods that will help his bones to heal. But if you wouldn't mind, maybe James and I could stop in here now and then for a meal."

"Anytime you want, girl. I'd love to have you."

Louisa could see the disappointment on the portly man's face, but she knew what was best for Martin, and it did not include Bert Large coming by periodically to wax philosophical.

A waitress came out and placed their food in front of them, and James reached out greedily for his bowl of spaghetti. Louisa moved quickly to cut it into bite-sized pieces before her son could complain too loudly.

"Well, I'll leave you three to enjoy your dinner, but I'll be back to take your puds order."

Bert waddled off, and Louisa smiled at Ruth. "He means well, but I can just picture Martin's face if he found himself having to endure Bert's questions. Let alone any of his unwanted medical advice."

"Yes. And how *is* my nephew?"

"They got him up on his feet on Saturday," she said as she scraped a piece of pasta from James's bib and spooned it into his mouth.

Ruth looked up from her plate apprehensively. "And how did it go?"

"It was obviously very painful, but he did it, and he did it very well. Over, and over, and over. *God*," she said, shaking her head.

"Yes, it's necessary. The weight placed on the bones speeds up the fracture repair process by increasing blood flow to his limbs.

"Martin's still in the inflammatory stage of his recovery. It's a painful period but the inflammation is crucial to increasing the blood flow to the fractured areas. Nutrient rich blood carries cells that become either osteoblasts, which form bone tissue, or chondroblasts, which form cartilage."

Ruth paused to chew a bite of salad. "The repair stage has begun now as well. Proteins formed by the osteoblasts and chondroblasts consolidate into a soft callus which eventually hardens.

"Have they discussed Martin's nutritional needs with you at all?" Ruth asked, laying down her fork and dabbing at her mouth with her napkin.

James began to fuss and Louisa pulled several toys out of the nappy bag, laying them on the high chair tray. "Not much. I do know it seems like he's eating all the time. The Parsons have been faithful in their daily delivery of meals. Martin seems to be eating well, better than I've ever seen him eat actually. I don't know how he can be staying so trim in fact ... laying in that bed most of the day."

"Fracture repair takes a surprising amount of energy, especially long bone fractures. Having suffered several of those, Martin's caloric demands now are probably three to four times higher than before the accident. It's really difficult to take in that many calories in a day eating the foods we normally eat." Ruth pushed back in her chair and turned to watch the fishing boats making their way into the harbour.

"I'm assuming then that all the shakes and smoothies he drinks are to boost the number of calories he's getting?"

"Oh, it's much more than that. Those cocktails have a very high protein content and are full of the extra vitamins and minerals he needs as well. I would imagine they'll send you home with a good supply of them, but you can also get them from Mrs. Tishell."

"Wonderful," Louisa groaned. "I never considered that *she* would have to be involved in Martin's care." She worried her lip and drummed her fingers on the table.

Ruth got to her feet. "Let me handle picking up any supplies from the chemist."

"Oh, Ruth, thank you. The woman just makes me so uncomfortable, and the way she talks about Martin is just ..." Louisa said as a shudder went through her.

"I honestly don't think you have anything to be concerned about, but if it makes you feel better, I'd be happy to help out."

Louisa gave her a sheepish glance. "I do appreciate it."

"Well, I need to be off. Places to go and people to see, as they say. Let me know if there are any new developments with my nephew."

Bert scurried over when he saw Ruth leaving. "Oh dear, oh dear. She missed her puds."

Louisa smiled at him. "It's all right, Bert. The meal was so satisfying in itself we just didn't feel the need for puds tonight."

"That's a shame. What about little James? Perhaps a biscuit?"

"No, thank you, Bert. I need to get him home and off to bed," Louisa said as she got up and started to gather James's things together.

Bert began to clear the table. "Right then. You'll let me know if there's anything I can do? Anything a'tall."

"Yes, Bert. I will. And thank you." Louisa laid a twenty pound note on the table and hurried off up the steps, her thoughts now turning to her regularly scheduled conversation with her husband.

With James tucked into bed, Louisa rang Martin's number.

"Louisa?" He answered in the soft, silky voice he reserved for his wife and son.

"Hello, Martin. How was your day?"

"Busy. And you?"

"Busy too, but productive. I got caught up on my paperwork yesterday and met with a couple of parents I'd been needing to consult with, today."

"Do you need help, Louisa? I mean, maybe you should consider hiring someone to help with the laundry, housework, and that sort of thing."

Louisa huffed out a breath. "Thank you, Martin, but I think I can handle things on my own."

"I wasn't suggesting otherwise. I just don't want you to get run down. Your immune system doesn't operate as efficiently when—"

"I'm fine, Martin."

He hesitated, hearing the tetchiness in her voice. "So, your day was productive. That's good."

"Yes, it is. I was able to work out a plan with Pippa at the school, so I can be there for you when you get home. And I think we figured out a strategy in case I need to take off in the middle of the day if you need me. So yes, it was productive."

As Martin listened to his wife, he was already feeling like he'd become a burden to her, and he wasn't even home yet. "You don't have to take off work, Louisa. I'm sure I can manage on my own. And the health aide will be there in the morning and evening. I'll be fine on my own."

"Let's play it by ear, okay? Regardless, I feel better knowing that there's a plan in place."

"Yes." He gave the book he had been reading a toss on to the table next to the bed.

"So, tell me about your day. Anything new?" she asked.

"Ed came in this morning, and we talked about when I might be able to go home," Martin said as he tried to get the bedding folded back neatly over his legs.

"And ...?"

"I have four requirements that I have to meet before he'll discharge me. I've ticked off two already, but the other two need work.

"He wants me to be able to get up and down the hills in Portwenn. I can't work on that on my own, for obvious reasons. I'll have to wait for a physiotherapist or occupational therapist to work with me.

"And I need to get the swelling down in my arm before I can meet the final requirement. I don't have a lot of control over that either. I can't pick things up until I have more dexterity in my fingers. Right now, it's just not there."

His discouragement could be heard in his voice. But Louisa knew he was always more pessimistic in the evening than he was in the morning.

"Just keep trying, Martin ... it'll come."

He rolled his eyes and changed the subject. "Chris and I had lunch together today."

"Good. I'm glad you're spending more time with Chris."

"Yes."

There was a period of awkward silence before Louisa asked, "Is there anything wrong, Martin?"

"No, not really." He breathed out a weary sigh. "Dr. Newell came by today, and we talked ... quite a lot actually."

Louisa walked into the kitchen and sat down at the table. "Oh? What about?"

"We talked about the conversation you and I had on Saturday ... what I said about Chris."

"Did he have any words of wisdom for you?"

"He has some things he wants me to think over. Louisa ... erm, what were you thinking when I said what I did about Chris?"

Louisa furrowed her brow. "Well, I thought what you said was unkind and unfair. Is that what you mean?"

"No, no, no, no, no. What were you thinking about me?"

"Martin, if you're wondering how I was *feeling* about you, I was disappointed but mostly shocked that you would say something like that about your friend. And yes, I was mad at you ... at first."

"At first?"

"Mm-hmm. After I had some time to cool off and think it through, I realised you didn't mean what you said. Then I was just worried about you and wanted to get back to the room to make sure you were all right."

Martin was quiet for several seconds before he said, "I would understand if you were—well, did you think—I mean, I would understand if you were—well if—"

"Martin, stop. Just stop and think about what it is you're trying to say. What do you want to know?"

Air hissed into the phone. "Are you disgusted by me when I say things I shouldn't? Do you ever regret marrying someone like me?"

"*No!* Absolutely not, Martin! *Remember,* I told you to not think for one minute that I didn't love you."

"It *is* possible to feel both things—to love someone but know they wouldn't make you happy," he said.

Now it was Louisa's turn to be quiet. He had just spoken words from the letter she wrote to him when they called off their first wedding. "Yes, you're right, it is." Her gaze settled on the platinum band on her left hand. "Martin, what I was feeling when you said what you did was temporary anger and disappointment. There will always be times when we anger and disappoint one another, though ... won't there?"

Martin tried to recall a time when he truly felt anger towards Louisa. Perhaps when she had been shifting furniture during her pregnancy. No, Martin knew what anger felt like and that wasn't it. That was concern that she and the baby could have been in danger.

Perhaps when she refused to take the antibiotic he had prescribed for her urinary tract infection. Yes, that had been anger. But most of the time, Louisa simply confused and frustrated him.

"Louisa."

"Hmm?"

"Mm, never mind."

"Martin Ellingham!" Louisa blew out a breath. "For goodness' sake, can't we have a normal husband and wife conversation?"

"I'm sorry."

Her elbow thunked on to the table, and her head dropped into her hand before she drew in a calming breath. "Martin, just because I have a moment of anger or disappointment with you doesn't mean I don't want you anymore. I will always want you ... love you."

She waited for a response but none came. "You know, there's a difference between the momentary flash of anger I had the other day and the hatred your parents had for you. Underneath the temporary emotions I may feel on occasion, I love you very much. And that will always win out in the end. Your parents never felt any love for you ... never had any love to give to you. There was no love there to ... well, I guess to neutralise the anger."

"Mm. I see."

"Do you, Martin? Are you sure you understand? Because I don't want you over there in Truro having any worries about us."

"No, I think I know what you're saying."

A nurse came into the room to check Martin's vital signs and give him one of the twice daily heparin injections he received.

"I'm going to have to say goodbye; someone's here. But ..."

She heard him clear his throat and could picture him pulling in his chin.

"I miss you," he mumbled.

"I miss you, too. And Martin, remember that underneath whatever emotions I might be displaying at the moment, I love you very much."

"Yes. I love you, too."

Chapter 16

"Dr. Ellingham ... *Dr. Ellingham*. Wake up, you're dreaming."
The nurse grabbed on to her patient's arm as he thrashed
violently in the bed.

An aide hurried into the room. He tried to hold on to
Martin's legs as he kicked at the blankets that were restraining
him.

"Dr. Ellingham, you need to wake up!" the nurse said,
shaking Martin's shoulder. "You're going to hurt yourself."

She stumbled backwards as her patient threw his arm out
forcefully, trying to free himself from his attacker.

*He had found himself alone in a room, an expansive room
devoid of colour—grey walls, grey ceiling. The floor was grey as
well, but spotlessly clean, and with such a shine he could see
himself reflected in it.*

*He was alone in the massive space, not lonely, just alone. He
was insignificant.*

*Martin felt something soft, warm, and wet touch his hand. It
left a trail of moisture that cooled as it began to evaporate into the
air. He turned and the dog's friendly accepting eyes looked back at
him.*

*It swung its tail eagerly back and forth, silently
communicating its desire for friendship. He knelt down and
stroked the animal's head, his actions being rewarded with a more
vigorous wag of the tail and more warm, wet affections applied to
his face.*

*Gathering the animal into his arms, he buried his face into its
furry body, the dog wriggling and panting its delight. Only
Auntie Joan had ever made him feel as he did now. He was*

significant to another living being, and it was wonderful. Martin felt his chest swell as he filled his lungs with air, relishing the moment.

Suddenly, the dog recoiled and began to trot away from him. He called to it and clapped his hands, beckoning it to return, but it continued to move farther away. He ran to catch up to it and reached out, wrapping his arms around its neck.

The dog whirled around, snarling and snapping at him. He jumped back, but the dog's teeth grabbed on to his arm. Pain shot through him as its jaws clamped down ever tighter, shaking him, like a rag doll, through the air. He kicked and hit at the dog, trying to free himself from its grip, and it pulled back momentarily, baring its fangs at him.

The friendly accepting eyes he had seen moments before had been replaced by his mother's cold and hateful ones. The dogs lolling tongue replaced by the smirk he would see on his mother's face as she watched his father carry out his punishments, seemingly entertained by her son's fear and misery.

The animal snarled and came at him again. Martin turned to run, but he tripped and fell on to his stomach. As he got to his knees, he saw his reflection in the shiny floor, and over him towered his mother, looking at him with disgust. He pushed himself to his feet and turned to see her disappear through the grey wall. He was alone again ... and insignificant.

"Dr. Ellingham, you need to calm down, or we'll have to sedate you. Do you understand?"

Voices around him began to register, and Martin forced his eyes open. The lights in the room were blinding at first, but as his eyes adjusted and he left his nightmare behind, he realised where he was. He was sitting upright in his hospital bed, his heart racing and breathing heavily. A sense of relief spread through him, followed quickly by embarrassment.

The nurse handed him a glass of water and excused the aide from the room.

"What time is it?" Martin asked as he squinted through bleary eyes, trying to see the clock on the wall.

"Just after half three," the nurse said as she pulled the blankets back and began to examine his legs. "I need to make sure you haven't done any damage here."

Having assured herself all of Martin's pins were still secure, she went to the small dresser by the sofa and pulled out a dry vest.

"Okay, mister. Off with the wet one," she said as she held up his left arm and began to peel his sweaty clothing from his body.

The woman was older, probably nearing retirement age, and she had a kindly face and a ruddy complexion. Martin watched her, taking note of her eyes. They were hazel like his mother's, but this woman's eyes held a warmth that his mother's lacked.

The nurse unfastened the brace and slipped his right arm out of the vest. She then went to the sink and came back with a wet flannel and a towel.

She eyed him for a moment before asking, "Do you want to do this yourself?"

Before she could respond she added, "No, of course you don't; you're all hog-tied with that contraption, aren't you?"

The nurse slapped the facecloth down on his chest and began to wipe the sweat from his body, but Martin pushed her hand away.

"I can do it, Auntie Joan!" he snapped before catching his mental slip.

The nurse hesitated but didn't say anything. She went to her patient's chart to update his notes.

Martin handed the cloth back to her, and she in turn handed him the towel to dry himself.

"Here, let me help you with the vest," she said as she began to thread his right arm and fixators through the sleeve. She tipped her head down and gave him a stern look. "I hope you don't think you can handle *this* yourself as well?"

"I *could* do," he grumbled back.

She slipped the neck over his head and he pushed his left arm through the opposite sleeve. Tugging it neatly down around his torso she gave him a pat on the back and stepped back to inspect her handiwork.

"Now, you look more comfortable."

Martin laid his head back on his pillow as the nurse pulled the blankets up and smoothed them out.

"You know, there's nothing wrong with allowing people to help you out once in a while," she said. "No one's immune to vulnerability, Martin. We all need a leg up now and then. And remember ..." She waggled a finger at him. "...helping you probably did as much good for *me* as it did for you. We all want to feel needed ... to be of significance in this world."

She dimmed the lights and stepped towards the door.

"Thank you," Martin said just before the door closed behind her.

Sticking her head back into the room she replied, "You're most welcome. Goodnight, Dr. Ellingham."

Martin slept well the rest of the night and woke feeling surprisingly refreshed considering the rather tumultuous night he'd had.

Carole Parsons came in with breakfast for him and stayed to visit a while.

"I spoke with Louisa last night. She said you're nearing the end of your stay here."

"Mm, I hope so. I have two more requirements that Ed wants me to meet, and then I can go home. Hopefully, I'll be able to work on those today. The physiotherapist should be in this morning."

Carole watched with amusement as Martin bolted down the four scrambled eggs, large bowl of fruit, and heavily buttered toast she had put in front of him.

"I'm going to have to bring you a bigger breakfast next time. I've never seen you eat like this, Martin!"

"Mm, sorry. I've been burning a lot of calories in therapy and the body requires a large amount of—"

"Yes, Martin. Chris has given me the full explanation of the physiological process of fracture repair. And you don't need to apologise; I love seeing you with a hearty appetite. And I like bringing meals over for you ... gives me a chance to get to know you better."

Martin picked up his napkin and wiped his face. "I ... want to thank you. Not just for the meals, for everything you've done to help Louisa and me through this."

Carole stood up and began to gather the dirty dishes from the tray table. "I'm very happy we could be of help to both of you. Martin ... the night of your accident was just awful. When I was introduced to Louisa that night she seemed so lost. It's very hard to see someone you love in pain, and Martin you were ..."

Carole came over and placed a chaste kiss on his cheek, causing a flush to spread up his neck. He cleared his throat and shifted uncomfortably in his bed.

"Anyway, you are very welcome," Carole said as she prepared to leave. "You know though, now that Louisa and I are friends, you and Chris will have to see more of each other."

"Mm, I think we can deal with that."

Chapter 17

Martin had been taken down to radiology around the middle of the morning for a series of x-rays and CT scans which had been ordered by Mr. Christianson. Tim Spalding was waiting outside his room when he returned.

"Good morning. They have you up with the chickens, I see," the therapist said as he watched Martin manoeuvre his chair through the doorway.

"Yes. I'm hopeful this is the last of it before I'm discharged." Martin jerked his hand back to prevent his fingers from being caught between his chair and the door jamb.

"Nice save. I'm glad to see you're watching out for that hand." Tim came into the room and took a seat as Martin shifted himself from the wheelchair to his bed. "Well, we're going to take a proper walk today, so why don't you get back into your chair and we'll get out of here for a while."

Martin turned a furrowed brow to the young man. "Why didn't you say that *before* I shifted myself into bed?"

The PT rose from his seat and gave his patient a roguish grin. "You need the practise."

"Mm, yes." Martin had practised the procedure so many times it was now more a matter of muscle memory than a thought process, and he made the transition flawlessly.

Tim led the way down the hall to the lift. "We're going down the street a few blocks to the rehab centre. It's the best place to practise ascent and descent manoeuvres. It won't be Portwenn sized hills, but it'll give you the general idea."

It was a pleasant fall day. The leaves, which had turned to the oranges, reds, and yellows of autumn, were painted on to a blue canvas of cloudless sky. Martin's thoughts turned to Louisa. She was probably sitting on the wall outside the school, looking out over the harbour and watching over the students as they took a break from their lessons.

"How are you holding up ... you want me to push for awhile?" Tim asked as he noticed his patient beginning to flag.

Martin was about to rebuff the young man's offer, but he remembered his words about guarding against over-use of his one healthy appendage. "Mm, that would be good," he said as he shook out his arm.

"So where are you from, Dr. Ellingham? I mean where did you grow up?"

"London," Martin replied, hoping this wouldn't turn into an interrogation.

"Oh yeah? I have family in London. What part of the city?"

"Kensington." Not wanting the conversation to lead to questions about his parents or his miserable years in boarding school, Martin tried to steer it in another direction. "Where did you go to school ... get your certification?"

"University of Plymouth. I have a sister who moved there after she got married, so I lived with them while I was at uni. Saved myself a lot of money and helped them out as well. They have a son with cerebral palsy. I worked with him quite a bit. He was my guinea pig ... poor kid," Tim said, chuckling.

Martin sat silent as they drew closer to the rehabilitation centre, partly out of a loss for words, partly because of the nervous tension he was experiencing. The use of the wheelchair on the hills in Portwenn didn't concern him. But the more he thought about an outing in the village, the more uncomfortable he grew, knowing he would be the star attraction and topic of conversation for the gossip and rumour mill.

"Actually, I probably won't even go out until I'm total weight bearing again. I should mention that to Mr.

Christianson. This might be an unnecessary step," Martin explained to the therapist.

"You've got another three weeks or more before you'll be weight bearing as tolerated, Martin. Aren't you going to be completely Bodmin by then, sitting inside the house?" Tim said, suspicious of his patient's dismissiveness. "I should warn you though, people *will* be curious at first. But generally, if you answer their questions right at the start, they tend to forget about the fixators."

"Hmph," Martin grunted. "You don't know the people in Portwenn. They'll be coming up with a myriad of excuses to come nosing around. It's like a daily competition to see who can dish up the biggest plate of gossip every morning ... *really*. And the biggest nosy parker of them all is Bert Large. He smells gossip before it even happens. Gawd, they'll be over me like flies on yesterday's fish."

"Well, try not to think about that now. Focus on what you need to do to get your discharge papers from Mr. Christianson," Tim said as they approached the building.

Martin spent most of the next two hours working on navigating the long ramps in the rehab centre. They varied in degree of grade, but none were as steep as Roscarrock Hill or even the hill that Ruth's cottage was on. But the therapist assured him he would indeed be able to manage his wheelchair in the village, if he were inclined to venture out.

"Okay, while we're over here, let's use some of the equipment," Tim said as he pushed his patient's chair across the room.

He wheeled Martin up to a table with varying sizes of round holes in the top. Martin's task was to pick up the matching round, wooden cylinders and put them into their respective holes. He no longer had any trouble picking up smaller objects but hanging on to them was still a trick.

He had been working at the exercise persistently for a solid half hour when Tim told him he needed to take a break. "Let's go and get some lunch at the restaurant next door. Then we'll come back to this."

The restaurant was small but adequately sized to accommodate the usual number of diners. Mostly staff from the hospital and the clinics on the campus.

They had just received their lunch orders when a loud penetrating voice rang out, causing Martin to groan internally. Adrian Pitts was a former pupil of Martin's and a surgeon on staff at the Royal Cornwall. He had also "outed" Martin to the village after he had refused the young man's request to convince Chris Parsons to promote him.

The revealing of his haemophobia had resulted in a very public practical joke played at the pub, and involving Bert Large and a bottle of ketchup. It also led to a shaking of the faith the villagers had in their doctor and continuous snide remarks in the years since.

"Martin! I heard a rumour you were here!" the cocky, womanising surgeon said. "What happened, Chief ... get caught snogging one of the village totties and her boyfriend didn't like it?" He chuckled at his own wit.

Martin gave the surgeon a look of disdain. "What do you want Adrian?"

"Just saw you sitting here and thought I'd stop and say hello. Seriously, what happened to you?"

"Car accident," Martin mumbled. "Was there something you wanted, Adrian? You're interrupting our lunch."

Adrian pulled a chair up alongside his former tutor and took a seat. "You're not still cheesed off about my letting it slip about your handicap, are you?"

"Go away, Adrian," Martin said as he turned back to the food in front of him.

"You should be thanking me, Chief. That stunner you were with that night at the hospital came back in to talk to me ... singing your praises ... defending your honour. I bet you could get *that* one to put out!"

Tim Spalding watched, nervously, as his patient's face reddened and fury began to burn in his eyes. Martin reached over with his left arm and grabbed hold of Adrian's tie, yanking the younger man over so he could look him in the eye.

"That *stunner* ... is my *wife,* you puerile little prat!" he spat out.

The therapist jumped to his feet and tried to loosen his patient's chokehold on the insolent surgeon, but Martin had wrapped the man's tie around his hand and had a firm hold. Tim reached across and grabbed a steak knife from the neighbouring table, cutting through the tie encircling Adrian's neck.

Martin leaned back in his chair, breathing heavily.

"Now, I think the man asked you to leave," the therapist said. "Next time you hassle a bloke, you better make sure you can handle him." He handed Pitts what was left of his tie and watched as he sheepishly walked out the door.

"You okay?" he asked as he dropped into his chair, trying to read his patient's facial expression.

"Yeah." Martin rubbed his head trying to ease the tension in the taut muscles across his temples.

"Care to talk about it?"

He sighed, and then reluctantly began to relate the the whole sordid tale to his therapist. He kept his eyes on the table, tracing circles around the rim of his glass.

"Hmph. I think you were being kind when you called him a puerile little prat," Tim said giving Martin a small grin.

"Mm."

"I don't mean to pry, Martin. Just don't answer this question if I am. But Dr. Newell's visits to your room ... is he helping you to figure out the blood sensitivity problem?"

Martin tipped his head to the side, breathing a heavy sigh. "My parents were ... harsh," he said before quickly averting his eyes.

Tim's brows drew together. "But your father was a well-respected surgeon."

"What does one have to do with the other?" Martin snapped. His father had gotten away with far too much over the years because of his *well-respected surgeon* image.

"Sorry, you're right ... it doesn't." The therapist spun his knife back and forth on the table in front of him. "Like I said, Dr. Ellingham, I didn't mean to pry."

Martin glanced over at the door. "Are you ready to go?"

"Sure."

When they returned to the centre, Tim started Martin back in on the ramps before again taking him to the table with the cylinders. He finally pulled him away when he could see his accuracy was waning.

"I'll push you to the hospital," he said as they crunched over the crisp fall leaves that had fallen from the trees. "I want you to rest up so you'll be ready to do some work when we get back to your room."

The two men walked in silence for the rest of the return trip. Martin was tired, and his therapist could see it.

When they reached the room, Tim helped Martin into bed before completing the range of motion exercises and lymphatic massage.

The stretching of his ligaments and muscles was still painful, but much less so than it had been in the beginning. Martin could see very positive results now. From both Tim's efforts as well as his own.

The massage his therapist performed never failed to relax Martin, and he dropped off to sleep quickly. Tim returned an hour later and worked with him on gripping common items he would need to be using every day—a hairbrush, spoon, toothbrush.

He practised with the spoon, eating a bowl of pudding. It wasn't pretty, but he managed to down the entire bowl with no more than a few spills on to the blankets.

"I know that at the moment it's more comfortable to use your left hand for these things, but force yourself to use that right hand. If you start feeling bone pain then switch to your left," Tim said as he took the spoon and laid it by the sink.

Tooth brushing required a tighter grip and proved more difficult, but Martin got the job done in the end. Both patient and therapist were pleased with the day's successes. A few more hours of practise and Martin felt confident he would be on his way home.

Chapter 18

Martin sat by the window in his room soaking up the rays of late afternoon sun. The days at hospital seemed nearly unbearable now. He had exhausted his supply of reading material, and although he was religious about doing the exercises given him by Tim Spalding, they weren't the mental stimulation he craved.

He had wheeled himself down to the canteen a little earlier in the afternoon and was now nursing the second of the two protein shakes he had picked up. He looked towards the door when he heard the soft squeak of its hinges.

Chris Parsons came in and pulled a chair up next to him. "Hey, Mart. How's it going?"

"I've never been so bored in my life," Martin grumbled. "Have you talked to Ed today?"

"I assume you mean about when you can go home," Chris said, taking a seat.

"Yeah. He had me down in radiology this morning. I thought I would have heard from him by now." Martin turned his chair and peered over the window ledge.

"He's going to stop by here in a few minutes, mate. I'm sure he'll bring us both up to speed." Chris watched as his friend gazed intently on something below. "What are you looking at, Mart?"

Martin turned back quickly, shaking his head. "Mm, nothing. Just thought I might have seen Louisa."

"Ah," said Chris, a knowing smile crossing his face. "I think my anti-social, solitary friend is lonely."

"I'm not *lonely*. I told you, I'm just ... bored." He drummed his fingers on the armrest of his chair.

"Hey, I get it. I imagine seeing *Carole* when I'm bored. Come on, Mart, admit it; you miss your wife."

Martin mumbled unintelligibly.

Chris sighed in exasperation. "There's nothing wrong with admitting you miss companionship, Martin. It's called being human. And when the companion looks like your wife, it's called being male."

Martin shot his friend a warning look. "You'd better stop right there, Chris."

"Sorry, mate."

The hinges on the door squeaked again, and Mr. Christianson entered the room.

"Hi, Ed." Chris got up and pulled another chair over near the window.

The surgeon gave them a nod of his head. "Chris ... Martin." He dropped into the seat with a heavy sigh. Well, Martin, your pictures looked good for the most part. About what we'd expect at this point. The hard callus formation has started on all of your fractures. The arm of course has been a bit slower to heal. There was a lot of damage there." He leaned forward, resting his elbows on his knees.

Martin furrowed his brow. "You said the pictures looked good *for the most part*. Is there a problem?"

"No, not really," the surgeon said, shaking his head. "It's just the soft tissue repair that you have ahead ... the reconstructive procedures. But we'll deal with those when the time comes."

Martin nodded. He had enough to worry about. He couldn't concern himself right now with what was to come months down the road. "When do you think I can go home?" he asked expectantly.

"I spoke with Tim Spalding before I came over here, and he thinks you're ready to go ... provided you keep working on things at home. I was reluctant, but he told me Jeremy Portman will be your home health nurse. He's a brilliant kid and will notice if any problems begin to develop. I also trust him to keep in close contact with Chris and me."

Ed leaned back, folding his hands behind his head. "We'll get you set up with the physiotherapists out of Wadebridge. They can do home visits until it's easier for you to travel. Chris, can you help Louisa get Martin back to Portwenn?"

"Yeah, sure. You won't be able to get in and out of a car until you're full weight bearing, Mart, so I'll call the ambulance service people ... line up a vehicle to transport you. Talk it over with Louisa. Then let me know when you want to leave, and I'll make the arrangements."

Ed cleared his throat and leaned forward, steepling his fingers. "Erm, Martin. I hear you had a bit of a disagreement with one of my surgeons earlier today."

Martin groaned and threw his head back. "Tim Spalding told you about it?"

"No, I actually heard about it from Dave Iverson, one of my other guys."

Chris looked back and forth between the two, perplexed.

"Adrian Pitts," Ed explained.

"Ah, I see."

"Care to tell me your version of the story, or should I take Iverson's rendition as gospel truth?" Ed asked, tipping his head down as he peered up at him.

Air hissed from Martin's nose. "The idiot made a sexually suggestive remark about my wife. Well, he didn't know she was my wife until after the comment was made, but that's neither here nor there. He was a royal arse when I had him on my team of registrars, and he's only gotten worse."

"So, you had him by the throat ... that part true?"

"Technically ... no. I had him by the tie."

"Martin, are you serious! Should I consider myself lucky I didn't get the same treatment after my comment a few minutes ago?" Chris shook his head as he gave Ed a grin.

"Chris, if he'd said what he did in reference to *your* wife, you would have done the same thing." Martin turned to Ed, "Talk to Tim Spalding, he was sitting right there. He was the one who took the steak knife to Pitts' tie, in fact."

Ed began to chuckle, "Oh, this just gets better and better. I wish I could have seen the look on Pitts' face."

Martin sat scowling. "I don't see the humour in this. The idiot insulted my wife, and I lost my temper."

"Martin! Since when do you care about losing your temper?" an incredulous Chris quipped.

"Forget it," Martin said as he slumped back in his chair.

Chris thought it best to let the subject drop for the time being, and he steered the conversation back to his friend's discharge from hospital. "So, Mart, talk to Louisa. Then let me know when you want to leave, and we'll make it happen."

"Right. I'll talk to her tonight."

Ed stood up and made a move towards the door. "I'll want to give you one last thorough exam before you go, Martin, and order a few tests. I don't want to send you home with something brewing under the surface. And I'd like to have a short meeting with you and Louisa before I cut you loose." He gave Chris a roguish grin. "No pun intended there."

"Very funny," Martin growled.

Chris waited until the surgeon had left the room before turning to his friend. "So, you want to talk about what happened with Pitts?"

"Oh, it's over Chris. Let's just forget the whole thing," Martin said as he wheeled himself back to his bed.

"I'm just curious, Mart. Why does losing your temper with Pitts upset you so much?"

Chris watched as Martin got himself out of the wheelchair before pivoting around and sliding back on to the mattress. Then, leaning forward he used his left hand to first hoist his right leg, then his left leg up on to the bed. Chris couldn't help but be impressed by the progress his friend had made.

He pulled the blankets up over Martin's legs, and then he stared at him, waiting for an answer.

Martin scratched at his head. "I lost my temper with a patient a while back ... an alcoholic. I suspected he'd been abusing his son, then I found the boy with a broken arm. The father called the child a bastard and said the boy deserved the punishment he'd gotten." He ran a palm over his face. "I've always been able to control myself ... physically."

Chris furrowed his brow and shook his head at him. "But you don't worry about hurling insults at people."

Martin picked up his therapy putty and began to knead it vigorously with his injured hand. He sat for a while, thinking about how to explain himself.

"Insults don't cause physical harm."

"So, is this about the Hippocratic oath?"

Martin screwed up his face. "No! It's about losing control and going too far!"

Chris stood up and walked over to the bed. "I'm not sure I understand what's worrying you, Mart. I do know though that this isn't typical behaviour for you. You should talk this over with Barrett Newell."

"*Yes*, I will," he answered sharply.

"Well, I need to get home before my wife-imposed curfew. Let me know when you want to get out of here, and I'll make the arrangements." Chris put his hand on his friend's shoulder. "What happened with Pitts ... no one's going to hold it against you. You'll probably be getting pats on the back from just about everyone in this hospital. Ed and I were just surprised."

"Mm."

Chapter 19

Martin picked at the unpleasant looking assortment of offerings on his dinner tray, taking a moment to bless the dried-out dinner roll with a curl of his lip. The menu had said he would be eating salmon tonight, but this tasted for all the world like chicken, Martin thought as he tried to wash it down with a glass of milk. At least the milk was palatable.

A young lady from the hospital food service staff had just stopped to pick up his partially cleaned plate when Barrett Newell stuck his head in the door.

"Mind a little company?" the therapist asked as he pulled up a chair, ready to take a seat regardless of his patient's answer.

"Erm, yes. That'd be fine." Martin gave his mouth a dab with his napkin and his hands one last wipe before folding it up and laying it on the table next to him.

"I heard from Chris Parsons that you're being paroled."

"Mm. Chris'll make arrangements for an ambulance service shuttle to take me back to Portwenn ... whenever it works for Louisa. I'm going to call her tonight."

Dr. Newell smiled and leaned back in his chair. "I'm very glad to hear that, Martin. It's been a tough battle to get back home, hasn't it?"

"Yes, it has." Martin tipped his head down self-consciously. "There was a period of time when I wasn't sure ... wasn't sure it was going to happen," he said with a hitch in his voice. He pushed the blankets back off his legs, preparing to shift himself from bed to wheelchair.

"You need some help there?" the psychiatrist asked, getting to his feet.

Martin gave him a dismissive wave of his hand. "Nope, I've got it." He grabbed hold of the external fixators on his legs, lowering his limbs one at a time over the side of the bed before sliding off and pivoting himself around to drop into the wheelchair.

"Very smooth, Dr. Ellingham. Very smooth," the psychiatrist said as he reached down and flipped the footrests for his patient. The therapist hesitated and then asked, "I was wondering how your day had gone ... lunch in particular."

Martin's head popped up. "Why would you want to know that?"

Dr. Newell gave a shrug of his shoulders. "Word travels through this building, Martin. There's a rumour going around that one of our surgeons had a set-to with a patient in a wheelchair ... two broken legs and a broken arm. Sound familiar?"

Martin let out a snort of air. "The man's a moron ... I had to ..."

The therapist rocked back on to the rear legs of his chair and put his feet up on the lower bed rail as he folded his hands behind his head. "Can you elaborate just a bit ... draw me a picture?" he asked as he rubbed his hand across his chin.

Dr. Newell observed his patient's body language—fist clenching, eyes narrowing, and his jaw set.

"He insulted my wife!"

"And you had to do what, may I ask?"

Martin shook his head, annoyed that he was being asked to revisit the whole miserable affair, yet again. "I lost my temper ... grabbed him by the tie and set the idiot straight."

The therapist cocked his head to the side and tipped his chin up, peering down at the man in front of him. "And was it effective? Did you set him straight?"

"I believe I did." Martin furrowed his brow and squirmed uncomfortably in his wheelchair.

"Well, that's good, isn't it?"

Swallowing the lump that had formed in his throat, Martin turned his head towards the window. "I lost control. What if ..." His gaze shifted back to his doctor. "What if I really hurt someone."

"You're a big fellow. Yes, you could hurt someone," the psychiatrist said nodding his head. "Is that what's bothering you, or is it a sense of disequilibrium you may have felt when you lost control."

"It's made me tense ... the whole incident. It's been eating at me. What if I *do* lose control sometime ... really hurt someone?"

Dr. Newell planted his feet back on the floor and rocked forward. "Do you really worry about that, Martin?"

"I just said I do; weren't you listening?" He closed his eyes for a few moments, trying to calm himself and gather his thoughts. "It's a fear I have. I used to have frequent nightmares about it when I was a boy."

"It might be helpful to both of us if you could tell me something about those nightmares. Can you remember any of them?"

Martin turned his gaze back to the window again and then began to relate the details of an oft-repeated dream that had haunted him since childhood.

"I was bullied a lot at boarding school. Belongings stolen, name calling, being pushed and tripped. I was the youngest at the school when I first arrived. I wasn't comfortable making friends ... didn't have a lot of confidence. I was an easy target and the others knew it."

He shifted his weight from his right hip. "I wet the bed a lot. I tried to keep it hidden from the other boys, but they found out one day. One of the year five boys made my life particularly miserable. Every morning he'd check to see if I'd managed to make it through the night with dry bedding. If I hadn't, which was most of the time, he'd pull the sheets off and parade up and down the hall with them, laughing … my classmates joining in."

He paused, wiping a hand down his face. "I started to have thoughts about what I'd like to do to him— torturing him physically the way he tortured me emotionally. It was shortly after I started having those fantasies that the nightmares began. In my dream, I'd kill him in some way, usually strangling him. I'd lose my temper and hurt him … kill him. When I realised what I'd done, I'd be in a panic—hide the body somewhere. I cut a slit in my mattress and stuffed him in it in one dream. I'd be so afraid my misdeed would be discovered, and I was overwhelmed by guilt. Then eventually, I couldn't take the fear of being found out anymore and I'd confess to the headmaster. There'd be a trial. My mother was always there, waiting to take me off to deliver my punishment. I'd be locked in the cupboard … spend the rest of my life in the cupboard."

Dr. Newell sighed and nodded his head. "You had absolutely no sense of control in your life as a child, did you Martin? No way to defend yourself."

Martin blinked slowly. "No, I suppose not."

The psychiatrist pulled a small pad out of his shirt pocket and jotted down a few notes. "I'd like you to make a list of words for me … words describing how you felt as a child when you were bullied or punished unfairly … unreasonably. Or just write it out in narrative form. Think about your feelings, and try to put a name to each of those feelings.

"I suspect, Martin, that what's bothering you about today's incident is not the actions you took but rather a sense you didn't make a conscious decision to take those actions. Try to remember … this was an incident. It doesn't define who you are.

"And you can learn strategies that will enable you to be in command of your actions in future. The next time you feel yourself losing control, I want you to mentally assign a name to your feelings. In doing that, you're shifting your brain activity from the right, or emotional side, to the left, or logical side, of your brain. I'll try to drop by with some journal articles on the subject. Let me know if this exercise seems to be helpful."

"I can do that," Martin said, relief spreading through him to have shared this burden of fear and guilt he had carried throughout his life. The man seemed to understand. He didn't react as if he was some sort of monster for having had those awful thoughts as a child.

Dr. Newell rose from his chair and took a step towards the door. "I have one other homework assignment for you. You're going to be stuck in either your bed or your wheelchair for a while, so I want you to turn on the television for an hour or so a day. But I want you to turn the sound off. Try to understand what's going on just by watching the people."

The therapist scrutinised his patient for a few moments. "This needs to be a program involving human interaction though, not a documentary that's being narrated. No surgical videos. The objective is to learn to focus on reading facial expressions and body language ... forcing yourself out of your comfort zone a bit ... to work that right brain."

This request earned the doctor a look of derision from his patient. "I don't watch television," Martin stated with finality.

Dr. Newell walked to the door and then turned "Well, you do now."

Martin had found an anxiety building in him as he watched the clock, waiting until he was sure James had gone to bed before ringing his wife. He looked forward to being back home with Louisa and James, but he did have concerns about how difficult the transition would be for all of them. The pressure in his chest eased when he heard his wife's voice.

"Hello, Martin."

"Hello. How are you?"

"Good. I've had a great day," Louisa said as she put the last of the dinner dishes into the dishwasher. "No detentions, got lots of work done at the school, and I feel like James and I are finally settling in here at Ruth's. How about your day? Anything exciting to report?"

"Why? I mean, why do you want to know. What do you mean—exciting?"

"I didn't mean it literally, Martin. I just meant, how was your day?"

"Ah." He breathed a sigh of relief that word hadn't gotten back to his wife about the dust-up at the restaurant. "Ed's given me the all clear to go home. Chris will make arrangements with the ambulance service shuttle to get me back to Portwenn."

"Martin! That's wonderful news! How soon can it be arranged?" Louisa scanned quickly around her, taking stock of what things needed to be done yet to prepare for her husband's homecoming.

"I'm to let Chris know when I want to leave, and he'll set it up. Ed wants to run some final tests before he releases me, but that won't take long. So it's entirely up to you."

"Martin, I would want you home tonight if it would would be possible. But ... I don't suppose it would be, would it?"

"No. I think tomorrow would be the soonest."

"Martin, set it up for the earliest opportunity. Then let me know, and Ruth and I'll come over." Louisa gazed out the window, picturing her husband as he sat in his hospital bed.

"Louisa, you don't need to come over. The service will bring me home."

"Martin Ellingham, this is a very big occasion, and I will not miss seeing you walk out the doors of Royal Cornwall!"

"Louisa, I'm afraid it's going to be some time yet before I'll be total weight bearing, let alone walking."

"I didn't mean that literally. But, Martin, this is an important milestone. I want to be there."

"It just seems a bit ridiculous for you to make an unnecessary trip over when—"

"Martin." Louisa said softly.

"Mm, yes. I'll talk to Chris and get back to you with the details." There was the merest hint of a smile on Martin's face as he said a final long distance goodnight to his wife.

Chapter 20

Martin woke the next morning, anxious to confirm with Ed and Chris that he would indeed be home by day's end. When the Parsons arrived with his breakfast, he immediately inquired about getting transportation arrangements made with the ambulance service.

"I'll see if they have a vehicle available later today, Mart. But we can't set up anything definitive until we get the final word from Ed."

"Well, when's Ed going to get the ball rolling on these tests he wants? Do you know what he has in mind?"

"I don't know, mate. Let me go and ring him ... see if he's submitted the lab orders."

He stepped out of the room to place his call and Carole tried to distract Martin with his breakfast. "Okay, while he's doing that, *you* eat. This may be the last chance I have to work on fattening you up, so I expect you to clean that plate," she said.

Martin worked his way through the food in front of him, keeping one eye on the door. When it finally opened and Chris re-entered the room his head shot up and he looked up at him expectantly.

"All right, Martin, Ed's ordering the tests. Eat up there; then I'll chase someone up to draw blood," Chris said.

Martin stared back at him for a few seconds. "Well ... are you going to get something lined up with the service?"

"Mart, relax! I'll handle it, I'll handle it!"

Martin gave his friend a sheepish look. "Mm, sorry."

Chris pulled up a chair and sat down next to his wife. "You know, Martin, Ed and I'll expect you to give one of us a call if you notice any problems developing after you're home. I'm sure Ed will cover all of this when Louisa gets here, but I'm going to nag you about it now, just to be sure you have it through that thick head of yours."

Martin screwed up his face. "Do I need to remind you that I'm a doctor? I know what to watch for."

Chris nodded his head as he dumped several more sausages on to his friend's plate. "All I'm saying is that if you can't convince Ed that you can be trusted to report any problems immediately, he won't let you go. So you'd better behave yourself."

"Yes, I know that!" Martin returned his attention to the breakfast in front of him, trying to dispose of the food quickly so he could get to the more urgent matter at hand—the tests that needed to be done before he could leave.

Carole gathered together all of the dirty dishes, packing them away to be taken back home one final time. "Well, Martin, I have an appointment I need to hurry off to, so I'll say goodbye for now."

Martin tensed as she leaned over to place a kiss on his cheek. "Mm, yes. Thank you for breakfast."

Chris stepped out the door to say goodbye to his wife then returned to the room with a nurse.

"Good morning, Dr. Ellingham," the woman said as she laid her basin of phlebotomy supplies on the tray table. "Let's get this blood drawn and see if we can't send you home today, all right"

She removed the cap from one of the three ports in his central line and drew the required samples.

"All done." She gave him a smile and hurried from the room.

"Okay Mart, let's go for a walk ... calm those nerves of yours," Chris said as he pulled the wheelchair over to the side of the bed.

Martin made his transition to the chair, and his friend leaned over to flip the footrests down. "I've got it, I've got it!" Martin said as he waved off his assistance.

He leaned over to get the necessary adjustments made, furrowing his brow and grimacing as the required movement pulled at his broken ribs as well as the tender abdominal and thoracic wounds.

Chris leaned over slightly and cocked his head at him. "You okay, mate?"

Martin sat back up and took a moment to catch his breath. "I'm fine. I appreciate your help, Chris, but I need to do these things myself."

"Yeah, you're right. It's hard though to stand back and watch you struggle when it'd be so much easier for me to do it for you."

Martin paused slightly, trying to get his head around his friend's comment. He couldn't remember a time when someone had wanted to make his life easier, and he found himself blinking back tears.

"Ready to go then, Mart?" Chris said as he held the door open.

"Erm ... yeah."

Martin was flipping aimlessly through the television channels when Mr. Christianson stopped in his room later that morning.

He pulled his stethoscope from around his neck. "Your bloodwork looks good, Martin. I emailed everything up to Dashwood and Simpson in London. I expect they'll say the same thing, so I guess you're free to go whenever you like. But I need to discuss a few things with you and Louisa before you leave ... if she's coming over that is."

"Yes, she is. She insisted on being here."

"Good. Let me know what time she's arriving, and I'll stop by for a chat." Ed took in a deep breath and let it out slowly, shaking his head. "I have to say, Martin ... it'll be a relief to have you back home safe and sound."

"Mm, yes." Martin brushed at a bit of lint on his warm-up pants. "I can't thank you enough, Ed. I ... I owe you my life. So, thank you."

"You're quite welcome ... a happy outcome in the end." Ed smiled as he moved back towards the door. "Let me know when Louisa arrives, and I'll come back down to go over a list of dos and don'ts with both of you."

He moved aside to let a visitor into the room. "Jeremy," he said, giving the young man a nod of his head as he slipped past him. "We'll see you sometime this afternoon, Martin," Ed said before heading down the hall.

The young man took several strides towards the bed. "Hello, Dr. Ellingham. I'm Jeremy Portman, the aide who'll be assisting you once you're home. I wanted to stop by and introduce myself," he said, extending his hand.

"Mm, yes. My wife mentioned she'd lined someone up." Martin scrutinised the young man, first for cleanliness, then for an outward appearance of professionalism.

"Would you mind if I sat down for a few minutes?" Jeremy asked.

Martin gestured to a chair and straightened himself in the bed.

The aide squirmed a bit under the eminent surgeon's penetrating gaze. "Tim Spalding's brought me up to speed on where you're at with the physiotherapy. Will you come over to Truro for further sessions, or go to Wadebridge?"

"Someone will come to Portwenn twice a week to work with me ... until I'm total weight bearing."

Jeremy pulled a pad of paper and a pen out of his jacket pocket. "Your wife has asked me to spend two to three hours with you each morning and evening on weekdays. She's given me a list of daily activities she thinks you might need assistance with, but I'd appreciate any suggestions you may have."

He handed Martin a piece of paper. "If you could review the list and tell me if there are any items you'd prefer to handle yourself or things you think we should add, I think we could get off to a smoother start."

Martin tried to tune out the negative thoughts that threatened to dwarf his previously elevated mood. He could not refute the fact that he would indeed need assistance with every item on the list in front of him. There were several other things in fact that he knew he would need help with, but he couldn't bring himself to add them to the list.

He handed the paper back to the young man. "That looks sufficient," he muttered.

His patient's change in affect was not missed by the aide. "I'll be there when you get home today ... just to help your wife with getting you settled in. I'll start my twice daily visits tomorrow and we'll get to work on eliminating some of the things on this list ... get you more independent," he said as he folded the paper and slipped it back into his pocket.

He held out his hand. "I'm glad I had a chance to meet you, Dr. Ellingham, and I'm looking forward to being a member of your support team. I'll be in touch with the ambulance service so I can be there to help out when you get home tonight."

Jeremy stopped with his hand on the door handle. "Going home can be a difficult transition. Give yourself some time to adjust, and don't expect changes to happen overnight. But I can tell you that once you get the go ahead to be weight bearing as tolerated, you'll see fairly rapid improvement."

Martin pulled in his chin and then picked up the television remote.

Chris stopped a short time later to let Martin know arrangements had been made with the ambulance service. He would be picked up at half three. Martin immediately rang Louisa to pass on the information he knew she'd been anxious to receive.

"Do you think you could be here at two-thirty? Ed wants to go over some things with both of us before he lets me out of here."

"I thought I'd take off at noon and head over. Pippa's already planning to fill in if need be," Louisa answered excitedly. "Martin, you have no idea how happy I am to have you coming home."

"Mm, yes." Martin tried not to let his own uncertainties cloud the moment for his wife, but he was feeling increasingly anxious as he watched the minutes tick by.

He rang off before slipping over the side of the bed and into his wheelchair, rolling himself out to the nurses station to let them know he was making a trip to the canteen. He had nervous energy to burn and he was also beginning to get hungry again.

He rolled through the doorway to his room just as he heard hurried footsteps approaching from behind.

"Hi Martin, I was hoping I could catch you before you went home." Tim Spalding watched as his patient spun his chair around adeptly.

"Ah ... yes. I leave at three-thirty this afternoon."

Tim sat himself down on the edge of the bed. "You don't sound real enthusiastic. What's up?"

Martin gave the young man an ambivalent shrug. "I'm just not sure about how this is going to go. My wife seems to be thrilled about it."

"But you not so much?"

"No. I *do* want to go home ... very much. But ... well, this could be very difficult."

"This *will* be very difficult ... for both of you."

"Oh, that's helpful!" Martin snapped.

Tim leaned forward and folded his hands in front of him. "Martin, I in no way mean that to be discouraging. I just want to be honest about what you can expect. You're going to experience highs and lows, maybe some pretty deep lows. And your wife may worry about every little grimace and groan you make. You'll cough and she'll come running. What seems like an expression of concern to her will probably feel like annoyingly excessive vigilance to you."

"Well, you just paint such a sunny picture," Martin grumbled.

"I'm just trying to say, Martin, you both need to be patient with each other ... encourage each other and expect frustrations. It's all normal, so don't let it throw you."

"Our marriage has been a bit ... shaky. I just hope this ..." Martin closed his eyes as air rushed from his lungs.

"The two of you have been through so much already, and you've handled it very well so far. You'll be fine, Martin. Just expect the bumpy patches. And don't turn away help if it's offered."

Tim stood up and put his hand on his patient's shoulder. "Well, I just wanted to wish you well before you left."

"Yes. Thank you ... for all your help. You're very good at what you do."

"Thank you, Dr. Ellingham. I appreciate that. Come by and look me up if you get over this way. Maybe we could have lunch together again. The last time proved entertaining," he said, giving Martin a sly grin before slipping out the door.

Chapter 21

When Louisa arrived at Martin's room she found him sitting in his wheelchair in front of the window ... head down and his eyes closed. She knelt in front of him, and as she took his hands in hers, the ever-present ball of therapy putty fell from his fingers before rolling on to the floor. Smiling to herself, she reached down to pick it up.

"Martin ... Martin," she said softly, reaching up to caress his cheek.

He startled. "Mm, sorry. I was watching for you. I must have nodded off."

"Yeah, you must've." Louisa got to her feet and leaned over to kiss his head before running her fingers through his hair. "Well, big day today, isn't it?"

"Mm." Martin searched his lap for the ball of putty.

"Looking for your companion?" she asked as she pressed the viscous material into his hand.

"It's an inanimate object, Louisa. I have no attachment to it whatsoever."

She stood back and crossed her arms over her chest. "That was meant to be a joke. Maybe I was off on my delivery, hmm?"

"Quite possibly." His eyes fixed on her face, and the corners of his mouth curled up ever so slightly. He reached for her hand and pulled her in before kissing her.

"That was very, very nice," she said.

"Yes." Their eyes locked and he swallowed hard. "I should let the nurses station know you're here," he said huskily. "They'll contact Ed."

Louisa fought her knee-jerk reaction to insist she make the trip out to the desk. "I'll just wait here then?"

"Mm, yes. I'll be right back."

She had just begun to wonder if she should go check up on him when he returned to the room, a cup of coffee balancing on the armrest of his chair. He had managed to get his fingers and thumb positioned on either side, giving it just enough support to keep it from tipping off in one direction or the other.

"I'm impressed! You have a lot more use of those fingers than the last time I was here." Louisa took his face in her hands and pressed her lips to his. "I'm so proud of you," she whispered.

She straightened herself, and Martin tried to pick the cup up to hand it to her. It tipped precariously to the side before he caught it with his left hand, preventing the hot liquid from spilling into his lap.

"Oh, oh, oh! Mind the future!" Louisa said, taking the cup from him.

He glanced up quickly, his eyes round. "What?"

"Maybe?" she said, giving him a coy smile.

"Mm." His uncomfortable gaze shifted to his lap.

There was a knock on the door, and Ed Christianson sauntered into the room. "Hello, Louisa. Big day, eh?"

"Yes, it is. I can't begin to tell you how excited I am to get things back to normal."

"Ah. That's one area of concern I'd like to address with both of you actually." Ed pulled two chairs over by his patient. "Please, take a seat, Louisa."

He sat down next to her and leaned forward on his elbows. "I think Martin is very aware there are going to be some difficult times ahead, but I wanted the opportunity to discuss it with you, too."

Martin watched the happy, expectant look that had been present on his wife's face fade.

"Some big challenges lie ahead for both of you, much more so for Martin, of course. But if you know what to expect, Louisa, I think it'll make it easier for you to understand where your husband's coming from when obstacles are encountered."

The surgeon leaned back in his chair, settling in for the discussion." First and foremost, you both need to understand that Martin is a long way from being back to normal. He'll get there eventually, but it'll be a slow process. It could be two years before we're completely done repairing the damage done in the accident."

A heaviness settled in Louisa's chest as Ed went on to explain about the surgeries that would be needed to mend the visible wounds, and also the immunocompromising effects of both her husband's recent splenectomy and the hypovolaemia.

"For the next two years or so he's going to pick up every contagion he's exposed to. In other words, Martin's likely to be sick a lot. It'll be important to hit you with a good broad spectrum antibiotic whenever you get sick, Martin."

"Yes, I'm aware of that," he said, irritated that his surgeon felt the need to remind him of the most basic medical facts. Ed took note of the dismissive look on his face.

He handed Louisa a slim binder. "I've put together some information that I hope will help you to understand the healing process Martin will go through, as well as a rough schedule of upcoming appointments, which either have already been made or will need to be made. There's also a breakdown of what surgical repairs will need to be done down the road. We can discuss how to approach those when the time comes.

"Most importantly though, I've included a list of symptoms to watch for. Any of them should prompt an immediate call to either Chris Parsons or me." Ed turned to his patient. *"Is— that—understood?"*

"I'm not a complete idiot! Of course, it is!" he snapped.

The surgeon held his hands up in front of him. "I'm just saying you don't have a great track record, my friend."

Louisa gave her husband an admonishing stare. "He does, without a doubt, understand you. *Don't* you Martin," she said in a soft but no-nonsense tone of voice.

"Mm, yes."

Ed pulled a folded piece of paper from his breast pocket. "Now, your medications ... The central line will stay in a while. We'll see if we can transition you to oral antibiotics and morphine once I clear you to be weight bearing as tolerated. I'll send plenty of additional bottles with you. Louisa, will you be comfortable changing those out when your health aide isn't available?"

"Sure. Martin can tell me how to do it," she said, giving her husband a smile.

"Good. I'll send some oral meds home with you as well, just in case a problem should arise with the drip."

He glanced at his sheet of notes. "Nutrition. It's vitally important that your husband is getting the proper balance of vitamins, minerals, and protein right now. He's burning a tremendous number of calories with all the bone and cartilage repair that's going on, so he'll be eating a lot."

"Yes, Martin's aunt explained that to me."

"Good. I'll send you home with an ample supply of the supplements he's been getting here, as well as a prescription for more when you need them. If you see his appetite decrease at all, you need to give us a call."

The surgeon rubbed a hand over his eyes and yawned. "Sorry, I was called in early this morning to do an emergency appendectomy. Which actually segues nicely into my next point. Get plenty of sleep, Martin. If you feel the need for it, go lie down and rest."

His finger worked its way down the list. "Martin, you need to keep changing position, but you also need to keep those limbs elevated. I'll send you home with a sling. You can use that periodically. It'd be safer for you to have that arm tucked close against you when you go out and about, but use the brace when you need help in keeping it elevated or if you're doing something that could result in another luxation. And remember to put those legs up if you're sitting. If you start to feel throbbing, get 'em up."

"Last, but not least ... sex."

Martin gave a barely perceptible groan, and Louisa gave him a nudge with her elbow.

"You have the all clear on that, but don't push things," Ed said. "And neither of you should expect too much at this point. No harps will be playing or rockets going off for a while. It'll probably prove to be an exercise in frustration until you get that hardware off, Martin."

Martin cleared his throat and rubbed his hand across the back of his neck.

"All right, that's about it then," Ed said slapping his hands to his knees and pulling himself to his feet. "Martin, it's been an honour," he said as he extended his hand.

"Mm, thank you, Ed."

"Louisa, let me know if you have any questions or concerns."

"I will," she said as she walked over and gave him a hug. "We can't thank you enough, Ed."

As soon as the door closed, Louisa stepped behind her husband. She wrapped her arms around him and nuzzled her face into his neck. "I'm looking forward to proving Ed wrong about those harps and rockets ... when you're ready."

Martin pull his head from her grip as he tried to contain her roaming hands. "Louisa ..." He breathed out a heavy sigh. "I'm

... just think a bit about what it's going to be like with me ... until I'm rid of the fixators."

"I have been," she purred in his ear. "It'll be a bit like making love to The Terminator, don't you think?"

He blinked his eyes at her. "The wha—?"

The door opened and Chris walked in.

"Hey, are you ready to have this big oaf back home, Louisa?"

"Very much so."

Chris disconnected the drip, laying the bottle in Martin's lap.

"I'll get the bags, if you can get the door, Louisa," he said.

Martin began to propel himself forward but changed direction suddenly, moving back to pick up a folded piece of paper from the top of the small dresser. He glanced down at the stick figures, and then he took one last look around the room before going through the door.

Chapter 22

Martin gazed out the window of the shuttle van as they passed through the Cornish countryside. It was visually apparent that time had passed him by. It had been a grey and drizzly day when he had last travelled this route, and the leaves on the trees were just beginning to show hints of their fall colours. Now, thanks to yesterday's gusty winds, most of the trees were bare of leaves.

He had always found the process of photosynthesis fascinating, but as a boy he would anxiously await those autumn days when the trees would cease their production of the chlorophyll that masked the true colours of their leaves.

He would inspect them every day. Watching as the green light that had been reflected back to his eyes all summer would fade, giving him a brief glimpse into their secret world as their rich reds, oranges and yellows were revealed.

It seemed a magical time, but it was fleeting. The wind would soon blow, tumbling them from their lofty perches to make way for the flush of new growth that would come in the spring.

This was the first year Martin could remember missing this spectacle of nature, and he breathed a heavy sigh at the thought of time lost.

"How are you doing?" Louisa asked when her husband's preoccupation became obvious.

"I'm ... fine," he said, straightening himself out in his chair to redirect his attention on the road ahead.

Louisa toyed with the soft curls that had grown out around the nape of his neck. "Care to share what you were thinking?"

"Nothing, really," he said shaking his head. "Just that things have changed since I made the trip over to Truro that night. The seasons I mean," he quickly added.

Louisa turned her head to watch as they passed by a small herd of wild ponies. "Things will get back to the way they were, you know. It'll just take some time for you to heal. But things *will* get back to the way they were. And until then, we'll adjust to this temporary reality. I'll be there for you, and you'll be there for me, right?"

"Mm, yes." Martin furrowed his brow, and his eyes drifted off again.

"What is it, Martin?"

He turned to look at her, his cheeks nudging up. "You said, things will get back to the way they were. Is that a *good* thing now?"

"Yes, Martin. That *is* a good thing now. We've made more progress than either of us realised, I think."

"Mm."

His abdominal muscles clenched as they approached the River Camel bridge. A flock of sandpipers scrambled across the mudflat below, in search of invertebrates hidden amongst the detritus deposited by the receding tide. *Some things never change*, he thought.

His wife's hand on his own nudged him from his reverie, and he glanced over at her.

"Almost home now, hmm?" she said, giving him a soft smile.

He swallowed hard and nodded his head.

The newly hired health aide, Jeremy Portman, was waiting at Ruth's cottage when they arrived, and he helped his patient navigate the ramp to the back door.

Martin pulled in a deep breath when they entered the house. It wasn't home, but it was familiar, and the ubiquitous odour of disinfectant and alcohol that permeated everything at

The hospital had been replaced by delicious smells coming from the cooker.

"Would you prefer to get settled into bed now, Dr. Ellingham, or would you rather be out here where the action is?" Jeremy asked.

"Erm, I want to be out here but—" He grimaced.

The aide grabbed the extra pillows that had been left on the sofa and put them on top of the coffee table. Then he positioned Martin's chair next to it and helped him to elevated his legs.

"*Well*, you look a little the worse for wear, but it's good to see you home again, Martin," Ruth said as she stood in the doorway watching the activities.

"Hello, Ruth. Whatever's in the cooker smells good."

"It's chicken with leeks and potatoes ... one of Joan's recipes. It didn't look terribly difficult, so I thought I'd give it a try ... in honour of the occasion." Ruth gave her nephew a crooked grin.

"Is it done yet?"

"No, but I suspected you might arrive with an appetite, so I made up a plate of cheese and fruit. Care for some?"

Martin made a clumsy attempt to not appear indecorously eager. "That would be good—fine. If you have it already prepared. Yes, that would be fine—good."

He craned his neck to see around his aunt. "Louisa. Louisa!" he called out.

She hurried out of the bedroom where she had been putting away his belongings. "What is it? Do you need something?"

"James. Where is he?"

She sat down on the coffee table next to his feet. "I had Poppy keep him at the surgery. She'll bring him over once you're settled."

"I *am* settled," he said as he gave her a small frown.

"I'll go ring her up then. Do you mind if she stays for supper?"

Martin screwed up his face and huffed out a breath. "I just got home, Louisa. I don't really feel like answering the girl's questions."

"I don't think you have anything to worry about. Poppy's still too afraid of you to ask any questions." She gave him an apologetic smile before dialling the childminder's number.

Poppy arrived with James in tow a few minutes later. The boy reached excitedly for his mother, and Louisa covered his face in kisses, inducing giggles. She tipped him back playfully, and his eyes connected with his father's. James squealed, "Da-ee!" and wriggled to free himself. As soon as all four limbs made contact with the floor he scrambled quickly to Martin's side.

"Oh, no you don't, Martin," Louisa chastened her husband as he leaned to the side and reached his hand out to the baby.

"I wasn't going to try to pick him up. I just wanted to touch him."

Louisa gathered the boy in her arms. "Jeremy, could you help me here? I want to let James sit with Martin for a bit. I think if we put him on the left side of your lap it might work, hmm?" she said as she gave her husband a nod.

"I'll hang on to him too, Dr. Ellingham, just to be on the safe side." Martin wrapped his left arm around his son, and Jeremy rested his hands on the boy's legs to keep him from squirming.

James's warm weight was comforting. Reassured that the bond they'd formed before the accident hadn't been weakened by their forced separation, the creases in Martin's forehead eased.

Jeremy observed them, realising that little James would be an important part of his father's recovery. When the child began to struggle to turn around, Jeremy repositioned him so that he could face his father. The child laid his head against Martin's chest and settled in, supported in the crook of his arm.

"Dr. Ellingham, I'll be happy to help you anytime you'd like to hold your son, but you will not be allowed to do this on your own for a while. And I'm sure I don't have to tell you that under no circumstances should you be left alone with him," the aide said, keeping a guarded eye on the pair of Ellingham men.

"We have Poppy to watch James," Louisa said. She glanced over at the girl. "Poppy, this is Jeremy Portman. We've hired him to help Dr. Ellingham out with daily activities. Jeremy, this is Poppy Flinn, James's childminder. Poppy's here Monday through Friday while I'm at the school, so you two will see quite a lot of each other."

Jeremy stepped forward and shook Poppy's hand, his gaze lingering on the girl.

Ruth announced that dinner was ready, and for the first time in almost six weeks, Martin joined his family at the table. All did not go completely smoothly as the table was not designed to accommodate a wheelchair. And Martin struggled to keep the food on his fork at times, resulting in one outburst. But adaptations would be made by everyone in time, and Martin's skills would improve as well.

After Poppy and Ruth said their goodbyes that evening, Louisa went upstairs with James to give him a bath before putting him to bed.

Jeremy tended to Martin's fixator pins and medications before assisting him with his nightly ablutions.

Martin was exhausted after the eventful day and found himself easily frustrated by the difficulty he was having in doing the most mundane tasks. He had no strength remaining in his injured right arm, and after dropping his toothbrush several times, he picked it up with his left hand to complete the task.

Louisa came into the bedroom, waiting in the wings as Jeremy changed the bottle on her husband's drip.

"I think that should hold you 'til morning, Dr. Ellingham. Is there anything else you need before I go?"

Martin rubbed his eyes and shook his head. "No, I should be fine now."

"All right. I'll go and let the two of you have the house back to yourselves for a while. I'll be here at seven tomorrow morning to help you get ready for your day."

Louisa saw the young man to the door before hurrying back to her husband.

"Well, here we are," she said as she watched him from the doorway.

Martin shifted himself over. "Care to join me?" he asked.

Louisa slid in alongside him, and he wrapped his arm around her. They lay quietly with their heads touching.

"I don't suppose you'd be comfortable sleeping here tonight?" Martin asked.

Louisa tipped her head back and pressed her lips to his. "Sounds a bit dangerous. One of us could end up on the floor."

"Yes. I suppose you're right."

"How 'bout I stay until you fall asleep, hmm?"

"That would be nice." He placed a lingering kiss on the top of her head.

Reaching under his vest, she slowly stroked her fingers back and forth across his chest. It wasn't long before his body relaxed, and the rhythmic up and down movement of his rib cage slowed.

After reluctantly leaving the warmth of his side, she leaned over and placed a kiss on his forehead. "I'm glad you're home, Martin," she whispered. "Sleep well."

Chapter 23

Louisa slept restlessly that first night, getting up several times to go downstairs to look in on Martin. Each time, she found him asleep and safe in his bed. But she couldn't shake the fear that he would wake and be disoriented in the darkened room, perhaps trying to walk to the lavatory. Or that he would forget where he was and find his strange surroundings upsetting. The narcotics provided him with relief from the pain but they also clouded his thinking, and his decisions were not always rational.

"I hate this sleeping apart, Ruth," she said as she sat drinking tea with her the next morning. "I suspect Martin would sleep better if we were together, and I know without a doubt that *I* would sleep better."

"They do make full sized adjustable beds. Maybe you should exchange the one you have," Ruth said, lowering the newspaper and peering over the top of her glasses at her.

Louisa went to the refrigerator, returning with a small plastic jug of milk. "I measured the room, and it's just too small to accommodate a larger bed. Martin needs enough space to manoeuvre his wheelchair around, too."

"Well, it wouldn't be ideal, but have you considered a cot? Something you could fold up and move out of his way during the day."

Louisa paused, milk bottle in hand. "Hmm, that's quite a good idea actually. Thank you, Ruth. I'll try to pick one up today."

She sat down and poured a splash of milk into the cup. "And I'm picking up another baby monitor. I want to be able

to hear if Martin needs something when I'm out of earshot."
Louisa hesitated before looking up at the elderly woman. "He's
going to take offense, isn't he?"

"No doubt. But I wouldn't let that stop you."

"Well, speaking of Martin, I should go and check on him."

Louisa got up from her chair and walked down the short
hallway. She stood in the doorway for a few moments,
watching him as he slept. The scars from the cuts to his face
had begun to fade, and eventually his more serious wounds
would heal as well. Those scars would remain, but he would
learn to live with them.

The wounds left by his horrible childhood, though, were
still gaping. Martin had hidden them well throughout his life,
but the pain they had caused had been, at times, debilitating. If
Dr. Newell could heal the wounds, perhaps he could learn to
live with those scars as well.

She slipped in quietly next to him and leaned over to kiss his
cheek. His eyes opened slightly, and his brow furrowed in
confusion when he caught sight of her.

"Louisa, what are you doing here?" he asked as his eyes
darted around the strange room.

"You're at Ruth's, remember? You came home from
hospital yesterday."

He wiped a palm across his face. "Mm, yes. How are you?"

"I'm good. Very happy to have my husband home." She
picked up the control and raised the head end of the bed.
"Would you like a cup of coffee? I brought your machine over
from the surgery."

"I would. But I'd like to get up first ... have some time with
you before you leave for the school."

"I'm taking today and tomorrow off; Pippa's filling in. That
okay with you?" she asked, cocking her head and giving him a
smile.

"That would be good. Nice actually."

"All right. So, what do we need to do to get you ready for your day?"

Martin looked around him. "I think if you could get a facecloth and a towel out for me ... lay it by the sink, I might be able to manage on my own."

Louisa bit her bottom lip. "Okay, I'll get things ready for you, but you have to promise you'll let me help if you need it."

"Yes. Yes, I will," Martin said with an edge to his voice.

Louisa gathered together what she thought he might need—razor, shaving gel, soap, toothbrush and toothpaste, as well as the requested towel and facecloth. She laid it all out on the counter next to the sink. "When will Ed let you start taking showers again?" she called out to him.

Martin's focus had shifted from the everyday practical matters to his wife's feminine curves, as he watched her moving about in the lavatory. *What was it she'd said? It'll be like making love to the terminator*? He'd have to look that up on the internet; he didn't want to disappoint her.

"Martin? Did you hear me?" she asked, as she stood in the doorway.

"Hmm?" he said.

"I asked you when you can take a shower again." She smiled at him, tapping the tube of toothpaste against her hand. Walking over, she ruffled his hair with her fingers. "Where is your mind at, Dr. Ellingham?"

He tipped his head down, peering up at her.

"You look like a guilty schoolboy," she said as she leaned over to kiss him.

"Mm. I can take a shower anytime now. The problem is, if I lift a foot up to step into the shower, then I'm bearing all of my weight on one leg. I can't do that yet."

"I see. And when *can* you do that?"

Martin swung himself around to get out of the bed. "I'll need to go over to Truro next week to have more pictures taken. If the fractures have healed sufficiently, then Ed will probably give me the go-ahead."

There was a knock on the back door and voices could be heard in the kitchen.

"Sounds like Jeremy's here. Maybe I'll let him take over helping you, and I'll go see if James is awake yet."

"James should be up by *now*. Is he sick?"

"He's fine, Martin. He's just gotten a bit lazy without you here to get him up at the crack of dawn every day. I'm afraid he's had to learn to wait for his mum in the morning."

Martin gave her a disapproving scowl.

"Good morning, Dr. Ellingham ... Mrs. Ellingham," Jeremy said as he stuck his head in the door.

"Good morning, Jeremy. I was wondering if you could help Martin wash and get dressed so I can tend to James," Louisa said as she slipped past the aide and headed towards the hall.

"Of course." Jeremy pulled the wheelchair up next to the bed, and Martin breathed out a sigh as he watched his wife hurry off.

"How long can you stand, Dr. Ellingham?" Jeremy asked as he watched him shift himself to the chair.

"I don't know. I just stand up long enough to make my transfers."

"I need to check in with Mr. Christianson first, but if he approves, I'd like to work on that today. If you can stand for a few minutes at a time it would make it easier for you to clean up in the morning, make yourself a sandwich at the counter, that sort of thing."

Martin worked his way towards the lavatory. "If you'll excuse me," he said uncomfortably, "I'd like to try getting washed on my own."

"That's fine, Dr. Ellingham. I'll wait around the corner in case you need some help. Just let me know if you do." Jeremy pulled a chair up against the bedroom wall and sat down to work on Martin's patient notes.

Martin managed to manoeuvre his wheelchair through the lavatory doorway, but he couldn't get himself turned in a direction that would allow him to reach the faucet. He struggled to back himself out of the lavatory again before starting from the beginning, this time using a different approach to get himself up to the sink. Success.

He turned the faucet on and let the water warm up before filling the sink in preparation for shaving. When he was in hospital, the nursing staff would bring him a small basin of water, and he would do his shaving in bed. Having to reach up and over the side of the sink to reach the water was a bit awkward, but he managed. Not yet trusting his right hand to apply a sharp razor blade to his face, he used his left hand for shaving.

He drained the sink and set about getting the facecloth wet and applying the body wash to it. This turned out to be a feat in itself when limited to the use of one hand. Wringing the excess water from the facecloth proved impossible. He squeezed as much of the moisture from the cloth as he could before leaving it lying on the edge of the sink.

He then turned his attention to removing his vest. Jeremy listened as Martin's patience began to wear thin, resulting in the utterance of words not normally allowed in the Ellingham home.

"Let me know if you'd like some help in there!" the aide called out.

Martin finally wrestled his left arm from the sleeve and peeled off the article of clothing. He set to work washing the upper half of his body. Water puddled up in his lap, and he began to shiver in the cool air. Now to rinse off the soap. He ran the cloth under the faucet, but bubbles oozed persistently from the cloth.

He threw a glance in the direction of the bedroom. Martin was resistant to asking for help—a lesson learned long ago. Asking for anything earned him the back of a hand or time in the cupboard, so he learned to fend for himself. To admit to needing assistance would reveal a vulnerability.

He continued his battle in the sink until he finally had the soap rinsed off completely. After drying himself with the towel Louisa had laid out, he picked up the clean vest and painstakingly worked it over the projections on the fixators holding his radius and ulna in alignment. He then pulled the neck over his head and slipped his left hand through the opposite sleeve.

"Bloody hell!" Martin erupted when he discovered he had managed to put the vest on backwards.

Jeremy forced himself to wait things out. Martin needed to learn to lean on others. To learn there would be times when he would need to ask for help.

The vest clung to Martin's still damp body, making it impossible for him to pull his left arm from the sleeve. He breathed out a heavy sigh and admitted defeat, calling out to his aide for assistance.

"Jeremy! Are you going to help me in here?" he sputtered.

The aide moved quickly. "Okay, relax and let me do the work." Jeremy held on to the sleeve and worked Martin's left arm out. Then he pulled the neck over his patient's head and worked the other sleeve over the fixators.

"Okay, let's try this again," he said, turning the shirt around and reversing the process. "I admire your efforts, Dr. Ellingham. You did a good job but just hit a stumbling block."

Martin leaned forward in his chair and the aide pulled the back of his vest down until it was smooth.

Jeremy went to the dresser and returned with dry warm-up pants and boxer shorts. "Let's not argue about this. Just let me help you this time around ... okay?" he said firmly.

"Mm, yes." Martin sat looking chagrined.

After pushing his patient's chair over to the assist pole, Jeremy instructed him to stand while he dried the chair. Then he undid the Velcro fasteners of the wet warm-up pants before pulling both pants and boxers down past his patient's knees.

"Okay, Dr. Ellingham, sit back down and take a little break. Then we'll get the dry clothes on you," the young man said. He covered Martin's lap with a towel and then pulled the wet clothing off completely.

"Ready?" he asked a few moments later as he pulled the clean boxers up over his patient's lower legs.

Martin closed his eyes briefly, beginning to feel as though he'd run a marathon.

"Yep." He grasped on to the assist pole and stood up. His aide worked the boxers up the rest of the way.

"Okay, back down again." Jeremy picked up the clean warm-up pants and pulled them up over the lower fixators.

"Okay, up again."

"Yes, I know," Martin said as he forced his muscles to raise his body from the chair one more time.

The aide worked the waistband of the pants up and over the fixators penetrating his patient's right thigh, then he closed the Velcro seams around the hardware.

Now washed and dressed, Martin collapsed into his wheelchair, feeling exhausted and disheartened. Jeremy sat down on the edge of the bed, facing him.

"Dr. Ellingham. You and your wife are paying me to help you with this sort of thing, but the money's not the only reason I'm here. You need help right now, and I *want* to help you. I find my job to be very rewarding ... helping people. I'm sure you can relate. Isn't that what you do as a doctor?"

There was truth in the young man's words, but the truth was not something that held any appeal for Martin at the moment.

He stared at him pointedly. "I'm a doctor. I diagnose and treat illnesses ... treat injuries. I enjoy the mental challenge. If you find fulfilment in mollycoddling patients, good for you. But I didn't go through years of medical training so that I could pat hands and rub backs."

It hadn't taken long for Martin to justify his churlish reputation.

Jeremy gathered together a pair of socks and slippers, working them over his patient's feet to complete the ensemble.

Louisa appeared in the doorway with James. "You look nice, Martin. Very well done."

"I had a little help," he confessed. He reached his hand out to his son and Louisa crouched down so the morning ritual could be carried out. James latched on to his father's ears and applied a slobbery kiss to his cheek.

"Good morning, James," Martin said as he pressed the backs of his fingers to the boy's forehead and stroked his thumb across his jaw.

"Maybe you need a little rest before having your coffee and breakfast, hmm?" Louisa said, noticing the fatigue in her husband's eyes.

"Yes. I am a little tired." Truth be told, Martin was exhausted.

Chapter 24

It was almost noon by the time Martin woke from his nap. Having missed breakfast, he was famished. Jeremy had finished up with his morning responsibilities and had left for the day. He would return again in the evening to help his patient get ready for bed.

Martin rubbed the sleep from his eyes and swung his legs over the side of the mattress. His aide had left the wheelchair where he could easily access it. He stood up, pivoted himself around, and then lowered his body into the chair.

Louisa and Poppy were having lunch with James, when he entered the kitchen.

"Well hello, sleepy head. Feeling a bit more rested now?" Louisa asked as she got up to move James's high chair over to make room for her husband at the table.

"I am, but I'm hungry." Martin wheeled himself to the refrigerator and pulled out several cans of his nutritional shakes, piling them on to his lap.

"I was going to make you a sandwich, Martin," Louisa said. "And we have a fruit salad that Poppy put together."

"Mm, that would be good. Maybe you could make two sandwiches, though."

Louisa stared back at him, and he quickly added, "Or, I can make them if you could help me get things together."

"No, no. I'm happy to do it!" She stroked a hand over his cheek as she walked by behind him.

Martin set two of the shakes on the table and popped the top on the other.

James, seeing his mother's attention had shifted to preparing his father's lunch, began to protest. Martin spun his chair around to face his son and then reached for the spoon in the boy's bowl of applesauce. Martin found something comforting and relaxing in tending to James. Perhaps it was the feeling of someone needing him.

Martin opened his jaws in an exaggerated example of what he expected from James and spooned the applesauce into the boy's obliging mouth. Using his right hand to complete this task proved somewhat messy for Martin as well as for James, but the two were making progress together.

Louisa swivelled around quickly when she heard the spoon drop to the floor and a strangled cry from her husband. Poppy was on her feet in an instant. She ran around the table, quickly prying James's fingers from one of the fixators on Martin's arm. By the time Louisa was able to react, Poppy had the situation under control.

Keeping one eye on her husband, Louisa took James to the sink to wash him off before setting him down on the floor with his toys.

Martin had his injured arm tucked tightly against his stomach as he rested his head on the table. He kept swallowing back the saliva that flooded his mouth, waiting for the waves of nausea to dissipate.

"I found these cold packs in the freezer, Dr. Ellingham ... if you want them," Poppy offered nervously.

Martin raised up and wiped the sweat from his brow. He nodded his head at the girl and reached out to take them from her hands.

Louisa knelt down by his side and examined his arm. "You're getting a little more colour back in your face. Is it feeling better?"

Martin sat, eyes closed, waiting for the sharp, deep, bone pain to ease into the throbbing that usually followed. He took in several deep breaths of air before turning to Poppy. "Thank you. You handled that very well."

Poppy's shoulders relaxed, and the fear on her face was replaced by a look of concern. "Is there anything else I can do to help?"

Martin shook his head vigorously. "No, just ... just let me have a few minutes.

"What happened, Martin?" Louisa asked. "The people at the hospital pulled on your fixators all the time, and it didn't hurt you."

"It has to do with shear forces ... the obliquity, or angle, of the fracture itself and angle at which James pulled the fixator. Just an unfortunate happenstance," he said, trying to wave off the incident.

Louisa lowered her head at him. "Don't try to minimise this, Martin Ellingham. And don't even think about keeping this from Ed and Chris. You promised them you'd let them know if there were any problems. *This* is a problem. So ... should I call, or do you want to?"

Martin waggled his head and put his nose in the air. "It really isn't a problem, Louisa. I'll check things out after a while to be sure, but it's really not a problem."

She stormed off and returned with her mobile in hand. "Last chance, Martin. Should I call, or do you want to?"

He lowered his head, sheepishly, then held out his left hand. "I'll do it," he muttered.

Louisa returned to the counter to finish making Martin's sandwiches, listening to his continued grumblings about needlessly interrupting the schedules of busy doctors and surgeons. She whirled around, giving him a look he knew to mean she'd reached her limit of tolerance. "Just ... do it, Martin!"

Poppy sat quietly throughout the exchange of words between her employers, shocked by the way Louisa handled the intimidating man the villagers thought Martin to be. Taken aback by the thank you and complimentary words he had uttered to her moments before.

Martin wheeled his chair into the living room before ringing Chris, downplaying the incident and apologising for any unnecessary inconvenience his phone call may have caused.

"Louisa was right. You should have called us," Chris said. "Will you *please* ... please let Ed or me decide whether something's a concern? All right, mate?"

"Yes, but do you see my point? The pins are tight, the pain has abated ... I really don't think any harm was done."

"I do see your point, Mart. But try to see things from Louisa's perspective too. If it makes her feel better, just call us. You're not inconveniencing me. It actually saves me a call to check up on you. So, how's everything else going?"

"Good. I slept well last night. It's frustrating to not be able to do things on my own, though."

"Yeah, I can imagine. But try to be patient. It'll come ... in time."

Martin rang off with Chris and returned to the kitchen.

"Poppy, would you take James upstairs ... see if you can get him to go down for a nap?" Louisa said.

She waited until the room had cleared and then turned to face her husband. "Well, what did they have to say?"

"Chris ... I just talked to Chris. He agrees that there's probably nothing to worry about."

She crossed her arms over her chest and raised her eyebrows at him. *"Oh?"*

Martin had an uncomfortable feeling in his stomach—the feeling he always had when he wasn't being completely forthcoming with his wife.

He drummed his fingers on his armrest and peered up at her. "He, erm ... also said you were correct to insist I ring him. I'm sorry, Louisa. It's not in my nature to do that."

"To do what?"

"Well, obviously, if I need to consult with someone on a medical issue, I do. But to—"

"This is a medical issue, Martin."

"Yes, but ... I mean, it's not as if I'm calling about a patient. This is a different situation entirely."

Louisa pulled a chair over and sat down next to him. "I'm not following; what's different about it?"

He breathed out a heavy sigh. "It's just not easy to do that."

"Martin, I'm not following you at all. To do what?"

"I'm not calling about a *patient,* Louisa. I'm calling about *me.* It's difficult!"

"What's difficult?"

"To ask for help! To ask other people for help! It's difficult."

"Martin, everyone needs help now and then. I do understand why you feel uncomfortable calling Chris and Ed. I mean, you're an esteemed doctor."

Martin shook his head. "No, Louisa."

She reached over and stroked the back of his neck. "I think you are, more than you realise. You know, when you were in hospital, the registrars over there at Truro were star-struck. Mr. Ellingham ... a patient in *their* hospital. But we're all human, Martin. Even esteemed doctors. No one will think less of you if you need help."

A weight descended on him as his wife smiled and nodded her head. She didn't understand, and he didn't have the words to make her understand.

He shook his head and rolled away from her. "You don't know everything. You think you understand me ... that you can fix everything." The ever-present cascade of vitriol was perched on the tip of his tongue, ready to spill over the edge the next time he opened his mouth.

"Martin, I'm just trying to help you to solve this problem," Louisa said perplexed.

"I didn't *ask* you to solve this problem! I don't *want* you to solve this problem! I just want you to listen to me for once and not tell me how I should or shouldn't—" He shook his head and spat out the word. "Feel! How the bloody hell can you tell me how I *feel* if I don't know myself?

"You don't know everything. You don't know anything about me Louisa because you never ask! And if you do ask and I give you a bloody answer, you correct me. Or you answer *for* me before I can even open my mouth, as if you know more about how I feel than I do myself!"

Martin rolled himself down the hallway and into the bedroom, giving the door a slam behind him.

Louisa heard James begin to cry upstairs. Their row had awakened him. She headed for the steps, leaving Martin to cool off.

Poppy sat rocking a now calmer James. The girl was understandably nervous, given the obvious tension in the household.

"I'm sorry about that, Poppy," Louisa said. "I hope you can appreciate how much stress my husband's been under. It just sort of came to a head down there."

The childminder squirmed, jostling James just as he was about to drift off to sleep again. The baby began to protest the interruption, and Louisa reached for him.

"Why don't you let me take him for a bit. Maybe you could run down to the green grocers for me? I need some ingredients for dinner tonight."

"Sure, whatever you want, Mrs. Ellingham," Poppy said as she folded her hands tightly in front of her.

"Could you get my purse for me? It's hanging on the coat rack by the front door."

When Poppy returned, Louisa gave her enough cash to purchase the needed supplies and then hesitated slightly before saying, "Poppy, about what went on downstairs a bit ago ... I'd appreciate it if you would keep that to yourself. What goes on under our roof is no one's business but our own."

"I'll keep it quiet, Mrs. Ellingham." She scurried out the door and down the stairs.

James fell back to sleep quickly, and once Louisa had laid him back down in his cot, she went to the downstairs bedroom door, tapping lightly. She waited for a response. When Martin failed to answer, she opened the door quietly and slipped inside.

He was lying uncovered on the bed. She assumed he had fallen asleep, but when she pulled the blankets up over him he opened his eyes.

"I'm sorry," he said. "I didn't mean all that."

Louisa sat down on the edge of the bed and rubbed her hand lightly across his chest. "I think you meant some of it though, hmm? Some of it's true, I'm afraid. More of it than I like to admit."

Martin flipped his left arm back and slid his hand under his head. "I can understand why you don't ask me questions. I don't really talk."

"That's not true though, is it ... that you don't talk." She gave him a gentle shove, and he slid himself over.

"I talk if I think there's something to talk about ... something someone would want to know about. But I'm not going to just prattle on about myself."

Curling up against him, she laid her head on his shoulder. "What is it you think people want you to talk about?"

Martin pulled his hand from under his head and stroked his fingers through her hair. "Things of significance, things that matter to them. I talk about health issues because they matter to everyone ... they should anyway."

"Yes, and I think many people *do* listen to you when you talk to them about those things."

"Oh, really? It's been my experience that people in this village show a clear preference for the medical information found online. Or in the vacuous rags sold at the checkout down at the market, equalled only in their vapidity by the the advice dished out by the likes of Bert Large."

Louisa's closed her eyes and pulled in a slow breath. "Martin, you said that you think people want you to talk about things of significance."

"Mm."

"What about you? Are you a thing of significance?"

He stared at her, blinking slowly.

"Well, Martin?"

"Why in God's name would people want me to talk about myself, Louisa?"

She propped herself up on an elbow and traced a fingertip up and down the bridge of his nose. "Maybe because they find you interesting, and they'd like to get to know you better."

He batted her hand away. "Louisa, that tickles."

"Sorry, is this better?" she asked as she placed kisses behind his ear and down his neck.

"Mm ... a bit," he said with a glimmer of a smile.

"Martin, do you feel insignificant ... as a doctor ... or to James and me."

He turned his head away before attempting to change the subject. "I think we were talking about our disagreement, weren't we?"

Louisa lowered her head at him and narrowed her eyes. "Yes, we were talking about our disagreement, if you want to call it that. I didn't actually have a chance to disagree with you though, did I?"

She ran her fingers through his hair, stopping to wrap a small curl around her finger. "Martin, you said I don't listen to you. And I'm afraid that's true. I'm sorry. I wish I could help you."

He wiped a tear from her cheek. "You can't fix anything for me, Louisa. But you *can* listen, and as ridiculous as it sounds, it seems to help. I, er ... I told Dr. Newell about thoughts I'd had as a child. Thoughts I felt guilty about ... still feel guilty about. Thoughts tha—"

"Oh, Martin. It's perfectly normal for children to think about those things, especially boys. Those hormones get going and—"

"*Louisa!* That's *not* what I'm referring to. This has nothing to do with pubescent hormonal surges, for goodness' sake."

"Sorry. Maybe ... I'm not listening again? Go ahead, and I'll try not to interrupt."

"Right." Martin hissed out a breath. "I felt guilty to the point I had nightmares about those thoughts. It was like a weight had been lifted from my shoulders just to have someone else know about it ... not think badly of me for it. That's a part of my childhood that will always be there, but I can let it go now."

Louisa held her husband's face in her hands and kissed him soundly. "I can listen, Martin. I *want* to listen. Now ... will you please answer my question? Do you feel insignificant?"

Martin closed his eyes and took in a deep breath before exhaling slowly. "Not anymore. Not to you and James. You make me feel significant, Louisa."

"You are without a doubt the most significant thing in my life. But I hope you can come to understand you're significant in so many other ways as well. To the many people whose lives you've saved, to the students who have learned from you, to Ruth, to Chris and Carole. There are many people who care about you. There are so many people who want to help you now, when everything's such a struggle for you to do on your own. Please, let people help you, Martin."

He brought a hand to his face and covered his eyes. "It's not that easy. And it's one of those things you won't be able to understand."

"Well, give me the chance to try to understand."

He grimaced. "I was taught from the very beginning to not ask for help. There were negative consequences if I did. As a result, I can hardly bring myself to do it."

Louisa ran her fingertip around his ear. "Maybe it's something you just need some practice with."

"I'll add it to my growing list of things I need to work on," he grumbled. "I still haven't made any progress on my crap list."

"Well, you were rather rudely interrupted by a lorry." Louisa nuzzled her nose into his neck. "I love you very much, Martin."

"I love you, too," he said, turning his head to give her a proper kiss. But Louisa, I'm very hungry. I never did get my sandwiches.

Chapter 25

Martin had created a list of things he needed to do during his convalescence, and at the moment, deducing what Louisa meant by her terminator comment was at the top of that list.

Completely satiated, having eaten the two sandwiches Louisa had prepared for him, as well as a large bowl of fruit salad and the remaining shakes he had left on the table, he went back to the bedroom. He opened up his laptop and typed *terminator* into the search engine.

Hmph. This source suggests it was quite a highly-acclaimed movie, Martin thought as he read the synopsis of the 1980's production. However, it didn't sound like something he would pay money to see. He would have to consider it though when determining what his wife might have been referring to with her comment the previous day.

He stared at the screen, absently, as his fingers tapped lightly against the laptop. *She could have been referencing one of the two scientific uses of the term. In astronomy, the terminator is the dividing line between the light, or daytime side, and the dark, or night-time side, of a planetary body.*

The term can also be used to define a DNA sequence that causes RNA to stop transcription.

Or, Martin thought, *she could have simply been referring to an ending to something ... or someone who puts an end to something.*

He was familiar with the last three of the four possibilities, so he would start with definition number two and deal with the movie later.

The astronomical term—the dividing line between light and dark. Maybe she was using it as a euphemism for the differences between males and females. Not likely. It doesn't fit with the phrasing she used.

The third possibility—Well, DNA and RNA do relate indirectly to sexual intercourse. This is a more logical connection to her comment than was the previous definition. It still doesn't make sense. He cocked his head and raised an eyebrow. *But then much of what Louisa says doesn't make sense.*

Possibility number four—an ending to something. Or maybe someone who ends something? Could be the Cornish vernacular for the ultimate partner in the bedroom. That would make sense ... to some degree. The more Martin thought about it, the more this seemed the most logical conclusion. *Oh, gawd! Is that what she means ... expects?*

He shook his head, trying to clear the tryptophan fog caused by his two large turkey sandwiches. *Maybe the effects of the morphine,* he thought. *Why can't Louisa just say what she means? Why does she do this?*

The confusion he was feeling at the moment was causing his head to pound. He rubbed at his temple as he set the terminator conundrum aside and moved on to the second item on his to-do list.

Dr. Newell wanted him to spend an hour a day watching the television. It would be a quiet activity, and perhaps it wouldn't exacerbate his headache. He could kill two birds with one stone by using the hour to watch *The Terminator.* He hoped that he wouldn't need to watch the entire movie to determine if it had anything to do with Louisa's remark.

He brought up his wife's online video account, and after plugging in his ear buds he settled back on the bed to complete his homework assignment for the day. The movie opened with a brief written prologue, which, in the end, Martin was thankful for. He would have been completely clueless without it.

Literary drivel, he thought as he read the words on the screen. He tried to focus on the faces of the characters in front of him, but he found the movie itself distracting. From the opening scene, it was filled with blood and violence. Mild waves of nausea rippled through his stomach as he watched a naked man, who he suspected was a steroid user, eviscerate one of several thugs who appeared to be taunting him for being out and about without clothes.

In the next scene, another naked man appeared, looking frantically for something to wear lest he be charged with indecent exposure. *Oh, gawd! How disgusting,* Martin thought as he watched the man take the trousers from a poor bloke who looked as though he'd gone some time without a proper scrubbing. It made his skin crawl to think of the innumerable communicable diseases and parasites that could be transmitted by those trousers.

The original naked man, now clothed, appeared to have an axe to grind with everyone he encountered, either blasting them with some sort of laser guided rifle or throwing them through a window or wall. *Must be the steroid use,* he reasoned.

He sat shaking his head at his laptop screen. *What's the story with the girl? She's being chased by two men who appear to want her dead. One of whom she bites on the arm, drawing blood and stupidly exposing herself to any number of horrid diseases— Hepatitis B, C, and D and AIDS to name a few.* He threw his head back. "God!" *The mindless twit's going to bed with the prat?*

"Is everyone in this movie an absolute moron?" he exclaimed aloud. *Driving recklessly. And at night without their headlights on, no less. And then there's the oaf who had the wherewithal to lock his car doors, but then left the window rolled down!* "Idiot. He deserved to have his car stolen," Martin muttered.

He had almost given up any hope of finding a connection between Louisa's remark and what he deemed a miserable excuse for a cinematic production when the assumed steroid user put a blade to his skin and made an incision, radial to the midline of the volar forearm, accessing an internal metal framework which the guileless theatre-goer was supposed to believe to be anatomically possible. "Oh, please. Tell me *this* isn't what she was referring to!" Martin moaned.

He watched until he couldn't stomach anymore. *They were certainly scraping the bottom of the understudy barrel when they cast that one,* he thought as he closed out of the site. *That pet lizard the girl seemed so attached to was the most convincing actor in the whole production. Maybe the movie would have been better with audio.*

He was still unclear about what Louisa meant with her terminator comment, but if it did relate to the movie, he could only assume she saw some vague resemblance between the ridiculous metallic skeletal system of the Terminator character and his own external fixators.

This scenario would certainly place less pressure on him than if she'd been referring to some Cornish vernacular suggesting he would be expected to provide her with an experience transcending all others.

Martin snapped the lid shut on his laptop and set it on the dresser next to his bed. Fatigue was descending on him once again. He laid his head back and quickly dropped off to sleep.

James would be waking from his nap soon, and Louisa wanted to check on Martin before she had a fidgety near-toddler to contain. She could see he was sleeping as soon as she entered the room. He was sprawled out on the bed uncovered, the way she usually found him when he had been left to his own devices.

She went to the closet and pulled a comforter from the top shelf and covered him up. He had regained much of the weight he'd lost immediately following the accident, but he could still do with a bit of fattening up in her opinion.

He looked younger when he slept than when he was awake, much as he did when he first came to the village. He was so shy around her for the first year after he arrived in Portwenn. He, of course, seemed much more comfortable in her presence now, but he still had his moments. She found it quite charming actually.

Louisa leaned over, leaving the kiss she intended to give him just above his head for fear of waking him. James's chatter could be heard emanating from upstairs, and she hurried off to tend to him.

Martin woke some time later to the sweet chortles and happy squeals of his son. After transferring himself to his wheelchair, he went into the lavatory and splashed cold water on his face. When he entered the kitchen moments later, James was playing happily in his high chair with his frog puppet, and Louisa was putting together a lettuce salad for supper.

"Well, hello." She strode over to give him the gesture of affection she had withheld earlier.

"Hello," he said before returning the kiss. He brushed the backs of his fingers across his son's cheek. "What's for dinner?"

"Are you hungry *again*?"

"Mm." He went to the refrigerator, removing one of his shakes.

"I've made a salad, and I had Ruth pick up some cod I thought—" Louisa was interrupted by a knock on the back door.

James whirled around, dropping his frog on to the floor. Martin groaned as he leaned over to pick it up for the boy, who was now kicking his feet and reaching frantically for the toy.

"Here, you better let me get it for you, Doc. You shouldn't be doin' that ya know. Someone in your condition an' all."

Martin's muscles began to tense at the sound of Bert Large's voice, knowing he was in for a pelting of questions from the rotund man. "Wonderful," he muttered.

"Oh, dear! Oh, dear! Al told me you were in a bad way. But that looks absolutely miserable, it does," he said as he leaned over to inspect Martin's arm, cocking his head one way, then the other.

"Mm. How are you, Bert?"

"I'm gettin' by. The old back gives me a bit of trouble, of course. I been icin' it, just like you said. Still hurts me some, though."

"Good." Martin turned his attention back to his shake.

"Hello there little James!" Bert said, laying a pudgy hand on the boy's head. He turned and retrieved the pot he had left on the counter. "I brought you some soup here, Doc."

He set it down on the table in front of Martin before lifting the lid and waving the aroma in his direction. "This here's a recipe handed down through generations of Larges ... sure to put a spring in yer step."

The man's jowls dropped and his head tipped to the side as he wagged a finger at Martin's legs. "You *know* ... you're not gonna be doin' much walking for a while," his said, quasi-conspiratorially.

"Yes, I'm aware of that."

"Bert, thank you so much for the soup," Louisa said as she placed a hand on the man's back and steered him towards the door. "It was very thoughtful of you. Martin tires easily though, so maybe he could stop by the restaurant to see you once he's feeling better."

"Of course. You come by anytime, Doc. But for now, you just get yer rest and don't be frugal with that soup. That there is guaranteed to put the lead back in yer pencil."

"Oh, Bert!" Martin said, wrinkling up his nose.

"What? What did I say?" He gave Louisa a guileless stare.

"Thanks again for the soup, Bert. It was so thoughtful of you."

"Not a problem. Goodnight, Louiser."

Louisa quickly closed the door behind him before returning to her Ellingham men. Leaning over behind her husband, she wrapped her arms around his shoulders. "He means well," she said softly in his ear.

"He's a busybody," Martin growled. "He always has to be the first to spread gossip around, doesn't he."

She patted his cheeks and then reached over to pick up the soup pot from the table. "He did bring you soup. Sure to put the lead back in your pencil, no less." She raised her eyebrows at him.

"The man has no sense of decorum."

"Hmm, possibly. So, shall we have the soup or the fish?"

Martin peered up at her sheepishly. "Maybe both?"

When Jeremy returned at seven o'clock, he got Martin up on his feet and recorded the length of time he could stand. Six weeks in a bed had caused the muscles in his legs to atrophy, and they soon refused to support him, forcing him back into his wheelchair.

When Louisa came downstairs after putting James to bed, she found her husband perspiring heavily and grimacing at the pain and effort it took to remain upright. He grasped the assist pole with his left hand and Jeremy supported him under his right arm.

Louisa watched for a few moments. "Are you sure he's not overdoing it, Jeremy?"

"Nope, he's really doing quite well, Mrs. Ellingham."

"Hmm, I don't know. Martin isn't very good about tell—"

"I'm fine, Louisa!" Martin snapped. He glanced at his aide. "What am I up to now?"

"Just under two minutes. Well done. Let's take a break, and then we'll go out to the kitchen ... see if you can stay up on those legs long enough to wash the last of the betadine out of your hair." Jeremy lowered him into the chair."

"Mrs. Ellingham, could you sort out what we'll need—shampoo and towel." Jeremy said.

"Sure."

The aide rested a hand on Martin's shoulder. "I'll go and get you a glass of water, okay?"

"Yes."

Martin stood in front of the kitchen sink a short time later, supported by his aide, as his wife gave him the first proper hair wash he'd had since his accident.

"Okay, now pivot," Jeremy said as his patient dropped back into the wheelchair, exhausted.

"Feel a little more human now, Dr. Ellingham?"

Martin looked up at the young man, screwing up his face and giving him a grunt.

The aide patted him on the shoulder. "Okay, let's go get you cleaned up and ready for bed. And you *will* let me help you this time around."

Martin was too tired to argue.

Jeremy helped him to wash and change into fresh boxers and vest. Then he changed out his IV bottles and administered his evening dose of heparin before saying goodnight.

Louisa hurried upstairs to look in on James and then slipped on her night dress before returning to her husband's room.

She stood in the doorway. "Well, here we are. Just the two of us ... finally." Walking to the side of the bed, she leaned over to give him a lingering kiss. "Okay, Dr. Ellingham, let's get that vest off and work on those lymphatics.

Martin groaned. "Louisa, I'm tired ... not tonight."

"You don't have to do anything but relax and fall asleep," she insisted as she pulled his left arm through the sleeve of his vest before removing it completely.

She lowered the head of the bed and Martin relented, sliding himself over to make room for her.

After dimming the light on the dresser, she crawled up next to him. "Now, you just close your eyes and try to relax those tired muscles," she said softly. Tipping his head back, she began to massage his throat with slow, circular motions. "Hmm, you *are* tense."

Martin lay perfectly still, his eyes closed. He felt exposed and vulnerable with his still-healing wounds on display.

Louisa continued, moving slowly down to his left shoulder, and then his chest. She pulled his left arm up over his head and massaged under it, trying to direct the lymph downward.

Her soft hands began the same motions on the opposite side, beginning at his right shoulder. She took a moment to gently move his arm away, exposing the long scar that ran from his chest and around his side before disappearing under his back. *The thoracotomy incision* she thought, remembering the sound of his gasps for air as the contusions and the ensuing infection made it difficult for him to breathe.

She wiped the tears from her cheeks with her sleeve and traced her fingertip around the scar. Drawing in a deep breath, she slid her hands back across his chest and began to move down his abdomen. It was awkward here to use the same circular motion. She needed to be careful not to pull on the sensitive mid-line scar that transected his torso—the incision that was made to stop the haemorrhaging that nearly took his life.

Martin opened his eyes when he noticed a cessation of movement. Louisa was sitting back on her heels, her hands over her face.

"Louisa?" He raised up.

She shook her head back and forth. "Martin, please ... be quiet." The soft, gentle voice he used when he said her name made it all but impossible to keep from breaking down.

His head sank back into the pillow. *Oh God, it's the damn scars.* He felt humiliated, hurt, and guilty for the distress he was causing her.

Having regained control of her emotions, she resumed the massage.

"Louisa, stop," he said.

"I'm almost finished."

He reached down and grabbed hold of her wrist. "Louisa, don't. *Stop.*"

She looked at him, taken aback by the vehemence in his voice. Tears welled in his eyes as he watched her. "Just—stop."

"Martin, what is it? Did I hurt you?"

"No. But you don't have to do this. I don't want you to; it upsets you. I'm sorry."

Louisa couldn't hold it in any longer and began to sob uncontrollably.

He tugged gently on her arm. "Louisa, come here."

She moved up the bed and buried her face in his shoulder. He held her until she had stopped shuddering and had quieted.

"I'm sorry," he said as he stroked his hand across her head. "I'm sorry. The reconstructive surgeries will improve the appearance ... after they heal. It won't be the same, but—"

She sat up. "You think I'm upset because of your scars? Martin, is that what you think? That I'm—that I'm repulsed by your scars ... how you look?"

He blinked as the furrow deepened between his brows.

"Martin, the scars reminded me of how much pain you've been through ... those horribly frightening days and nights after the accident ... how close I came to losing you." She cupped his face in her hands. "But they also reminded me of how very, very lucky I am to have you here with me now. And for that ... for that, Martin, I think they're beautiful." She leaned down and pressed her lips to his. "I was just overwhelmed by emotion ... that's all."

"Oh." His gaze flitted away for a moment. "You don't mind that ... being overwhelmed by emotion?"

She smiled at her brilliant, talented, but in some respects, oh-so-naive husband. "No, Martin. Not in this case."

He reached up and pulled her head to his, placing his lips against hers. The tender kiss deepened quickly into something more passionate as he pulled her tighter to him.

He couldn't get close enough. He wanted to feel his body against hers, her soft skin against his.

His amorous feelings were obvious. Louisa worked her hands down to the waistband of his boxers, easing them over the fixators and tossing them aside.

Leaving a trail of kisses up his legs and torso, she returned to nuzzle her nose into his neck—behind his ears. "I love you, Martin. More than anything in this world, I love you."

She slipped her night dress over her head, letting it drop to the floor as her husband's palm caressed her thigh before continuing up the gentle widening of her hips.

He stopped at the curve of her waist to stroke his thumb lightly across her stomach before reaching to caress her face. A low growl escaped his lips as his hand brushed her breast, and his words floated out on a breath. "Louisa, you are so beautiful."

He slid over on the bed and rolled to his side, and Louisa lay down next to him, pressing her back against him. He slowly appeased the hunger for intimacy which had been building in him over the last weeks. The scent of her perfume whetted his passion as he moved closer, rolling into her. He needed to feel every inch of her against him.

Louisa felt his lips on the back of her neck as she sensed his urgency. His intimate touches and her increasing awareness of his state of arousal heightened her own, and she clung to his arm as he tightened his grip. Tighter and tighter until she felt a shudder go through him. Gradually, the tension eased and they grew drowsy together.

Martin woke some time later, his arm numb. He kissed her shoulder and murmured her name. "Louisa."

"Hmm?"

"My arm's fallen asleep; I need to move it."

She slid over reluctantly and turned to face him, propping herself up on an elbow. Her finger traced languid circles around his ear. "That was lovely, Martin. Just ... absolutely lovely. Thank you."

He hesitated before asking, "Was it—erm, I mean, has it ever been better?"

She stared back at him. "What do you mean?"

Must not have been the Cornish vernacular, he thought. "Mm, it's not important."

He brushed a wisp of hair from her face, tucking it behind her ear. "Erm, I need the lavatory. Could you ..."

"Oh, right. Sorry."

Louisa got up and slipped her nightdress on before positioning the wheelchair next to the assist pole. Martin pulled himself up and pivoted into it.

He wheeled himself towards the bathroom, stopping part way before turning. "I'll be back," he said, channelling a cyborg wearing a Germanic accent.

He continued on towards the lavatory, leaving his wife gobsmacked. She slapped a hand to her mouth a second later when she realised her notably restrained and socially unaware husband had parodied a figure from pop culture.

She was still giggling when he transferred himself back into the bed. "Have you seen that movie?" she asked.

"Mm. Earlier today. Dr. Newell wants me to watch the television with the sound off. He thinks it will strengthen my ability to read facial expressions. I wanted to know what you meant yesterday ... what you said about me being like the terminator."

"You watched *The Terminator?* For me? Martin, that's so romantic. And with the sound off no less," she said, shaking her head. "I hope you know it's a bit ... hmm, how can I put this delicately?"

"Ghastly?"

"I'm not sure that was delicately put, but yeah, it was ghastly."

"That's a bit of a stretch, don't you think? I mean, a cyborg isn't even a medical possibility. Whereas external fixators have been used, quite successfully, for more than a hundred years."

"I was joking, Martin."

"Ah." Her cheeks glowed a lovely shade of pink as her eyes sparkled back at him. "You look happy," he said, the corners of his mouth nudging up as he studied her face.

She touched her forehead to his. "I am happy, Martin. Very happy."

"Good."

A puzzled expression grew on her face. "If you had the sound off, how did you know what the Terminator said ... and the accent?"

Martin looked at her slyly. "I watched the trailer."

Chapter 26

"Louisa! What are you doing out there?" Martin called out.

The slap of his wife's feet could be heard on the hallway floor before she appeared in the doorway, her brow furrowed and her forefinger pressed to her lips. "Shh! You'll wake James."

"What on earth are you doing out there?"

"I'll be right back, Martin. I have something I need to do first."

Martin groaned and dropped back on to the bed, rubbing at his tired eyes. He was exhausted, and it was getting late, but he didn't want to go to sleep before saying goodnight to his wife.

When Louisa finally returned to the room, she was in a somewhat dishevelled state. "What in the world have you been doing?" Martin asked as he reached up and tried to smooth out her hair.

She sat herself down on the side of the bed and took his hand. "Martin, promise you won't argue with me about this, okay?"

"I can't promise you anything if I don't know what you're going to say, Louisa." The warm feelings left by their lovemaking minutes before were quickly growing tepid. He had hoped his wife would crawl back into bed with him until he drifted off to sleep, but she seemed to have become involved in some sort of project.

"All right then, you'll just have to accept that you're going to have a roommate, because I can't sleep upstairs when you're all the way down here.

"I picked up an airbed today at Tesco's in Wadebridge. Ruth suggested a cot, but they didn't look very comfortable. This I can just slide under your bed during the day. Quite brilliant on my part, don't you think?"

Martin opened his mouth to disagree, but Louisa was up and halfway out the door. "Wait here a minute," She said before disappearing around the corner.

"I'm not going anywhere," he grumbled.

She returned, dragging a mattress behind her, which she dropped unceremoniously on to the floor next to the bed. "I'm going to sleep in here with you until you're well enough to make it up the stairs."

Martin stared down at the fleece covered lilo and shook his head, wagging a finger at it. "You can't sleep on that, Louisa. It won't adequately support your back, which could lead to any number of spinal and nerve conditions.

"And it's cold down there on the floor. Draughts increase as you get closer to the ground, and the air in that thing will conduct the heat away from your body and into the floor. It won't be comfortable. Not to mention that dust and allergens in the air settle and are in much higher concentra—"

"Martin. Stop talking," Louisa said, pre-empting the long-winded and tenaciously argumentative diatribe her husband was gearing up for.

He eyed her taut features warily, and then clamped his mouth shut.

"That's better," she said softly. "Now, you may not like this arrangement, but this is the way it's going to be. So just accept it."

She leaned forward and kissed him before setting about making up her temporary sleeping accommodations. Martin looked on, not saying a word.

She ran back up the stairs and returned with her pillow which she dropped on to the mattress below.

"Louisa, I—"

"*Mar-tin.*"

His wife had the no-nonsense look on her face that meant she wasn't to be messed with. He hesitated, and then let the words race from his mouth before she could shush him again. "I just want to say that if you get cold you can come up here and I'll warm you up."

With that, he laid back down and closed his eyes.

A smile spread across her face as she turned out the light and crawled into her nest.

They were awakened the next day by James's happy morning sounds coming through the baby monitor. Louisa had spent part of the night on her new bed, but she found her husband to be correct; it was cold on the air mattress. She had slipped in next to him shortly before the sun came up. It was crowded on the small bed, but Louisa found his warm, solid presence to be both comforting and relaxing, lulling her back to sleep.

"Good morning," Martin said as he watched his wife's eyes flutter open.

"Good morning." Louisa rolled over to look at the clock, slapping a hand to her forehead. "Ugh, six thirty," she groaned. "Now that *you're* home, James seems to think he needs to get up with the seagulls."

"Mm, sorry."

She wedged her elbow under her and leaned forward to kiss him. "That's not what I meant."

"Ah." His eyes flitted away for a moment before he drew in a breath and said hesitantly, "Louisa ... I should point out, it's just gulls."

"What's that?"

"You said seagulls. They're just gulls. There are better than fifty different gull species actually, but none of them are called *sea*gulls. The most common species in our area is the European herring gull, or just herring gull. Not herring seagull."

She narrowed her eyes at him, and he pulled in his chin. "Just thought you'd like to know."

"Thank you, Martin. I better go see to our son, hmm?"

"Yes."

His fixators caught on the sheets as he tried to roll over to kiss her, pulling him up short. He cursed them as he watched her slip from the bed and out of reach.

Jeremy arrived while the Ellinghams were eating breakfast, and Louisa invited him to join them at the table.

"I've already eaten, but I wouldn't say no to a cup of coffee. Let me get it though," the aide said as he slid behind Martin's wheelchair to get to the machine.

"How are those muscles after all the activity yesterday, Dr. Ellingham?"

Martin's head shot up, and he glanced at Louisa with a panicked expression on his face.

"After all the exercise you got ..." She nodded her head at him. *You* know ... working with Jeremy."

"Erm, yes. I'm fine, Jeremy."

"Good. I think we should work on increasing the time you can stay on your feet today. A couple more weeks, and you might have the all clear from Mr. Christianson to be weight bearing as tolerated. Strengthening those legs now will get you walking sooner. This will also improve your balance. That'll minimise your chances of taking a tumble."

"I see. Yes, that sounds sensible," Martin said as he poured more dry cereal on to James's high chair tray. "Louisa, I could really use a haircut. And maybe some different clothes."

Louisa brushed the toast crumbs from her fingers. "I'd be happy to help you with that, Martin. But I'm not sure how we'd get you to the barber in Wadebridge ... or get you to a tailor. I'm sorry, but I think you're going to have to wait a couple more weeks. Just until you can be walking a bit."

Martin closed his eyes tightly and sighed softly. For some reason, his wife's answer hit him especially hard.

Jeremy pulled a chair out and sat down next to him. "Let me see what I can do, Dr. Ellingham. Sometimes we need to get a little creative to get these kinds of things done. But I might be able to make it happen."

Martin looked over at the young man and straightened himself in his chair. "That would be good."

"Well, let's go and get some work done. Then we'll get you ready for your day," Jeremy said as he rinsed his cup and put it in the dishwasher.

By the time patient and aide had finished their work more than an hour later, Martin could stay on his feet more than twice as long as he had the day before.

"All right. That's enough for now. We'll work on this a bit more when I come this evening."

Jeremy helped Martin back into his wheelchair before heading for the door. "I need to collect some things from my car, Dr. Ellingham. When I get back, we'll get you ready for the day."

The aide returned with a box in his arms, and he set it down on the floor in front of him. He pulled the flap open, dumped the contents out, and began to screw the pieces of plastic together.

"I'm assuming the occupational therapist at the hospital didn't mention this gadget to your wife, or I would have seen one in the bathroom. It's a shower chair with a swivelling seat. I think between the two of us we can give you a proper washing this morning."

Martin almost smiled. "Thank you, Jeremy. Pass the receipt on to me, and I'll reimburse you."

Louisa scooped up the baby and walked into the room. "Why wasn't this on the list of items I was supposed to pick up? It was never even mentioned."

Jeremy nodded. "It should have been discussed with you, and it should have been included on the list. When you interviewed me, Mrs. Ellingham, I mentioned I was interested in improving the job our health care system does in preparing patients for their return home. Not having this shower chair isn't a life or death issue by any stretch of the imagination, but I think it'll improve your quality of life over the course of the next weeks, Doctor."

"You don't think we do an adequate job with home health care?" Martin asked.

"No, I really don't. In my work as a nurse at the Royal Cornwall, it wasn't uncommon to have a patient readmitted after being discharged. Often due to falls or infections, which could have been prevented if they'd had adequate health care at home."

Martin thought of Beth Sawle, a patient of his who'd had knee replacement surgery. She subsequently developed an infection. The woman's sister, a former employee at Porton Down, the government's military science park, had been manufacturing antibiotics and using her as a human test subject. If there had been an aide checking up on her, the unfortunate situation might never have occurred.

Jeremy stood and picked up the assembled chair. "I'll mount this to the bathtub, and then I'll help you into the shower."

There was no assist pole next to the bathtub, so Jeremy held on to Martin's left arm as he pivoted and sat down on the shower chair. His aide then laid a towel over his patient's lap before unlocking the swivel seat. Martin tried to lift his right leg up and over the side of the tub, but he lacked the strength.

"Here, let me help," Jeremy said as he grasped the fixators and swung Martin's legs around. The aide lifted the detachable shower head from the bar on the wall and adjusted the water to a temperature his patient found comfortable.

He made sure Martin had soap and shampoo close at hand, showed him a hook on the side of the chair where he could hang the shower head when he needed to put it down, then pulled the shower curtain shut. "I'll be just outside the door. Don't hesitate to call if you'd like some assistance."

"I can do it on my own," Martin said more tersely than he had intended. He was a private man, and privacy had been in short supply lately, putting him on edge.

He spent the first few minutes allowing the warm water to soothe his many aches and pains before tending to the task at hand. Washing around the fixators proved tricky, but he got the job done. Feeling the cleanest he had in weeks, he called for his aide.

Jeremy shut the water off and handed Martin a towel. "Do what you can there, Dr. Ellingham, then let me know what you need help with." The aide closed the curtain and stepped back out the door.

Martin cursed under his breath as the bath towel snagged on a pin. It had caught on the fixator holding his radius together, and Martin could not untangle it with his one good hand. "Jeremy, I need you in here!" he called out gruffly.

The aide came back into the room. "You hang on to the towel, and I'll untangle the thread," he said as he unwound the terry loop from the pin. "There you go. You ready to get out now?"

"Mm, yes. I think so."

Jeremy helped Martin into a clean pair of boxers and a vest before thoroughly drying his fixators and cleaning the pin sites.

Martin couldn't honestly say he felt like a new man, but the shower had improved his spirits. By the time he was dressed and had eaten a snack, he was feeling more positive.

"Jeremy, I'd like to hear more about the weaknesses you've found in our healthcare system. Is this something you decided to tackle on your own, or are you working in tandem with the patient outreach people at the Royal Cornwall?"

"No, no. It's my own thing. I couldn't get the people at RCH interested. I'm hoping to submit an article to the *BJN* at some point. I guess you could say I'm on a sabbatical of sorts."

"It's an impressive undertaking," Martin said before tipping his cup back to catch the remaining drizzle of espresso.

"It's an area that interests me, and I thought working in the home health care field would help me to understand what needs to be addressed. I'm hopeful it might legitimise any writing I do as well."

"I'd be very interested in reading your article. As a surgeon, my job was conducted in the operating theatre. Working as a GP for five years now has proved enlightening." He grimaced. "In some respects."

"I'd be honoured to have you be the first to see it."

The aide went to the refrigerator and returned to the table with one of Martin's shakes. "Drink up."

Chapter 27

Martin rolled his chair into the living room where Louisa was working on school papers and James was practicing his walking skills, traversing the perimeter of the coffee table.

Parking himself next to the sofa, he watched with a growing sense of pride at the little boy's persistence. He lost his balance periodically, his nappy crinkling softly as his bum made contact with the floor. Each time, he gave his father a bright smile and pulled himself back up to begin his attempts anew.

Martin noticed a new addition to James's collection of toys littering the table top—a small toy fire truck that made the familiar *wee-wah* siren sound when a button on its top was pressed. He couldn't resist and gave it a small push with his finger, sending the toy rolling. James squealed, and his face lit up to see his father joining in with his play. He smacked a hand down on top of the toy, and the truck sprang to life, the noise causing giggles to bubble from the child's mouth.

Louisa left her work at the desk to join them, crouching down next to her husband. "Are you having fun, James?" she said.

Her son picked up one of his alphabet blocks before working his way around the table to hand it, somewhat clumsily, to his father.

"Thank you, James," Martin said softly as he set the block down on the table. James worked his way back to his starting point and picked up a second block, which he carried over and pushed into Martin's hand. As Martin leaned to the side to set the block next to the first, his son slapped his small hand down on top of his father's much larger hand. "Da-ee." He gave Martin a wonky grin.

Martin gazed down at James's hand, a replica of his own, but in miniature. The same straight, sturdy fingers and broad palm. Hands that looked slightly too large for the arms to which they were attached.

Dr. Newell told him he would need to keep reminding himself it was his parents' own failures that had resulted in the sterile and often abusive relationship they had. He did his best to remember it, but at times such as this, when he felt an intimate connection with his son, a cloud seemed to descend on him, darkening the moment.

He noticed his wife's gaze, now focused on him, and he turned his head away.

"What is it, Martin?"

He shook his head. "I don't know."

She stood up and moved behind the wheelchair, wrapping her arms around him. He took in a deep breath as he fought the urge to snap at her and push her away.

"Are you having pain?" she asked.

"I said I don't know what it is, Louisa."

She placed her cheek against his. "I really wish you would talk to me about these things, Martin."

He hissed out a breath. "I made my parents miserable, Louisa. And no matter how hard I tried, I couldn't change that. I couldn't make them proud. My mother didn't want me touching her, so I couldn't put my hand on hers like James did with me just now. I couldn't hug her ... show her I love her."

Louisa struggled to get her head around his last words. *Show her I love her?* How could he possibly still harbour any love for Margaret Ellingham?

"Are you happy now?" he asked quietly. "Did I tell you what you wanted to hear?"

"Martin ... this isn't about me. It's about you." She reached a hand up to stroke his cheek. "I just want to help you if I can. To help you forget the awful childhood you had so that you can enjoy the rest of your life."

He looked at his wife with a deep sadness in his eyes. "I'll never be able to forget my childhood, Louisa. I'm sorry. It's always going to affect me. And because it affects me, it will affect you and James, too. I'm so sorry for that."

Hearing his father say his name, the baby cruised around the table to him. Martin reached out to stroke his son's finger with his own. "His hands look just like mine. We share the same genes."

"Yes, they do look just like yours, don't they?" Louisa took his hand and held it next to James's. "And he'll probably do great things with *his* hands too someday. If he grows up to be just like you, Martin, he'll be an extraordinary man. The difference is that James will be happy and confident, knowing he has two parents who love him dearly.

"James will be able to laugh and enjoy life to the fullest. He'll never have to endure the feeling of being unwanted or insignificant. He'll have those wonderful Martin Ellingham genes but none of the horrible memories you've had to carry through life."

Martin watched his son as he stretched himself across the table to reach his frog puppet. "Louisa, could you set him on my lap?"

She looked apprehensively from her husband to her son. "I don't know, Martin. Maybe we should wait until Jeremy comes tonight."

"Please, Louisa. Put him on my lap."

She hesitated before getting to her feet and gathering her son into her arms. "I have to hang on to his feet though ... agreed?"

"Mm, yes." Martin wrapped his left arm around James's body, pulling him in close to his own.

The boy settled in, relaxing against his father's chest. It wasn't long before his eyes began to get heavy, and he soon drifted off to sleep.

Martin watched his sleeping son, marvelling at his perfect features and flawlessly smooth skin.

With the baby now napping, Louisa left Martin's side to pull a chair up next to him.

"Louisa, I couldn't go back to the way my life used to be. I couldn't live with that anymore," Martin said.

She rested her arm on the back of his chair and toyed with the short locks on the back of his head. "It's a good thing you won't have to then, hmm?"

Martin shifted and James stirred slightly before settling back into the crook of his arm.

"I know I'm a difficult person ... that you can get frustrated with me," he said as he kept his gaze fixed on the baby. "I know I fail miserably when it comes to romance and that I infuriate you at times. And I realise there have been times you haven't wanted me in your life. But I can't do it again ... to be unwanted."

"Martin, it's not that I—"

"Please, just let me *finish*." He gave her a pained scowl. "I know I said you have as many chances as are necessary ... for you to earn my trust back. But I realise now I can't do it again ... be unwanted again. And if that's the case, I'm not being honest if I tell you that you have as many chances as are necessary."

Louisa sat frozen in her chair. "Are you giving me an ultimatum, Martin? Are you're saying if I leave you again, that's it?"

"Mm. I think that's the way it has to be ... for both of us. And for James. We both need to make a commitment to our marriage, and I don't think you can do that if you've left that door open. Or more correctly, if I've left that door open *for* you.

"I can't do this ... work through all of my problems if I have the possibility of you leaving hanging over my head. And you won't have the sense of security you need either if that possibility exists. And what kind of parents would we be for James if you left every time we hit a difficult patch ... if I *let* you leave? We've been through a lot together in the last weeks. You've been there for me every step of the way. I really don't think you need those extra chances anymore ... do you?"

Louisa studied her husband's face. "You're saying you'll trust me if I tell you I won't leave you again ... is that right?"

"Mm-hmm."

She put her hands on his cheeks and turned his face towards hers. "Martin Ellingham, I will never—*ever* walk away from you again. We're guaranteed to have our share of difficulties, but I promise you I *will* stay and work through them with you. And just to be clear, there has never been a time I haven't wanted you, Martin.

"When I was pregnant with James, I didn't handle things very well. Not telling you for six months, then springing it on you the way I did. I'm sorry about that. I *did* want you to be involved with the pregnancy, but things got off to a bad start."

She brushed her hair back away from her face and shook her head. "I should have given you a little time to absorb it all. I didn't give you any time to prepare ... just showed up at your door and ... *surprise*, you're going to be a father! Then when it didn't go well ... you know, when I told you ... well I s'pose I let my pride get in the way. But I wanted you very much."

She leaned over and gave him a lingering kiss. He began to mumble something as her lips pressed against his, and she pulled back, furrowing her brow at him.

"What did you say?"

He looked down at his lap. "Can you take James? His nappy leaked. Gawd, it must be like Niagara Falls in there!"

Chapter 28

Ruth joined Martin and Louisa for dinner Friday night, updating them on the progress with the renovations to the old farmhouse. According to Ruth, both her assistants, Al Large and Morwenna Newcross, Martin's receptionist, had been putting in long hours at the farm, working on the yard and outbuildings.

"The yard certainly needed a bit of attention," Martin said. He polished off his last bite of broiled Pollock before ladling more of Bert's heirloom soup into a bowl. It was a surprisingly succulent dish, especially when compared to the substandard fare usually served up at Large Restaurant. He had to wonder why it wasn't on the menu.

Louisa carried a load of dishes to the sink and then returned with a facecloth to clean the pureed peas from her son's face. "When do you hope to be able to start hosting guests, Ruth?"

"Well, *I* don't see any point in opening the place up until the spring tourist season begins, but Al thinks we should try a dry run over the holidays—family gatherings, company Christmas parties ... that sort of thing.

"Could be he's on to something, I suppose. It *would* give us a chance to work any bugs out of the system before the hordes of guests descend on us in May and June."

Ruth watched her nephew over the top of her teacup. "I'm glad to see you're putting some weight back on those battered bones of yours, Martin. You were getting terribly thin."

Martin winced at his aunt's remark, and his spoon clanked sharply as it dropped into his bowl. "You sound like my mother."

Ruth's head shot up, and she stared at him, deadpan, from across the table. "Then I'll choose my words more carefully in future."

There was a knock on the door and Louisa went to answer it with James perched on her hip. "Jeremy, hi. Come on in." It was a brisk evening and the cold wind whipped in across the floor, bringing with it a tornado of leaves.

The aide hurried into the little kitchen, blowing air into his hands to try to warm them. "Hello, Dr. Ellingham. Feeding those fractures?"

"Yes. I have a bit more soup to eat, and then we can crack on."

"Take your time." The young man pulled out a chair and sat down across from Ruth. "How are you, Dr. Ellingham?"

"Oh, I'm getting by ... for a woman my age," she said, giving Martin a wry smile. "What do you have planned for my nephew tonight?"

"We've been working on building the strength back up in his legs, as well as improving his balance. We'll do more of that." His gaze shifted to his patient. "And I—and if you're not comfortable with this, Dr. Ellingham, please say so. But I brought my cousin over with me so she could visit a friend who lives here in the village. She's a stylist. Works at a salon in Truro. If you'd still like that haircut, she could do it for you this evening."

Martin hesitated. He was comfortable with his barber in Wadebridge, and this cousin of Jeremy's might be an incessant chatterer, full of questions about his accident. Or even worse, she could be like the giggling girls who loitered outside his surgery. But desperation won out over trepidation and he gave the young man a nod. "As long as she doesn't blather—"

Louisa caught his eye, tipping her head down and raising her eyebrows, a gesture Martin knew to be a reminder to mind his manners.

"Yes, that would be fine. Good," he said. "Thank you, Jeremy."

"Great. I'll give her a call."

The aide stepped out of the room to ring his cousin, and Louisa seized the opportunity to admonish her husband. "Martin, it's very nice of Jeremy's cousin to help you out, so be nice."

He hissed out a breath. "Why do you always assume I'm going to behave abominably?"

She glanced over at Ruth who raised an eyebrow at her nephew.

He scowled as his wife came over and kissed his head before whispering in his ear. "I'm going to miss running my fingers through those curls you know."

"Mm. Well ... yes." He squirmed under his aunt's smirking gaze.

"Okay, it's all set. She'll stop by in about a half hour," Jeremy said as he re-entered the room. "You ready to get to work, Dr. Ellingham?"

"Yes." Martin untangled himself from his wife's grasp and headed in to the living room.

Louisa sat back down at the table with James on her lap.

"And how are you dear? Holding up alright having the patient at home?" Ruth asked as she observed the weariness on the younger woman's face.

"I'm *very* happy to have Martin home again, Ruth." Louisa reached for a toy on the high chair tray and handed it to the baby.

"That doesn't really answer my question, does it? You look tired."

James began to squirm and fuss, unhappy about being restrained, and his mother set him down on the floor.

"Well, I haven't been sleeping very well. But really, I'm very glad Martin's back home and improving."

Ruth got up and refilled the tea kettle before plugging it into the socket above the counter. "More tea?"

"Yes, please, Ruth." Louisa picked up her empty cup and stared into it absentmindedly. "Ruth, Martin said something today that surprised me."

"Oh?" The elderly woman took the cup from Louisa's hands and set it back on the table before dropping a teabag into it.

"He said he loves his mother. He was sorry she wouldn't let him touch her ... that it prevented him from expressing his feelings for her in that way. *Show her that I love her* is what he said. Present tense ... not past. That just struck me as odd. How could he possibly still love that woman after all the years she mistreated him ... rebuffed him? She's an absolutely horrid woman."

"Do you love your mother and father? They haven't exactly been model parents either," Ruth said as she poured hot water into their cups.

"Yes. But I never doubted their love for me. They may be selfish people, but they're far from the cruel and unloving parents Christopher and Margaret were to Martin."

Ruth set the kettle back on the counter and returned to the table. "You told me once Martin said he spent the first forty years of his life trying to earn his parents' love. I'm sure it's going to take time for him to completely accept that the love he felt for them will never be reciprocated, and he will probably never stop loving them. Outside of Joan, they were the only people in his life when he was young. The only people he had to hang on to. And he may come to realise that what he felt ... or feels ... for his parents isn't really love but rather a childhood fantasy of *having* a loving mother and father."

Louisa gazed at her son playing contentedly on the floor at her feet. "That is just so sad, Ruth. A childhood *fantasy* of having loving parents."

"Yes, it is. But that's the hand your husband was dealt."

Ruth gazed pensively as she ran her fingers along the edge of the table. "You know, it's quite possible Martin's working through a grieving process. That he keeps coming back to the denial stage because he's not ready to move on. He's displayed signs of all but one of the five stages—denial and isolation, anger, bargaining, depression."

Louisa cocked her head at her husband's aunt. "I know what you mean by the denial and isolation, and he certainly went through a period of depression. And anger ... anyone who's met Martin has likely been on the receiving end of that one. I'm not sure what you mean by bargaining, though."

"Oh, Louisa. Your husband's been bargaining all his life. Doing whatever he could to try to win favour with Christopher and Margaret. Excusing their lack of love for him by placing the blame on himself. Convincing himself his parents sent him away to boarding school because they wanted to make sure he received the best education possible. I suspect that's why he pushed so hard to get James registered at St. Benedict's."

"But his mother came right out and told him she sent him to boarding school to get rid of him."

Ruth nodded. "Yes, but those feelings can persist long after the truth is realised."

"Hmm." Louisa sipped at her tea. "You said five stages, though. What's the fifth stage?"

"Acceptance. And hopefully that's a stage he can reach in all of this. I think part of the difficulty for Martin is he keeps having new events thrown at him that he needs to process ... work through. It's almost like he has to start at the beginning again every time."

James spotted the little pile of leaves that had blown in the door and scrambled over to reach them before his mother could put up a road block.

"No, no, James. Leave that be," Louisa said as she pulled some of the fibrous material from her son's mouth and tossed it in the bin. The baby let out a resentful wail.

She scooped him into her arms. "Let's go and check on your daddy, okay?"

They found Martin and Jeremy finishing up in the living room. Martin was standing much straighter now than he had been just a few days before, and his sense of balance seemed to have improved.

"Very well done, Martin!"

He turned his head quickly at the sound of her voice, and the movement caused him to become disoriented and fall backwards.

"Martin!" Louise cried out.

Jeremy grabbed hold of him under his arm, and Martin latched on to the assist pole. The aide lowered him back into the wheelchair.

"He's fine, Mrs. Ellingham. This is why your husband will be working on these skills under close supervision for a while. His proprioceptive sense has been impaired by the injuries to his musculoskeletal system. The physiotherapists will be doing a lot of work with him on getting that back when they come next week."

"Proprio ... I'm sorry, say that again."

"Proprioception. It can really be considered one of the senses ... like sight or smell. Proprioception is our position sense. It can be damaged by a stroke, or in your husband's case, by his injuries. Even a sprained ankle can throw it off, so you can imagine the challenges your husband has ahead of him. It's an important sense. Without it patients fall and suffer further injuries which obviously slow the recuperation process."

Louisa set James down by the coffee table. "So, this is different from having a sense of balance?"

"Yes. It does involve balance, though." Jeremy tried to think of a better way to explain himself. "When you walked across the room just now, you did need a sense of balance, but you also needed to know exactly when your foot was going to touch the floor with each step you took. The nerves in your muscles, tendons and joints sent signals to your brain, and your brain in turn sent signals back, telling your limbs which way to move and how far to move. Your husband's had a lot of damage to those nerves, but they're intact. They just need to be retrained."

"I see."

Louisa worried her lip, and Martin reached for her hand. "It'll be fine. I'll need to work on it, but it'll be fine," he said as he gave her a reassuring nod.

The rest of the evening passed quickly. Jeremy's cousin arrived, giving Martin the haircut he needed without unduly aggravating him with small talk. The aide then helped him to wash and change before administering the necessary medications.

"I don't know what we'd do without Jeremy," Louisa said as she pulled her air mattress out from under the bed that night.

Martin watched his wife wrestle with the bedding. "Yes, he was a good choice. Thank you."

Louisa stopped what she was doing and smiled up at him. "You're welcome. I'm glad you approve."

"Erm, Louisa. Maybe you should lay a couple of rugs down on the mattress before you put the sheets on. It might be warmer. Or ..."

Louisa went to her husband's side and wrapped her arms around him, touching her forehead to his.

"Yes, Martin?"

"I was just going to say ... well, the bed's small, but I can slide over. And I really can't move around much at night, so I don't need a lot of space."

Giving the air mattress a shove with her foot, Louisa returned it to its position under the bed. She turned out the light and then climbed in, nestling up against him.

Martin rested his injured right arm on her hip and burrowed his face into her neck.

"Hmm, that's very, very nice ... husband."

"Yes, it is, Mrs. Ellingham," Martin pulled her in close for the night.

His touch was warm and tender but she also sensed a certain firmness about him. "Martin."

"Hmm?"

"Should I see about getting that recipe from Bert?"

Chapter 29

Martin woke Saturday morning in the same position he was in when he fell asleep the night before. Louisa had shifted, however, and lay facing him. He watched her as she dozed, her weight numbing his left arm which was trapped beneath her. He wiggled his fingers, trying to get the blood flowing again without disturbing her, but she began to stir.

"Good morning," she said as she reached a hand out to caress his cheek. "Did you sleep well?"

She raised up on an elbow, and Martin quickly rescued his now cold and tingling appendage, pulling it up to his chest.

"Erm ... yes, fine." His fingers began to warm as blood rushed back into them.

"Problem?" she asked, concern quickly shadowing her face.

Martin shook his head, "No. My hand just fell asleep."

She sat up next to him and took hold of his arm, caressing it. "Why don't you lie back and I'll do your lymphatic massage," she said as she moved to make room for him.

He struggled to pull himself towards the centre of the mattress.

"Can I help?" Louisa asked sympathetically as she watched him fight friction.

"No!" he snapped as his muscles began to burn with the exertion it took to make headway.

He stopped and huffed out a breath. "Maybe you need to use the lavatory, or get a glass of water," Martin suggested with tetchiness in his voice. It seemed to add insult to injury to have his wife looking on as he struggled to do things.

"Oh ... I see." Louisa dropped down from the bed and wrapped her dressing gown around herself before heading towards the kitchen, feeling the sting of rejection. She filled a glass with water and stood staring out the window as a fine mist silently hit the outside of the panes of glass, building up until the moisture trickled down in tiny rivulets where it puddled on the sill.

At the moment, with the grey and damp day contributing to her mood, the future seemed daunting. Martin had come so far, but he had an even longer journey ahead of him.

Louisa suddenly felt ashamed of the way she had reacted to her husband's request moments before. *Martin has all he can do to keep himself together. Don't expect him to try to do it while walking on your emotional eggshells,* her conscience told her.

She headed back to the bedroom with a readjusted attitude. Peeking around the doorway, she saw him grimace as he allowed his body to roll backwards. He put his hand over his face and shuddered as he swallowed back a groan.

She stepped back into the room. "Get yourself all sorted?" she asked with faux cheerfulness.

"Mm, yes. Sorry to keep you waiting."

Louisa leaned over to press her cheek to his. He had wiped the tears from his eyes before she returned, but the moisture remaining on his face was cool against her skin.

Brushing her fingers through his now close-cropped hair, she raised a question she'd been reluctant to ask. "Martin, how much do you hurt?"

He responded with unintelligible mumbling and cast a dismissive wave through the air.

She took his face in her hands and gave him a penetrating stare. "I asked you a question, Martin, and I expect an honest answer."

He gazed back at her for a few moments, and then sighed. "Some days are worse than others."

"I see. And this is a bad day, isn't it."

He winced as pain shot through his left leg. "It's probably the change in barometric pressure." Patting the mattress next to him he said, "I think I'm ready for that massage now," effectively putting an end to the conversation.

When Jeremy arrived a short while later, he helped Martin with his shower and medications before joining them at the table for breakfast.

Louisa scrambled the eggs rather than preparing them in the more traditional boiled-with-soldiers fashion, having learned it was easier to get more of the protein rich food into her husband that way. She could also cook them with a bit of butter, getting extra fat into his diet without him being any the wiser.

Martin balked at the bangers on his plate but did nothing more than to give them a sneer before ingesting them. The toast and orange marmalade was a breakfast staple in the Ellingham household and one which Martin relished. The intake of the refined sugars and empty calories in the preserves was one of the very few dietary vices Louisa was aware her husband could admit to having.

"That was delicious, Mrs. Ellingham. Thank you very much," Jeremy said as he pulled the napkin from his neck and laid it on the table.

"Jeremy, I think Louisa might be more comfortable if you used her Christian name," Martin said. "And ... you can call me Martin if you like." He cleared his throat and quickly turned his attention to James Henry, who was sat next to him in his high chair, squeezing scrambled eggs through his fingers.

"If you're comfortable with that, Dr. Ellingham," the said.

Louisa began to clear the dishes from the table. "Martin, I asked Jeremy to look into something for me. He found a car hire company in Truro that has wheelchair accessible vans. He returned the car I had picked up in Wadebridge, and his cousin gave him a ride back to Truro. He picked a van up for us and drove it over here today."

"Oh, Louisa," Martin groaned. "You shouldn't have done that. You hate driving the Lexus through the village. A van will be much worse. You'll never be able to—"

Louisa raised her hands to stem the flow of words coming from her husband's mouth. "Martin, hear me out ... please."

She waited until she saw him purse his lips, a clear indication he was making a concerted effort to hold his tongue.

"I don't use a vehicle when I'm in the village, and the Murphys, up on Silvershell Road, said we could park the van in their driveway while they're abroad. So, finding a parking place large enough isn't a problem. And I've rented a *small* van. Just big enough for one wheelchair and three other people. It's not like we have to get through the narrow lanes on the way to the surgery."

Martin rubbed his palm across his forehead. "Look, I appreciate that—"

"Martin. I'm done talking about this," she said, raising a hand and her eyebrows simultaneously. The discussion was over.

"Yes."

Louisa gave him a feeble smile. "Now, Jeremy's going to ride over to Truro with us today. He needs a ride back to the rental place. We'll drop him then stop in at Jaeger's, and one of their tailors will look into modifying some shirts and trousers for you."

"Oh."

Louisa put her hands on her hips and cocked her head at him. "Just, oh?"

"No, that would be fine ... good."

"Good." She kissed his cheek, and a red flush raced up his neck as he glanced at his aide.

Louisa finished the breakfast clean-up while Jeremy went to get the van and Martin went to use the lavatory. She was slipping the baby into his jacket when the aide came back in the door.

She glanced down the hall. "Jeremy, I was wanting a word with you ... before Martin comes back," she undertoned. "Is he supposed to be having much pain?"

"Well, there will be some discomfort, even on the morphine. Probably for a number of months yet, but it should improve with time. He may always experience some pain, especially with weather changes and physical activity ... cold temperatures. It varies from one patient to the next. Why do you ask?"

"Well, I could tell he was really hurting this morning. He downplayed it, but I think it was worse than he let on."

"I'll keep an eye on him. I'm sure your husband's hating the mentally dulling effects of the meds, so he may be reluctant to admit to having any discomfort. I'll mention it to Mr. Christianson and Dr. Parsons as well."

Louisa heard the sound of her husband's wheelchair, and she leaned over to pick her coat up from the table.

Martin had removed the brace from his arm and had the sling Ed Christianson had sent him home with laying on his lap. "Could you help me with this, Louisa?"

"Certainly. What do you want me to do?"

"Pull the Velcro apart on the piece that goes around my arm, then I'll need you to wrap the strap around my neck and fasten the buckle."

Once Martin's arm was secured in the sling Louisa tucked his coat in around him. "There, snug as a bug in a rug," she said as she leaned over to place a kiss on his cheek.

He gave her a blank stare and a grunt. "Sounds awful."

"It's just a saying, Martin," she said before pulling the door open.

The trip to the city began reasonably well. They dropped Jeremy at the rental company where he had left his car, and then continued on to Jaeger's.

The Jaeger's saleswoman had an ingratiating manner, which instantly put Martin on edge.

She hurried over to them as they stepped into the store. "Oh, love! What's happened to you?"

Martin looked at her askance. "None of your business."

She reached out to put a hand on his shoulder, and he quickly rolled his chair back. "For goodness' sake woman, keep your hands to yourself!" he barked.

Louisa reached down, pressing her palm against his chest. "My husband was in a car accident. We'd like to look at some shirts and trousers that we can have altered to fit around the external fixators on his legs and his right arm. A looser style, maybe?"

"Of course, let me go and see what I can find. You just wait right there sir and relax." She started off for the racks of clothes.

"Good gawd!" he said, rolling his eyes.

"Martin, she's just trying to be sympathetic."

"I didn't *come* here for sympathy. I came to get some bloody shirts and trousers!"

"I'm just saying she's not trying to be intrusive. She just—"

James began to complain about being restrained in his pushchair, and Louisa dug around in the nappy bag for his new toy fire engine.

Martin grumbled under his breath before rolling himself towards a rack of suits.

The clerk returned with an armload of possibilities, laying them out on a nearby counter. Martin wrinkled his nose at her selection. "I'm a doctor, not a used car salesman."

"Mar-tin," Louisa hissed.

"I'm sorry sir, what did you have in mind?" the woman asked, giving him a saccharine smile.

He pointed with his thumb in the direction of the more formal attire. "Don't you have something over there?"

The clerk folded her hands in front of her and sighed loudly. "The fine wool in a suit just won't stand up to the wear from your ... um ... the metal pieces. Would you like to look at something in a polyester, perhaps?"

Martin stared at her incredulously for a moment, his jaw clenching. "No—thank you."

"I was thinking more in terms of some nice casual trousers and loose fitting shirts," Louisa said as she leaned over to straighten her son out in the push chair. The boy shrieked his resentment at having to begin his struggle to free himself anew, and she unsnapped the safety harness before lifting him up.

The clerk gave her a strained smile. "A stretch cotton would be a more practical choice. Maybe a full-leg chino. It would be a compromise between the wool trousers and these more casual trousers I already brought out. If you go with a darker colour the—" She wagged her finger at Martin's legs— "the doodahs won't be as—"

"They're called fixators," Louisa said with an edge to her voice.

"Yes, yes. As I was saying, they won't be as noticeable with the darker coloured trousers. Of course, this is all completely up to you, but the dark coloured stretch chinos are what I would recommend, sir."

The chinos lacked the look of professionalism to which Martin was accustomed, but in the end, practicality won out over style. He scowled at his wife. "I guess they'll have to do."

"Good, that's one decision made. Now we better look at shirts," Louisa said.

Martin selected six casual button down shirts as well as six dress shirts he could pair with ties.

The tailor emerged from the back end of the store. He seemed to be familiar with the needs of patients being treated with external fixators, and he didn't waste time with what Martin would consider to be idle chatter.

He took the measurements he needed so he could adapt the trousers to work with Martin's hardware. The shirts were roomy enough that the sleeve could be fitted over his arm, so the decision was made to leave the right cuff unbuttoned, and he would roll the sleeve back.

"We need to be here again on Wednesday. Is there any possibility you could you have things ready by then?" Louisa asked the man.

"That doesn't give me much time. I'll do what I can, but I might not have everything done by then."

By the time they left the clothing store, the clouds had cleared and the wind had died down. Louisa slowed as they neared the van.

"Martin, I told the Parsons we'd be in town today. I thought maybe we could meet someplace for lunch."

He groaned. "Louisa, I'm tired. Maybe we could have dinner with them on Wednesday."

"Your appointment isn't until half four. By the time we finish up at the hospital and have dinner it'll be getting awfully late for James. And I told Carole we were going to be here ... I don't want to appear anti-social."

"Yes ... I get the idea! But we do need to get back before my drip needs to be changed."

Louisa leaned over and kissed his head. "I brought an extra bottle with me. And thank you for being agreeable."

Martin's scowl deepened. "Did I have a choice?" he mumbled.

He looked on as his wife pulled out her mobile and rang up their friends, silently hoping they wouldn't answer.

Chapter 30

When Louisa reached the Parsons on her mobile, Chris suggested they meet for lunch at an out of the way bistro on the outskirts of town.

The Ellinghams arrived at the restaurant before the Parsons, much to Martin's relief. He was anxious to be spared an audience as he adjusted to manoeuvring his wheelchair in and out of the van.

Getting up and down the ramp was not a problem, due in great part to the time he had spent working with Tim Spalding, ascending and descending inclines. But getting the chair positioned so the automatic restraint system would work properly was much more challenging, and by the time they left Jaeger's Martin's level of frustration had increased exponentially.

When they arrived at the Trennick Mill Restaurant Louisa activated the automatic sliding door/ramp mechanism and unlocked the restraint system. The van was not designed for someone of Martin's stature, and in his haste to disembark before the Parsons arrived, he failed to duck as he passed through the doorway.

Louisa was just coming around the back of the vehicle when she heard a loud thud. She looked up to see Martin raise his hand to his head, trying to soothe the ache and sting of his most recent injury.

"Oh, Martin!" she said as she rushed to him. "Here, let me see." She pulled at his arm to move his hand away.

An angry red line had already formed on his forehead. "We need to get some ice on that. They'll have some in the restaurant."

Martin was both annoyed and embarrassed by his own carelessness. He pushed his wife's hand away.

"I'm fine, Louisa. Just—get James."

Louisa gathered together the baby and the nappy bag before walking around to close the sliding door.

"Martin, are you sure you're all right?"

He closed his eyes and took in a slow breath. "Yes, I'm fine. Let's just ..." He jerked his head towards the restaurant and wheeled himself forward.

Louisa felt a growing sense of foreboding as she held the door open for her husband. They found a table in a back corner and sat down to wait for their friends.

Pulling a bag of dry cereal from the nappy bag, Louisa busied James in a high chair. She saw the Parsons and stood up, waving them over.

Carole leaned over to kiss Martin's cheek. He recoiled and glared at her, and she put a hand on his shoulder. "How are you doing, Martin?"

"Fine. Sit down so we can eat ... please."

Chris scrutinised his friend's face as he lowered himself into the chair next to him. "What happened to you!" he asked as he grasped him by the head to inspect the welt that had developed.

"I hit my head coming out of the bloody van," he spat. "It's fine!" He glanced at the patrons around them.

Chris shifted immediately into doctor mode. "Follow my finger."

"I need to use the lavatory," Martin said as he backed away from the table and spun his wheelchair around.

Carole wagged a finger at their departing friend. "Follow him, Chris. He's going to need help."

Chris trotted off to catch up with him, slipping ahead of him in time to hold the door open.

"I can manage, Chris!" Martin snapped.

"Oh, really? Just how are you going to do that?" He leaned back against the lavatory wall, crossing his arms over his chest.

Martin looked at the line-up of urinals in front of him, realising he would be without the use of an assist pole.

"All right! Help!"

Chris hooked his right arm under his friend's left arm and helped him to his feet before turning his head to give him some privacy. Once Martin was settled back in his chair, Chris returned to his previous position against the wall.

"That wasn't really so bad now, was it, Mart? Letting me help you?"

Martin tapped his fingers on the armrest of the chair and glared back at him. Gradually his expression softened. "Sorry. I appreciate your help."

"You're welcome, mate. Now, may I *please* take a look at that bump on your head?"

Martin rolled his eyes before giving him a nod.

"Any headache, blurred vision, confusion?" Chris asked as he turned his friend's head towards the light coming in the window.

"Yes, yes, and yes. But it's the morphine ... nothing to worry about."

"He shaded Martin's eyes one at a time, checking his pupillary reflexes. "What about nausea?"

"Some. But again, it's the morphine. Chris, I'm fine!" Martin pushed the doctor's hand away.

"How many fingers am I holding up?"

"Two, but you're going to have one less if you don't stop it!" Martin said, exasperated.

Chris straightened up, reasonably satisfied his friend was not concussed.

While the men were in the lavatory, Louisa had some time to chat with Carole about life with her temporarily disabled husband.

"I tend to push him too hard, Carole. I always have. But now, I think I'm anxious to have things back to normal. It feels like we're seeing snail's-paced improvement."

"Louisa! Think back just six weeks ago. Six weeks ago yesterday, you were in the trauma centre with him. Remember that? I think he's made remarkable progress."

Carole picked up her water glass and took a sip. She looked sympathetically at her friend. "I do understand, though. It's been a nightmare for both of you. You just want to put the whole thing behind you, I'm sure."

"That's exactly it. Those days in the hospital were just awful, and I really want to forget them. And I worry about Martin constantly ... and he knows it. Which is terrible because then he hides things from me so I don't worry about him any more than I already am.

"I talked to our home health aide this morning in fact. Martin's having a lot more pain than he lets on ... which is completely unnecessary. He could be on a much higher dose of pain medication than he is, but for some reason he's chosen to hide the pain. Jeremy, Martin's aide, suspects he doesn't like the negative effect it has on him mentally."

Carole picked up a menu and began to peruse it. "He's probably right. Chris would be the same way."

Louisa reached into the small basket of saltines on the table and opened a packet, breaking off a piece for her son. "On a more positive note, Martin agreed to get some more casual trousers this morning."

"However did you manage that? You must be some kind of miracle worker." Carole laid her menu down on the table and stroked a hand over James Henry's head.

"He doesn't have much choice. The fabric in his suits wouldn't hold up to the wear from the fixators."

James began to fuss so Louisa dug through the nappy bag for his frog puppet. "He's going to hate it, though. He practically lives in a suit." She broke another saltine in half, giving part of it to James before popping the rest in her mouth. "He's going to feel very unprofessional."

"Well, what about other times ... when he has a day off?"

"A day off? Believe me, Carole, Martin doesn't take days off. He'd be the first to admit he's always working. I swear, I have to put the man to *bed* to get him out of his consulting room."

Carole gave her an impish grin. "Yes, I've been wondering how that's been going. A bit fiddly I would imagine."

"Carole!"

"Sorry, you don't have to answer that. I'm just curious is all."

Louisa smiled at her friend. "Let's just say it hasn't been a problem ... in the least."

Carole glanced up as their husbands approached. "Shh, here they come."

Martin's fatigue grew more apparent as they waited for their food to arrive, as did Chris's concern for him. "You hanging in there okay, Mart?" he asked.

Martin cast a quick glance towards his wife who was involved in happy conversation with Carole. "I'm fine."

The food arrived, and Martin's spirits seemed to rise with a bit of sustenance.

"Carole dabbed at her mouth with her napkin. "That was delicious," she said. "How was your chicken, Martin?"

"Mm, quite good. Both savoury and satisfactorily nutritious."

"Louisa, you need to get him home now. He won't admit it, but he's exhausted," Chris said as he reached into his back pocket for his wallet.

She gave him an uneasy smile. "I'll take him home straight away." She was about to declare the outing a success when her husband's plain-spoken and surly nature was put on display.

"Is there anything else I can get you?" a waiter asked as he began to clear the empty dishes from the table, reaching over Martin and knocking him in the head with his elbow in the process.

Martin put a hand up, defensively, as he erupted. "Watch what you're doing you stupid nit! Good God, were you trained by barbarians?"

The young man jumped back at the unexpected verbal attack. The earthenware dishes on his tray slid forward, some landing with a crash on the floor and some in Martin's lap.

Martin emitted an agonised cry of pain as they collided with the sensitive wound in his thigh and the fixator in his femur.

Chris was at his side immediately, clearing the debris away and taking a hurried mental inventory of possible damage from the incident.

"Where's your pain at, Mart?"

Martin was blinking back tears and trying to catch his breath. *"Jeez, it hurts,"* he squeaked out.

"Yeah, I bet it does. But, one to ten, Martin ... where's your pain at?"

"Eight," he forced out as his hand gripped the armrest of his chair. He swallowed repeatedly as saliva flooded his mouth.

Chris reached over to the IV line and adjusted the speed of the drip. "Hang on, Mart. It should start getting better pretty quick here."

Louisa held her breath, waiting for the morphine to free her husband from his pain.

A bit of colour began to return to his face, and he wiped the tears from his eyes.

"Doing better now, Mart?" Chris asked as he crouched next to the wheelchair.

"Yeah."

The incident had attracted the attention of both patrons and management personnel. Martin became aware that all eyes in the restaurant were on him. "Louisa, can we go? *Please* ... I jus' wanna go."

Chris covered Martin with his coat while Louisa bundled James into his parka, and they slipped out of the restaurant as discreetly as they could.

Once Martin was in the van and his wheelchair was locked in place, Chris stepped away, pulling out his mobile and ringing Ed Christianson.

"Ed's on call at the hospital, Mart," he said when he returned. "He wants to lay eyes on you before you head back to Portwenn."

"I'm fine now, Chris. It doesn't hurd anymore."

"Yeah, I bet it doesn't. But we're going to have Ed check you over anyway, just to be on the safe side."

"Louissa, I jus wanna go."

"We will Martin, but not until Ed takes a look at you. Now, shush."

Martin was agitated while they waited for Ed to arrive in A&E. The additional morphine was causing him confusion. "This isn't my room, Louissa."

"I know, Martin. Ed's on his way down. Once he's checked you over I'll take you home, okay?" she said as she caressed his hand.

"Yess."

CT images were taken, and Ed carefully examined the pins in Martin's fixators. "I think you check out fine my friend."

"Good. Can I go home now?"

"Yep. We'll get a full series of pictures when you come in next week, but I think all is fine."

Chris adjusted the drip so Martin was receiving a lower dosage of morphine, and then helped Louisa get him into the van. Al Large would meet them at Ruth's to help her get him from the van to the cottage.

As she tucked the blanket Carole had loaned them in around her husband's legs, he looked at her with tired eyes. "Could we please just eat at home next time?"

"Yes, Martin. We can eat at home next time."

But there will have to be a discussion about the risks of terrorising wait staff, she thought.

Chapter 31

Chris had sent instructions for Jeremy to increase Martin's morphine dosage for the night, and by the time the aide left, his patient was sleeping soundly with his limbs elevated and iced.

Louisa was in the kitchen making breakfast when he woke the next morning. He blinked, trying to focus his eyes on his fuzzy surroundings. "Louissa! Louissa!" He sat up in bed, and the room began to spin.

Louisa set the carton of eggs she had in her hand down on the counter and hurried to his room.

"Good morning. Did you sleep well?" she asked as she pulled the curtains back to let the rays of sunshine stream in the window.

"I don' feel well." He let his head drop back on to the pillow and squeezed his eyes shut as the bright light sent pain through his head.

"What do you mean, does something hurt?"

"Iss hard to think. I'm dizzy."

"It's probably the morphine. Chris wanted to make sure you didn't have pain in the night, so he had Jeremy increase your dosage."

"I don' like it. Jus' shut it off." Martin pulled at the blankets and reached out, trying to grab at the IV line.

Louisa wrapped her arms around him and held on until he quieted, and then she pushed him back down on to the bed. Leaning over, she kissed him, and his eyes closed reflexively.

"Go back to sleep," she whispered.

She looked at her watch then back to her now sleeping husband. It was a half an hour yet before Jeremy was due to arrive.

The rattling sound of Ruth's key in the lock on the back door made its way to the bedroom, and Louisa hurried out to the kitchen.

"Ruth, I'm glad you're here. Martin's getting extra morphine, and when he woke up a little while ago, he was worked up. He said he was dizzy and couldn't think. He's gone back to sleep now, but I was afraid he'd wake up again before Jeremy got here."

"I'll look in on him," Ruth said as she patted her on the arm. "Maybe you could make us each a cup of espresso."

Louisa started the coffee brewing getting the bottle of milk from the refrigerator and setting it on the table. As she gazed down the hall towards her husband's room, the tension and concerns that had been building in her for the last several days bubbled over and tears began to stream down her cheeks.

Ruth returned to the kitchen to find her seated at the table, sobbing into a tea towel. "Oh, for goodness' sake, what's the matter?" Ruth asked as she took a seat beside her.

Louisa took several deep breaths before spilling her heart out to the elderly woman. "I just want Martin to be well again ... to have things the way they were. I'm so worried about him. This morning ... Ruth, what if he'd tried to get up out of bed? What if he pulled his IV out? I wouldn't have known what to do. I *don't* have the proper training to be doing this!"

"Take a *deeep* breath, Louisa, and try to calm yourself down."

Louisa pulled in a gulp of air as her ponytail whipped side to side. "I'm doing a *horrible* job of taking care of him. Yesterday, I took him over to Truro to get a tailor to alter some clothes for him. I thought it would be good for him. I wanted to do something normal. I suggested we meet the Parsons for lunch.

He *tried* to talk me out of it. He *told* me he was too tired. But I was so sure seeing Chris and Carole ... doing something normal, would be good for him. Then he hit his head coming out of the van. And the waiter dumped a tray of dishes in his lap. We ended up in A&E at the hospital!"

"Good grief. How incompetent."

Louisa worried the tea towel in her lap. "Well, it wasn't really the *waiter's* fault. He was reaching over Martin, and he bumped him in the head with his elbow. You can imagine how your nephew reacted to that. The waiter was startled when Martin yelled, and he spilled the tray."

"Well if it wasn't the waiter's fault, I certainly hope you're not suggesting it was Martin's fault. That waiter shouldn't have been reaching over him in the first place. Yes, Martin can be very abrupt, to say the least. But in this case, it sounds like a good lambasting was warranted."

Ruth got up and went to the sink for a glass of water. "But that's really not important. I assume everything checked out all right or your husband wouldn't be asleep down the hall."

Louisa took in a ragged breath and sighed heavily. "He's fine. Sore, but fine. I should have taken him home, though, when he said he was tired."

Ruth poured two cups of espresso and set them on the table. "Well, it doesn't sound like any serious damage was done. It does concern me that you don't trust Martin to know what he needs or to know when something's too much for him. He's not a child, Louisa. He's been on his own pretty much all his life. He's certainly capable of knowing what he *is* or is *not* up to doing."

Louisa looked nervously down the hall. "I think I'll just ..." she said as she gestured towards her husband's room.

"I'm sure he's fine, but suit yourself," Ruth said.

Having satisfied herself that Martin was still safely asleep in his bed Louisa returned to the kitchen.

"You're right, Ruth," she said as she sat back down at the table. Her fingernails tapped against the side of her teacup. "Martin just seems so vulnerable right now. But I do tend to treat him like a child at times."

Ruth reached across the table for the sugar bowl. "Yes, he *is* vulnerable right now, but far from helpless. I would suggest you try to remember to encourage but not push. My nephew neither needs pushing nor does he respond well to it—a typical Ellingham."

A loud wail came through the baby monitor, and Louisa set her cup down to go check on her son.

"Will you keep an eye on Martin, Ruth? I'll be right back."

"I'll hold down the fort." The elderly woman sighed and shook her head.

Jeremy had arrived by the time Louisa returned with James, and Ruth had apprised him of the morning's goings-on.

"Good morning, Mrs ... er, Louisa. I was just going to check on your husband."

"Hi, Jeremy. Martin wants his morphine dose cut back. He woke up feeling pretty miserable. I was afraid he was going to pull that IV out completely. Maybe you could talk to him about it?"

"Certainly, Mrs. Ellingham."

"It's Louisa, Jeremy. Just Louisa," she said as she gave him a smile.

"Yes, sorry about that. I'll try to remember."

Louisa put James in his high chair and got him started on his breakfast. "Another cup of coffee, Ruth? Or tea?"

"Maybe a cup of tea. Thank you."

"We did get a bit of good news yesterday," Louisa said as she set a bowl of tea bags in the centre of the table. "Ed said Martin's fractured femur showed good callus formation. He'll likely give him the okay to be total weight bearing when we go in on Wednesday."

"That is good news. That should speed the recovery process up immensely."

"Why is that?"

"The physiotherapists can do so much more with him, and he'll be up on his feet more, putting weight on those bones. There's typically marked improvement once patients are up and walking."

"Oh, Ruth, I'm excited for Martin."

"Well, don't set your hopes too high. Mr. Christianson will have to get pictures of the right and left tibia and fibula before he makes a decision. That left leg is going to be lagging behind the right one. And Martin has a long road ahead of him yet, so don't expect things to improve overnight."

"I'll try to curb my enthusiasm."

"Just temper it with pragmatism, dear. Being able to get around easier will be a big step in itself."

Louisa dumped dry cereal on to James's high chair tray and gave him a Sippy cup full of milk. "I'm going to go see how things are going in the other room. Could you watch James?"

Ruth moved herself to the chair next to the baby. "I think I can manage for a little while."

Martin was awake, and Louisa could hear his slurred mumblings as she approached the room. Jeremy had the blankets pulled back and was examining his legs when she reached the doorway.

"All okay in here?" she asked.

"Louisa, tell Jerrmy to shut the drip off. I don' need it."

"Martin, I agree with you. I *did* cut your morphine back, but you know as well as I do we need to taper you off or you'll end up with problems," Jeremy said before trying to direct his patient's attention away from the contentious issue of pain medication.

"The oedema in these legs has gone down nicely overnight. Let's get you sitting up a bit and when the extra drugs have cleared your system we'll get you in the shower. Sound like a good plan?"

"Mm, I s'pose so."

The aide raised the bed, and Martin shook his head trying to clear the fog from his brain.

"Do you have an appetite? I could get you something to eat," Louisa said.

Martin's face paled at the very suggestion, and he could feel his stomach begin to churn.

"Oh, gawd no," he groaned. "Jerrmy, I need to lay back down."

The aide readjusted the bed and pulled the blankets back up. "You're the boss. Take a few hours to sleep it off, Then, we'll see how you're doing ... okay?"

"Yes."

Jeremy pulled Louisa aside as they walked down the hall. "Mrs. Ellingham, could I have a word with you, please?"

"Sure. Let's go into the living room." She glanced towards the kitchen, hoping Ruth was faring all right with James.

She took a seat on the sofa, and Jeremy sat down next to her.

"I think we need to discuss how much activity is too much for your husband," the aide began. "He was really exhausted last night, and the discomfort he was in was obvious."

"I know, Jeremy. I should have just brought him home after we got done at Jaeger's. That's what Martin wanted. I should have listened to him," she said as she drummed her fingers on the armrest.

Jeremy was venturing into dangerous territory by interfering in a couple's relationship, but Martin was his patient ... his responsibility.

"Mrs. Ellingham—Louisa, it's none of my business how you and your husband make decisions—under ordinary circumstances. But these aren't ordinary circumstances. You really *must* let Dr. Ellingham set the limits right now.

"I met with Dr. Parsons and Mr. Christianson last week, and they cautioned me to watch that your husband didn't overdo ... that he's not a patient who needs to be pushed, but he might not recognise when he needs to ease up a bit. Would you agree with their assessment?"

Louisa laughed nervously. "Chris and Ed know my husband very well. In some ways, Chris knows him better than I do. Martin hasn't been able to accomplish what he has in his life without a great deal of determination.

"But what happened yesterday has nothing to do with Martin, Jeremy. When he said he was tired and wanted to head home rather than meet our friends for lunch, I should have listened." Louisa rubbed at her temples. "I *will* need to talk to him though. He didn't have to be so harsh with that waiter. He certainly didn't need to yell at him the way he did."

Jeremy hesitated. "Would you like to hear my thoughts on that?"

"I have a feeling you're going to tell me whether I want you to or not," she said, giving him a contrite smile.

"I think your husband had been pushed too far. He was tired, probably hurting, and it was an uncomfortable situation for him ... knowing people were looking at him. And he'd had to navigate getting in and out of the van, hitting his head in the process. I think you should give him a pass on this one. Let the subject drop."

"Hmm, you might be right."

A loud clatter came from the kitchen. "Oh, James Henry Ellingham! You're going to be the death of your old Aunt Ruth."

Louisa gave the aide a quick smile. "I better go see to that."

Jeremy sighed as he watched her hurry off.

Chapter 32

It was after eleven o'clock that morning when Martin finally began to stir. Given a bit of time to adjust, he was able to sit up on the edge of the bed with neither dizziness nor nausea.

Jeremy was only expected to spend two hours in the morning and two hours in the evening in the Ellingham home, but with his patient sleeping off the heavy narcotics he'd received, the aide stayed until Martin had awakened, helping him into the shower and then into clean clothes.

"Bet you feel like a new man now, hmm?" Jeremy said in jest.

Martin looked down at his fractured limbs, then back up at his aide. "Ah. That was a joke, wasn't it?"

"Yep, that was a joke. I think your wife's been working on a nice dinner, so let's go get something to eat."

Louisa breathed a sigh of relief when she saw her now lucid husband enter the kitchen, and she turned away from the cooker to lean over and give him a kiss—a kiss that lingered long enough to cause a restrained Martin to squirm in his wheelchair.

"Louisa, people are watching!" he whispered stridently as he glanced uncomfortably at his aide and his aunt.

"Good, then they'll see how much I enjoy loving you, won't they," she whispered into his ear.

He cleared his throat and rolled his chair back. "I'll just go ... wait for dinner. Mm."

"Jeremy, you can stay and eat with us I hope?" Louisa said as she placed a large bowl of roasted broccoli on the table.

"I'd like that. I'm not a great cook myself, so I tend to eat a lot of sandwiches. Can I help with anything?"

"No, you've been working. Just sit down and relax," Louisa said.

The aide pulled out a chair and took a seat next to Ruth.

Martin stopped beside his son and reached his hand up to brush his fingers across his jaw.

"How are you James?" Martin asked. The boy pulled himself to the side, peering down at his father's wheelchair. He slapped a hand against Martin's cheek and gave him a wonky grin.

Louisa pulled the pièce de résistance from the cooker, and with much pomp, set the large platter down in front of her husband.

"Broiled monkfish ... no butter—just the way you like it," Louisa said.

"Thank you, it looks delicious." Martin's mouth salivated as he stared at the dish in front of him. "Erm, what did you make for everyone else?"

Louisa stood frozen in place, staring back at him. "I thought this would be enough ... for everyone."

"Mm, sorry. It was meant to be a joke," he said, dipping his head.

Louisa's moment of panic dissolved into relief, then into a smile. "It was a good joke, Martin."

His cheeks nudged up as her eyes sparkled back at him.

Sunday progressed much more uneventfully than Saturday had. The added morphine that had upset Martin in the morning had worn off completely by mid-afternoon, and his hearty appetite had returned. Louisa watched him as he sat in his wheelchair working on his laptop, pausing now and again to take a swig from one of the two protein shakes on the small table next to him. If he wasn't working on exercises with Jeremy or napping, he was sure to be eating. The number of calories the man was ingesting everyday was astounding to Louisa, especially given the fact he was still struggling to put on weight.

"What are you doing there?" she asked as she walked up from behind and wrapped her arms around him.

He jumped, startled by her sudden presence. He quickly moused over and closed the window he'd been looking at, but not before she glimpsed enough to know the web page had to do with child abuse.

"Mm, just doing some reading. How are you? Did James go down for a nap?"

She nuzzled her nose into his neck. "Yes, he did. He's a very good little sleeper."

Martin's thoughts wandered from the present to the past briefly, remembering the long sleepless nights he experienced as a child. Often having been awakened by a nightmare, he would be afraid to close his eyes again for fear he would fall back into the same horror. Instead, he would reach for the copy of *Gray's Anatomy* his grandfather had passed on to him. The Latin and Greek word roots and combining forms were predictable, and they gave him a sense of reassurance.

His wife's lips on the back of his neck prodded him out of the past. "... going to need you to remind me, okay?"

When he realised he had no clue as to what his wife had been talking about he began to squirm. She came around in front of him and crouched down.

"Martin, you weren't listening to me, were you? Did you hear *anything* I just said?"

"*Yes*. Yes, I did." He tugged at his ear and shifted his gaze to the ceiling. "I may have missed a bit of it ... before the part about reminding you."

She patted his cheeks and gave him an understanding smile. "I was apologising for what happened yesterday."

"But that's not your fault, Louisa. If that moronic twit hadn't—"

Louisa pressed a finger to his lips. "Martin, stop talking."

"Mm. Yes."

"I'm sorry for not listening to you when you said you wanted to go home ... that you were tired. I'm sorry I've fallen into a habit of making decisions for you ... about what you need or don't need. That day I insisted you take James to Millie's Playgroup, how you should spend your time with James, and yesterday ... Well, I thought it would be good for you to spend some time with the Parsons."

"I did enjoy some of it. The chicken was quite good."

"Yeah, well it didn't end very enjoyably." She got to her feet and leaned down to press her cheek to his. "You're my husband. My very responsible—intelligent—and gifted man. And you got through life splendidly before I came along, and you can continue to get through life without me deciding what *is* and *is not* good for you. That's what I need you to remind me about, Martin."

"I see." He pulled his head back and stared at her, his gaze penetrating. "I wasn't really getting through life splendidly, Louisa. I was just ... getting through."

Louisa stood up and kissed the top of his head. "Do you feel like a nap while James is sleeping?"

"Mm, I'm really not very tired. After sleeping all morn—"

Martin found his words cut off abruptly as his wife pressed her lips to his and kissed him passionately. "It wouldn't have to be that kind of nap then, would it?"

Martin and Louisa "woke from their nap" shortly before the first chortles and coos from baby James could be heard upstairs. Louisa collected the boy and set him in his high chair with his afternoon snack before preparing a sandwich for her husband.

"There you go. One turkey and provolone sandwich with lettuce and tomato. Can I get you anything else?" she asked as she brushed a hand across his head.

"No, this is good, thank you."

She pulled out a chair and sat down across from him. "Martin, if Ed gives you permission to be weight bearing as tolerated, does that mean you can go for walks with James and me again?"

Martin washed his bite of sandwich down with a sip of his shake. "That'll be a while yet. I need to work on my balance and strength, as well as my proprioception skills. And I don't have to tell you Portwenn isn't exactly flat. So, try not to expect too—to get your hopes up."

"Hmm, Ruth said the same thing."

Louisa's noticeable disappointment was felt by Martin as guilt. Guilt for the inconvenience his long convalescence was causing her, as well as guilt for the anxiety and worry he knew his wife was feeling. And he had become more aware of the years he had spent "lonely and miserable", as Auntie Joan would say. Years lost to the effects of his upbringing. And it made the awareness of the time ticking by during his recovery all the more acute.

"I'll work as hard as the physical therapy people will allow me to."

Louisa reached across the table and took his hand. "Martin, I have no doubt you will. But do try to remember to not overdo, all right."

"Mm ... yes."

There was a rhythmic knock on the door, and the legs of Louisa's chair screeched across the floor as she got up to answer it.

"Joe! Come on in!" Louisa returned to the table. "Martin, Joe's stopped for a visit."

"Yes, I can see that," he grumbled.

"Hi ya, Doc! You're lookin' better ... a bit. Glad to be home I bet!"

Martin's scowl deepened further. "Yes. Is there a purpose to this visit, Penhale?"

"Well, it's not really a visit, as such. More of a police matter. Are you up to a little cha-*t*? You're still looking kinda' peaky." He put his hands up in front of him. "I mean you always look good. You're just maybe looking a little—less good."

A headache set in behind Martin's eyes as the policeman's nasal voice grated in his ears, and his habit of dragging out the words he found to be particularly relevant prolonged the conversation.

"You know, with you not havin' your *suit*. And your *tie* all *tied*. So, we can do this anoth—"

"*Penhale*. What do you want?"

"Right, Doc. I'll get right to it. You asked me to check up on the Hanleys. I heard you were home—well not *home* exactly— but anyway, I thought I'd stop and give you a report."

"Have a seat, Joe. Can I get you a cup of tea ... or coffee?" Louisa asked.

"A cup of tea would be nice. If you got any of that orangey tea that comes in the little tin ... the one that's shaped like a cat, that'd be nice," Joe said as he laid his baton on the table, hoisted up his tool belt and sat down.

A low grumble caused Louisa's eyes to snap a warning at her husband. She turned back to their guest and gave him a tense smile. "Sorry, Joe. All I have is tea bags." She set the bowl on the table in front of him.

"Oh, that's too bad." He wrinkled up his nose as he picked through his options.

Louisa poured hot water into his cup and then lifted the baby from the high chair. "I'm assuming this is confidential, so I'll just take James upstairs for a while."

Martin's eyes widened as he watched his wife disappear around the corner, suddenly feeling defenceless, left at the mercy of Joe Penhale.

"So, what is it Penhale?" he asked, his lip curling as he watched the man spill tea on to the tablecloth before brushing it away with his hand, shaking the excess on to the floor.

"I checked up on the Hanleys, like you asked."

Martin's jaw clenched. "And?"

"All seemed to checked out okay ... I think."

"What do you mean, *you think*? Did the children seem healthy? Was Mr. Hanley sober when you looked in on them?"

"Well, it's not like I did a breathalyser on him. Didn't have probable cause. If there'd been reason to suspect drink-driving, that'd be probable cause. But he was just sittin' there ... watchin' the telly."

Martin let out a heavy sigh and closed his eyes. What was it Dr. Newell had said ... give a name to his emotions? He had too many negative feelings churning in him at the moment to make heads or tails of any of them, so he named the physical sensations instead. Chest pain and tightness, throbbing in the temples, muscle cramps in his clenched jaw.

He drew in a slow breath. "What was his affect?"

Joe looked back at the doctor blankly. "I don't think I have a device for measuring that one, Doc. And even if I did ... you know ... the whole probable cause *di*-lemma again."

A rush of air hissed from Martin's nose. "How—would you describe—his outward appearance?" he asked through clenched teeth.

The lights appeared to come on in Joe's eyes and he snapped his fingers. "Gotcha, Doc. He looked quite nice actually. Blue plaid flannel *shirt*—it complimented his eyes quite nicely. Brown *pants*— a bit smudgy maybe, but not bad. He might'a even had a fresh haircut—all slicked back, kinda like that guy in the commercials that—"

"Penhale! Did the man seem intoxicated!"

"Oh no, Doc. If that's what you wanted to know, you should'a just asked that in the first place. It's not good for you to get all worked up ... what with your condition and all."

Martin screwed up his face. "I *did* ask that in the first place, you idiot!"

"I must'a missed it, I guess. All those questions about his attire got me distracted. In future, it'd be best to get right to the point."

Joe stood up and returned his baton to the loop on his belt and then walked to the door. "Well, it was nice visiting, Doc. I'll stop back when I have more time ... keep you company for a while."

"Oh, gawd," Martin groaned.

Chapter 33

Monday morning came with bright sunshine, warm temperatures, and calm winds—an unusually pleasant day for Portwenn in late October. Inside the Ellingham home though, the morning was getting off to a rocky start.

James's unhappy cries of distress had roused his parents with a start. He had woken with a runny nose, a cough, and was understandably irritable. He was also cutting another tooth, which only added to his misery.

"Let me take a look at him, Louisa," Martin said as his wife stood in the doorway with James clinging to her, crying into her shoulder.

"I don't want you any closer than you are now, Martin. You're probably going to pick this bug up anyway, but I'm not going to deliberately expose you."

James took in a ragged breath, triggering a coughing spell. Mucous rattled around in his airway as his father looked on helplessly. "What's his temperature?" Martin asked, knitting his brow.

"If I did it right it's one hundred point four. I had to get a new thermometer a few weeks ago, and Mrs. Tishell recommended the infrared kind."

Martin straightened himself up and craned his neck to get a better look at his son. "Tympanic or temporal artery?"

"What?"

"Is it a tympanic or a temporal artery thermometer?"

"Oh Martin, I don't know. I stuck the thing in his ear and it beeped. Mrs. Tishell said this kind of thermometer is very accurate though."

"Well, she must be slipping because she's wrong. You need to get his rectal temperature using a digital thermometer. Call Ruth and have her pick one up at the chemist. And have Poppy give him five millilitres of Calpol every four hours today. But no more unless she consults with me first."

Louisa glanced at her watch. "Yes, Martin," she said before hurrying down the hall.

"And tell her to let me know if the Calpol doesn't knock his fever down ... or if it goes any higher!" Martin slumped back in his bed and breathed out a heavy sigh.

Poppy arrived a few minutes later, and Louisa passed the baby off to her. Preparations for the first day back at school since Martin's return home were not going according to Louisa's original plan.

"Don't worry, Mrs. Ellingham. We covered childhood illnesses in the childminder course Dr. Ellingham enrolled me in. I know what to do. And if there's something I don't know, I'll ask your husband ... or his aide."

Louisa looked anxiously from her son back to Poppy before rushing off to shower and dress for work.

Jeremy arrived while she was upstairs, and by the time Louisa was ready to head off for the school, the childminder and the health aide had things under control.

James had eaten a bit of breakfast and was now being rocked by Poppy, his eyes showing an obvious heaviness. Louisa kissed him lightly on his fuzzy blonde head before scrubbing her hands and going to say goodbye to the other ailing member of the family.

"I need to run. Can I get you anything before I leave?" she asked as she eyed him nervously.

"I'm fine. I have Jeremy if I need something," Martin said, giving a nod towards his aide.

"Hmm, okay. He'll be leaving in a couple of hours though, so make sure you're all set before he goes." Louisa turned her attention to the young man. "You *will* call me immediately if you have any concerns ... if anything happens?"

Jeremy looked up from the patient notes he was working on. "Don't worry, Mrs. Ellingham. We'll be fine here."

Louisa blew her husband a kiss and reluctantly headed out the door.

Jeremy pulled the blankets back from Martin's legs and inspected the wounds for any sign of redness or drainage. "I think the swelling's come down since you came home last week. Hopefully, getting you walking will speed that along a bit more. How's the pain today?"

Martin shifted his gaze to his lap. "There's a bit of discomfort but nothing I can't deal with."

Jeremy tipped his head, trying to make eye contact, but Martin kept his eyes averted. "You know, Martin, the physio people will be starting in with more intense therapy today. You're going to have pain."

"Yes, I'm aware of that!" he snapped.

"Okay. I'll help you clean up and get dressed then."

The aide let the issue of pain medication drop for the time being.

Two therapists from the North Cornwall Physiotherapy Centre arrived mid-morning. They introduced themselves as Max Spencer and Kieran McPherson. Max was a tall, slender fellow who seemed to bear a perpetual grin, which Martin hoped would not get tiresome. And Kieran was a soft-spoken, curly-haired blonde with a thick Scottish brogue—the type who went about his business, seemingly happy in his work.

Kieran began the range of motion exercises Tim Spalding had been doing with Martin, while Max began bringing in equipment they would use later.

Jeremy had been trying to keep his patient's muscles and joints limber, but physiotherapy wasn't his area of expertise, so he had to proceed in a conservative manner. Therefore,

Martin's muscles and ligaments had contracted in the days since his last session with Tim Spalding. So, the same exercises that had been done a week ago, were proving too painful when done with Kieran.

"I'm sorry, Dr. Ellingham. You've stiffened up since your last session in hospital. We can't start with the more intensive exercises today until we get things to relax a bit," Kieran said apologetically.

Martin had been able to swallow back the groans when his left leg was being manipulated. But when the therapist moved to his right leg, the muscles, which had contracted from his calf all the way up the side of his thigh, pulled sharply on the fracture in his femur, left tender by the unfortunate incident at the restaurant. A sudden wail raced from his throat and resonated through the room before he could suppress it.

Poppy, who was preparing lunch in the kitchen, found the stifled groans agonising to listen to. The harsh reality of what the Ellinghams had endured in the last month and a half hit her, and she blinked back tears.

James began to cry upstairs, and Poppy hurried off to retrieve him from his cot.

She took the child's temperature. It had risen slightly, probably because he was due for another dose of Calpol. But the childminder had strict instructions to notify Dr. Ellingham if the boy's fever went any higher, and she had also noticed the baby pulling at his ear.

She vacillated between interrupting Martin's therapy session to inform him of the new developments or waiting until there seemed to be a lull in the activity. This was Dr. Ellingham's son, though, and everyone in Portwenn knew how fiercely protective he was of James.

She tapped lightly on the door jamb and Kieran waved her into the room.

"I'm not s'posed to let James get too close to his dad," she said hanging back in the doorway.

The therapist had been working on Martin's arm and pain was now pulsating through it, radiating into his shoulder. "What do you *want*, Poppy?" Martin growled.

She recoiled, intimidated by the gruff doctor. What sounded to her like anger instantly shattered the little confidence she had gained in the last two months working for the Ellinghams.

Tears came to her eyes and she said timidly, "You wanted to know about James. His— his temperature is one hundred and one."

The pain began to abate in his arm, and Martin wiped the sweat from his face with a towel. Poppy watched nervously, noticing his trembling hand as he gave the towel back to the therapist.

He squeezed his eyes shut momentarily, swallowing several times in an effort to quell his nausea. He took in a deep breath and then looked over at Poppy. She took a step back and turned her head away, but not before Martin saw the tears that had gathered in her eyes.

"Poppy ... erm, when did James last have Calpol?" Martin asked, trying to focus his thoughts on his son's symptoms.

"Four hours ago. But—but he's been pulling at his ear, too." Poppy pulled her shoulders in. "I thought you'd wanna know."

Martin rubbed his palm across his forehead and nodded at the girl. "Yes, I *do* want to know. Could you please call my aunt and ask her to bring my otoscope over for me?"

"Yes sir," Poppy said as she turned and began to move quickly down the hall.

"Poppy! Have her bring my stethoscope and prescription pad from the top drawer in my desk, as well!" Martin called after her.

She returned to the doorway long enough to deliver another, "Yes sir," before she fled down the hall again.

Kieran emerged from the lavatory with a glass of water for his patient. "We're going to take a break, and then we'll start in on the real work, Dr. Ellingham."

Martin collapsed back on his pillow and put his arm up over his face. The image of the childminder's fearful expression popped into his head. He knew he upset people at times. He'd even seen patients leave his office in tears on more than one occasion. But he'd always attributed it to nervous constitutions. Or in the case of his female patients—premenstrual hormones. He had never noticed fear in them. He knew he could be an angry person, but was he a frightening person? Louisa had accused him of scaring her students once. And Morwenna told him a few months ago, people were too afraid of him to bring their children in to be jabbed for measles.

Martin drifted off to sleep but was awakened a short time later by his therapist.

"Would you like some assistance with getting in your wheelchair, Dr. Ellingham?" Kieran asked as he moved the chair over next to the bed.

Martin waved him off. "No. I can do it." He had repeated the transfer manoeuvre so many times he could do it in his sleep.

Wheeling himself down the hall, Martin looked around for James and Poppy. "I'll be back in a minute," he told the therapist before continuing on to the kitchen. He could hear voices as he approached. He found his aunt sitting at the table with the childminder and James in his highchair eating a bowl of chopped peaches.

"Hello," Ruth said, eyeing him curiously as he came around the corner.

He acknowledged her with a grunt before stopping next to the high chair to touch the backs of his fingers to his son's forehead. "Did you bring my otoscope?"

"I did. But should you be so close to him if he's sick? You're immunocompromised."

"Yes, I'm aware of that."

Ruth pushed herself up from the table and stood by her nephew's side. "Here you go, Martin," she said, holding out the instrument.

"Mm. Thank you."

"Poppy, could you put James on your lap so I can look in his ears, please?" he said.

The girl picked James up and sat down next to Martin.

"All right, now hold him against you and grasp his head so that he can't turn away from me."

When the baby began to protest, his father spoke softly to him. "It's all right, James. I'm just going to look in your ears ... see what you have going on in there."

"Maybe I should hold on to him, Martin," Ruth said as she eyed the childminder uncertainly.

"No. Poppy can do this. James is comfortable with her."

Poppy ducked her head as a glimmer of a smile crept across her face.

Martin inspected the right ear first—pink and healthy.

"Poppy, could you turn him around for me?"

The girl shifted the child so his left side was facing the doctor and then held him firmly. Martin distracted him when he began to struggle, shining the otoscope light on to the back of his hand.

"I'm just going to shine this in your ear, James," he said as he stroked his hand slowly across the top of his son's head.

James began to cry when Martin inserted the tip of the specula into his ear, and he pulled at his father's hand.

"I'm sorry, James. I had to see what was bothering you in there." He placed his palm protectively over the boy's ear. "We'll get some medicine for you that'll clear that right up."

"My stethoscope ..." Martin said as he reached towards his aunt.

Ruth handed him the instrument and watched as her nephew worked it under the child's vest.

"Ruth, if I write out a prescription, could you run to Mrs. Tishell's and get it filled?"

"Certainly. Otitis, I assume?"

"Mm-hmm. His lungs sound clear, but he has a pretty angry looking ear. I'm glad Poppy noticed he was pulling at it. The eardrum is bulging significantly." Martin glanced at the girl and did his best to give her a smile.

He scrawled out instructions for the chemist, struggling to grip the biro with his disabled hand. Then he added his signature at the bottom of the sheet of paper before tearing it off and giving it to his aunt.

"Well, I'll be off then," Ruth said as she buttoned up her coat.

"Thank you, Ruth. Tell Mrs. Tishell to put it on my personal account."

Martin waited for her to leave the room and then turned to the childminder. "Erm, Poppy, I'm sorry I yelled at you. I didn't mean to ... I mean, I wasn't angry with you. It had been a difficult session and it ... erm, I was very uncomfortable. You did the right thing by letting me know about James's fever right away. And you showed good observational skills when you noticed him tugging at his ear ... recognised there could be an ear infection."

The childminder blinked back at him. "Okay."

Martin returned to the living room, an uneasiness descending on him. *Louisa's not going to be happy about this* he thought. How was he going to explain to her that he couldn't stand to watch James suffer? That it was genuinely painful for him to sit back and not do anything when he knew exactly what the little boy needed.

Chapter 34

The two physiotherapists helped Martin out of his warm-up pants and vest and on to the portable table, which had been set up in the living room, before beginning the second round of the day's therapy. They put him through the same exercises Tim Spalding had used to strengthen his quadriceps, hamstrings, and calf muscles.

"Sit up as straight as you can, Dr. Ellingham," Max said as he swung Martin legs up on to the table and tucked a rolled-up towel under his left knee. "I want you to straighten your leg for me, and hold it there for five seconds. Repeat that four more times. We'll do five sets of these quad contractions and then add to the length of time you hold the position."

The therapist put his hand on Martin's thigh, assessing the strength of the contractions. "You have surprisingly good muscle tone for a bloke who's been off his feet for six weeks. Tim Spalding must be a slave driver."

Martin's ears, focused on the sounds coming from the kitchen, garbled Max's words. He shook his head and crinkled his eyes at him. "I haven't the foggiest idea. We didn't discuss hobbies."

Kieran and Max exchanged befuddled glances.

Why would they think a reasonably intelligent person like Tim would get involved in something as dangerous as cave diving? Martin wondered.

He refocused his attention on the task at hand, setting his jaw as his recalcitrant muscles fought against him.

"Excellent," Max said. He rubbed cocoa butter on to his hands and massaged his patient's left thigh before moving to the opposite side of the table. "All right, let's work the right leg. Go easy though. I don't want you to be feeling excruciating pain. It's going to hurt, but it should be tolerable."

There was a clatter in the kitchen, and Martin's head whipped to the side, following the sound.

The therapist leaned over and peered into his face. "Dr. Ellingham, did you hear what I just said?"

"I'm sorry?"

"I said this will hurt, but don't overdo it with this fractured femur. I don't want you to be in agony tonight."

Martin heard the back door open and Ruth's voice in the kitchen. "I'll be back in a minute," he said as he swung his legs over the side of the table. Max and Kieran hurried to his side as he slid from the table and dropped into his wheelchair without the benefit of an assist pole.

"But, Dr. Ellingham, we're not finished yet," Kieran said as Martin disappeared down the hallway. He looked over at Max, shrugging his shoulders.

"Did you get the amoxicillin?" Martin asked as he entered the kitchen.

"Yes, I did and—" Ruth eyed her nephew, giving him a lopsided smile. "Poppy and I can manage medicating the child, Martin. I am a doctor you know."

"Yes, I realise that." He craned his neck to see around the elderly woman. "Poppy, try using a bottle teat. Some babies will—"

Poppy was already prepared, pouring the measured dose of medicine into the teat she had placed next to her on the kitchen table.

"Oh." Martin gave a sharp nod of his head. "Very good."

The childminder smiled, watching the white liquid disappear as the ever-hungry little Ellingham sucked it down.

She looked up at the doctor. Her gaze was drawn downward before flitting to the side as a flush spread across her face.

Martin glanced at his lap, realising he was sitting in front of her in nothing but his boxer shorts. "I'll just ... be off then," he mumbled, ducking his head and moving quickly from the room.

The therapists put Martin through a series of exercises, working different muscle groups in his legs. By the time they finished, Jeremy's words of warning were echoing through his head as the pain seemed to be intensifying rather than abating.

Kieran took over, and Max took a seat on the sofa.

"They tell me I'm the upper limb specialist, so Max and I'll split some of the duties with your therapy. He's especially good with the lower limbs, so we make a good team," the young man said as he rested Martin's arm on a small shelf attached to the edge of the table.

"I spoke with Mr. Christianson about starting in with the palmar pronation/supination exercise. He thinks you're ready, but he gave me strict instructions to proceed carefully. I was surprised to hear the occupational therapist at the hospital had tried this more than two weeks ago."

"Mm, it didn't go very well," Martin said, grimacing at the memory.

"Yeah, I bet. You would have been putting way more force on those bones than they could take at that point. I bet my mum heard you all the way to Glasgow."

"Mm." Martin grunted as he shifted his weight from his throbbing right femur.

"All right, Dr. Ellingham, we'll start out with the basics. Keep your hand on the shelf, palm down. Then lift your fingers one at a time for me."

This was an exercise Martin had done ad nauseam over the course of the last two weeks, and his efforts were rewarded by the therapist's broad grin.

"Now let me see you touch each of your fingers to your thumb."

Martin found this particular activity more difficult, and at first it had been agonising. But he thought he'd seen improvement with time, in both the level of discomfort as well as with the strength and dexterity in his hand and fingers.

"Good. Now I want you to hold that right arm out in front of you, palm down. Then, very slowly, turn it palm up."

Martin began to raise his arm, but a sudden snap in his shoulder caused him to drop it back to his side as he tried to squelch the accompanying yelp. Kieran moved forward quickly and placed his hands under his patient's upper arm to give him some support.

"Anytime you're ready, Dr. Ellingham, slowly turn that palm up."

Martin began to rotate his hand, trying to ignore the excruciating movement of the bones in his forearm.

"Where's your pain at?" Kieran asked as he closely watched his patient.

At the moment, the pain Martin was experiencing was compounded by the sickening sensation of the pin movement in his muscles as the bones rotated. "Maybe a six—or a seven."

He had come to appreciate during his hospitalisation how difficult it could be for a patient to accurately quantify and describe pain. The quality of his own pain affected the degree of perceived intensity.

His pain had varied from dull to sharp, stabbing to persistent, a burning pain compared to an ache. He found he had a tendency to rate a persistent pain lower than he might a stabbing pain. It was frustratingly difficult to accurately describe what he was feeling to his doctors and nurses.

"Okay, stop rotating your hand. Just hold that position for a moment." A pallor had become apparent on Martin's face. "Is the pain letting up at all, getting worse, or is it staying the same?"

"Mm, I think it's letting up a bit."

"All right, turn your hand a little more, but if the pain gets any more intense than it was before, I want you to stop again."

It was difficult and painful, but Martin eventually had his hand in a palm up position.

Kieran then had him reverse the process. Going from palm up to palm down was excruciating, and Martin's groans could be heard by Poppy and Ruth in the kitchen.

"It doesn't sound like a fun time for my nephew." Ruth took a sip of tea and tried to return her attention to her newspaper.

Poppy took James upstairs for a nap shortly before Louisa arrived home for lunch.

"Hello, Ruth. You're a nice surprise. Can you stay for lunch?" Louisa slipped her coat off and hung it up on a hook by the door, setting her bag on the floor.

"Yes, I do believe I can. I'm afraid my refrigerator is empty at the moment, so my next stop will have to be the market."

Louisa set the salad that Poppy had prepared on the table. "Well, how do you think Martin seems to be doing?"

Ruth went to the sink and filled her teacup with water. "I haven't seen much of him. He's been busy with his therapists, and I had to make a trip to the chemist for James's prescription."

"Why? Has his cold gotten worse?" Louisa said, glancing towards the hall.

"He's fine, dear. Martin checked him over and discovered he has an ear infection. He's on antibiotics and will soon be on the mend, I'm sure."

"Martin? Martin checked him over?" Louisa's eyes narrowed as she pursed her lips. "Excuse me, I'll be back in a minute."

Her shoes hit heavily on the floor as she went in search of her husband. She found him in the lavatory, washing up.

"Martin Ellingham! Ruth just told me you were handling James. Is that true?" She stood in the doorway with her hand perched on her hip, glaring down at him imperiously.

He glanced up at her before returning to his laboured attempts to remove the sweat from his body. "Poppy noticed James pulling on his ear. His temperature was up slightly, and he was irritable. I strongly suspected an infection. I couldn't ignore it, Louisa."

"I could have taken him over to Wadebridge later, Martin. You *unnecessarily* exposed yourself to whatever James has. Do you *really* think that was a smart thing to do? Hmm? I'm not happy with you, Martin."

He released a heavy breath and tossed the face cloth over the edge of the bathtub before turning his wheelchair around. "Excuse me," he said. He waited for his wife to step aside and then rolled himself into the bedroom, pulling open a dresser drawer and removing a clean vest.

Louisa watched him struggle to work the right sleeve over his arm, the stretchy fabric repeatedly snagging on the pins that protruded through his skin. His movements became more and more frenetic until his arm dropped to his lap, and he seemed to surrender to the garment.

He sat motionless for a moment, his back to her. Then he reached out and slammed the drawer shut.

His hand came up to cover his face, and Louisa could just make out the sound of his ragged inhalations. She pressed her fingers to her temples and drew in a slow breath before walking over to crouch down next to him.

"Tough morning?" she asked as she rubbed her hand gently across his shoulders.

He sat silent, his head turned away.

"Here, let me help you." After untangling the fabric from her husband's fixators, she worked the sleeve carefully back over the pins. Then she slipped the neck over his head and held the left sleeve while he pushed his arm through.

"Martin, did I overreact just now?" she asked as she pulled the shirt down around his torso.

"No, of course not." He sat quietly, gently massaging his aching right hand. "But ... maybe you need to hear me out *before* you react."

"Martin, I can't imagine what you could say to justify what you did. I can't understand why you would deliberately expose yourself to James's germs."

"And I don't know if I can explain it so you *can* understand why I did what I did."

She put a hand against his cheek. "Why don't you give it a try."

He turned a pained gaze to her. "I'm a doctor. I couldn't let James suffer longer than was necessary. I could help him. He's my son, and I could help him."

"I'm very aware you're a doctor, Martin. But you're also a patient who's recovering from a *very* serious accident. A patient who's immunocompromised. I could have made an appointment for James over in Wadebridge."

"Yes, but they wouldn't get him in over there until later today. I couldn't leave him to suffer on his own when I knew I could help him." Martin dropped his head into his hand. "I couldn't stand it, Louisa. Knowing he was hurting and not doing anything. I just wanted to stop him from hurting."

He sat with his eyes closed for a few moments, finally mumbling, "I'm not like my father. I don't ever—" He pulled in a breath. "I don't *ever* want to be like my father."

"I think I see." Louisa reached out and took hold of his fingers, gently caressing them with her thumb. "You were afraid James would feel what you felt when your father left you to suffer with your broken arm. Having the medical skills to help you, but leaving you to suffer."

"Mm."

She cocked her head at him. "I do understand now, Martin. And I'm very glad you're *not* like your father. And James is very, very lucky to have a father who loves him enough to risk getting sick to come to his aid."

"It's a rhinovirus, Louisa. I can deal with a sore throat and a snotty nose."

"Well, still." She got to her feet and leaned over to kiss his cheek. "I'm sure you wore a mask. That will have reduced your chances of picking up whatever James has, I'm sure."

Her brow furrowed as her husband began to fidget in his chair. "Martin, please tell me you at least took *that* precaution!"

He blew a sharp hiss of air from his nose. "I didn't want to frighten him. When I had young surgical patients, they were terrified of the masks."

Louisa shook her head. "You don't want James to be afraid of you ... the way you were afraid of your father. Is that it?"

"Mm." Martin hesitated before asking, "Louisa, do people find me frightening?"

She gave him an apologetic smile. "Sometimes you can be a little intimidating, yes."

"I see." He stared off across the room.

"But only if they don't know you very well. I think once people get to know you, they see you differently. You're a big man, Martin. And an imposing personality. You pull that illusion off very well anyway."

She patted his shoulder. "We better go and eat the lunch Poppy's worked so hard to prepare, hmm?"

Martin's ears began to burn at the thought of the girl. "Could you help me get some warm-up pants on first?"

Chapter 35

The aroma of food cooking led Martin to the kitchen for lunch, while, with her maternal instincts calling, Louisa had made her way upstairs to check on the baby. He was sleeping soundly but with the tell-tale snuffly breath sounds of a child with a cold. With her fingertips, she transferred a kiss from her lips to the baby's head before re-joining the rest of the family downstairs.

Louisa had warned Poppy about Martin's ravenous appetite, so the childminder had more than compensated, preparing enough tossed salad and chicken soup to feed a small army.

"Poppy, this soup is delicious!" Louisa said, giving her husband the overly vigorous nod of her head that was his cue to reinforce the compliment.

"Yes," he mumbled.

She shot him a warning glance, and he added flatly, "It is."

Martin really didn't find the meal to be anything more than adequate, and his forced cajolery seemed less than honest. He had planned to thank the girl for making the meal and leave it at that. He found the disciplinary style his wife used with him to be both annoying and belittling, and he made a mental note to raise the issue with Dr. Newell.

The afternoon seemed to drag on interminably. Ruth had set off to get her groceries, Louisa had returned to the school, and James slept most of the day.

Martin worked on the assignment from his psychiatrist, watching a rebroadcast of a television program called *Coronation Street*. There were definitely plenty of facial expressions to analyse and what seemed to Martin to be an excessive use of exaggerated body language. One of the characters, a ruddy-faced, white-haired woman, bore an uncanny resemblance to his Auntie Joan.

He pressed the power button and tossed the remote aside. What would the last year have been like if Joan were still alive, he wondered. She would have delighted in spending time with James Henry, been completely at sixes and sevens over his and Louisa's marriage, and been ... The last six weeks would have been very hard on her. It was maybe just as well she hadn't been here. But he missed her terribly.

He laid his head back on the pillow and closed his eyes. The therapy earlier in the day had left him with a persistent pounding in his limbs, and it was perhaps best to try to sleep the rest of the afternoon away if he could. He tried to allow his body to relax and his mind to block out all of his many fears and worries of late. He soon drifted off into a fitful slumber.

He sat in Ed Christianson's office, entertaining himself by batting a crumpled-up piece of paper around on the desktop. He'd been to radiology for his CT scans, and he was now forced to wait to find out whether or not he would be allowed to start bearing full weight on his fractured legs.

The door opened suddenly, and Mr. Christianson strode into the room, brows bumped together in a scowl.

"Martin. How are you today?"

"I'm fine. Hoping you have good news for me." He pulled at his collar, trying to loosen the tie that seemed to be preventing adequate oxygen from reaching his lungs.

"I'm afraid it's bad news, my friend. You compromised your recovery when you recklessly exposed yourself to your son's illness the other day. We have malunions in every one of your fractures. We're going to need to delay your fixator procedure."

The surgeon leaned back in his chair, folding his hands behind his head and throwing his feet on to his desk. The fixators on his lower limbs clanked against the metallic piece of furniture.

Martin looked with envy at the man's hardware. It was so unfair. He had only wanted to help James, and now it seemed as if he was being punished for caring about his son.

He felt a heaviness in his chest. This meant more weeks, possibly months, of waiting to be able to get out of the bloody wheelchair. He nodded his head in resignation then turned his chair and wheeled out the door to head down the hall.

"Hey, Mart! What's the verdict?" Chris Parsons called out as he approached from the other end of the corridor, his fixators jutting proudly through the side seams of his trousers.

Martin heaved a heavy sigh. "I bollocksed it up, Chris. I'm going to have to wait. The cold I picked up from James has set me back."

"I'm sorry, mate." Chris looked down at him sympathetically. "Buck up, though; it'll happen for you. Keep up with the physical therapy, get plenty of rest, eat an optimally nutritious diet, and you'll get there. You'll have your fixators, just like everybody else."

Chris patted him on the shoulder before moving down the hallway.

Wheeling himself forward, Martin stopped at the lift and pressed the down button. When the doors opened, his lovely wife was standing in front of him. She looked stunning—her fixators following the curves of her legs in a strangely seductive manner. He couldn't keep his gaze from lingering on them. He found his heart palpitating and the colour rising in his cheeks.

"Oh, Louisa," he murmured.

"Are you ready to go ... go home and maybe take a romantic walk along the Coastal Path? Then we could head off to bed a little early tonight, hmm?" She gave him a coquettish smile.

"Louisa, I can't. Ed said we need to postpone my procedure. I'll have to wait for my fixators. I still can't be the man you want me to be ... not in that way."

Louisa pursed her lips and crossed her arms in front of her. "I told you, Martin! You never should have exposed yourself to James," she said crossly as she turned her back to him.

She drove him back to Portwenn in stony silence.

Ruth walked into the kitchen with James in her arms as Martin and Louisa entered the back door of her cottage. He gazed with a heavy heart at the shiny metallic three pointed star logos on the sides of his aunt's fixators. They matched the hood ornament on her car and announced the superior quality of the Mercedes brand as they reflected flashes of light back into his eyes.

Ruth set little James down on the floor, and he toddled over to his father, the special hardware on his short legs keeping him upright.

"How did the appointment go? Do you get your fixators? Are you going to be back up on your legs again?" Ruth asked.

"Martin has to wait," Louisa said through clenched teeth. "His illness has set him back, I'm afraid." She blew out a breath and threw her purse on to the kitchen table.

Martin tipped his head down. "I'm sorry, Louisa. I really am sorry." He couldn't possibly feel any lower than he did at that moment.

There was a loud banging at the door before Joe Penhale burst through, his police issued hardware jangling noisily. "Doc! It's Bert Large. I think he's havin' a heart attack or something!"

The doctor's mind immediately began to formulate a plan of action. "Louisa, call Morwenna. Tell her to go to the surgery and get my defibrillator kit ... bring it to Bert's. And tell her to hurry!"

He wheeled his chair out the door and down the ramp before propelling himself down Dolphin Street to Middle Street, racing towards the Platt. He slowed slightly before making a sharp right turn on to Roscarrock Hill, the cornering forces and inertia causing the left wheels of his chair to lift into the air.

Joe raced ahead of him, his baton clattering loudly against his fixators, beating a steady rhythm as he hurried up the steep grade.

His arm aching intensely, Martin laboured to pump the lever on his wheelchair back and forth, moving himself frustratingly slowly up the hill. Heat began to build in him, and his vest was soon soaked with sweat.

Martin stirred from his sleep slightly. He knew he was hot. Terribly hot. He pulled impotently at the blankets covering him, sapping the little strength he had. He tried to wake himself from the ridiculous nightmare but fatigue sucked him back into the implausible delusion.

A feeling of panic set in when he reached the restaurant and looked down the long, steep stairway leading to the terrace. He could never make it down those steps! Not without fixators. He could see Bert sitting in a chair, his body listing heavily. The man had a plump hand to his chest, and he was gasping like a fish out of water.

Footsteps could be heard approaching from behind, and the singsongy voice of Mrs. Tishell rang out.

"Helloo, Dr. Ellinghamm!"

Martin twisted in his chair as the women ran up from behind. He looked up at her, horrified by what he saw. Her ubiquitous white cervical collar had been replaced by a ring of metal, held up in Frankensteinian fashion by pins jutting from the sides of her neck.

"Mrs. Tishell, what's happened to you?" he asked, wracking his brain to come up with any sort of medical explanation for the absurd apparatus.

The chemist ran her finger slowly and suggestively along the ring on the front side of her neck. "Oh, this? Do you like it Doctor?" she purred.

"Of course not, it's hideous!"

A disturbingly seductive smile spread across her face as she undid the top button of her jumper and leaned over, wrapping her arms around him.

"Oh, Dr. Ellingham! You do like to tease me, don't you!"

"*Oh, dear, oh, dear! You better be careful there, Doc. Louiser's not goin' to be happy to hear about this. Not happy a'tall!*" Bert Large said chuckling jovially.

Martin pushed defensively at Mrs. Tishell's roaming hands as he craned his neck around her to get a look at his possible cardiac case. The portly man stood in front of him, his industrial strength fixators revealing themselves from behind his green apron.

"*Bert! Your chest pain ... it could be an ischemic attack! Sit down for God's sake!*"

"*Oh, don't worry about that, Doc. Just a touch of heartburn, it was. A bit too many bowls of my special soup. Fast as I slurp it down, Jenny fills it back up. And I keep eatin'!*" He chuckled again.

Martin felt helpless, trapped in his wheelchair in the clutches of the potty chemist. "*Mrs. Tishell! For goodness' sake, let go of me!*"

"Martin. Martin, wake up. You're dreaming. You need to wake up," Louisa said. She shook him, trying to rouse him. "Martin, wake up!"

Martin yanked his arm away from her. "I said *let—go!*" He tried to roll away, but his movement was restricted by the hardware on his limbs.

Louisa wrapped her arms around his body and put her cheek against his, talking softly in his ear. "You were having a nightmare. Open your eyes and it'll all go away."

Martin's gaze darted as the ceiling stared back at him. He locked a wild-eyed stare on his wife's face, and then slapped his hand over his eyes, rubbing them vigorously as he attempted to erase the disturbing images left from his dream.

"You lie still, and I'll get you a glass of water," Louisa said as she walked towards the door.

He shook his head as he tried to make sense of what was going on.

Louisa hurried back into the room, setting the glass down on the nightstand. "Let's sit you up, okay?" she said as she raised the head of the bed.

Martin let out a low groan as he brought himself to vertical, his entire body complaining.

"What is it? Does something hurt?"

"Everything hurts!"

"I'm calling, Chris. Stay there, I'm going to get my mobile."

"Louisa!" He groaned. *"Louisa!"* he called after her.

Louisa came back into the room and stood by her husband's bed, wringing her hands.

"Don't—call Chris, just give me a—a minute."

"Martin, you feel hot. I think you're sick. Do you feel sick?"

"Yes, but it's Mrs. Tishell. Don't call, Chris."

"But you said everything hurts."

"No, I think I'm having pain from the therapy this morning is all."

She cocked her head at him. "What *about* Mrs. Tishell, Martin?"

He patted the mattress beside him. "Just come and sit down. Give me a chance to get my head together."

Louisa passed him the glass of water and then went around, climbing on to the mattress before taking his hand in hers. "That must have been some dream you were having. Why don't you tell me about it, hmm?"

Martin gave her a scowl. "It was utter nonsense is what it was," he muttered. "Nonsense."

"Still, I'd like to hear about it."

He heaved out a heavy breath and rolled his eyes. "It was absolutely ridiculous." He eyed his wife uncertainly, and then cleared his throat. "Everyone had fixators except for me; you couldn't walk without them. And I had to wait for my fractures to heal to get mine. I'd bollocksed things up by catching

James's cold. Somehow, being ill caused malunions in my fractures and— See, I told you it was absolutely ridiculous!"

Louisa caressed his arm. "I'm finding it quite interesting actually—go on."

He let out a long groan as his chin dropped to his chest. "Everybody had them. Chris, Ed ... even James."

"Really?" Louisa looked at him wide-eyed, her interest in the story now piqued. "Little, tiny, baby fixators! How cute!"

"You can't be serious, Louisa. There was nothing cute about it. Without them, James wouldn't have been able to walk! They were the only thing holding him up!"

She gave him a small smile. "Well still, it sounds quite cute to me. But go on, I want to hear more. Did Ruth have them?"

"Mm." Martin looked at his lap. "They had the Mercedes emblem on them," he mumbled.

Louisa's hand went to her mouth, trying to stifle a giggle.

"Louisa! It's not funny! It was strange ... *creepy*."

He picked at the blanket. "Joe Penhale came barging in the door of the kitchen at one point—his baton clanking away against his metal hardware. He said Bert Large was having a heart attack. *Idiot*. It turned out to be heartburn from eating too much of his soup. I'd raced down to the restaurant— risking life and limb by the way! Then Mrs. Tishell showed up and... Oh, gawd." He covered his eyes.

"And?" His wife's eyes narrowed, and her lips pulled into a thin line. "I want to hear it, Martin."

"No, no, no, no, no. It's nothing like that." A shudder rippled through his body. "She wasn't wearing her cervical collar. She had a metal ring around her neck ... pins protruding from the sides. She looked like Dr. Frankenstein's bloody monster. Then she was grabbing on to me. I couldn't get her off!"

Louisa began to giggle again, pulling her hands up over her face.

"Louisa, it's really *not* funny."

Her giggles grew until she was doubled over and in tears. "I'm sorry, Martin. It *is*!"

"Louisa!"

She took in a deep breath and held it until she had regained her composure.

Martin screwed up his face. "It's not funny. It was *awful*! I couldn't get the woman to let go of me."

"You're right, it's not funny. I mean ... it is funny, but I shouldn't laugh." She pulled a tissue from the box by the bed and dabbed at her eyes. "Oh, dear."

A restrained smirk appeared on her face. "So, what were mine like?"

"Your what?"

"My fixators. Anything special or just your everyday, run-of-the-mill fixators?"

Martin could feel the blood rushing from his neck up to his cheeks and ears. He tipped his head down as he answered her. "They were ... special. They, er ... They curved—nicely. They matched the shape of your legs."

A gentle smile slipped across Louisa's face. "Well, at least I'm special in your dreams," she said as she nuzzled her face into her husband's neck.

Martin pulled back and looked at her, his eyes slightly glazed. "You are *always* special." He tipped his head so he could reach her lips with his and he kissed her, the intimacy of the moment quickly intensifying. His hand slipped under her blouse, working its way up.

Louisa caressed his cheeks with her palms before pulling back quickly. "You *are* hot, Martin. I'm going for the thermometer. I hope you're not getting sick."

Martin watched as his wife disappeared around the corner, along with his hopes for something more. "Bugger," he muttered.

Chapter 36

"Thirty-eight point two. You *have* a fever," Louisa announced emphatically as she held the thermometer up to her husband's face to prove her point. "I'm calling Chris."

"Louisa, I feel fine. Let's just wait an hour or two and see where it's at then."

She pushed him back on to the bed and pulled the blankets up around him. "See, you're not thinking clearly either. Now I'm sure I should call Chris. I'm going to ask Poppy to stay a bit longer until we get this sorted."

"But, Louisa it's—" Martin watched her hurry off. "Pffft. Fine. Call Chris. How could I possibly know what I'm talking about? Why can no one seem to remember I'm a bloody doctor?" he grumbled to himself.

Voices could be heard in the kitchen, and it wasn't long before Ruth appeared in the doorway, her purse slung over her shoulder.

"Martin, Louisa mentioned you're unwell," she said as she walked slowly over to the bedside.

"Aay! I'm fine. It's just a low-grade fever."

Ruth pressed her hand to her nephew's forehead. "Hmm, yes. Well, she *is* right to be concerned, you know."

"It's being handled, Ruth. It's most likely just an inflammatory response to the physiotherapy today. Is there any other reason you're here?"

Ruth gave the blankets a gentle tug up around his neck. "As a matter of fact, there is. I was wondering if, since you're at a loose end at the moment, you might consider doing a bit of work for me. The old grandfather clock at the farm has quit working, and Al and I don't seem to be able to diagnose the problem."

"I would most certainly be interested in taking a look at it, but I'm a bit cack-handed to do the job right now, don't you think?" Martin pulled the blankets back down and sat up.

"Oh, I don't know. Maybe you could look at it as therapy?" She plopped her purse down on to the bed.

"I'm likely to make a hash of it, you know."

"Really, Martin. I've never known you to make a hash of anything."

Martin's thoughts went immediately to his romantic history with Louisa. Obviously, his wife hadn't shared his many less than stellar moments with his aunt.

He rubbed a hand over his head. "I could take a look at it for you sometime and do what I can, but I won't make any promises."

Ruth picked up her purse and moved towards the door. "Fair enough. Perhaps this weekend? You and Louisa and the child could ride out there with me. Al and I could show you around."

Martin reached over to the dresser and picked up his glass of water. "Mm, I'll discuss it with her and get back to you. Erm, how are things working out for you ... staying at the surgery?"

"Reasonably well. I get the occasional uninformed villager looking for medical assistance, but they're usually easy enough to move along." She stopped in the doorway and stared back at him.

"Don't take any chances with this fever, Martin. After all you've been through, even something that seems trivial now could bring everything down on top of you. You need to stay ahead of things."

"Yes, I realise that."

After Ruth had gone, Martin slipped into his wheelchair and headed down the hall to look for his wife. As he neared the end of the corridor, he could hear her voice in the living room. He stopped, trying to make out who she was talking to. She was on her mobile. *Must be Chris,* he thought. But she sounded upset. He had just begun to move his chair forward when she uttered words that brought him to a stop.

"We'll see what Wednesday's appointment brings, but I'm afraid if there hasn't been considerable improvement, that's it. I just can't deal with this anymore."

There was a pause on his wife's end of the conversation, and Martin sat waiting in his chair, his brow furrowed as his stomach began to churn.

"I'm sorry if that sounds harsh, but there's a limit to what can be asked of a person, and I'm afraid I passed that limit long ago."

His heart was pounding, and it felt as if he'd been sucker punched. He waited anxiously to hear her next words.

"Yes, I realise he's your friend. And I *do* feel for him ... you know I do; I'm not completely heartless. I just can't take having to deal with any more problems, and that's all I see in the future, I'm afraid."

There was a long pause before Martin heard Louisa speak again. "I'm sorry. He'll have to find someone else to lick his wounds for him. I'm just too tired to keep nursing the man along. If we don't get a good report on Wednesday, that's *it.*"

Martin turned his chair around and headed back to his room, just catching her parting words. "Fine, I'll see you on Wednesday."

Louisa heard soft cries beginning upstairs and hurried to her son. She laid him on the changing table and took his temperature. She knew Martin would be requesting that information. The baby had soaked through his nappy, so she quickly wiped him down with a wet flannel before changing him into clean clothes. After pulling off the sheets in the baby cot she headed back downstairs.

As she passed through the hallway, with James on one hip and the laundry under her other arm, she stopped to look in on her husband. He was sprawled out on the bed in his usual daytime fashion, with an arm flung up over his face. She continued towards the kitchen and dropped the laundry in front of the washing machine before settling James into his high chair.

"There we are, James, some of Poppy's delicious soup." Louisa set a bowl down in front of the boy and sat down at the table. She worked through some of the paperwork she had brought home with her, glancing up occasionally to watch as her son picked at the bits of vegetables and chicken she had strained from the lunch leftovers.

Trying to eat with a stuffy nose was making James irritable, and he pushed the bowl over the lip of the highchair tray and on to the floor.

"Oh, James Henry. You *do* have your father's temper, don't you."

Louisa was wiping up the floor, and James was just starting in on his bananas, when Jeremy arrived for his evening shift. He greeted Louisa and tousled James's hair as he passed by.

"Jeremy, it seems Martin's running a fever. Both he and Chris Parsons think it's from the physiotherapy this morning, but I'm not so sure. You might want to check his temperature. The thermometer's upstairs on the changing table in James's room."

A sneeze squeaked from the baby's mouth, and Louisa was hit with a shower of macerated banana and saliva. Jeremy grabbed the facecloth from by the sink and ran it under the faucet before handing it to Louisa.

"Thank you, Jeremy. Erm, you should know ... Martin had contact with James this morning. Poppy noticed him pulling on his ear, so of course your patient couldn't resist checking him over. James has an ear infection, so Martin prescribed amoxicillin."

"All right, I'll go check in on him," Jeremy said as he headed towards the hall.

"He might be sleeping. He was just a bit ago."

His patient was still lying on his back when Jeremy looked in on him, but his eyes were open and he was staring at the ceiling.

Martin couldn't quit thinking about Louisa's words. Just three days ago, she had promised she would never walk out on him again. And he had said he would trust her. Had she had a change of heart? He had been difficult. Maybe she hadn't realised how much he would need from her.

I do trust you, Louisa. The fear of being unwanted again was lurking just beneath the surface. *But please don't leave.*

Jeremy tapped lightly on the door, reluctant to interrupt what he could see was a contemplative moment. "Martin, may I come in?"

He raised up quickly, the movement eliciting a groan. Jeremy hurried to lend him assistance before raising the head of the bed.

"How did the therapy go this morning?"

Martin closed his eyes and shook his head.

"Ah, kinda brutal, eh?"

"Yeah. It was harder than I'd anticipated."

The aide reached into the bag he had placed on the dresser and pulled out a thermometer.

"Hmm, one hundred and one." He began to check Martin's surgical wounds and pin sites. "How are you feeling ... apart from the soreness from therapy?"

"I'm fine ... just tired."

Jeremy pulled a stethoscope from his bag and placed the diaphragm against his patient's chest, shifting it periodically.

"Okay, Martin, lean forward for me." The aide's brow lowered as he moved the instrument around.

"I'm hearing pleural rubs on the right side. See if you concur, Doctor," Jeremy said as he handed Martin the stethoscope.

Martin nodded his head. "Mm. I agree."

He looked up at his aide, and the left corner of his mouth curled ever so slightly as he gave him another nod.

"Are you having chest pain?" Jeremy asked as he thumped his fingers against Martin's back.

"Yes. I thought it was from the thoracotomy."

He tipped Martin back on to the pillow. "Could be, but you and I both know it's likely pneumonia. I'll give Dr. Parsons a call."

He hurried from the room, returning a few minutes later.

"Dr. Parsons and Mr. Christianson want me to get you started right away on a heavy hit of broad spectrum antibiotics. They want chest films as soon as possible, so they've shifted your appointment with Mr. Christianson up a day—get everything done in one fell swoop."

"Mm. So I'll find out about weight bearing tomorrow then?"

"'Fraid so. Let's wait until morning to do the shower. I think your body's been stressed enough for today."

"I'm fine with that," Martin said, rubbing his hand over his eyes.

"I'll call over and cancel your session tomorrow. Dr. Parsons is calling in a prescription to the chemist here in Portwenn. If they don't have it on hand here, it can be picked up in Wadebridge."

Jeremy stepped out of the room to fill Louisa in on the latest developments.

"I hate to take James out in the chilly air. I'll call Ruth, and she can pick up the prescription," Louisa said as she reached for her mobile.

"Oh, I was planning to pick it up," Jeremy said as he lifted his coat from the hook by the door.

Martin wheeled his chair into the kitchen. "What's this?"

"Jeremy volunteered to pick up your antibiotic. And what are you doing out of bed, Martin?" Louisa asked.

"I'm hungry," he said as he reached for the handle on the refrigerator door.

Louisa snapped her fingers at him. "Back to bed, now! I'll *bring* you something to eat."

He gave her an indignant look before pulling the door open quickly, grabbing two of his shakes, and turning to head back to his room.

When Jeremy returned from Mrs. Tishell's with the necessary medication and supplies, he piggybacked the antibiotic on to Martin's drip. They would know after the scans the next day about the extent of the pneumonia.

Martin lay awake that night, long after Louisa had drifted off to sleep, spooned up against him. The worries about tomorrow's appointment churned in his head. He tried to focus on the warmth and softness of the woman next to him, nestling his face into her neck and breathing in the sweet smell that never failed to send his senses reeling. "I trust you," he whispered softly as he pulled her close.

Chapter 37

Louisa's eyes slowly drifted open. The room was bathed in the soft light of early morning. She listened to Martin's slow, rhythmic breathing and determined he was still asleep. Rolling over, she studied his face, reaching a hand out to brush her fingers ever so lightly across the top of his head. Baby James had inherited so many of his father's physical characteristics. The blonde hair, sturdy build, and of course, the hands.

She delayed leaving the warmth of their shared small bed, resting her eyes and mentally going through the day's schedule. When she opened them again, Martin was looking back at her.

"Good morning," he said, pushing her hair away from her face. "Did you sleep well?"

"I did. How about you?"

"Fine." Martin took in a short breath before his mouth opened and closed several times.

"What?" Louisa asked.

"Mm. Nothing—nothing."

She was familiar with the look on his face. The first time she saw it was the morning in the taxi, after the horrible incident with her student, Peter Cronk. It was the look that meant he had a question but was afraid to ask it. As if he instinctively knew it would get him into trouble if he opened his mouth and let the words spill out.

Sometimes he could hold the words back, and other times it seemed he just couldn't help himself. That morning in the taxi was, unfortunately, the latter. But this morning, Louisa's instincts told her to risk whatever embarrassing medical discourse might be perched on his tongue and prod him further. "Martin, what were you going to say?"

He was looking at her, gazing into her eyes in such a penetrating manner that it made her self-conscious.

She sat up and pushed him on to his back. Leaning over, she locked eyes with him. "Martin Ellingham, you have a question you want to ask, and I *want* you to ask it. I won't be angry, no matter what words come out of that mouth of yours. So just ask it."

Martin took in a breath and licked his lips. "What if the news isn't what you'd—what we'd hoped to hear today?"

She furrowed her brow and cocked her head at him. "Well, I suppose I'd be disappointed."

He blinked his eyes slowly as he stared at her. "I mean, will you be—or are you—especially now with the pneumonia—are these problems getting to be too much? Or if Ed says the fractures need more time to heal, how will you feel about that?"

Louisa shook her head. "Well, of course, my first concern is for those lungs of yours. It'll be a huge relief if that all checks out okay. The bones will heal in their own time. We'll just need to be patient a bit longer if your legs aren't ready for you to be putting full weight on them yet."

She traced the outline of his mouth with her fingertip. "I know you'll be disappointed if Ed says you have to wait, but try to remember, Martin ... it's only been six weeks. We can be patient a little longer, hmm? And I'll do my best to keep you distracted while we wait."

She reached under his vest and ran her hand across his chest before leaning over to kiss him, her lips lingering before she pulled back to look at him.

"Is there more you wanted to ask?"

"Erm, who—who were you talking to on the phone yesterday ... after work?"

"Remember, I called Chris ... about your fever."

"Ah. I thought as much." He shifted his eyes away from her and looked distractedly out the window at the brightening sky. "No one else then ... that you talked to?"

"Well, Stu Mackenzie called me." Her brows pulled together. "Why do you ask?"

"Stu Mackenzie? Who's Stu Mackenzie?"

"Mar-tin, he's on the Board of Governors ... you served with him." Louisa nodded her head, willing him to remember.

"Ah. Yes."

"Do you recall the mess that was created when the year two teacher got sick and had to quit?"

He gave her a vacant stare.

"Oh, *Mar-tin!*" She huffed. "*Remember?* I couldn't find a replacement, so I had to do all that shuffling around." She circled her hand in the air. "When I moved Trisha Soames from year five to year two."

"Who?"

"Martin, you are impossible sometimes! Trisha Soames ... the reason you didn't show up that night we were supposed to meet for drinks at the pub."

"Ah, yes. Short, high-strung woman with chapped hands. She should've been wearing gloves when she did the washing up."

"Rrright. Anyway, Stu suggested we hire his best friend from college. A recent divorcee who couldn't bear living in the same town as his ex-wife. The man was looking for a teaching position elsewhere, but he didn't want to teach a younger lot. So, against my better judgement, I let Stu talk me into hiring him to teach year five, and I moved Trisha to year two."

She sat back on her heels and screwed up her face at him. "Martin, I've told you about all of this before! Weren't you listening?"

He deepened his scowl. "I'm sorry, I don't follow. Why did you hire him if it went against your better judgement?"

"Oh, Martin. That's not the point!"

"What is the point then?" he asked, shaking his head.

Louisa huffed out another breath. "The point is, Martin, it's been a nightmare having the man on staff. He's like Mark Mylow times ten, only without the sweet side. Constant whinging about how miserable his life is ... things never working out for him. We all have to listen to him moan and groan about it ... dragging the staff right down with him. He even depresses the kids! At least Mark seemed to enjoy being our constable. This guy complains constantly about being a teacher.

"And he refuses to follow the school's teaching outline, doesn't show up for meetings, you name it.

"There's an appointment on Wednesday with a woman from the district office ... a liaison. I've tried to work with the man, but I just can't take the stress of having him on staff for another term. I'm going to have to dismiss him if the liaison can't convince me tomorrow the man can and *will* make a concerted effort to right himself."

"Ah."

Louisa gave her husband a sideways glance. "Are you smiling? Do you find this humorous, Martin? Because I assure you, it isn't! And if you've picked now, of all times, to bless me with a rare Martin Ellingham smile ..."

Martin pushed himself up on the bed. "No! No, no, no, no! I'm just—just—" He let out a sigh. "I overheard your conversation. I thought you were talking to Chris."

"I don't understand. Why would I talk to Chris about a teacher at the—"

Louisa squeezed her eyes shut and winced. "Oh, dear. You thought I was talking to Chris about the *doctor's* appointment? Martin, I would never, ever, *ever* abandon you to deal with something like this on your own. How could you possibly think tha—"

Louisa realised suddenly that less than three months ago, she was doing just that. It may not have been physical wounds her husband had been dealing with at that time, but he was wounded nonetheless.

She put her hands on his cheeks. "I told you— *promised* you I would never leave you again. You still don't trust me, do you?"

Martin looked back at her, his cheeks nudging up. "*That's* why I was smiling, Louisa. I did trust you, and you—you didn't let me down." He raised his head to look at her.

Her eyes were moist with tears. "I think we're improving. You're trusting me more, and I'm becoming more worthy of that trust."

She took hold of his hand. "I do understand, Martin, that your trust in me may be shaky at times. That's to be expected. The important thing is that your trust in me continues to grow stronger. And if you ever feel shaky, *talk* to me, because I think it's going to eat away at any trust we've built up between us if either of us is harbouring any doubts."

"Mm, yes." Martin's gaze was fixed on her. He reached up and buried his fingers in her hair, pulling her back down on the bed with him. Then he kissed her passionately before giving the day a proper start.

Martin and Louisa sat in Ed Christianson's office later that morning, listening as the man spoke from the opposite side of the desk.

"Your CT images look excellent, Martin. There's a good amount of soft callus formation at the fracture sites, and we're starting to see some hard callus development, too. The left leg is lagging behind the right, but that's not a surprise. I sent the pictures to Robert, and he was pleased as well. So, here's how we'd like to proceed.

"I'm recommending we get you over to Wadebridge ... get you into the hydrotherapy pool at the physiotherapy centre. That's doable now, isn't it? Chris says you've rented a van?"

"Yes, we've rented a wheelchair accessible van. So yes, we can make trips to Wadebridge," Louisa said.

"Good. I'd like to see you in the pool everyday this week. Then next week we'll try putting full weight on those legs when you're on dry land." Ed tapped his biro on the desktop as he flipped through Martin's patient notes.

"Okay ... next order of business ... that arm. We're seeing slow progress there, but it *is* happening. You need to accept that the fixators on your arm are going to be your constant companions for another seven to ten months or so. We'll need to make adjustments to the amount of tension we have on them as well as tweaking the alignment of the bones as we go along, but I'm optimistic."

Ed rolled his chair back and stretched his feet out in front of him. He reached out to grab a large envelope, giving it a shove across the desk. "Your chest films, my friend. Tell me what you think."

Martin took the envelope and passed it to Louisa. "Could you hold on to that, please?" he said before pulling the plastic sheets from their protective sleeve. He held them up to the light overhead, scanning over them carefully. "Some consolidation in the lower lobe of the right lung, ill defined borders, no significant volume loss. A simple segmental pneumonia."

"I'd concur with you on that. And given the fact that your temperature is down today—probably streptococcal. I'm glad your aide caught the pleural rubs."

"Yes. I was attributing the chest pain to the thoracotomy and the fever to the rigorous therapy session yesterday."

Ed rose from his chair. "A lesson learned about the lack of objectivity when a doctor tries to diagnose himself, maybe?"

"Mm."

Louisa sat, her head swivelling back and forth between the two men. "Excuse me. Are one of you two doctors going to translate this into layman's terms for me, so I'll know if I can stop worrying?"

Ed quickly reclaimed his seat. "I'm sorry, Louisa. Your husband has a strep bacterium pneumonia. It's confined to the lower lobe of his right lung—probably just getting a toehold in there. The antibiotics we have him on seem to be doing the job, though."

"So ... no need to worry?"

The surgeon shrugged his shoulders. "We need to keep tabs on it, but it's not unexpected given Martin's recent medical history. I think it'll rectify itself within the next couple of weeks."

Rolling his chair forward, Ed rested his elbows on his desk, steepling his fingers. "Louisa, the day Martin was dismissed from hospital, I told you he was going to be sick a lot. This is round one, and I think he'll weather it with no problems. Just don't let this stubborn bloke dismiss any concerns you may have. Call if you're worried about something. Chris or I will let you know if it's nothing to fret over."

Ed rose from his chair again and saw them to the door. "Martin, again, it's been a pleasure. Keep up the good work. It really *is* paying off, mate."

As he rolled his wheelchair out into the warm rays of the October sun, Martin felt a huge weight lifted from his shoulders. Louisa followed behind him as he made a left turn towards the bench where he sat with Tim Spalding a few short weeks before. The therapist had shared some wise advice with him that day, and Martin had taken it to heart.

"I thought we could sit for a little while," he said shyly.

Louisa lowered herself on to the bench, taking his hand in hers and giving it a reassuring squeeze. Martin was feeling quite optimistic about the future as he sat here in the same spot, this time with a positive prognosis and with his wife.

Chapter 38

Aside from a quick diversion to Jaeger's to pick up Martin's altered clothing, there were no extra stops between Truro and Portwenn on this trip.

Martin had felt energised after the good report they received, but by the time they arrived back at Ruth's, he was ready for a lie-down. Louisa looked in on James, napping in his cot upstairs, and then grabbed a bite of lunch and hurried off to the school.

The baby woke shortly after his mother left the house. He was, as is any baby with a cold, irritable and unsettled. Poppy brought him downstairs to the kitchen and sat him in his high chair while she measured out his amoxicillin.

Jeremy arrived just as she laid the baby on her lap to dose him with the medication. "Here, let me give you a hand," he said. He poured the white liquid into the bottle teat while the childminder held on to James.

His hand brushed Poppy's as he wiped a bit of the sticky liquid from the boy's face. "Thanks," she said, pulling up her shoulders and giving him a shy smile. She glanced at her watch. "Yer awful early. You and Dr. Ellingham working on your paper again?"

The aide's fingernails clicked against the tabletop as he averted his eyes. "No ... no. I just thought I'd—well ... I was having lunch at The Mote with a friend. I thought I'd stop and see how things went over in Truro. They back yet?"

"Yeah. Mrs. Ellingham's gone back to the school and I think the doc's sleeping."

"Ah. I better not disturb him then," the aide said as he picked up the spoon Poppy had used to measure the baby's medication and took it to the sink. "Are you from the village?" he asked.

"Yeah. I was born here. My mum and dad were, too." She shook her head. "Well, not *here*—here," she stammered. "I mean in Portwenn. Well, no—not in Portwenn. At the hospital in Truro."

"Yeah, I figured." Jeremy gave her a crooked grin and grabbed the tea towel from the door of the cooker.

"I can't imagine living in the same place that long," he said as he dried the clean items and laid them on the kitchen table. "So, your parents have never lived anyplace other than Portwenn?"

Poppy spooned the last of the baby's peas into his mouth, and then placed a bowl of bite-sized pieces of hard-boiled egg on his tray. "Nope. That's the way it is with a lot of people around here. I guess they're happy in the village and don't see much point in goin' anywhere else."

Poppy stood up and went to the refrigerator to find her own lunch. "Can I get you something to eat? I'm going to have a sandwich. I could make you one, too ... if you want."

Jeremy hesitated. He had actually already eaten a rather hearty lunch and had no room left in his stomach, but this was an opportunity to get to know this girl. There was something about her he found quite charming.

"Yes, a sandwich sounds good, thank you. Can I help you with anything?" he asked.

Poppy glanced over at the table. "Erm, maybe you could make some tea? If you want tea. I don't mean you have to have tea. There's milk or coffee if you..." Poppy's gaze wandered to the young man's face. Their eyes fixed momentarily on one another before shifting to their appointed tasks.

"No, no. Tea's good. For you, too?" the aide asked as he filled the tea kettle with water and plugged it in.

"Yes, please." Poppy focused her attention on the slices of bread on the countertop but reeled around quickly when she heard a strangled cry coming from the baby. She hurried over to him. James's face had turned red and he was kicking his feet wildly, pulling at his bib.

"Jeremy! He's choking on something!" Poppy said as she quickly unbuckled him and pulled him from the high chair.

James screwed up his face as if to cry, but no sound was heard. Poppy dropped into a chair and peered into the boy's mouth. Not seeing anything, she flipped him on to his stomach, laying him across her forearm, and gave him several sharp slaps on his back. Nothing. "Get Dr. Ellingham!" The childminder turned James on to his back and looked again for the obstruction—nothing.

Martin had just woken from his nap when the commotion began, and he hurried into the kitchen, nearly colliding with Jeremy. He watched helplessly as the girl worked to clear his son's airway.

After two several unsuccessful thrusts to James's chest and two more slaps to his back, a chunk of boiled egg popped from his mouth, followed quickly by a gasp for air and a loud wail. The child made eye contact with his father and reached his arms out to him.

Martin gestured to Poppy to give him the baby. She looked at him uncertainly before Jeremy stepped in and took James, setting him carefully on Martin's thigh.

James pulled at his father's vest, seeking a more soothing position against his chest. Martin boosted his son up, his bum in the crook of his left arm, and the baby buried his face in his shoulder.

"It's all right now, James. Shh-shh-shh-shh-shh. You're all right," Martin said softly.

Poppy watched the tender moment between the sweet child, James, and his gruff and intimidating father, seeing a different side to the man.

He looked over at Poppy. "What was he choking on?" he asked, his voice trembling as he struggled to control his knee-jerk reaction to lash out at the girl.

"It was hard boiled egg. I'm sorry, Dr. Ellingham, I thought I'd chopped it up enough that he wouldn't..." Poppy's eyes began to fill with tears as the realisation of what had happened hit her. She hurried out of the kitchen and took refuge in the living room.

Martin took in a deep breath, trying to loosen the vise-like tightness in his chest as he watched her hurry away. Jeremy walked over to clean up the blob of food that had been blocking the baby's airway.

"Jeremy, let me see that before you bin it."

The aide dropped it into his patient's hand.

"Could you take James, please," he said as he passed the now calmer baby to the aide.

Martin wheeled his chair down the hall, looking for the childminder. He found her sitting on the sofa, her hands shaking as she held them between her knees. She lowered her eyes to the floor when she saw him enter the room.

"James is fine now," he said as he wheeled his chair up next to her. He got no more response from the girl than a small nod.

He sat awkwardly, trying to find words that might comfort her, but none of the prepared phrases he had stored away in his head seemed appropriate. He decided to take a more direct and impersonal approach—an approach that felt more natural to him.

"Poppy, you did everything correctly. James's nasal passages are swollen due to the viral infection he has; therefore, airflow through his nose is very limited so he breathes through his mouth. I believe he had a mouthful of food, and when he inhaled through his mouth, he aspirated the egg he'd been chewing. What he brought up when you performed the Heimlich manoeuvre was very small bits of food. His choking had nothing to do with improper food preparation."

Martin waited for any sort of response but got none.

"You performed the manoeuvre perfectly, Poppy. James could have choked to death, but he didn't because you knew what to do. You stayed calm, and you did your job. You did it well."

Still no response from the girl.

Martin scratched at his head. "Poppy, is there anything I can say to make you feel better?"

The childminder shook her head, her eyes still focused on the floor.

"I know this was a frightening experience," Martin continued. "When things like this happen it's always frightening. But you need to stay calm and focus on what steps need to be taken at the moment, then let yourself feel the fear later. That's what you did."

Poppy raised her head up and looked at Martin. "Thank you, Dr. Ellingham. You're a good teacher," she said giving him a timid smile.

He cleared his throat and pulled in his chin. "Mm. I don't know about that. You better get back to the kitchen."

Martin wheeled himself into his bedroom and took a moment to steady his nerves. Seeing his son in such a serious state had shaken him to the core. He didn't even want to consider the outcome had Poppy not been able to jar the obstruction free from James's throat. He could have tried to perform a tracheotomy with his injured hand, but he knew he could have done more harm than good during the attempt.

In the seconds James was without air, Martin's thoughts were on nothing but the best treatment options should Poppy's attempts fail to help his son. But once the obstruction had been cleared, it had taken every ounce of self-restraint in him to not allow his fear for James's safety to come out in a rage towards the childminder.

After he had regained his sense of composure, he realised it would have been not only an unfair reaction, but an unreasonable one as well. He recalled his psychiatrist's recent words to him about how anger can mask other emotions. He hadn't given it a lot of thought before today, but this was his typical response to fear. Fear that he felt internally was quite often displayed outwardly as anger.

"Well, I believe tranquillity has returned to the kitchen," Jeremy said as he stuck his head into the bedroom. "How did the appointment go this morning?" The aide asked, drumming his fingers on the doorjamb.

"It went very well. I received an excellent report on the fractures—good soft callus formation on the lower limb fractures. The arm's a bit slow, but it's coming. Mr. Christianson would like me to go over to Wadebridge every day this week to work with the therapists in the pool. I was wondering if you might be available to help out with transportation."

"Sure. Let me know what time you need to be there, and I'll make it work. What about the lungs? How did they look?" Jeremy asked.

"Not too bad. You were correct though—a lower lobe simple segmental pneumonia in the right lung. The antibiotics seem to be effective, so it's likely streptococcal. Both Mr. Christianson and I are impressed you caught the pleural rubs. Well done."

The aide stood, momentarily speechless. He had heard enough about Martin Ellingham to know he was very economical with the accolades, and that he didn't give them unless they were well deserved. "Thank you, Dr. Ellingham."

Martin shifted his gaze quickly to his lap. "Mm."

Jeremy crossed his arms in front of him. "Can I get you anything? You're probably hungry."

"Yes. Yes, I am. And, er ... after lunch I'd like to take a shower. Louisa picked up some new clothes for me this morning ... if you could give me a hand."

"Certainly."

When Louisa came home from work that afternoon she found Martin and Jeremy hovered over papers that were strewn across the kitchen table. James was in his high chair next to his father, playing with his new fire engine and his purple dinosaur.

"What are you doing?" Louisa asked, peering over her husband's shoulder.

"It's Jeremy's paper on deficiencies in our home health care system," Martin mumbled, his eyes not leaving the work in front of him.

"Your husband's agreed to help me with formatting, deciding what to stress in the paper, that sort of thing."

Jeremy was obviously thrilled to have Martin's assistance with the work, but Louisa wasn't as keen on the idea.

She placed her hand on her husband's shoulder. "Don't you think you should be in bed? You *are* sick you know."

"I'm fine, I've had *plenty* of sleep today." Martin turned his attention to his aide. "Jeremy, you don't need all of this in your first page," he said as he drew a red circle around the sentences in question.

"But those are important issues that need to be addressed," the aide said.

"Yes, I realise that. But the majority of the people who make these decisions are self-important, parsimonious nits. They aren't going to remember *any* of this if you throw too much at them at once. You can take it up in a later paper.

"And they're too enamoured with themselves to give a tinker's damn about whether or not increasing funding would benefit a handful of people living out in the back of beyond. Emphasise the expenditures that will result in cost savings. You have to appeal to their tight-arsed—"

"Martin!" Louisa pulled her hand back away from his shoulder, and for the first time since she arrived home, he turned to look at her. She stared back at him, gimlet-eyed.

"What?" he asked.

Her ponytail whipped back and forth. "Oh, Mar-tin!" She gave a huff before shifting her focus to dinner preparations.

Martin looked over at his aide, pulling up his bottom lip and giving his head a tip to the side. "Stress the most important issues first and then tie up the loose ends later. You're not likely to keep their attention past the first page. If you haven't persuaded them by page two, the rest is irrelevant."

Jeremy had a meeting in Truro that evening. So, after giving Martin his daily injections, he showed Louisa how to change out the bottle on her husband's drip and then left early.

As she was coming downstairs after putting the baby to bed, Louisa noticed Martin sitting on the sofa with his feet up, reviewing the changes Jeremy had made to his paper. The aide had helped him into some of the new clothes she had picked up earlier in the day, and from her position on the stairs, Martin looked like his old self again. *Well, minus the suit,* she thought. She stood for a while, watching him as he flipped through the pages. *Oh, Martin, you do look handsome tonight.* She remembered how the day had started off and it made her smile.

He looked up when he heard the steps creak, and his breath quickened at the sight of her. "Hello."

"Hello," she said as she approached from behind, putting her hands on his cheeks. "We're all alone."

"Mm, I noticed that." He reached back and grasped her wrist, pulling her forward. "It's a nice evening. Do you want to go sit outside for a bit?"

"Oh, Martin. We better not; you're sick."

"Louisa ... please."

Martin was getting tired of being confined to his aunt's cottage, and it *was* an unseasonably warm evening.

"You have to wear a jacket ... and let me put a blanket over your legs."

He opened his mouth to argue but thought better of it. "Yes."

Ruth's cottage didn't provide the spectacular view that the surgery did, but it was picturesque in its own way. Quaint old buildings flowed down the hill on either side of them, visitors welcomed by their illuminated doors.

Louisa had helped Martin shift from his chair to the bench on the front porch, and he sat with his arm wrapped tightly around her shoulders. He filled his lungs with the sea air. How he had missed this during those weeks in hospital.

The old school was perched on the cliff, like a soldier standing sentinel over the children in the village.

The steady pounding of the ocean waves on the cliff rocks was a mere whisper by the time it reached their ears, the noise muffled by the houses around them.

"This is very nice, Martin. It was a good idea," Louisa said, laying her head on his shoulder.

"Mm, it is nice." He hesitated. "Erm ... I'm sorry to spoil the moment, but..."

She reached her hand up and pressed a finger to his lips. "Then don't, Martin."

He stared at her for a moment before tipping his head down to place a kiss on her lips, lingering. He pulled back, brushing his fingers across her cheek.

Her thoughts turned again to how their day had begun. "Maybe we should go ..." she said, giving a hesitant nod towards the door.

"Mm." He kissed her again. "Louisa ... I should tell you ..."

She became lost in his eyes as they fixed on hers. "*Shhh,* you are *not* obliged, Martin. Remember?" she said softly.

"Mm. I do remember," he said, his words flowing in the soft, velvety voice that could make her weak in the knees. "Your horrid friend's concert."

"Mar-tin," she said, shaking her head.

"Wasn't that the night?"

"Yes, but why do you—" She sighed softly as his hand settled on hers before sliding slowly up her arm.

"I asked if you were wearing perfume," he said, his fingers teasing open the buttons of her cardigan. "It was Kenzo Flower ... am I right?"

"Martin ... don't—" She drew in a breath as he leaned forward to brush his lips along her collarbone.

Pulling back, he looked at her, his eyes glistening in the light from the street lamp at the bottom of the hill. "That was one of the most memorable, most—" There was a little hitch in his voice. "—most painful nights of my life."

"I'm sorry, Martin," she said, tipping her head back to gaze up at him. "I hurt you."

"Mm. It was painful because I hurt you. I didn't mean to. I was trying to explain—"

She silenced him with a kiss.

"Louisa ... I really do have to spoil the moment, I'm afraid. Something happened today I need to tell you about."

She stiffened. "Yes?"

"Everything's fine now, of course, but there was an incident with James. He choked while he was eating lunch."

"What do you mean, he choked?" Louisa said, getting to her feet.

"He had no air getting through."

"Oh, Martin! I need to go check on him!"

Martin grasped her hand. "He's fine, Louisa. By the time I reached the kitchen, Poppy had things in hand. She knew what to do. She stayed calm and everything's fine. I just wanted you to know."

She shook her head. "I still think I should go check on him."

"Okay. Go check on him. But ... maybe you could come back. I liked where things were going ... before I spoiled it."

"I liked where things were headed as well." She bent down and held his head to her breast. "Don't go anywhere." She lowered her voice and gave him an impish grin. "*I'll be back.*"

"Louisa, that's not becoming for a lady," he gently admonished her.

Chapter 39

Martin woke Wednesday morning feeling tired and out of sorts. He had insisted Louisa sleep upstairs, so when Jeremy arrived at six o'clock to help him get ready for his physiotherapy appointment, her sleep would not be disturbed. He found himself regretting that decision as he tossed and turned, unable to fall asleep until after 2:00 a.m.

When Jeremy arrived, he helped him shower and dress. The two men then went to the kitchen, and the aide boiled four eggs for Martin and two for himself.

"I rang Mr. Christianson yesterday, Martin. I thought I'd better check in with him to see what he wanted me to do with your central line," Jeremy said as he set a plate of toast and a jar of marmalade on the kitchen table. "We're going to pull that out this morning—see how you do on the oral analgesics."

"That will certainly make it easier to move around. I feel like I've been on the end of a leash for the last six weeks," Martin said as he scooped marmalade on to a slice of toast, smearing it around the best he could using his right hand and the back of the spoon.

"Jeremy, I'd like you to give some consideration to an idea I had while I was lying in bed awake last night."

"What's that?" the aide said as he peeled the top of the shells on his eggs and set them aside.

"I think I'm going to go completely barmy if I sit around here for the next four months. If I work hard at it, I could be fit enough to start seeing patients sooner than that, perhaps in a few weeks ... *if* I have an assistant. I'd like you to think about helping out in the surgery for a while." Martin peered up from his plate.

Jeremy quit chewing and stared across the table at him. "Are you serious? You're bloody serious! Martin, you—you're—" the aide stammered, waving his spoon at his patient's broken limbs.

"*Yes*, I'm aware of my current condition. But I think this could be a workable solution. I would of course compensate you fairly for your contribution to the practice." Martin poured milk into his tea and stirred it in.

"What do you think Mrs. Ellingham will think of this idea? Or Dr. Parsons ... Mr. Christianson?"

Martin picked up a toast soldier from his plate and poked around absentmindedly in his boiled egg. "I think I can persuade them ... *if* you're on board with it."

Jeremy washed down his toast with a sip of tea and set his cup down slowly. "Martin, it's been a little more than six weeks since you sustained your injuries ... very major trauma I should remind you. You need to be realistic; your body needs more time to heal."

Martin set his toast down on his plate and brushed his hands off, preparing for the verbal duel he sensed was coming. He looked his aide in the eye, squared his shoulders, and began to systematically defend his position.

"I am a doctor. I'm fully aware of what happened to me six weeks ago. I am also aware of my limitations. I *do* agree I need more time. I need to be more ambulatory. I need to get some strength back and improve the dexterity in my hand. I at least need to be capable of *dressing* my goddamn self in the morning! But I also know what I'm capable of. Only once in my life has an obstacle kept me from doing what I wanted to do, and I'm not going to let it happen again. This is not some flight of fancy. I *can* be ready in a few weeks, but I need your help. Chris and Ed will never agree to this if you're not on board with it."

Martin reached up and rubbed a large palm over his face. "Jeremy, I can work with you. I trust your judgement. I won't need to explain to you every step of the way what I may or may not need assistance with. I would appreciate it if you'd give the idea some serious consideration. I can't just sit around here for four more months. I *can't*."

Jeremy saw a desperation in Martin's eyes, and he fought his impulse to acquiesce to his request. "Martin, you know what the medical impracticalities are, and I won't go through the checklist of reasons for not rushing back into things. But it's not just your health I have to think about. I don't think I'm as confident of my abilities as you seem to be. It would be rather intimidating to be working under the aegis of someone with your reputation."

Martin shook his head, furrowing his brow at the young man. "What do you think you're doing right now?"

"I'm doing what I was trained to do—nursing. You're asking a whole lot more of me, I just don't know if I can handle that kind of responsibility."

Martin slapped his hand down on the table, causing the plates and utensils to dance on its surface. "Good God, Jeremy! You do realise the nursing profession requires a *very* high level of responsibility, don't you!"

Louisa appeared in the doorway, rubbing the sleep from her eyes. "Martin! What in the world is the shouting about? It's not even seven o'clock; you're going to wake James!"

Martin quieted. "Mm, sorry. Jeremy and I were just ... discussing something."

"Well, keep your end of the discussion in a lower decibel range, please," she said, shaking her head as she turned to go back upstairs.

Martin breathed a slow hiss of air from his nose. "I'm sorry, Jeremy." He rubbed his tired eyes, "I'm curious ... did you ever consider medical school?"

The aide spun his knife back and forth as his head dropped to the side. "I did. It just seemed very risky to me—sinking all that time and money into something, which could ultimately end in failure."

"What makes you think you wouldn't be able to make it through? You're a hard worker ... intelligent." Martin tipped his cup back, draining the last of the warm liquid into his mouth. "More importantly, you have good instincts."

Jeremy shrugged his shoulders and sat quietly for a few moments. "I—er, my dad didn't think I was cut out for it."

Martin was familiar with the aide's father. They were in medical school together. He had found the man to be loud, self-important, and a womaniser. Adrian Pitts came to mind, and Martin's hand clenched involuntarily. "I'm not sure it really matters what your father thinks. Do *you* think you could do it?"

Jeremy shrugged his shoulders and got up from the table to take the remaining dirty dishes to the sink. "I thought at one time I could. I really wanted to be a surgeon, but I decided it wasn't for me. I don't think I have the kind of ballsiness it would take."

"There's an old adage about surgeons, Jeremy. Sometimes wrong, never in doubt. It means, we take a patient into theatre knowing that much in the field of medicine is ambiguous. We don't know with certainty our patient will wake up after a procedure better off than they were before. Or that they'll even make it off the table for that matter. But you have to set that aside and proceed with confidence. If you can't do that, then surgery's not your calling."

Martin winced and rolled himself back away from the table to massage a cramp from his leg.

Jeremy came around and knelt down. "Just sit back. Think about relaxing that muscle," the aide said as he tried to work the knot from his patient's thigh.

"What about a non-sur—" Martin grimaced and pressed his fingers to his eyes, trying to hold back the tears.

"Any better?" the aide asked.

"Yeah." Martin took a few slow breaths and nodded his head. "Yeah, it's better."

"Good."

"What about a non-surgical specialty ... or general practice?" Martin asked.

The aide shrugged his shoulders. "I don't know. It's a long haul through medical school. Like I said, I'd be risking a lot of time and money."

"Well, I *know* you could do it. And as far as it being a risky proposition ... there's usually an element of risk involved in anything worth doing." Martin looked up at the clock. "We'd better get going or we'll be late."

Jeremy stood back up before making eye contact with him. "I'll give your proposal some thought."

"Good. Jeremy, I really *can't* just sit here for four more months."

"You'd make a horrible prisoner, you know," the aide said, giving Martin a grin. "Let's go take that central line out and get you to your appointment."

The physiotherapy centre was located, ironically, at the bottom of the River Camel bridge, just yards from where Martin's accident occurred. It was a relatively new building, with the newest innovations in therapy equipment. The pool was equipped with pumps which, when activated, generated a current action to provide resistance once a patient was strong enough to ambulate through the motionless water. And the water was heated to ninety degrees Fahrenheit, an optimal thermotherapeutic temperature.

Jeremy helped Martin to change into the swimming trunks Louisa had picked up when she stopped at Jaeger's the day before. He was grateful for his early appointment time when he saw the only other people in or around the pool were his therapists. Jeremy pulled up a chair and sat down to observe the session.

There was a lift on the side of the pool that was used to get patients in and out of the water. When they lowered Martin into the water, the initial effect of the pressure on his swollen limbs was painful.

"We're going to give you a few minutes to adjust to the sensation, Dr. Ellingham. Then we'll get you up on your feet," Kieran said as he and Max each held on to an arm to steady him. Once the discomfort had abated, Martin found the warmth and buoyancy of the water provided some relief from the pain.

"All right, we'll support you while you stand," Max said as they helped him to his feet.

"Get used to that sensation, then try to pull your left leg forward first."

Jeremy pulled his chair closer to the pool.

Martin didn't have a lot of difficulty moving his left leg, but the movement threw him off balance, and his therapists had to steady him. Moving the right leg forward was much more difficult, and it caused a deep, intense pain in his fractured femur. He managed to walk the length of the pool and back, an achievement that seemed monumental.

By the end of the first hour, Martin was relying less on his therapists for balance and support, but his right leg dragged with every other step.

Once finished in the pool, Jeremy helped his patient back into his vest and boxers.

"Well, that was pretty ugly," Martin said as he watched his aide wipe the moisture from his fixators.

"I actually thought you did very well. Your stamina is great. That in itself puts you ahead of the curve. And it'll be of great benefit to you as you work on getting ambulatory."

"Mm. I have a lot of work to do yet. It could be a while before I can get back to ... before I'm able to do things again."

"Hang in there, Martin. I know it was a rough morning, but you'll see pretty rapid improvement in your gait over the course of the next couple of weeks," the aide said. He patted his foot. "Come on. Those two gorillas are waiting to work that arm and those legs some more."

Martin was exhausted by both the time in the pool and the painful manipulations of his limbs. He collapsed on to his bed when they arrived back at Ruth's but was awakened shortly before eleven by a growling in his stomach.

He went to the kitchen and removed two of his shakes from the refrigerator.

"James is takin' a nap right now, so I can make you some lunch if you want me to," Poppy said.

"Mm. That would be good. Thank you."

The childminders blue eyes sparkled as she gave him a smile.

Wheeling himself up to the table, Martin flipped through the newspaper until Poppy placed a bowl of soup, a sandwich, and a salad down in front of him.

He pulled in his chin and picked up his spoon. "Thank you."

She pulled up her shoulders and ducked her head before heading off to check on her charge.

After he finished with his lunch, Jeremy helped Martin with a shower. They were in the bathroom, and the aide was drying his fixators, when Louisa arrived home for lunch.

"How did it go this morning?" she asked cheerfully as she peered in the door.

Martin shrugged his shoulders, mumbling unintelligibly. She cocked her head at the aide, and he gave her a discreet shake of his head.

"I'm going to grab some lunch ... look in on James," she said as she looked back at Jeremy, worry tempering her smile. She turned to leave, and Martin called out to her.

"What's James's temperature today?"

"Back down to normal, Doctor. And the cold symptoms are much improved as well. He's still working on that new tooth, though."

He gave her a nod of his head. "I'll be out in a minute."

Her husband seemed discouraged, and in general just not himself. Louisa was hesitant to leave him to head back to work, but she had her meeting with the district liaison at half three, and she didn't dare to miss it.

Martin's demeanour hadn't improved by the time she arrived home late that afternoon, and he was, even for Martin, unusually quiet. She was anxious to talk to him, and as soon as James was down for the night, she joined him in the living room.

"Are you all right, Martin?" she asked as she worked another pillow in under his legs.

He laid his *BMJ* down on his lap. "I'm just tired. Maybe we'll go to bed early tonight?" he asked, peering up at her.

She leaned down and placed a kiss on his forehead. "Is that an invitation?"

"Mm, yes. I intended it to be."

"Then I accept. But ... could we please talk about what you have on your mind first?"

He glanced up at her before returning his attention to his medical journal.

"Martin, what is it? Did something happen today?"

He shook his head. "No, not really. It was just hard. Very hard."

Louisa dropped down beside him and nestled in under his arm.

He was silent for several moments before he spoke again. "Louisa ... trying to walk was terribly difficult. I could do it, but my right leg—it took so much effort to pull it forward. I couldn't wa—" his breath caught in his throat. "It's not normal."

Louisa pulled his hand up and pressed it to her lips. "And it's frightening, hmm?"

He took a deep breath in and blew it out. "Yeah."

"Martin, it *will* be all right. It'll take time and a lot of work, but things are going to improve. I'm sure they'll improve a lot. Try not to get discouraged."

He breathed out a heavy sigh as he turned his gaze towards the floor.

Louisa laid her head on his shoulder. "Whenever you get down ... have a tough day ... come home to your wife and get your hugs and kisses, reassurances, whatever you need. I'll always be here for you, okay?" She pulled back and looked at him, wiping the moisture from the corner of his eye.

"Do you know that—that I draw a lot of strength from you?" he asked as he ran his hand over her ponytail.

"Really, Martin?"

"Mm, I do."

"That makes me very happy ... to know I can do that for you." She slowly undid the buttons of his shirt, pausing to trickle kisses down his chest.

"Louisa, I think I'm ready for bed now," he said hoarsely.

She gave him an amused smile. "Yes, I noticed."

Chapter 40

"So, what was the pool like today?" Louisa asked as she lay facing him, propped up on her elbow.

"It's just a pool ... about ten by twenty feet, I'd say. The water temperature's kept at around ninety degrees Fahrenheit, or so I'm told. It's equipped with pumps that generate a current in the water to provide resistance when needed."

Louisa leaned forward and touched her nose to his. "A little bit more than the pool specifications, please."

He pulled back, blinking his eyes. "Ah, I assume you're referring to my physical sensations in the water then?"

"Yes, Martin."

"I see." His gaze settled on her cleavage before he lifted his head and nuzzled into her neck.

"Martin!" she said with a giggle.

"Hmm?"

She pushed him back on to the pillow, "You didn't answer my question. How did it feel for you to get in the water today?"

He rubbed his eyes, trying to stave off the sleepiness that was threatening to spoil the evening he had been hoping for. "It was uncomfortable at first. The pressure of the water on my legs caused some pain. But the buoyancy was nice. It seemed to actually relieve the discomfort after a while. Walking hurt, especially the right leg ... trying to bring it forward."

Louisa reached over, gently stroking his injured arm as it rested across his stomach. "What about here? Did it seem to help to have your arm in the water?"

He watched his wife's mouth as she spoke—the soft, sensuous curve of her lips, and he brushed his thumb gently over them.

"Mar-tin. She said softly, drawing out his name.

His gaze shifted back to her eyes. "Mm. I was distracted."

"Oh, sorry."

"It's quite all right. You can't help it," he said as he worked his way down the buttons of her cardigan before flipping the two sides back, letting his palm loiter over her shoulder.

Louisa reached her arms behind her to let the jumper slide to the floor, but in doing so, it caught on one of the fixators on Martin's arm.

He tried to free the garment from the pin, sending a sharp pain through his arm and hand.

"Martin, what's wrong?" Louisa asked when she saw her husband's face contort in pain.

"Your jumper's gotten hung up!" he squeaked out.

Louisa turned around and untangled the knitting from its restraint, tossing it on to the dresser before turning her attention to her distressed husband.

"Are you all right?"

His clenched jaw began to relax, and he gave her a nod of his head. "It's better now ... yeah, I'm okay," he said, letting out a small sigh over the interruption to their romantic moment.

Louisa leaned over and pressed her lips to his. "Now, let's see ... where were we?"

Martin wove his fingers into her hair and pulled her head back down, searching with his lips for a special spot on her neck. Just below her ear was skin so soft it felt like velvet. Her name floated out on a breath. "Louisa."

He reached his arms around her, feeling for the clasp on her bra, careful to avoid any twisting motions that could induce further pain. He fumbled for a few moments before he could free the hooks. He heard a small gasp from his wife as he pulled his arms forward to remove the undergarment.

"Ow!" she yelped, placing a hand to the back of her arm.

"What's happened?"

"One of your pins ... it scratched me."

He pulled at her arm. "Let me take a look."

"It's *okay*. Just leave it," Louisa said, sensing their evening being threatened once again.

Martin sat himself up, taking hold of her arm again. "Louisa, let—me—see."

He scrutinised the wound carefully. "Mm, it's okay ... just a small scratch. I'll clean that up and put a plaster on it later."

Louisa dropped back on her heels and tipped her head down, narrowing her eyes at him. "I *told* you it was okay." She stretched up to kiss his forehead. "Shall we try this again?"

"Yes. But it might be safer if we skip the first step. My undressing you seems to be rather hazardous."

"Hmm, maybe you're right. It *is* a shame though," she said as she tugged her husband's left arm through the sleeve of his vest. As she pulled the right sleeve over his hardware, a loose thread snagged on a pin, requiring yet another delay while she untangled it.

Martin sighed heavily as his wife worked his boxers over the metal on his legs. "I'm sorry, Louisa. This isn't very romantic."

She paused and gave him a sly grin. "It *could* be." Leaning over, she trailed kisses down the inside of his thigh, eliciting a small gasp from him.

Dropping his boxers to the floor, she slowly peeled away the last of her impediments, trying to supress a self-satisfied smile as her husband's eyes followed her every languid move. She climbed on to the bed next to him and pulled the covers up over them.

Martin tried to roll to his side, hanging up on the sheets. "I bet the Terminator never had this much trouble," he grumbled, tugging at the bedding in frustration.

"Maybe, but as they say in America, the Terminator never made it to first base. So, shush." Louisa straightened out the sheets, then nestled in next to him. "Ahh, this is much better, don't you think?"

As Martin stared back at her, his eyes darkened, and a dazed expression slipped across his face. "Mm. Much better."

Louisa reached behind her and turned out the light. And then, as they say in America, Martin hit a homerun.

After a tiring day and sex's somnolent sway, Martin had fallen asleep quickly. He woke the following morning feeling more rested than he had in six and a half weeks.

"I've been thinking about our conversation yesterday morning," Jeremy said as he slipped a towel over the rack in the bathroom. "Just what did you have in mind for me to do *if* I agree to be your assistant in this hair-brained scheme of yours?"

Martin rubbed at the metal on his arm. "Well, your chief responsibility would be to screen the patients. Chris and Ed will never approve this if it would result in my exposure to pathogens. So, I'd need you to identify those people with possible viral infections or contagious bacterial infections. They can be sent over to Wadebridge. I'd also need you to draw blood and give injections, at least until I have better control of my hand. I don't think my patients would want to see me coming at them with a needle right now. And ..." Martin hesitated. "If you had the training necessary, you could do some basic wound sutures. I could watch you ... give you some pointers. But you'd need to spend some time in Plymouth doing a course in wound management training."

Jeremy smiled back at him. "I've already done the course. I worked in A&E when I was first hired by the Royal Cornwall. They sent me for the training."

"Good ... good!" Martin said, a smile trying to creep on to his face. "So ... you think you might be interested?"

Jeremy sighed. "It's going against my better judgement, but yes ... I'm interested. If, of course, your doctors and your wife approve."

"Yes. Yes, of course. I'll ring up Parsons today and bounce it off him. He can talk to Ed Christianson."

Martin knew his chances of persuading Chris Parsons were better than his chances of getting Ed Christianson to agree to his plan. If he could convince Chris, he felt confident Chris could then convince Ed that it was a reasonable idea.

He sequestered himself in his bedroom later that morning before ringing his friend.

"No, Martin, absolutely not! I knew you were going to do this to me! I just knew it! In fact, I have a bet going with Carole. She guessed it would be at least two months before you'd be pushing for this. I told her it be more like two weeks. Geesh! You've surprised even me this time, Mart."

Chris paused to catch his breath and regain his composure. "No, absolutely not. It's way too soon!"

"Chris, I have a pla—"

"Martin! You can't be exposing yourself to the kinds of viruses that would be parading through your surgery. It's just way too soon."

"Chris, hear me out ... please. I don't want to put you in a difficult position, but I can't sit at home for the next four months. I've thought this through, and I think my idea will work."

Martin heard his friend sigh into the phone. "All right, Mart. Tell me about this bloody plan of yours."

"My home health aide, Jeremy Portman, is bright, responsible, and from what I've seen of him so far, I think he would do an excellent job as my assistant. Any sick patients—"

"No, Martin! You're immunocompromised! You can't be *treating* sick patients!"

"I could send any cases I can't handle over to Wadebridge and—"

Chris groaned on the other end of the line, and Martin swallowed back the tightness that was rapidly developing in his throat. "I thought you were going to hear me out, Chris."

"Okay, go on."

"Well not all sick patients are contagious, are they? A good percentage of my patients have chronic conditions that need to be monitored—cardiac issues, diabetes, thyroid disease. I also have a fair number of minor injuries—fishermen impaled by fish hooks, farmers with lacerations and crush injuries and—"

"And how do you propose handling those cases? Are you going to suture wounds with one hand? Your non-dominant hand no less!"

Martin mumbled unintelligibly.

"What's that, Martin?"

"Has Carole ever told you you're not a very good listener?" He exhaled forcefully. "Don't close your mind to this without hearing me out."

Chris rubbed at the tension forming in his temples. "Fine, Martin. Go ahead."

Martin cleared his throat, attempting to loosen the persistent lump. "My aide has taken the wound management course over in Plymouth. He could handle any suturing or wound treatment. I can supervise. And as for the contagion issue ... Jeremy can screen patients before they come into the consulting room."

"Oh, mate. I don't know."

Martin could hear a weakening of resolve in his friend's voice, and he pushed a bit more. "Look, Chris, you wouldn't expect me to stay inside for the next four months, would you? I could go to see a movie, or go out to eat ... right?"

"You're not likely to do either one of those things unless Louisa drags you there, so yes, I can, with confidence, say—you may go out to eat or to a movie. And by all means, feel free to attend any heavy metal concerts or bring-a-dish dinners that might interest you, as well."

"Ohh, now you're just being ridiculous, Chris! You know what I'm saying, don't you? I'm going to be exposed to these things to a certain degree. It's unavoidable. I think if Jeremy and I take precautions, this can be done without increasing my level of exposure."

"Martin, why can't you just kick back and take it easy for once? Why is this so important to you?"

There was a period of silence before Chris heard his friend's voice again. "I—I'm feeling that fog I was in a while back ... the depression. I *can't* take this for four more months, Chris."

Martin listened as the seconds ticked off Ruth's old mantel clock.

"Okay, mate. Give me a day or two to think it over ... maybe bounce it off Ed. Then I'll let you know."

"Thanks, Chris." Martin rang off feeling less than optimistic.

Chapter 41

Each day brought longer and harder sessions in the hydrotherapy pool. And although it was hard and often discouraging work, Martin was seeing noticeable improvement in his ability to bring his right leg forward.

His sessions would begin with time in the water before Max and Kieran put him through the gruelling range of motion exercises. Max pushed Martin's limbs farther than Tim Spalding ever had, and although the warm water helped to relax the muscles, the exercises still caused pain in his fractured bones and stiffened joints.

Now that he was total weight bearing, the therapists had begun intensive strength and stability exercises, spending a full hour each day working with Martin on his balance—something that would become increasingly important as he began to spend less time in his wheelchair and more time on his feet.

The balance exercises proved especially frustrating as Martin's proprioception was significantly diminished due to the extent of his leg injuries.

Ed had spoken with Martin by phone about working on building up his arm strength in preparation for his use of crutches. The bones had not yet developed enough callus to support more than a very limited amount of weight, even with the added benefit of the buoyancy the pool provided. But some stress put on the fracture sites would promote new bone formation.

Kieran started him out with low-stress arm movements with nothing more than the resistance provided by the water. They would later add increasingly heavy weights and, finally, the resistance of current in the water.

Martin was seeing slow but noticeable gains in his overall health. But always lurking in the back of his mind was the uncertainty about how much improvement there would ultimately be.

Louisa had seen her husband withdraw over the recent days. His sullen demeanour and short temper had created a tense atmosphere in the household that even James had picked up on. Something was on his mind, but she couldn't get him to open up about it.

The trip to the farm with Ruth had been planned for Saturday afternoon. Martin had a therapy session in Wadebridge early in the morning and it was lunchtime before he and Jeremy arrived back in Portwenn. Jeremy dropped him at Ruth's and then went to meet a friend at the pub.

Louisa was working on lunch preparations, and Ruth was reading the paper at the table as James played in his highchair next to her.

"Martin, you look knackered. Why don't you go have a lie-down? I'll come wake you up for lunch in a little while," she said as she chopped up fruit for a salad.

Martin pulled his mobile out of the pocket of his warm up pants, scowling when he saw there were no new messages. He tossed the phone on to the kitchen table, sending it sliding across to the other side, over the edge, and on to the slate below.

"Bugger!" He rolled himself over to retrieve the device from the floor. He let out a yelp of pain as he leaned carelessly over the side of his chair, the armrest digging into the thoracotomy wound in his side.

"Martin! Are you all right?" Louisa hurried to him.

"I'm—fine!" he sputtered as he doubled over with a hand pressed to his ribcage.

Louisa picked up the phone and handed it to him.

He snatched it from her. "Oh, that's just great! It's broken now!"

Louisa stared at him, cocking her head. "Martin, it's okay. It's just a little crack in the screen. It still—"

"What do you mean, just a little crack in the screen? It's *ruined*!"

James began to whimper in his high chair, and his mother handed him a piece of Melba toast to distract him.

"Martin," Louisa said softly. "You're tired. Go have a lie-down, hmm? You'll feel much better when you're rested." Laying her hand on his shoulder, she leaned over to kiss him on the cheek.

He pulled away abruptly, whirling his head around, his eyes flashing. "I'm *not* tired! And stop telling me what will make me feel better!"

Louisa's shoulders sagged as she watched him move off down the hall.

Ruth lowered the newspaper. "Well, this is interesting," she said as she stared at the now empty hallway. "How long has he been behaving like this?"

Louisa worried her wedding band. "The last few days he's been difficult. Something's bothering him, but he insists nothing's wrong."

She dropped the towel on to the kitchen table and collapsed into a chair. "Ruth, this is scary. He's been acting like he did before my accident on Sports Day, and I'm afraid he's falling apart again. What do I do?"

"First of all, you calm yourself down." Ruth went to the cupboard and got a teacup, putting it down in front of her nephew's wife before dropping a teabag into it. "It's going to be of absolutely no help to him if he feels you're panicking.

"Martin's endured a harrowing ordeal, and he's going through a very frustrating and frightening process right now.

He's bound to feel overwhelmed at times. He needs you to be the calm and confident voice—the voice of reason."

As Ruth poured hot water into her cup, Louisa fidgeted, casting worried glances down the hall.

"I think I should go check on him ... see how he's getting on," she said as she began to get to her feet.

Ruth put her hand on her wrist. "Give him a little space, Louisa. I don't have to tell you, my nephew isn't one to seek the limelight, and for the last seven weeks he's had people fussing over him left and right ... hovering over him constantly."

Louisa looked at her husband's aunt sceptically. "There must be something I can do to help him."

Ruth nudged the teacup closer to her. "Drink your tea, dear."

The elderly woman folded her hands, resting them on the table in front of her. "Now, I can't say this with reasonable certainty, but I would imagine what Martin needs more than anything, is to regain some sense of control in his life. He grew up in a loveless environment. He never really had a home. He spent decades perfecting a craft where he feels confident, safe, accepted, and if not loved, at least respected.

"I doubt my nephew is even aware of it, but medicine became his home, really. At least he felt he was wanted and that he belonged in the medical environment. He was in control of his life. When he developed his blood sensitivity, he lost some of that control. And now, even the little control that was left has been taken away. I suspect it could make him feel rather insecure and at a very frightening time in his life, I might add."

Louisa took a sip from her cup before setting it down on the table. "I'd never thought of medicine as being a place of security for Martin. It makes me rather sad actually ... to think he sees medicine as home. I'd like to believe James and I ... and you would be home to him."

Ruth nodded her head. "I think we *have* become that. But to some degree, he'll always cling to medicine as a sort of safety net, and right now that safety net's been taken away. And I doubt he feels certain he'll get it back."

"I think I see what you're saying, Ruth. It adds to the sense of vulnerability he's already feeling."

"That's right. You *must* show him you're completely confident in your relationship ... that this accident and its aftermath is of no threat to your marriage. I know it's asking a lot of you, Louisa, but he needs you to be rock solid through all of this."

Louisa stood up and went back to her lunch preparations. Once the table was set she went to her husband's room and tapped softly on the door. Getting no answer, she opened it, expecting to find him sleeping. But he was lying on the bed, staring absently, seemingly deep in thought.

"Martin," she said softly.

He raised his head up.

"Lunch is ready. Do you want to come and join us?"

"Mm. I'll use the lavatory and be right there," he said as he propped himself up on his elbow.

Louisa approached, hesitantly. "Martin, may I sit for just a bit?"

He moved himself over, and she dropped down next to him, wrapping her arms around his shoulders. She held him, not saying a word. Before getting back to her feet, she leaned over and kissed him.

"I'll leave you to it then," she said as she stood to leave.

He opened his mouth as if to say something, but closed it again, the words left unspoken. "I'll be out in a minute."

He was on the sofa, reading one of his journals, and Louisa had just put James down for his afternoon nap when there was a knock on the front door.

"Dr. Newell! Come in ... please," Louisa said, stepping aside to allow the therapist in from the porch.

"Thank you, Louisa. I came over with my wife and daughter today. They wanted to visit that pottery shop over by the harbour, and I thought I'd accompany them ... stop in to see how Martin's doing while I'm here in the village. Is this a good time?"

"Yes, he's in here," she said as she led him towards the living room. "Martin, you have a visitor."

Martin sat himself up, and the therapist pulled a chair closer to the sofa before taking a seat.

"Well, you're looking more like yourself than when I saw you last. Feeling better too, I hope."

Martin gave the journal he'd been reading a toss on to the coffee table. "Yes. Progress seems slow, but things are moving in the right direction, I think."

"Good, glad to hear it." The doctor hesitated, glancing in Louisa's direction.

"I, erm ... should go and get some laundry sorted upstairs," Louisa said as she headed for the steps. "Can I leave you to keep an eye on my husband ... make sure he doesn't walk off anywhere?"

The psychiatrist gave her a nod. "I'll call if I need any help subduing him."

He waited until Louisa was out of sight before speaking. "Martin, I'll forgo the prevarications and get right to why I'm here. Chris Parsons, Ed Christianson, and I had a bit of a chinwag yesterday. Chris gave us a recap of your conversation the other day"

"I think I know where this is going, so let me save you some time. I'm going to compromise my health if I go back to work too soon. Ed wants to see more hard callus formation on my fractures. Chris thinks I'll be exposing myself to too many pathogens. And you don't think I'm ready mentally. Is that about right?" Martin snipped as he reached over and picked up his journal.

"No, that's *not* right. Hear me out before you say any more." Dr. Newell leaned forward, tapping his fingertips together. "Yes, all three of us have legitimate concerns—"

"Legitimate concerns I've already addressed with—"

The therapist put a hand up in the air. "As I was saying, we have concerns. *But* ... you've thought this through carefully, and given the fact that Jeremy Portman would be assisting you, we'll give you the go ahead. *Provided* you come over to Truro for a thorough physical with both Ed and Chris. And you will never see patients without your assistant in attendance. If there are any cases Mr. Portman feels could expose you to a contagion, they must be sent to Wadebridge.

"You know your limitations in regard to muscle strength and dexterity. And given that those two variables will change over time, we'll leave it up to you to decide what you can or can't handle. Chris will be in contact with you about proper protocols when ferreting out the contagious patients."

Martin stared at the man. "I'm ... surprised. When I hadn't heard from Chris, I thought you weren't going to allow it."

Dr. Newell crossed his ankle over his knee and leaned back in the chair. "Well, you made some valid points. If this is handled properly, you shouldn't be putting yourself at a high risk of exposure. And we're as concerned about your mental health as we are your physical health. Which brings me to my next question. How *are* you doing, mentally?"

Martin closed his eyes and heaved out a heavy sigh. "I'm worried about that. I think I'm sliding backwards."

"Explain what you mean by that. What does that feel like?"

Martin tossed pillows on to the coffee table before lifting his feet on to them.

"It's like I'm looking through a window. I can see what's going on around me, but there's a barrier there ... like I'm not really a part of things."

The therapist leaned forward, his elbows on his knees. "And you've had this feeling before?"

"It started several years ago. There was a party at the pub once for Louisa. She'd just been given the job of head teacher at the school, and she'd invited me to the party she was having that night. I watched from the surgery terrace, but there was that barrier there. I wanted to be there with her ... be a part of things, but I couldn't."

"Had this problem improved for a while ... before the accident occurred?"

"Yes, to some extent. I at least felt I was a part of things with James and Louisa ... and Ruth. But for the last week or two, that same ..." He shook his head. "I don't know, something's not right."

Dr. Newell furrowed his brow. "Have you had any medication changes recently?"

"The morphine. Ed had my aide remove the central line, and he switched me over to oral morphine."

The psychiatrist tipped his head back as the pieces began to come together. "I'll discuss this with Ed Christianson and get back to you. I suspect this slip back into some depressive symptoms may be a drug issue.

"Try not to let this worry you, Martin ... let it start to snowball on you. We'll get it sorted." The therapist got to his feet and put a hand on his patient's shoulder.

"Be sure you talk with Louisa about this. If she senses a problem, it will likely get blown out of proportion in her head. Discuss it before that can happen."

Chapter 42

"Oh, did Dr. Newell leave already?" Louisa asked when she came back into the living room.

"Mm." Martin moved over to make room for her. "Have a seat," he said. "There's something we need to discuss."

Her breath caught in her chest. "Should I brace myself for bad news?"

"Noo! It's nothing to worry about. I, erm..." Martin rubbed palm on his trousers as he tried to choose his words carefully. "I've been talking with Jeremy and Chris about something, and I discussed it with Dr. Newell as well."

"Martin, just tell me what it is. You're making me nervous."

He licked his lips and tried to swallow back the lump in his throat. "Please don't say no to this, Louisa. I can't be stuck here in Ruth's cottage for much longer. Dr. Newell thinks the change that was made to my medications earlier in the week could be contributing to some of the problems I've been experiencing, but I know there's more to it than that. I just can't sit around here. It's making me anxious."

"Are you talking about a holiday ... taking a holiday somewhere? Oh, Martin. I don't really think you're ready for that, do you? And you have your physical therapy ... doctor's appointments ... you wouldn't have Jeremy around to help you. And I certainly don't have the know-how to take care of all the things Jeremy takes care of. No, Martin. That's not practical."

"I didn't mean a holiday. I want to start seeing patients again."

"What do you mean?" Louisa's brow began to furrow. "Tell me how you think you can do that. Physical therapy takes up a good chunk of your time, and you already come home from Wadebridge exhausted!"

"Yes, I'm aware of that. But I think by the end of November, I'll have enough strength back to work half days at the surgery."

Louisa's ponytail flicked back and forth like the tail on a fractious feline. "Martin, don't—rush things. You've had so many setbacks. Can't you just give yourself time to recover completely? And you shouldn't be exposing yourself to sick patients anyway!"

Martin could hear anger creeping into her voice, and he felt his chest tightening in response. "I've thought this through carefully and discussed it with Jeremy and Chris ... and today with Dr. Newell. They all think it's a reasonable plan; so does Ed," he said, trying to project more confidence than he was feeling at the moment.

The disapproving expression on Louisa's face intensified. "Oh really? You discussed it with Jeremy, Chris, Ed *and* Dr. Newell? Do I have any say in this, or has the decision already been made by your little—*medical fraternity*? Hmm, *Mar-tin?*" she said, her tone becoming increasingly strident.

Martin sat silent, anxiety beginning to suck the air from his lungs. He tried to slow his breathing, but it was coming in rapid, ragged breaths now, and the room seemed to be closing in on him.

"Well *Mar-tin*? Why am I the last to be included in this conversation? I'm your wife!"

Martin squeezed his eyes shut tightly and tried to tune her out until he could regain a sense of control.

"I didn't know—well if—if they didn't go along—well, I didn't want to worry you unnecessarily, so I thought it best..." There was a steady throbbing in his ears as his now pounding heart sent the blood coursing ever more rapidly through his body. His stomach began to churn violently, his palms grew moist, and he swallowed back saliva as it flooded his mouth.

Louisa suddenly became aware of her husband's growing pallor and obvious distress.

"Martin, are you all right?" she asked before laying a hand on his arm.

He jerked it away, "No! Don't touch me!" Struggling to his feet, he took several steps, trying to move forward, but he lost his balance and fell to the floor.

"Martin!" Louisa dropped to her knees next to him. "Martin? Martin, are you all right?"

The jolt had broken the grip of the panic attack, and Martin looked around in confusion.

"I'm going to be sick," he said, desperately trying to stave off the waves of nausea.

Louisa grabbed the bin next to Ruth's desk and returned to her husband's side.

Martin pushed himself into an upright position before ceding to the queasiness.

Louisa hurried off to the bathroom and returned with a cool, wet facecloth. She heard the back door open as she was wiping the cloth over her husband's sweaty face, and Jeremy's footsteps could be heard in the hallway.

"Jeremy, we're in here! I need your help!"

"What's happened?" Jeremy asked as he hurried over.

"Martin fell. He tried to stand up and walk."

Jeremy took his patient's wrist in his hand, palpating for a pulse point. "Well, his heart's racing." He looked at his eyes, checking his pupillary reflexes and the conjunctival membrane inside his lids. Then the aide began examining his patient for any outward signs of injury or damage to the external fixators.

"Martin, did you lose consciousness?"

"No. Louisa's right. It was a panic attack. I'm fine now, just help me back up."

Jeremy stepped back to scrutinise the situation and figure out how best to get Martin up off the floor. "Let me go and get a gait belt. Just sit there until I get back.

Louisa stood to the side, tapping her fingers together nervously. When Jeremy returned, he wrapped the belt around Martin's waist, and with the help of his good arm and Jeremy's assistance, Martin was able to boost himself back up on to the sofa.

"Let's get you cleaned up. We'll check you over again after that," Jeremy said. "And, you're due out at the farm in a couple of hours."

"Could I have a glass of water?"

Jeremy gave Louisa a jerk of his head, and she headed towards the kitchen.

She returned shortly with a glass in her hand." Here you go, Martin."

By the time he was finished with his shower, Martin seemed to be back to normal. Jeremy knelt on the floor as he rubbed the moisture from his patient's fixators. "May I ask what triggered the panic attack?"

Martin sat for some time without saying a word. "I'm not sure. We were discussing my getting back to seeing patients and..."

He could hear Louisa's voice in his head, the building anger in her tone. Then he realised it wasn't his wife's voice he had heard but rather his mother's. He had heard Louisa's words, but it was his mother's mocking and condescending tone.

He returned his gaze to the aide. "My childhood was ... difficult. I think something reminded me of my childhood, that's all."

"I see." Jeremy got to his feet. "Okay, let's get you dressed."

Helping him with his shower had given Jeremy the opportunity to check his patient over more thoroughly, yet discreetly. Everything seemed fine, aside from a rather nasty scrape where Martin's upper arm had made contact with the corner of the coffee table. Jeremy disinfected and bandaged the wound before helping him into clean clothes.

"I need to run down to the chemist to pick up some supplies. Can I turn him over to you for a while?" Jeremy asked Louisa as he came back through the kitchen. "I left him in bed to rest for a bit."

"Certainly, Jeremy. You'd be very welcome to join us when we go out to the farm if you like. Martin might enjoy showing you around. He spent a number of summers there when he was a boy, and he has very fond memories of those times."

"I'll think on that. I might just take you up on it," Jeremy said before he pulled the door shut behind him.

As soon as the therapist had left the house, Louisa walked down the hall to her husband's room. He was lying on his side facing away from her and appeared to be asleep, so she slipped in carefully behind him, wrapping her arm around him. His body was still warm from the shower, and the pleasant clean smell of soap emanated from him. She had begun to drift off to sleep when his voice awakened her.

"Louisa?"

He felt her stir slightly against his back. "Louisa, can we talk?"

She propped herself up on her elbow and buried her face in the side of his neck, tightening her grip on him.

"I think talking's a very good idea, Martin."

He rolled over on his back and looked up at her. "I didn't intend to leave you out of this decision, you know. I just didn't really expect Chris and Ed to agree to it in the first place. It didn't seem like it made sense to prattle on about something that wasn't likely to happen anyway. *You* would have had the final say no matter what anyone else said."

Louisa stroked her fingernails lightly across his chest. "Maybe we should prattle on about it now. Now that they *have* agreed to it."

"Is it going to upset you again?"

"No, Martin. It won't upset me. I'm sorry I let it upset me before. I guess maybe I had my own sort of panic attack. I don't think I'm ever going to be ready for you to go back to work. It would be so much easier to keep you at home where I know you're safe."

Martin shook his head. "Louisa, more than half of all accidents happen at home. Last year alone there were almost five thousand deaths as a result of a home accident. In fact, you might be interested to know, more accidents occur in the lounge or living room than anywhere else in the house. The UK spends more than forty-five million pou—"

Pressing her hand to his mouth, she shook her head. "Shhh! I get it, Martin. And I know you're right. I'm just trying to say I'm sorry for not having given you a fair chance to explain this plan of yours. And I'm trying to tell you ... I love you very, very much. And that after what's happened ... what I saw you go through ... Well, maybe I got a bit hysterical."

She brushed her fingers over his arm and dipped her head. "I *would* like to hear about your plan, and I *will* try to keep an open mind."

Martin proceeded to fill her in on all that had been discussed, stressing that he would not be allowed to treat patients who could be contagious. "So, we'll have Morwenna screen the patients when they call in, and Jeremy will screen them again in an area set up in the lounge. No one will be allowed in the consulting room until they've first been seen by Jeremy."

Louisa sat for a few moments. "But what if they're coming down with something and they don't know it?"

"That *is* a risk. But I'll be at a lower risk of exposure in my practice than if we were to go out to eat or go shopping. I can't spend the next two years waiting for my disease resistance to build back up, sequestered away in Ruth's cottage. I'll be more susceptible to illnesses all my life. It's just a matter of taking precautions where possible and being proactive in treatment when I do get sick."

"Maybe you should consider an administrative position. Chris seems to like his job."

Martin's eyes drifted shut as a ragged breath brushed Louisa's cheek. "I'm a doctor ... a good doctor. And I love *being* a doctor ... most of the time. Please don't ask me to give that up, Louisa."

She watched her husband's pleading eyes and remembered Ruth's sage advice about the importance of medicine in his life. "If Ed and Chris think you're strong enough, then I agree. I'll support you *one hundred percent*, Martin."

Martin reached up and pulled her to him, squeezing her as tightly as his aches and pains would allow. "Thank you," he whispered in her ear. "Thank you."

Don't miss out!

Click the button below and you can sign up to receive emails whenever Kris Morris publishes a new book. There's no charge and no obligation.

Sign Me Up!

https://books2read.com/r/B-A-PAJD-TFCL

BOOKS 2 READ

Connecting independent readers to independent writers.

Also by Kris Morris

Battling Demons
Battling Demons
Fractured
Fragile
Headway
Insights
A Cornwall Christmas

About the Author

Kris Morris was born and raised in a small Iowa town. She spent her childhood barely tolerating school, hand rearing orphaned animals, and squirrel taming. At Iowa State University she studied elementary education. But after discovering a loathing for traditional pedagogy and a love for a certain tall, handsome, Upstate New Yorker, she abandoned the academic life to marry, raise two sons, and become an unconventional piano teacher. When she's not writing, Kris builds boats and marimbas with her husband, who she has captivated for thirty years with her delightful personality, quick wit, and culinary masterpieces. They now reside in Iowa and have replaced their sons with ducks.

Read more at www.ktmorris.com.

Made in United States
North Haven, CT
30 January 2022

15410456R00205